BODY SUIT

by Suzanne Hagelin

Peter,

Life is an adventure!

Suzanne Hagelin

The journey you go on is your pain, and perhaps your cure: for you must be either mad or brave before it is ended.

"Out of the Silent Planet" C.S. Lewis

Stephen, your help has made all the difference in this book, editing, encouraging, challenging, advising—every author's dream. I have no other way to appropriately credit you except with two heartfelt words: thank you.

Body Suit
Copyright © Second edition 2018 by Suzanne Hagelin
Varida Publishing & Resources LLC
www.varida.com
Cover redesigned by Roslyn McFarland.
Original cover design includes image courtesy of NASA/JPL-Caltech.

ISBN: 978-1-937046-14-9

CONTENTS

BODY SUIT

Mercury—the store not the planet—shone like a jewel, a brilliant, glass enclosed, egg shaped dome, wreathed with clouds, at the center of the Columbian Sky Mall. Walter gazed through the center panel of the curved walls of the most prestigious spacewear showroom in the western hemisphere. He watched for only the most distinguished customers, dressed in a subtle but well stated Orbitwalk suit, his brown eyes snapping with energy and life, black boots glinting dully at the heel with a metallic sheen. Persons of lesser budgets and more common status naturally found themselves siphoned to the side doors where a less ostentatious entry gave them a more suitable welcome.

As a persuasive defender of the theory that extraterrestrial suits were meant to be personal spaceships, Walter specialized in promoting luxury gear like XenoTek and Angyon to the wealthy. He knew his job and was good at it.

"Every model comes with skin stabilizing technology and atmospheric controls for your comfort," he projected with a friendly, rich voice, gesturing with an aristocratic wave of his hand toward the display floor as he surveyed a handful of visitors who braved the main entrance.

A business man in an Italian suit glanced at him and moved past on the left without speaking. On his right, an older woman with a hardened face and heavy makeup looked toward him expectantly, and he discerned instantly that she would be a tedious burden, impossible to please. He much preferred to attend the attractive woman striding confidently through the entrance directly in front.

She was dressed in classic designer clothes in gray tones with cobalt blue accents; matching shoes and purse. This was the customer of choice. He turned toward her and waited for her approach. Glancing at him, she read his intent and neither responding nor rejecting it, glided into the showroom.

There was something familiar about her.

1

He followed her into the main area where robotic mannequins pantomimed their way through modeling poses in a dream state; on standby until their warehouse graveyard shift began. Swiveling and moving their limbs artistically, fitted in off-world body suits, they circled by, one after another, in a profusion of designs. They entered through a luminous cloud, traveled around the showroom through waterfalls, rings of fire, neon green orbs that simulated radioactive debris, and departed unharmed down a windy tunnel.

The woman fixed her eyes on one model after another as they paraded by. Her mental chatter jumped from one topic to another at lightning speed in her head, never fixing long enough to really complete a thought. "*Strong enough to handle exposure to natural forces.... Never tearing... warm enough.... I want to look good... forget about the fact that I'm wearing a suit.... What if I can't afford what I need?... I can't believe Belymer betrayed me... He should have that suit and look stupid in it... Will I be exposed to radioactive waste?*" and so on.

"Ah!" Walter intoned in a soothing voice next to her, "Such a troubled look for an attractive woman with the entire solar system at her disposal!" He had interrupted her thoughts after watching for a few moments to discern the limits of what she could and would spend once his powers of persuasion and flattery were fully executed.

"Allow me to help narrow down the choices for you," he offered with raised eyebrows, a nod and a gracious manner that would've flattered an interplanetary ambassador, "This range of suits is designed for miners and quarry workers and would be entirely unsuitable for a lady of your carriage. Let me just adjust…" Whipping out a flat hand-sized disk, he touched its smooth surface with a few quick taps and the modeling robots narrowed to a certain range of tasteful options within their quadrant. The rest cycled elsewhere.

"There! If you would step this way, Lady…" he paused expectantly, waiting for a name.

"Operative Frandelle, of the…" she hesitated, not really wanting to say 'Mars Expedition' and give away her situation. She had been forced to indenture herself to pay off her former business partner's debts and had barely escaped prison.

"No need to say more," Walter interjected quickly, a model of discretion. He always kept up on the news and her name was enough for him to remember the case. He understood completely where she was going, and what she would need. "I have served many honorable citizens who elected to increase their net worth through service contracts off world." This was his way of adding some dignity to her need for a Hostile Environment Work suit (HEW).

Most HEW customers were adventurous contractors looking for lucrative returns on a year or two of labor somewhere in the near solar system. Those who signed on with the Mars Expedition, the newest and most risky pioneering effort in the world of interstellar colonization and resource extraction, were looking at the greatest opportunities in the galaxy: wealth, new skills, developing new science and technology, being a formative part of the next stage in human expansion. It was a heady prospect for any person willing to take the dive. Walter had considered it himself though not for the best reasons; his desire to escape was stronger than the longing for adventure. A lack of money to buy space gear had kept him out this time, but maybe by the time the next team was recruited he would be able to afford the suit he wanted.

Operative arrangements were another matter, more of a limited work release program that gave debtors to society a way to pay off non-violent crimes or exorbitant legal settlement costs. Once on site, they were equal to contractors but received no pay until their debts were covered. For most, that could be accomplished in one to two years on the Moon – much quicker on Mars, he was sure.

Seating her in an elegant, white leather chair, and offering her a tall glass of mint iced tea, the rep introduced himself.

"Walter," he smiled engagingly and took her hand with a warm, friendly handshake. "Honored to be of service, Contractor Frandelle. Let me describe the concerns your new enterprise opens up and the variety of solutions we have to solve them."

"Thank you," the attractive woman accepted as she tasted the tea. She usually went by Sil but declined to give him the advantage of her first name.

He began the understated performance that had earned him his reputation in sales, weaving, introducing, alternating, speaking, waiting, and artfully leading her to the one suit he knew she would want the most. It took two hours of interaction and culminated with the now lovely woman standing before him clothed in beauty and style, exuding all the confidence that belonged to a masterpiece.

Sil stood in front of a full length mirror clothed in the burgundy HEW suit. The leather like material framed her figure better than any other suit. Her hair was pulled back tightly in a utilitarian bun from her face and she wore only the faintest makeup, but the effect was startling. It transformed her from a stressed, intense, pale faced, thirty-something woman to a calm, even mysterious, woman with a purpose. She posed, turned, smiled faintly, looked at her hazel eyes and remembered that they were the feature she was most proud of.

Not bad, she thought. *But it's got to be way out of my price range. I have expensive tastes.*

"The XT-247 is very popular in the diplomatic circles. Not only is it beautiful and flexible, but it has the highest level of puncture and bullet resistance ever made. We like to say it's 'anti-assassin'," Walter informed her with an appraising look. The shade of the suit was adjustable but he had chosen the burgundy to flatter her coloring and he knew it had done what it needed to do.

"How much is it?" Sil asked attempting to be offhanded, hiding how much she wanted it.

"I'm afraid this is one of our most expensive models," Walter responded apologetically, "I knew you would want to make an informed decision so I have shown you a full range of our Hews. All of them are effective. This one is the best."

Sil glanced over at the pile of other suits she had tried on and the selection of models hanging that remained to be tried. None of them begged to be owned like this one.

"How much is it?" she asked again.

"With the highest measure of toxin safety, radioactive waste collection systems, uv-ray shielding, air quality adjustments in addition to all our standard features, you are getting top value for your money. Not to mention that it comes with a lifetime guarantee on all parts, and free labor for the first year."

"But, how much…" Sil tried yet again.

"Consumer Analysis has reported no failures and complete satisfaction with this model from its introduction on the market until today and company stock has skyrocketed because of its sales. No other model has even close to the number of sales on the Moon and it's second on the list for…"

"Excuse me, Walter," Sil interrupted, a tight-lipped look spreading across her face as the suit's charm began to lose hold in the face of sticker dread, "I have limited funds and no credit. Don't hold me in suspense."

"I wouldn't dream of it," Walter effused warmth and sincerity. "I wanted you to understand how great a value this suit entails because, though it is expensive, the offer I can make today is rare. We've moved a lot of our inventory and I can afford to be generous."

Sil became suddenly tired of his game – and Walter saw the look that crossed her face.

"600 universals is over 20% off the retail value and…" he purred in his most soothing voice as she fled shuddering to the changing room.

"I don't care!" she shot back over her shoulder, "I'll take the cheapest one that will do the trick no matter how ugly it is."

"Who am I kidding?" She murmured bitterly to herself as she changed into her own clothing. "My days of style, high society, money, success and respect are over." She choked back an angry tear and gritted her teeth to shove the wave of discouragement back into its cage in her belly. *Face of steel*, she reminded herself as she returned to the rep, *face of steel*.

Walter matched her chill expression with a stone face of his own. He smelled the threat of a small commission and allowed her the only taste of disapproval he ever extended.

"Of course the BAV-21 has been a sturdy model for generations. We have some refurbished ones that are quite affordable even for the most frugal of speculators…" he breathed disdainfully, letting the last word hang in the air.

She shuddered ever so slightly and grew still, delaying the moment when she must pick up the inferior suit.

Walter was watching her and waiting, comfortable in his role, and completely unprepared for what happened next.

She turned and lifted her eyes. A passing glance in his direction caught him. Her gaze, unguarded, reached him, pierced him, and for an instant he was only human and so was she. He saw her soul and witnessed the desolation that resided there. Suddenly he knew. The sorrow and weariness he had glimpsed was familiar. He identified with the gut-wrenching drama playing out under the surface of her calm exterior. He had lived it before.

His sales brain warned him not to allow the human connection but it was too late. Maintaining an appearance of detachment was still possible, though.

Sil looked away again and picked up the 'sturdy model'. She felt the heavy material and tried to read the tag.

"Made of metal alloys, organic and composite materials. R26-vx capacitor. Double headed four chambered multi-purpose waste storage, trion technology heating and cooling system…"

Her vision blurred a little and that sick feeling in her stomach began to surface again. This suit, only 47 universals, made her feel like a cow in a trashcan.

Then her mind flashed on her former business partner's deceitful face and it boosted her morale and hardened her resolve. She couldn't prevent what he had done to her, but she was still the same person she had always been and knew how to get what she wanted.

"Some contractors have taken an interest in our co-investment plan," Walter allured gently as he coaxed his compassion into a back corner of his mind, "It requires a mere 20 universals to cover the cost of paperwork."

He picked up discarded Hews, arranged them on their models and sent them gliding back to the showroom conveyor. This was a task the mannequins usually did for themselves but he found it a useful tactic in making a better sale. There was something compelling about removing options one by one.

"Co-investment plan? What is that?" Sil took a deep breath and entered what she thought of as her transaction-mode. She gave Walter her face of steel, raised an eyebrow and cocked her head slightly. This was a posture she had often adopted when negotiating with clients in her previous life. Separated as she was from her former power, it still had an effect, even on Walter.

He turned to look at her and understood the time had come for solid negotiation. Fortunately, he had himself back in hand and was ready.

"It's a contract added onto your indentureship. Basically, you add however much time to it that's needed to cover the cost of the suit after you've paid off your debts – before," he emphasized, "Before earning any money of your own to make a new start."

"What is the interest?" she shot the words at him in a staccato, fixing a tiger's gaze on him and pulling herself up tall. It added a sense of danger to the process.

"4% the first two years, 15% the next and it goes up two points a year after that," Walter responded flatly, unable to look away, unwilling to yield to her stare. Her transition into a force to be reckoned with, knowing as he did what lay underneath, made her interesting.

"What penalties?" she pressed taking a step closer and leaning toward him. Her eyes smoldered with an animal's intensity. She became even more compelling.

Walter inhaled deeply before he answered. "The..." he brushed his forehead, sensing a higher risk if he looked away. "The penalty for defaulting before the end of ten years is..." His words failed him and the room felt dark as he searched for the logical conclusion to his sentence. Her proximity was making it hard to think.

"Is what?" she asked with a veneer of politeness, as though she were not the one in control. "Death?" Her eyes blazed with fire and his heart raced.

"Ha..." he gasped lamely but realized she wasn't joking. The pathos and intensity he had seen in her combined to grip him. Whatever the penalty actually was, she could see no life beyond the ten year default. "Fines, or work penalties if the fines aren't paid."

"A work prison," Sil hissed, releasing him from her gaze and turning away.

Walter reached for his throat unconsciously as though to soothe it and examined her figure with a new respect. He cleared his throat and brushed off the front of his suit attempting to regain his composure and objectivity.

"A woman of your talents would shine better in the XT model," he urged with undisguised admiration. "There must be a way we can fine tune the contract to make it palatable."

She continued to stand with her back to him, calculating her debts and the barest of expenses down to the tenth in her mind, several times over, as she had been doing night and day since the verdict was handed down. There was no way around it. Six years was the earliest she could pay off the debts. And a suit like this would add another year at least to the indenture.

Swiveling slowly around, first the head, then the shoulders, and finally the hips, Sil locked her gaze onto Walter and the fascination took hold of him again. He held his breath until she spoke.

"You will take off the default penalties," she established.

7

"Of course, it may be difficult but for someone in your situation I will certainly do my best…" Walter hedged, staring into her eyes.

She faced him head on, stepped very close and rested her index finger on his chest. It seemed crazy that she had touched him. The image split in his mind into two parts, one appealing for help; the other tapping him with the point of a sword.

"How much of a commission do you make off the XT-247, Walter?"

"I can't discuss…" he swallowed.

"How much, Walter?" the finger tapped gently and the eyes bore into his mind; the threat, the appeal.

"15% is often what they give me but sometimes with taxes and fees it's greatly reduced…" he rattled off, unwilling to move a muscle or even straighten his shoulders.

"A pound of flesh, is it, Walter? Is that the share you get of my two years of slavery in the outer reaches of the solar system? Is that what you live off of? Go to the Bahamas? To Paris?" She continued to stare into his eyes and tap him with her fingertip.

"Paris is nice…" he babbled absurdly, "But I don't think one sale… well, maybe it helps…"

"Not a drop of blood, Walter," she smiled disarmingly, stepping back from the personal space she had invaded.

"Blood?" he melted with relief. "What do you mean?"

"One day," she reasoned, "That's all. You have spent half a day with me and in those few hours will skim off the cream of a whole season of my life. My sweat, my torment and loneliness, my agony, everything I have to live on… the staff of life, Walter. Is that all my life is worth to you? A few hours and then your trip to Hawaii?"

Walter was beyond confusion. On the one hand, he was enjoying the strange negotiation and the sense of a sale won without having a clue what she was talking about. On the other, he had seen the loneliness and realized she was battling for her life the only way she could. He had never had an encounter remotely like this before in all his years of retail.

"I would like to see Hawaii someday," he searched for his footing, "but your life is surely worth a thousand trips." He warmed his face with his most charming and dimpled smile.

"Ah!" she said agreeably, "That is so kind! I knew you were an understanding man."

"Thank you!" he nodded slightly, "I'm not sure…"

"So, with the 20% discount you mentioned and your lavishly generous offer to forgo your cut for my sake, I may be able throw myself off the deep end and buy the XT-247…" All her previous anxiety and discouragement were now quelled in the comfortable practice of engagement. For the moment, the offensive indenture contract had become a tool.

"Now just a minute, Contractor," Walter finally picked up on the tightening of the snare around his pocketbook, dissolving the web of enchantment she had begun to wrap around his soul. "I am not willing to work without pay and shouldn't be expected to…"

"A few hours?" Sil's eyes narrowed into slits, piercing his heart with shame, "Years of my life without pay mean nothing but I must sympathize with your morning time of drudgery spent with me? You are paid a salary but it's not enough. No! You crave a pound of flesh… but you have no right to a drop of blood, Walter."

For a moment, Walter was appalled at his own greed – that he had hoped to make a profit off her added years of indenture, and lowered his eyes.

"The company no doubt pays you for charging me interest during my time of slavery, Walter," she shook her head in amazement, looping the silvery web around him again.

"No!" he protested, caught and snared. "I make nothing off of that!"

"And why should they, I wonder?" Sil swiveled around again with the ease of control she had learned from years of securing her influence. "It doesn't seem fair…"

"It's despicable," Walter complained with a furrowed brow, "I don't think you should be charged any interest at all."

"That's so sweet," she whipped around and rewarded him with loving eyes full of gratitude. "What would I have done if another rep had come up? No one could have helped me like you." Walter didn't even think of resisting the full impact of that thrill and only a strong restraint fueled by concern for his job kept him from sweeping her into a passionate kiss.

In twenty minutes, she walked out with the latest, most expensive Hew suit model on the market, marked down to a cost of 390 universals (less than half the retail price), at zero interest with no default penalties and 150 universals worth of accessories thrown in at the last minute.

Walter had landed the biggest sale of the day, but was hardly able to work. His thoughts made no sense. She was impressive. No, he was a fool. She had needed his help and he had kept his cool. No, she had fenced and beaten him. He had been outmaneuvered. She was very attractive. *So am I*, he reassured himself. But, that hadn't made an impression on her. She was exciting.

I'm exciting... Walter wanted to add, but it wasn't true. He could have been in that expedition and had hesitated. *I always choose the safer way*, he reproved himself.

As the sun went down and he walked toward the public transport, he knew this day would soon be behind him and all would be as it had been. The attractive woman would be propelled far into space, immersed in a life of servitude, maybe never returning, her spirit broken, her individuality faded, her beauty erased. And he would forget her.

But Walter didn't *want* to forget her. Her enchantment still held and he didn't want it to fade. He hated the thought that he would never see her again or even know what became of her. There *must* be a way he could create a connection with her. If he could just come up with a good excuse to talk to her again or stay in contact with her, maybe he could create a link.

But how could a guy like me ever hope to come up with something a girl like her could want? He sighed, leaning his head against the trolley window and gazed into the darkening sky.

Ideas didn't have to be good though, just decent enough for a working sales pitch.

2—PORT

The Walla Walla spaceport was full of people without the condensed feeling of a big city subway station at rush hour. The expansive walls of transparent, platinum-infused glass dulled the racket of trans-atmospheric commuter ships and softened the glare of the August sun. Shops and advertisements vied for last minute impulse shopping decisions; flavor enhancers for the bland inflight food, gaming/sleeping headgear, first aid for weightless ailments, and similar items selling for ten times their value.

Sil sat comfortably in the premier lounge where no one even considered checking her boarding status. Her XT-247 headgear, no more obtrusive than an archaic hearing aid, was streaming a crystal-clear, holographic image into her cornea with sound funneled into her ears. Her own skull formed the antenna and enabled her to speak articulately without moving her lips.

Her eyes looked pleased and her mouth was shaped charmingly with a gentle quirk in one corner, almost a smile. It was one of those looks that the recipient would read as very personal and warm. And though a number of travelers glanced her way hoping to catch her eyes and become that recipient, it was plain she was 'hollowing', conversing with someone via holographic chat.

"Why would you want to stay in touch with me?" she cooed like a dove, "I will be hopelessly far away." She rested comfortably on the leather chair; arms relaxing on the rests, legs crossed, and head tipped, coffee in hand.

"You may need a contact on earth, don't you think? A business contact?" Walter had dressed in a richly colored plum dress shirt and a dark tie for the call.

"I have no business left on this planet. Everything I had was taken away from me." She sipped her espresso and savored the cinnamon, wondering if it would be her last taste of it for years.

"You could say I have an investment in you," Walter smiled disarmingly. "My entire commission went into your future and it makes sense that someday I would benefit from it." He watched her image as she sipped her coffee again and smoothed her hair with her free hand.

"Oh?" Another faint smile lit her face. Another sip of coffee.

"Drinking caffeinated beverages before an Earth orbit launch is not recommended," a suave, slightly foreign sounding woman cautioned in the passageways of the spaceport.

"I have some experience in space futures and interstellar investments," he continued, tilting his head slightly and intentionally emitting as much confidence and trustworthiness as he knew how. "Not as risky as some, I prefer to take a more conservative, stable approach, but I have a history of steady growth and a knack for selecting the right ventures to invest in."

"I won't have finances to invest for years," Sil answered flatly with a hint of brass in her tone.

"It might be of use to me to have another over-space contact to keep me updated," he added, unable to ignore the thrill he felt at creating a link with her. He knew he was offering her something she would appreciate.

Her eyes locked onto his intently, reaching in and gripping him somehow. Sinking into the fascination she had snared him with a few days before, he began once again to breathe shallowly, his mouth falling open slightly.

"Why should I trust you?" she tested, tossing the empty coffee cup into the de-materializer where it vanished, and leaned forward. Announcements in the background wafted by without interrupting the contest he had begun.

"I'll give you…" he thrust.

"I'll need…" she countered at the same instant.

"Access codes," they landed on the words simultaneously.

"You send them to me now and I evaluate them before I leave or no deal," Sil jumped to her feet and tossed her head as if to shake off a fly. The muffled tapping of her boot disturbed the focus-field of the executive next to her, who twisted his face in disgust and reset the envelope a few inches away.

"Sending…" Walter reposted, also leaping to a stand. He had set up an interstellar account the day before and had the access ready to link to her eye-Ds and vocal-slots.

"Money upfront," she hissed, "or no deal."

"No," he said, posing for her, knowing only she could see, in a mock fencing stance where his extended hand was the weapon reaching out in a friendly way for the 'point'. "Nothing illegal."

"It's not technically illegal..."

"No." With the art of holograph, he drew her image closer.

"What then?" she smiled, softening her tone. Proximity merely gave her an advantage. It freed her to wait for him to play his hand.

"You will be behind 'enemy lines', as it were, of the Mars industry with access to key information days to months ahead of the public. I'd be willing to reward you with stocks and investments in whatever company you feed me tips about." Walter restrained the impulse to laugh. He had spent all week trying to figure out not only how to entice her into a partnership but also how to maintain a measure of control in it. The delight at his own cleverness and the excitement of interacting with her was something of a rush. He shifted his pose to a different fencing stance, whipping the friendly hand around a few times as though he held a rapier.

"What do you intend to do with my inside tips, Walter?" Sil parried so smoothly he didn't realize what had happened. "Will you invest at the same level as me? Or will you draw in other investors and take a cut? Will you sell my intel? Will you build your career in the world of interplanetary speculation with my widow's mite?"

Walter had no idea what a mite was or what his suggestion had to do with widowhood. Operative Frandelle was no widow. He dropped his arms and stood awkwardly, a little disconcerted.

"Well?" she didn't allow him the luxury of backing away now that the hollowing had been adjusted for proximity. Her finger reached toward his chest as if to tap it. "I can borrow money and hire a broker to do whatever I want." This was mere boasting. She had tried a thousand ways to make it happen and the difficulties were too great. But he didn't know that.

"Who would loan you money?" he began, allowing his fascination with her eyes to keep him from puzzling out her position. He was glad for the debate even if nothing more ever came of it, making him both easier and harder to manipulate.

"And why should you sell my tips when I am far more capable of marketing them cleverly?" she reasoned with a gentle tilt of her head, raising her eyebrows and adding warmth to her hazel eyes. All her contacts were burned and her name was mud. No one would touch her tips with an optic link.

Walter didn't know that.

"Let me talk to some of your investors," Sil maneuvered with a silky voice, "and find out for myself what your standing is among them." She stroked her cheek in a strange way that put off careless observers in the lounge but filled Walter with a desire to protect her.

His fingers extended slowly and his arms stretched around her image.

"Lady," he whispered without thinking. "I don't have any investors. I just want to help you."

It never crossed her mind to gloat. Her image had been so tarnished and her treatment universally cold, that she hungered for kindness. She also feared being vulnerable.

"Operative Frandelle," she corrected with a hint of irritation, though she also extended a hand toward him and captivated him with a binding gaze. "Are you saying you want to loan me money *and* be my broker?"

"Operative Frandelle…" he conceded. "Maybe I can spare you the brutal payment the contract demands of you and help you set up something worth coming home to." He hardly knew what he was saying any more. Now that his preplanned script was ended and her answers had flown far off the page, he let slip whatever came to mind without restraint. He tried to convince himself he was almost in love with her but that was too far of a stretch. He wasn't really hinting that she could come home to him. It hadn't even occurred to him yet.

"Walter…" she spoke carefully, trying to balance the undercurrent of his attraction to her with the risk he seemed prepared to take. "I couldn't ask you to take a gamble like that—though my business instinct is killer and my intel would be valuable. I could never pay it if an unforeseen crisis wiped out what I borrowed." Her eyes pleaded with him, pulling on that soft side of his heart, blurring the practical half of his brain.

"Excalibur is about to embark. All contract and indentured workers report immediately to the docking bay for clearance and loading." The foreign voice powerfully interposed itself into their hollow. "Repeat message: Excalibur is about to embark…"

Ignoring the offended glares of the elite travelers in the premier lounge where she had been relaxing when her wristband ticket began flashing, Sil gathered her belongings and strode away. The summons broadcast incessantly in her ears until she reached the waiting area she should have occupied all along.

"…Are you there?" Walter's voice broke in when it had finally fallen silent. His tone of anguish was hardly fitting and it surprised her.

"Yes," she answered hesitantly as she got in line. "Only for a few moments longer. Then all communication must end."

"Give me your contact code so we can complete arrangements when you're in space. You'll have daily transmissions, won't you?" He had grown very serious. It wasn't love. It was a frail connection to vicarious adventure and he hated to lose it.

"Sending," she responded straightforwardly, "but, keep in mind that anything over three minutes will cost me and be added to my debt."

"I'll pay for the transmissions," he replied artlessly, "You may need the time to talk to family or friends."

Sil laughed bitterly. "Not likely!" The greedy bunch had all turned their backs on her in their scramble to preserve their own nest eggs, fortunes *she* had made for them. Not one of them had offered to help her out of the disaster or even loan her funds for the trip to Mars. Every tenth was coming from her contract.

"Walter," she began tentatively, about to let a little humanity show through a crack in her façade again.

"Operative Frandelle, boarding!" burst into the hollow.

"What?" he begged urgently.

"Never mind," she dismissed him resolutely and flipped off the connection.

Stepping into the scanning chamber, she walked carefully though the various bands of light that confirmed identity, health, financial status, completion of training modules and packing requirements, and an evaluation of her HEW suit.

"Satisfactory," the examining AI announced and the doors opened before her with a deep whoosh. Air wafted forward, pulling her down a ramp into the tunnel-like passageway. With a silent click the doors closed behind her.

Walter sighed deeply as he found his favorite chair and fell into it exhausted. The sun shone through the open window and a faint breeze ruffled the branches outside.

"Daisy, what's my status?" he asked his manager, a personal, sibling-D model AI who was an established member of the family.

"Your supplemental retirement fund has been cashed and the universals deposited in your new interstellar account, ready for disbursal," she began, sitting down in a chair across from him. "Your vacation ends in three days and the high season begins in two weeks. Sales projected to be 15% greater than last year. You're expected to bring in over 32% of those sales alone."

"However," Daisy interposed in her friendly way, with a sweet smile. "Economic downturns suggest that the increase in sales will not lead to higher profits. Time for you to shine!"

She folded her hands in her lap. Designed to resemble a young woman, barely twenty, her smooth cheeks and bright eyes were the picture of health and cheer. Her blond hair, so real it looked human, curled upwards at the tips and framed her face. She wore a black and white, window-paned dress with sunflowers in the design, white belt and shoes, and a flower in her hair.

"You seemed tired and perhaps a little discouraged from the hollow. Did your arrangements go as planned?" Daisy requested. "Would you like me to talk to the birds?"

"It went well enough," Walter responded. "I think it may lead to something, but we didn't complete the negotiation."

"Yes, I could use some birds," he added.

Daisy leaned out the window, opened her mouth and sang flawless bird song from her memory banks. Joyful, beautiful chirpings came from her lips and soon, several little feathered creatures had accepted the invitation and began to sing for her. She smiled, pointed her face to the window, and grew still.

The cat, too old to be a threat, but still feisty enough to think about it, jumped into Walter's lap and settled down to listen and watch.

"Ah! My old friend," Walter murmured to him. "Are you the one that has made me a home body and kept me from venturing beyond my own planet?"

The old friend purred and said nothing.

3—SERF

"Contractor housing is straight ahead," the same voice that had made the earthside spaceport announcements sounded in her ears. Sil wondered if it was provided by her suit.

"Is there a bathroom facility I can visit first?" she asked the voice. Visual imaging in her optical nerves showed her the way to the closest one. It was filled with clean, sterile, compact stalls without any color or design; utilitarian, functional. Simple instructions on the door taught her how to use a toilet in low gravity, and cold lighting blanched her face as she mist-cleaned her hands, making a ghostly reflection in the mirror.

Returning to the stream of operatives disembarking from the inter-lunar transport shuttle, she headed to her assigned room. Her contract started immediately at 0800 the next day. Work details would be handed out at breakfast and she would be serving the Guam Base guests for the next two months. This was considered a reasonable period to learn about the company that owned her contract, adjust to low gravity and settle into the practical aspects of her indentureship.

"Guam is a fully equipped miniature city orbiting in a wide ring around the earth roughly halfway between the moon and the terran sea level," the welcome clip in her room explained in a warm friendly voice. She was so relieved at having the bunk room to herself that she hardly listened to the recording. A bed, closet, drawers, desk and chair, made up the meager furniture of her quarters, with just enough empty room to stand in the middle and take one step in each direction.

"Generous funding from Director of Science Kaldeen has made the luxury of the base's many amenities possible," the clip continued. Gentle, happy music lapped around the tiny room almost warming the cold gray walls and white furnishings.

17

"Where can I find Supervisor Mandel?" Sil interrupted the welcome. "Is it possible to speak with him right away?"

"You must be thoroughly processed before ascending into the public regions of Guam to speak with company leaders." The female voice shifted subtly, less benevolent and slightly more authoritative. "Do you wish to proceed with the welcome or continue it later?"

"Later. What must I do to finish processing?"

"Place your hand on the blue lit door panel and stare into the light. You will be screened."

She placed her right hand on the panel and gazed into the blue light. A light tingling in her skin was all she noticed of the panel of tests that were executed in the space of half a second.

"Identity confirmed. DNA sampled, T-cells stored, length of life calculated, subject quality assessed for company project participation." The voice uttered calmly, growing more sterile.

"Operative Frandelle," it continued, "Do you agree to all aspects of the contract that was delivered to you in its entirety? Do you have any objections to make to any of its restrictions, limitations, parameters, promises or factors?" The voice lowered in pitch and increased its air of command.

"Are you referring to the contract I reviewed with my lawyer on earth during the enacting of my verdict?" Sil questioned uneasily, dropping her arm to her side.

"The contract is the same, but some of the parameters were to be received after you left earth due to their confidential nature. These have been added to your data banks and can now be reviewed at any time."

Touching the belt at her waist, Sil summoned her virtual computer screen.

"Show me the Operative Parameters that have been added to my contract," she subvocalized.

Two hundred and seventy six pages opened before her.

"It figures!" she snapped in disgust, throwing herself down on the bed and stretching out. She might as well be comfortable if she was stuck reading all this.

After several pages of extremely tedious verbiage, she lifted her eyes to the door panel.

"What if I have a problem with something listed here?" she challenged.

"You have already signed the contract and bound yourself to it. The company will make a record of your objection and in the event of a lawsuit, it will be taken into consideration." Was that a sneer in the welcomer's voice?

"What if I don't understand something? Will you explain it to me?"

"Yes. I have the capability of providing explanations within certain limitations."

"Which are...?" Sil demanded in exasperation.

"Based on my programming and your level of clearance."

"Clearance? It's not like this is a military operation. It's a private enterprise serving investors and stockholders."

"I can't say," the welcomer countered absurdly, "Your employee status doesn't give you access to that information."

The narrow pallet was beginning to feel a little firmer than was comfortable and the lack of windows seemed suddenly constricting. There wasn't even a bland piece of art projected on the blank wall.

"Do I have to approve it all now?" Sil asked glumly, "Before I can complete processing?"

"Processing will only be considered complete when you have finalized your contract. Until then you have access only to the operative quarters." The room grew a little dimmer as the instructions continued. "Your Guam work assignment would restrict you to this level and you would have no job assigned for Mars. Those who complete processing are placed in a queue for assessment." The voice was no longer clearly feminine. It seemed to be dropping gradually in pitch with every sentence.

"Meaning all the good jobs will go to those who are processed first regardless of their qualifications? Is that what you're saying?" She sat up in alarm.

"That is correct."

"Do you know what my skills are? Do they understand what I could do for them and how I could help to make this operation profitable?!" her voice rising as she jumped to her feet. A metallic ring echoed as her toes bumped the edge of the wall.

"All of that is meaningless until you accept the terms sent to you." The voice responded flatly.

19

Sil looked around her room distractedly, measuring the width, breadth, height; noting the vent and the gentle flow of clean air that blew through it, the crisp lines of the shelves and doors, the neutral colors of the room, almost colorless actually.

"I am Companion," the voice informed. "That is the name you will use to address me as long as you are a member of this venture."

"You're giving me orders?" Sil gasped. She had never debated an AI as an equal before, let alone as an underling. Her arms crossed involuntarily as if she were cold, but the ambient temperature was quite comfortable for sleeping quarters.

"The title is meant to inspire trust between us. My architect thought it better than Taskmaster which is what I actually am. I have access to your headset as well as all the speakers in the base. Your first assignment is to complete your processing. For the next eighteen hours, until you report for duty at 0800, you have the freedom to interact with me or not. After that, I will define the context for our communication at all times."

A fear she had never known before slipped into her chest and pressed on her lungs. She had never been deprived of the refuge of silence before. She had always had the privilege of quiet within her own mind. This AI was calmly telling her it would be able to broadcast in her ears at any time.

"Companion…" she spoke carefully, dropping her hands to her side and breathing deeply, trying to slow down her heart rate. "What is your normal context for communication with operatives like me?"

"Most of the time, the operatives and I find a middle ground we both find acceptable. As long as they listen to me during working hours, I maintain silence during off hours."

"That sounds reasonable," she replied cautiously, "Will that arrangement work with me?"

"Once you have completed your processing, I will answer that question." Companion said. The once female voice had morphed into a male tenor with an emotionless timbre. It was melodic but without a hint of human warmth.

Resolve to crest every wave that threatened to capsize her came to her aid once again, as it had so many times before and her eyes began to flash intensely as she thought furiously.

"Could I accept the parameters now to finish processing and then come back and review the document carefully? Would I still be allowed to voice objections?"

"Objections can be made at any time."

"Will they carry any legal weight?"

Companion hesitated. Strange for an AI, Sil thought, why would they program hesitation? Was it really an AI? Was it being managed by a live person? Was the program allowed to defer to a person because it was programmed to never lie and a lie was needed?

"There is insufficient data to answer that question," Companion stated. "The occasion has never arisen and is considered unimportant."

Sil crossed her arms and tapped her foot rapidly. Two, three deep breaths, and she reached a decision.

"Companion," she ventured, "I want to register an objection in the document." She saw it being added to the page in her virtual screen as she spoke. "I object to the severely limited time and opportunity given to me to read these parameters and agree to them. I believe that I am under duress at this time because of my fear of being stuck with a job I am not suited for on Mars.

"Furthermore, I reserve the right to read this document in the future and add objections for an indefinite period of time up until the completion of my contract and the pay-off of my debt."

She swiveled on her heel, took a step and continued.

"If legal action is initiated at any time in the future, by either party, the company or myself, I require that all my objections be included in the court records and allowed into consideration, whether recorded in this document or by some other means on Mars."

She turned and walked two steps in the other direction, then faced the door panel again. Though she guessed Companion wasn't really in any particular direction, it pleased her to interact this way. And actually, Companion automatically accepted her pattern and chose to record the visual from the door panel.

"That is the restriction I am adding to the contract in order to complete my processing. Companion, do you agree?"

"On behalf of the Mars Venture Conglomerate and the specific company that owns your contract, I record your restriction and accept your processing. You may now exit the operative region through any of the exit doors and have access to the public regions. You are seventy-third in the queue for interviewing with Supervisor Mandel and will be summoned when the time for your appointment approaches. Welcome to Guam!" The tenor voice mellowed with a hint of friendliness while articulating the last sentence.

"Seventy-third?" she bit her lip in frustration. "Really? Have I been that slow to complete processing?"

"Of the three hundred and forty six operatives contracted for employment, seventy two of them took care of processing in the waiting area in Walla Walla and the others are putting it off till later. Most have not read more than a few sentences of the document."

"I could have done this on earth?" she uttered wryly.

"If you had proceeded to the general operative waiting area on time, you would have had the opportunity," Companion said. Sil was sure she heard a smirk in his voice.

Blast! That's what she got for grasping at a few final moments of elite status before becoming a bonded worker! That – and a sore bladder because of the espresso she drank just before take-off.

She opened the door to her bunker. "How much time do I have to explore?" she asked before venturing out.

"At least two hours, possibly three," Companion affirmed calmly.

Companion! Sil snorted to herself as she climbed the ladder to the bunker hallway. More like Compression, she thought.

"I am oblivious to insults," Companion's voice commented softly in her ear. "And, no, I am not reading your mind. But I have worked with people enough to recognize the meaning behind small gestures."

"I request silence until it is necessary for you to speak to me," Sil said icily, infuriated by the invasion of her privacy and the demeaning interpretation of her manner. It hadn't been meant as an insult, but as humor to cheer herself up.

Shaking off the annoyance, she popped out into the corridor and began heading toward the exit to the public regions as fast as she could in low gravity. It was more than comical and she chuckled to herself as she leapt forward step by step in what felt like slow motion. Her lightly gravetized shoes clicked into contact with the corridor floor and snap-released with each stride. Compared to most of the new arrivals, she was graceful as a gazelle with the sophisticated programming of her suit. The others were either leaping with too much power and banging into the ceiling or battling their legs, grabbing them in their hands to free them from the deck, and tipping into the wall and snap-clicking into a crazy position with a foot twisted around behind or even on the wall itself.

The corridor opened into a wide common area where operatives could mingle, be fed, receive orders, and enjoy a break during off hours. Comfortable chairs, tables, misting fountains and fake garden plants were spread out in an English garden design. Sil ignored them and sped to the main chutes.

Many people were being knocked back as they tried to enter a chute, obviously still unprocessed, but Sil breezed through, leaping into one of the windy tunnels and rocketing up to the public level. I love that feeling, she gloated to herself, zooming ahead of a crowd.

The Hanging Gardens of Babylon, as they were called, opened before her in breathtaking, majestic splendor. It was a series of hydroponic domes cascading above and below linked by slides, stairs, and even swinging ropes for the playful guest. Sunshine, filtered through protective glass, was streaming into the domes like liquid light, pooling and flooding the gardens. Some were tropical, with birds, lizards, insects, trees and flowers mirroring famous jungles of Earth. Some were crisp, towering forests with redwoods, cedars, and trees of the Pacific Northwest. Some were filled with farm beds, lush with an abundance of food, vegetables, fruits, bushes, trees, vines, herbs.

Water, rich and luxurious, poured over in streams from one dome to another, sparkling with light. The music of nature in all its glory filled the panorama.

"Whoa!" Sil exclaimed out loud in spite of herself, riveted to her place as she gaped at the sight. After a few moments she noticed the people, the shops and cafes, the reading nooks, the chess and game tables, and shaking herself, she set out to explore. The ropes begged to be tried first.

It was barely two hours and one cappuccino later that Companion summoned her for the appointment with Supervisor Mandel and gave her illuminated directions. She had visited only a few of the domes, since she lacked the access to the higher and more inviting levels, but she had already mapped out the sections she hoped to work in for the next two months.

Once again, Sil found herself in a queue with ordinary people, waiting for an appointment that would apparently not last longer than five to ten minutes. She rehearsed what she would say and avoided eye contact with anyone around her.

Soon the door swiveled and her name was announced and one person exited on the left as she entered confidently on the right. The office was relatively small and functional with bland furnishings that melted into inconsequence next to a breathtaking window with a startling cut-out view of the earth and myriad stars. It was like a bizarre commentary on the pitiful inferiority of the human business being conducted within the confining walls.

Mandel was a shriveled, red faced, shrimp of a man that sniffed periodically when he spoke. He barely glanced up at her from the skill sheet displayed on his monitor.

"Business, finance, marketing…*sniff*… we have little use for any of this on Mars," he began unceremoniously.

"I read people and manage them very well. Also, I'm an excellent operations analyst, able to improve and streamline procedures, redistribute funds, resources, and people, for their most effective use…" Sil assumed her most persuasive air of confidence, exuding strength and competence, with a hint of a smile.

"It hardly matters," Mandel sniffed and rubbed his nose with a cloth, without deigning to give her even a passing glance.

"Mars is certainly a very costly venture and with my experience, I am sure I could help increase profits in a number of ways, if I had the authority to examine and evaluate – and make changes to the operation." Sil crossed her legs and resisted the urge to cross her arms, as well. Something about this wasn't right at all.

"Let's see, how much do you weigh on Earth? A hundred and fifteen pounds? Hardly enough to break rocks even with the machinery… *sniff*… No medical background, no computer tech," Mandel seemed to read very slowly.

"I am quite skilled at computer tech," she countered, straining out the irritation that tried to creep into her voice.

"Not the kind we would be interested in," he responded blandly. "No, uh… feminine skills, parenting, mothering, fostering, babysitting, not even cooking or cleaning…"

"What?" she gasped, horrified, "What are you saying? What are you talking about?"

"There is a small circle of ambassadors, executives, and master scientists on hand who have a use for personal staff… *sniff*… but other than that, all the jobs are extremely functional with no skills or previous experience required."

"I speak several languages…" she whispered, not realizing she had begun to wring her hands anxiously. She had never done that before.

"We have automated translators and all the latest technology," he fixed his little eyes on her appraisingly, as though noticing her for the first time and scanned her with a squinty glare. "Do you have any courtesan skills? That could be an alternative for you. We would provide…"

"No!" she spat out, her eyes growing wild and her fists clenching. "Absolutely not!"

"You are assigned to the mines," he responded resolutely, clicking something on the screen and waving her away without another glance.

"You must be joking," she fumbled, "Would you really ignore everything I have to offer and make me a common worker in the mines?"

"It doesn't matter," he spun his chair around to give her his back.

Sil stood and walked slowly out of the room. The fear she had begun to feel in the bunk gripped her chest again and rose to her head, throbbing like a headache, chilling her fingers and making them tremble.

"I have no control over what's happening," she said softly as she passed through the swivel door and moved like a shadow toward the wide public avenues that so recently had delighted her.

"I have more control than you do," Companion sneered in her ear.

"You don't sound like an AI," she snapped back and for a moment she was sure a living person had spoken.

"I was programmed by real people," Companion responded cleverly, and immediately she doubted what she had known instinctively in her gut.

"Companion, do you have any influence on the assignment I get here at the base?" she asked, adding some respect to her voice in case it was programmed to be offended or flattered by small things.

"I can add your name to a specific work group but 'real' people will be assigning jobs," he replied coolly.

"I would like to work in…"

"You have been placed in the food service group and I see no point in switching you," Companion stated.

25

Sil hesitated, debating within herself whether showing annoyance or submission would be more effective with this AI.

"I…" she ventured tentatively.

"…have no skills in mechanics or electronics or space repairs, or gardening, or sewage management," Companion suggested. Sil gulped at the 'sewage' reference.

"Ok," she surrendered. Actually, that was the one she would have requested. "I request silence till 0800."

"Silence from me till 0700 when I will wake you for breakfast," the AI corrected.

Sil merely nodded and set out to explore as much as she was allowed before necessity drove her back to her quarters for sleep.

4—GUAM

"How do you like Guam?" Walter asked, once the initial greetings had been said. His choice of coral tie and dark brown dress shirt were oddly complimentary and Sil found herself wondering how he had settled on his sense of style.

She hadn't changed out of her black and white serving clothes or the somber skull cap she was expected to wear while waiting tables. But then, she knew it was flattering and wanted Walter to see her in it. She intended to maintain whatever element of intrigue she could for as long as possible. Her tie to him was very slim and it was beginning to seem like he held the strings.

"It's beautiful," she answered with warmth. "You really should see it. The lower gardens and the general viewing deck alone, which are the only ones I have access to, are worth the trip. But the luxury sections are supposed to be the most spectacular of all and I find them hard to picture. And I can't even imagine the Disney Space Rides that make Guam the most coveted vacation spot in the Solar System." She smiled with a head tilt and one lifted eyebrow.

Walter smiled back and found himself noticing that she looked good in a server's cap.

"I have some tips for you, I think," she continued. Holograms being too expensive in trans-space, they were communicating via a flat screen image. "I've heard some rumors on the business deck. I have the day shift at a café there and hear a lot of chatter."

"I'm listening," Walter smiled, using his most friendly and disarming grin without thinking. Instinct had taught him to encourage the sharing of information this way. Sil responded with her own friendly manner, but she did it intentionally.

"Hammer & Tongs have sent some execs up here to meet with Moon real estate reps," she narrowed her eyes and nodded knowingly. "And we know what that means."

"Ah… yes," Walter hesitated, disconcertedly. "Well, that is…"

"They have an extraction plant on the Moon and intend to expand their operation over the next six to eight months, of course," she explained without adding even a hint of condescension to her voice. "They must have found the investors they needed and now, before they announce the lease of Moon property, is the perfect time to buy stock."

"I see," Walter responded. He was still processing what she said, but didn't want her to know it. "So, are you saying no one else has this information? Is our line secure?"

Her eyes bore into him for a moment. She had specifically given him generic, easily obtained info to see how he would handle it. Plus, she was testing to see if he had received the letter she had had sent to him from her lawyer with instructions on coded dialogue.

"All lines of communication are bound to be monitored, Walter," she breathed softly, deciding to be sweet instead of irritated. "It was wise of you to think of it. It may be commonly known information but, it will be half a day at least before most people have access to it. It may be a good deal. But, I have no problem waiting for some better options, if you prefer. You could pass this tip on to your investors."

"Good idea," he replied brightly, as though pleased, but he was troubled by the undercurrent in the conversation. Somehow he had already developed a sense of what she actually meant when she spoke and the two didn't always line up. "I have set up an investor's tips site and have a number of clients already signed up."

"Glad to hear it," she said, watching his face carefully. What if he had gotten the letter and didn't understand what she was doing? Or was he cleverer than that – he hadn't got it yet but sensed her test and was confused by it?

"Operative Frandelle," Walter allowed puzzlement on his face. "Could I make a suggestion?"

"Yes…" she twisted her mouth a little, not sure she wanted to hear it.

"I've submitted a recommendation to XenoTek, the manufacturers of the XT-247, that they should consider endorsing you as a live subject."

"What?" she interrupted testily, crossing her arms and frowning.

"Most of their customers are soft living, wealthy people like ambassadors and company directors who never approach even 5% of the circumstances the suit was designed to handle and it's not much of an endorsement." He paused to see if he should continue explaining.

"Go on," she sighed and wiped the frown off her face.

"Most of the suits that are selling in that range are inferior and now even the latest XenoTek models coming out lack a number of key features essential to life in adverse conditions," he explained without any of the sales slick that normally accompanied this topic.

"I'm not going to be facing adverse conditions, Walter," Sil spoke calmly but her eyes flared. "I am not the ideal test subject."

"It's not a prediction," Walter held up a hand as though to soothe her. "All I need to do is persuade them that it could be and they might sign you on. As your investing agent, I have authority to broker a deal, but I wanted to find out if you would be willing to go for it."

"What would they require of me?" Sil asked, interested in spite of herself.

"You would have to thoroughly study the full length version of the manual – which is included in the suit, by the way – and report back on different features as you have the opportunity to try them out."

Sil tapped her arm with a finger and thought. Walter watched her, wishing she would turn on some of the intensity she had focused on him in the past. He liked the feeling of being drawn into the unknown and unpredictable.

As if sensing his wish, she shot a look at him and smiled mysteriously, moving closer to the camera. "Walter," she said somewhat menacingly, "You wouldn't double cross me, would you?"

"No!" he laughed awkwardly, both unnerved and pleased. "I have no reason to. I don't know how I could…"

"You don't want to be on my bad side, Walter," she gazed deeply into his eyes. "I don't mind if you make money off my investment tips, but you had better not make your fortune off of broadcasting my suffering in the mines of Mars."

"I would never do that," he softened visibly, his brow creasing with concern. "Are you really assigned to the mines?"

"Yes," she whispered. For the briefest moment, he glimpsed sorrow in her eyes. Sorrow, and... was that fear?

"I'm glad you got that suit, Frandelle," he said soberly. "It sounds like you could need it. I wouldn't want anything to happen to you."

"Call me Sil," she gave him a wry, half sided grin, squelching the emotion that had gotten past her veneer. "All my friends call me... well, used to call me that."

"Silvariah," she added with a shrug, "but I never use the full name."

"Sil..." he experimented and liked the way it sounded. "If I get this deal for you, what sounds fair? Realistically."

"What were you planning on negotiating?" she countered.

"Stocks, upgrades, covering the cost of your suit, cash payments graded to reflect the success of your material... maybe some money up front."

"They'll never do that," Sil shook her head and pursed her lips. "They won't pay out a dime till they see some profits brought in because of me. And how much would you take? Fifty percent?"

"Fifty?" Walter choked. The thought had crossed his mind, since he would have to do some of the work to make it happen, but now that she confronted him, he was insecure about it. Were they joint investors? What was their business relationship exactly? How was it supposed to pan out?

"Fifty percent isn't a crime, Walter," she chuckled. "At this point..." She stopped herself before letting on that he was her only friend. It felt so humiliating and she wasn't able to bring herself to say it.

"Really?" He was astonished. It would be a really good deal for him, actually quite exciting. "That would be great!"

"I'm a business woman, Walter. A deal that is good for both of us makes us want to keep working together, and I would feel better if I knew you were invested in our arrangement."

"I am," he responded but as he spoke it was a revelation. I guess I am, he added in his mind. He was beginning to want more than just a momentary thrill at talking to an attractive woman heading into a dangerous frontier.

"I... I like you," he followed up clumsily raising both hands with a shrug.

Sil eyed him thoughtfully for a moment. "I guess you do," she decided finally, "and I like you, too, Walter, though I'm not the kind of person to just blindly trust you. Not yet, anyway."

"Set it up," she resolved, "and get whatever you can for me. Take your fifty percent and invest my share for me. I will send updates when I can."

"Sil..." he pleaded gently, sensing she was about to end the call.

"Well?" It was getting late and she wanted down time before bed.

"I don't know you very well. Can you give me something... to learn about you, or, I don't know, satisfy my curiosity about you?" He appealed to her with disarming sincerity.

"More than the thousands of news reports, interviews and clips that have covered my scandalous fall from wealth and power?" Sil stood with her finger on the disconnect switch, only her waist visible, centered in the screen.

He didn't answer. His disappointment at the end of the call tugged against his elation over the sponsorship contract he was authorized to pursue. Plus, viewing her waist was distracting.

"I'll think about it," she said and the screen went dark.

"You're growing attached to her, Brother," Daisy smiled sweetly at his side.

$-\Diamond-$

"I tested the clothing app on the XT-247 today. The 200 series comes with an extensive selection of the latest fashion designer mods by names like Dome Consortium and the Bolivian Enfoque. After work I wanted to transition from an incognito peon to ambassador's daughter with a simple tap of a button so I programmed it ahead of time and this is what happened..."

The plain, undecorated face of a serving girl in a white skull cap faded into an overhead shot, seamlessly put together by a friendly tech in the security division from a grand assortment of Guam base cameras. High above the discount shopping street, it swept across a sea of ordinary people in plain overalls and jumpsuits of various colors and with a sense of falling over a waterfall it zoomed toward one white head moving calmly through the crowd. Panning around to the front, Sil's face came into view, her eyes indistinct, lips colorless, expression bland. And with a hint of three D, her utilitarian suit stood gently out from the crowd; black with a white apron and a small emblem over the pocket representing the restaurant where she worked. The apron fluttered gently as she passed people heading toward the float tubes.

The camera slipped in closer on her face again and her lips moved ever so slightly. "Custom outfit change, test-one, in three… two… one…" She mouthed as she entered the darker halls and the flow of air swooshed her upwards to the promenade of the public regions. The cameras caught the sense of flying, switching from one angle to another as an amazing transformation took place. When she landed in the lobby, her suit had become a full length, dark green dress, slim cut with one strap over the left shoulder. It had a deep red shimmery under-suit with a single long sleeve on the right arm, and rustling folds of red bursting through the knee high slit on the other side. Her hair was smoothly pulled into a braid at the top of her head from where it stretched like a rope interwoven with gold threads down to her shoulder, across her chest, and around the waist. The makeup lighting had made her gray eyes startling with dark green accents and her cheeks tinted with a gentle bronze. Her lips were full and red. Her shoes looked like soles shaped for heels and the faintest gold chains networked across the tops of her feet. Gold bracelets wrapped her bare arm and red jewels hung glistening from her ears.

The cameras continued to pan around her, catching the passersby who turned to stare and whisper. She walked purposefully toward Sheiks, the prestigious club at the highest dome her clearance would allow and the doors swept open for her. The camera watched as she entered and the doors closed behind her.

"Picture, as well," Sil's plain servant face returned to the screen, "the aroma of my designer perfume that the suit was also able to recreate in those few moments of ascent to the lobby. My reception inside the club was just as impressive and only the club's discretion kept me from including it in the footage.

"The programming was extremely practical. I explained what I wanted and was given holographic examples to consider. It took all of five minutes to scan through the shading and choose makeup, hair, shoes, and accessories. As a woman familiar with fashion I can say with confidence that Test #1 was a success."

"This is Space Correspondent GP…" she concluded, assuming the company would add whatever they wanted to spruce it up.

Walter had loved it and according to his latest transmission, the company had said they would consider the material and get back to them. "In the meantime," they had told Walter, "Have her keep reporting till we come to an agreement and decide what suit aspects we want her to test."

Sil assumed they were still unsure about her notoriety or the value of her reports. She had made up her mind to start with the most obvious test their average customer would be interested in, even though there were already many reports and ads focusing on fashion. It would give them a sense of how she presented herself and hopefully build a little trust. She really didn't expect them to pay anything until they had seen some footage worth buying.

They'll come around, she thought, *once they realize what I can offer*.

"Operatives, assemble in the workers' lobby in twenty minutes," Companion interrupted her train of thought as she lay on her bunk. Her suit was hanging in the closet and she had just slipped into sweats.

"What?" She couldn't help exclaiming. "I just got off work and my feet…"

"Objection noted," Companion snapped coldly.

"Why are we…?" Sil requested, slightly intimidated.

"Your contract specifies that you will be present at any and all meetings, posted events, communications, interviews, and interactions announced by the company for your job code. This constitutes your notification."

"But, what is the purpose of…" she tried again, turning toward the door and leaning on one elbow.

"The purpose will be made clear at the meeting," Companion's voice had a hint of arrogance, she was sure.

Sil didn't respond, realizing that she was wasting the twenty minutes arguing with an AI. She closed her eyes and lay her head on the pillow.

"Your attendance is required," Companion pushed.

"I'll be there," Sil answered meekly, hiding her annoyance.

"Do I annoy you?" Companion poked. Why did he keep talking?

"I am not complaining and will be on time," she responded with a hint of desperation. *Please, please, don't keep talking!* She cried out in her mind.

"I have access to all your bio data and it's clear to me that my voice provokes unseemly reactions in you," Companion pressed mercilessly.

She gritted her teeth and blew out a puff of air. Her fists clenched in spite of her attempts to restrain them.

"I think you can guess what I am registering on my charts." Companion's voice grated on her.

"Is it against my contract to have feelings that are less than friendly toward you?" she groaned.

"It has been determined that docile workers who let their bodies and minds rest when they are inactive, are better subjects for our contracts."

Sil managed not to display her misgiving at this statement and kept silent though the AI had given her a moment to reply.

"Herding new contractors into acquiescence has proven most beneficial to productivity," Companion continued smugly.

She kept assigning feelings to this AI taskmaster, but she wasn't sure if those emotional traces were there or she was imagining them.

He wasn't speaking but she felt him waiting for a response.

"Herding?" she questioned softly, "What does that mean?"

"Some contractors have a stronger streak of independence than others," Companion continued, sounding pleased. "But it's a simple thing to tame a rebel... to wear them down... wear them out..." The voice faded toward the end.

Sil had no heart to ask any more. She couldn't bear to hear what he might say. There was no doubt he was warning her. She had always been very, very independent.

Fortunately, Companion ceased explaining.

At the required time, Sil made her way to the workers' lobby. It was packed with operatives of all shapes and sizes, predominantly men, and everyone's suit, including her own, was identically coded to be a bright green jumpsuit with three gray triangles across the shoulder blades. A powerfully built man in black stood on a platform at one end looking over the throng.

"Operatives!" he boomed, though yelling was unnecessary with the voice amplification system. "Your training for work begins today!" He folded his arms behind his back so his muscle definition could be seen through his sleeves and planted his feet about a meter apart. "You will be working in adverse conditions and the things you learn, can and will save your life many times over!"

There was little stirring in the crowd, as though no one was bothered by the clear admission of the danger involved. Looking around surreptitiously, Sil realized that she seemed to be the only one who hadn't expected to be working the mines.

Her suit was different than all the others, too, like the quality of fine, supple lambskin compared to a full grain hide. Would that matter?

"Gravity Training! Working with Hazardous Chemicals! High Heat! Danger of Falling!" were some of the aspects of daily life in the mines that a contractor needed to be trained to handle. Sub-zero temperatures, limited water and air, pressurization, managing illness, mental disturbances, and more, were added to the list. By the time the massive bulk of a man had finished listing the myriad circumstances threatening life and limb on Mars, many had lost interest and were whispering things like, "Want to get a beer when we're done here?" and "Have you heard the score for the big game last night?"

No one besides herself, not even the other women, seemed in the least perturbed – and some of them were as slight as she was.

I don't belong in this group! She protested in her own mind. And apparently everyone else agreed. They ignored her and parted when the meeting ended, chatting, planning, acting as though it were a normal day in their lives. She stood still in the lobby watching them and once again, feeling a hint of fear.

"The new training has been added to your schedule," Companion's voice whispered in her ear unnaturally close and it made her jump out of her skin shuddering.

"Don't do that!" she subvocalized back to him as she made her way down the halls back to the operative quarters. "It's like hitting me in the head!"

"Actually," Companion spoke normally in her headgear, "the bio response was remarkably similar to being slapped. Interesting…"

It didn't seem right for an AI to find her interesting. Is this how he interacted with all the workers?

"None of the other workers jump like that," Companion shared confidentially. "Your sense of privacy is stronger than theirs."

His words seem to echo in her head… your sense of privacy… privacy… privacy… She had thought she had plumbed the depths of losing her privacy when the whole world tore through her life in the tabloids and ripped it to shreds. But this – this invasion of her inner being – was horrifying. She didn't think the AI could read her mind, but what if it had enough data on her brain activity and records of her speaking, that it could guess what she was thinking?

"I'm pretty good at guessing what you're thinking," Companion said innocently.

Sil sucked in a breath and held it for a moment, standing still with a hand lightly touching the rail on the wall. Her eyes stared blankly in front of her as people streamed by and around her in both directions.

"What am I thinking?" she asked, letting the air out of her lungs.

"Well…" again the AI hesitated in a very human way. Was there a human behind this?

"You don't want me reading your bio data and evaluating your state of mind. You resent the invasion of your privacy. You're scared of the coming training and possibly of me."

"That's pretty perceptive," she responded, but deep within, she was slightly relieved. It wasn't true mind reading. She had been thinking of Walter and the XenoTek contract.

"Then again," Companion's voice almost hissed, "I may not be telling you everything."

Sil said nothing. Walking calmly back to her quarters, she dressed for bed, turned out the lights and lay thinking intensely till falling into a troubled, restless sleep.

She had no intention of being herded into acquiescence or worn down to docility. But she must find a way to survive.

5—TRAIN

"Extensive and thorough training is an integral part of our investment in these candidates – all prime, quality, top-of-their-field contractors, with a sense of adventure and a love of pioneering in the Great Unknown…"

These words were being uttered by a strikingly beautiful woman with dark smooth skin, black hair flowing loosely down to her waist and a perfect figure. On a balcony overlooking the operative's gymnasium, she posed before a group of elegant, expressionless VIPs with a graceful arm outstretched toward the prime, quality candidates below. The observing execs nodded, raised eyebrows, 'ah'ed and glided gently forward on their travel disks, which both carried them and anchored them in the gravity free environment, as the guide walked forward fluidly.

Boots magnetized to the deck below, working in teams of three in a weightless environment, the operatives practiced using mining machinery. The melodious voice drifted down and Sil turned to look in spite of herself. One of the executive women was wearing a suit like her own. She recognized the programmed outfit, a clean, businesslike selection much too unassuming for her. She smirked under her mask, evaluating and categorizing the various people. She would have had this little group under her thumb in five minutes.

"Watch out!" someone yelled and she ducked just in time to miss a massive valve ring someone had tossed too aggressively. It rolled and turned on itself in several planes as it followed a slow trajectory through the air.

"What's the protocol?" the bulky man bellowed, pointing a sculpted arm and finger at the leisurely projectile.

There was a chorus of 'oh's from the observing cream puffs above, curious to see an impromptu demonstration. "In zero gravity you may imagine a massive object will do no damage, especially at that speed," the glamorous guide explained. "…but its mass and inertia are the same,

37

whatever the gravity. If it hit someone, they could be severely injured and even mild damage could destroy the precarious shelter of the HEW suit."

"But, don't worry!" she breathed through glistening, smiling, red lips. "Our contractors are well equipped and prepared for the challenges of their daring – and exciting – careers." An unfamiliar operative jumped up, trotted alongside the valve ring and tossed a rope through it, catching and pulling it on the other side. He lassoed it and with gentle pulls, tamed it, bringing it to a hovering stop in the air.

The suited cream puffs applauded from their floating disks. The elegant tour leader smiled knowingly and with a swivel of hips, led the way through an exit at the opposite end of the balcony. The pampered group followed, coasting in a swoosh after her.

"Staged," muttered a square faced mug in her group, as they returned to their task of assembling the machine.

"Yup," the other man, pale, thin headed, nodded with a bland expression.

"What do you mean, 'staged'?" Sil piped up, shattering their impression of her as a mousy, insecure, clerical type. They both stared at her and then glanced at each other. She had forgotten for the moment her desire to be unnoticed and allowed her natural confidence to show.

"Look," said the thin headed one, pointing at the operative who had lassoed the valve ring. He was walking calmly up to the dais where the muscled man presided over them. The square faced one watched her just long enough to see that she had understood and returned to his task of clamping in an interlocking part.

"Who tossed it in the first place?" she asked as she stretched the insulating blanket around the drilling core, and Thin-head machine-screwed it into place.

They looked at each other again, almost smirking, as though she were pretty stupid.

"He did," the pale, thin headed one spoke again. Both men set their mouths into firm thin lines, making it quite clear they had nothing more to say. She gathered he meant that the man who had caught it also was the one who tossed it to begin with.

They continued working in silence with occasional instructions shouted from Mr. Universe.

After three evenings of working with lines, safety gear, and basic machinery, Sil felt as though there couldn't possibly be anything more tedious than mining on Mars and she found herself seething with anger at her old partner who had gotten her into it. Wherever he was, gloating and spending the company money, she hoped he would get a terrible disease and die a long, painful, lingering death.

Work groups were regularly shuffled and it was easy to remain inconspicuous. She found herself naming people so she could remember them, not out of interest or a desire to make friends, but for her convenience. It always came in handy to read and evaluate people, even if she made a wrong judgment – though she usually didn't.

Square Jaw must have said something she missed because Thin Head (which seemed to fit better than Pale Head) was laughing silently, his lipless mouth open and his teeth showing. A glance around revealed the source of amusement. A woman was flailing, rolling around in the air, gradually getting higher, because her boots had detached and she had lost her magnetic grip on the metal floor. Most of the operatives were watching with grins, but one snatched a flexible tube and looping it, caught her around a leg and drew her back down. She may have been grateful, but the discomfort of looking foolish in front of the other operatives made her sulk instead. She grabbed his arm, planted her feet and pushed past him to clank her way back to her group.

The rescuer just nodded as though he understood, rolled up the tubing, and returned to his work, as well.

He has a nice face, Sil thought as she searched for something to name him. She didn't want to think of him as the rescuer. But there was nothing obtuse or humorous about him. Average height, average build, average face.

A sudden lurch threw everyone down onto the deck, on their knees, faces, or backs. Many found tools or machine parts in their hands slamming down and cutting or bruising flesh.

"Who turned on the gravity?" someone shouted and choruses of yelling and cursing followed. Some struggled to their feet, some held gloves tightly over bleeding cuts, some moaned grasping an arm or a leg. The nice guy was pulling a lever off of his partner's back and turning him over to see if he was alright.

Sil had been thrown forward onto the machine because she had been leaning over it at the time, and a thin bar had cracked her smartly across the cheek. Dazed for a moment, she merely clung to the machine gasping for breath before getting back on her feet. Then, touching her face she felt the cheekbone tentatively and decided it wasn't broken, but it would be a shiner, for sure.

I hate bruises on my face, she thought, gritting her teeth.

"Gravity is not a constant anymore!" the annoying, over-muscled trainer boomed at them. "You never know when you may be caught in an area with a malfunctioning gravity field!"

With another sickening lurch, the field was turned off again and they were all weightless. Several went floating and many vomited. The cursing and yelling became angrier and one man threw a machine part at the trainer who caught it easily and grinned.

"Now, it's getting interesting," he growled. The room grew quiet as they waited to see what he would do. His grin kept growing bigger as though he relished the attention and the power he had. He reached up with the part as though to throw it back but then, thinking better of it, he merely said ominously, "We will talk later."

Sil had been one of the sick ones and while at first she was humiliated at having been weak, she was soon relieved when it turned out that all the vomiting operatives were allowed to quit training for the rest of the evening. They hobbled to their rooms clutching the walls. Behind them the door swung shut on the trainer's blasting voice mocking them for their weak stomachs.

Making her way down the corridor, leaning on the left wall, Sil came across one of the many windows facing earth and a heartbreakingly beautiful view of her home planet was centered there, brilliant blue waters, swirling white clouds, green and brown land masses on the sunny side and just a hint of sparkles from cities in the night side.

She spread her hands on the glass (actually a clear composite they called 'GlaS™'), and a tear rolled down her bruised and swelling cheek. Her body trembled with queasiness.

"I want to go home," she whispered in a rare moment of vulnerable anguish.

"Of course you do," Companion smirked in her ear. "That's what makes you so easy to manage."

This was the last time she was unprepared for the AI's interruption. It unnerved her so thoroughly, making her vomit again though there was nothing left in her stomach, that she decided she would never again be caught off guard.

"You may think you can get rid of my voice by taking off the head gear but I have an excellent image of the bones of your skull and can project my voice waves directly to your ears using your own head as an antenna."

"Curse you!" she allowed herself one final expression of hatred for the invasive oppressor. "I hate you! I hate you! I hate you!"

Companion laughed. AI's didn't understand humor, did they? Either people were involved or had programmed their own attitudes into it.

"Yes, of course!" he responded reasonably in a milky, friendly voice.

Earth shone through the window, so close but so, so far away.

$- \Diamond -$

The camera focused on Sil's helmeted face, her eyes, accented in gold and burgundy, snapped with excitement and her mouth held a gentle mysterious smile through the clear face guard.

"Being cast adrift in space would be a terrifying experience for most people but I'm looking forward to today's training with anticipation," Sil enunciated her words clearly making it seem natural and spontaneous, though she had practiced numerous times.

As the camera panned away from her face, she fell backward into a black expanse, rapidly growing smaller as she was propelled away, no air, no drag, no restraints to slow her fall. "Oh!" her bronze lipped mouth shaped an expression of fear and surprise as she grew tinier and tinier.

Space. Solid, tiny, unflickering spots of light shone in the dark emptiness. The camera gazed at it for a few long seconds until a flashing beam began to grow in the spot where she had vanished. Quickly the figure expanded. Sil coasted gracefully back, arms and legs posed as though she were gliding, soft beams shooting behind her from her shoulders and waist like a rippling cape. She glided directly back to the opening, the mysterious smile still hovering about her mouth, and just before reaching the hatch, the beams vanished. Twirling artistically, carried forward by her momentum, she landed lightly on her toes.

Sil raised her eyebrows and glanced back over her shoulder where some poor souls turned and shot awkwardly back and forth, bumping into one another, bumping into the hull of the training deck, their bodies held rigidly in the shape of their suits. The camera swept closer. Some had buttons on their chest plate, some had handheld devices, but all were floundering in space as they turned their tiny propelling jets on and off. It was comical.

41

Trainers coasted around from one operative to another, giving instructions, as Sil's figure came back into focus.

"I've heard it rumored that I could travel back to earth on my own in this suit if I wanted – it's that space worthy – but I wouldn't give up this adventure for anything!" She winked. "Correspondent GP signing out."

The clip ended and the wall display in Walter's living room went blank.

"This is the one that will seal the deal, Sil, well done!" he said out loud, smiling. "Back up and freeze at 74 seconds," he added, and the clip reappeared and stopped at the place where Sil was about to land on deck, her toes stretched out to touch.

He searched her face for some hint of personal warmth but she was all sophistication.   Had she lost weight?   The suit would adjust without wrinkling or sagging, but he worried that her limbs seemed longer and thinner.

"Daisy," he turned to his AI sister. "Analyze the broadcast and the message with it according to the code she sent." He could have asked the computer but since he couldn't talk to Sil directly, he wanted to at least have a conversation with a type of person.

The code was a blend of color, music, and numbers.   The lighting she chose to makeup her face, the clothing, the melodic tones in her voice combined with numeric values to the words she used were quickly translated into her latest investment tips.

"She was wearing gold and burgundy eye color accents," Daisy began, tilting her head, tossing her bouncy hair, and folding her hands in her lap. "Which opens the gold and precious metals code. Her voice music indicates that an opportunity to invest in the stocks she flagged will be showing up in the next few days after they bottom out at the listed amounts."

About seven stocks reflected on the wall with predicted lows and highs for the next few days and weeks.

"She also referred to flaws in mining equipment that will cripple the Moon extraction project being touted right now and recommends buying into corresponding earth mining operations even if they seem steep. Avoid any Moon mining companies for the next six months till the problem is solved."

"She said all that?" Walter interrupted in astonishment.

"Each number coded in the message, which is very simply achieved by reading the nine bit code in a seven bit format, refers to a specific term. I will display the dictionary for you." Daisy responded thoughtfully as the text scrolled on a different wall.

"Hmmmmmm," a ring tone hummed nearby.

"Hello, Cuevas residence, this is Daisy," she turned toward the window. "One moment, Madeline, I will check." She rotated back to look at him.

Walter shook his head vehemently back and forth.

"Walter, your ex-wife says she is suing you for back alimony and tax fraud and..." Daisy turned her head away for a moment as though to listen better. "Yes, Madeline? Did you say embezzlement? I will let him know. Of course! No problem. Thank you. Yes, you have a nice day, too. Good bye."

"Daisy! How many times have I told you NOT to wish her a nice day?" Walter slapped his hands down on his knees in exasperation.

"Sixteen times not counting the first seven times when you didn't finish the sentence. But as you know, I'm equipped with extra social skills and it is to your advantage for me to be gracious. I don't mind repeating myself, if it helps." She smiled lovingly.

"What could she possibly be suing me for this time?" he groaned, grasping his forehead and kneading it anxiously.

"She didn't say any more than what I already told you. Don't be worried. She has lost the last three lawsuits and you have rebuilt a little of your wealth since the dreadful divorce and the first lawsuit. I think you're safe at this point."

"But the anguish and cost of defending myself..." Walter shook his head and moaned. "I just don't want to do it anymore. Why did I ever marry her?"

"I believe that is a rhetorical question, and a reply is not expected. I'm learning to be silent even when it seems like I ought to answer." Daisy showed her adorable dimples.

"Thank you, Daisy. You're good to me and I appreciate it." He closed his eyes and leaned back. His warm, tanned face had grown pale and sickly. "If you would contact my lawyer and ask him to begin whatever it is he needs to begin."

"Yes, Walter, gladly," Daisy raised her eyebrows and smiled. "And there are a few more things you should know. First of all, you've made enough money on recent investments to cover the cost of fighting the lawsuits. And second, Operative Frandelle included an address and a name in the end of her message."

Walter opened his bloodshot eyes and looked at her in confusion.

"An address?"

"In Boston. I will begin researching the name and looking for video footage on the place."

Walter furrowed his brow and stared at the floor. Was this the personal connection he had asked for? Had she actually given him a clue to who she was apart from the public figure?

He closed his eyes again and sighed deeply.

"I just don't know..." he left the thought unspoken. Did he really want to care about a woman again? He glanced at Daisy and for the thousandth time asked himself if he really preferred to isolate himself with an AI rather than try to find someone and possibly be ripped apart again.

His parents had perished in a shipwreck off the coast of Bali. His sister had died after a tragic illness with a rare, incurable disease. The woman he had been in love with in those days grew tired of his grief and left him. Madeline, the creature from the deep, had swept in imperiously about the time he had decided to drown his heart in whiskey and just not care anymore. She was fun at first, demanding but entertaining, a pleasant addition to the world of alcohol he had been making for himself, a mind numbing distraction. But one day, she took him by the hand and marched him to the nearest justice of the peace, and swept him through a quick marriage ceremony that he was too apathetic to resist.

Then the torment had begun. She demanded money and more money and drove him mercilessly to work harder and find better paying jobs. For six years she had bullied him and bled him dry till she found another victim and divorced him. The settlement had been devastating but he had felt only an immense relief over his miraculous escape. He didn't even care about losing everything he owned and starting over.

"She's found out about my investments," Walter sat up suddenly, flooded with a rush of adrenaline. He curled his lips with a scowl. "You aren't going to touch a cent of it, MaddenLier."

"That must be a derogatory label for your ex-wife," Daisy surmised brightly. "If you wish I can make your investments much harder to track and give the appearance of losing money so she will leave you alone in the future."

"Oh, Daisy, if you can do that, I would adopt you as a real member of the family," he replied jumping to his feet and grasping her shoulders. "Yes! Do it! Free me of the curse of the Maddening Lying Madeline!!"

"Done!" Daisy declared triumphantly only a few moments later.

Walter dropped his head back and raised his arms in a victory salute and thanking the AI profusely, told her she was upgraded to Sister.

"I am pleased," was Daisy's cheerful response.

6—DEPART

Elegant and important people were sipping drinks in the Sheiks Lounge. Tourists were strolling along the Milky Way Avenue shopping district. Gardeners and their AI underlings were unobtrusively tending the vast gardens. Botanists, ornithologists, apiculturists, zoologists and a profusion of specialists cared for their realms in the base. Agriculturists, chefs, nutritionists, ecologists, naturists, and many more cared for the human inhabitants.

Everything was functioning smoothly as it should and Sil was taking a lunch order from a table of customers when the unexpected announcement came.

"Operatives. Report to Launch Bay Five at 16 hundred hours sharp for immediate departure for Mars," a generic voice, not Companion's, sounded in her ears.

"Did you get that, Serving Girl?" a frowning man grumped at her. "No tomatoes on that club sandwich!"

"Yes, sir," she responded submissively, ignoring the put down. She steeled herself against the surprise of the summons. They were supposed to have had three more weeks of training and adjustment at Guam before embarking on the Mars transport at the beginning of April. It was still early in March.

"Your shift ends early in two hours," Companion added impassively. "That will give you two hours to pack." She distinctly heard a snicker. Why would they program a snicker?

"Did you get my martini? Honestly! How did you get this job?" an aging, skinny woman with expensive jewels, fashion clothes, and heavy makeup on her wrinkled skin exhaled in disgust. "I have a mind to speak with your manager!"

Something clicked inside Sil. She turned toward the woman and leveled her gaze.

"Madam Donatelli," she identified, and placing both hands on the table, she leaned forward into her face. As she did so, Sil tapped a button on the belt of her own suit that transformed her humble serving garb into a sleek, black, glistening outfit such as a diver or a space racer would wear. She kept this one on hand for fun and would switch it on occasionally during her free time.

"Three months tops. That's what I would give your Cays investments before they start free falling. All this here…" she gestured toward the suited people at the table, "can't change that. You should've listened to my advice a long time ago when you paid me top consulting fees for ten minutes of my time. You should've fired him and put Bertelo in his place, the only man with any market sense."

The woman gasped at her, astonished, outraged and speechless.

"How dare you say such things to me!" no-tomato man, the 'him' she had referred to, sputtered in fury.

"Forget the martini, the club, and the tip," she concluded stretching up to her full height, "I quit."

Striding away with a fleeting sense of elation, Sil didn't look back and didn't care what happened behind her.

"That was a cute display," Companion commented mildly. "It will be your last."

"Then I'm glad I chose that crew to dump on. They deserve it as much as any of the vicious piranhas that fed on the dissolution of my assets and gloated over my fall." Crowds parted as she walked toward them radiating the heat of her disapproval. She kept her momentum and her core of anger constant until she reached the chutes. Then jumping in and falling rapidly down to the operative level, she passed out and crashed onto the floor at the entrance.

People walked around her, ignoring her. A few commented idly on the dangers of alcohol in low gravity environments. She grew very white and lay there drooling from the corner of her mouth for more than five minutes before someone with a hint of mercy came upon her.

"What happened?" he exclaimed. "Did anyone see? Didn't anyone stop to check?"

Someone explained that there were health attendants whose job it was to take care of that kind of thing and it was better not to intervene. They didn't want to be blamed for an accident they didn't cause.

He knelt down and turned her over, wiping her cheek with his sleeve. He felt her pulse, counted her breaths, and called to her gently. "Wake up!" he suggested, patting her face. "Operative! Wake up and report. Why are you on the floor?"

A woman with a concerned face sidled up carefully.

"She should not be on the floor," she whispered confidentially. "You do not want to be here when they come. Either get her up and go, or get out of here. Trust me. It's not good."

"Why?" he asked, but he heeded her advice and lifted Sil into his arms easily. She weighed only forty pounds on the operative level.

"Slip into the men's room," the concerned woman added turning away and walking off.

The door to the men's room was right there. He jumped up and carried Sil inside, shutting the door behind them. "This is crazy," he muttered to himself wondering why it mattered. Weren't there cameras everywhere?

Not in the bathrooms, by law. There were motion sensors, but not cameras.

The bathroom was empty, so he set her down on the floor by the sink, wet his hands and slapped her face with the water. She didn't respond.

Looking at her belt, he noticed a flashing light that read '*Revive*'. He pressed it and her whole body jolted. She opened her eyes and groaned. She tried to talk but gurgled instead and wove her head dizzily from side to side with bleary eyes. The button now flashed '*Calm*' and he pushed it again. She closed her eyes and swallowed. She shuddered and hiccupped or maybe choked down a sob as if she had begun to cry but stopped. She opened fearful eyes and stared at him.

"Out of the way," commanding voices filtered through the crack under the door. "Make way for the Health Security Team. Isolation protocol in effect. This hallway is under Blue Quarantine." Blue light streamed under the door.

"What's happening?" Sil whispered. Her eyes focused clearly and she saw the nice man squatting next to her. "Why am I sitting here like this?"

"I found you unconscious on the floor next to the chutes and everyone was stepping around you. I tried to help and someone warned me that I needed to either get away or hide you in here. So I brought you in here." He spoke softly. Her natural inclination would have been to bash him in the face first and ask questions later but she remembered, as her mind was clearing, time and again where she had seen him help someone in trouble and she didn't doubt he was telling the truth.

Loud sonar began booming rhythmically in the hallway, throbbing in time to blue lights flashing. It was overwhelming and disturbing. Both the nice guy and Sil touched their headgear and the shell spread out around their heads, sheltering them from the noise. With a click on the ear, the nice guy synchronized their communications and they could talk.

"I saw your suitbelt flashing a message, 'Revive', and after I pressed it and it woke you, it said, 'Calm' and I pushed it again. That seemed to work." He said simply.

"What happened to me and what is that noise out there?" Sil's voice was almost normal now.

"That noise is some form of decontamination protocol that was initiated after you fell. I'm not sure by whom. I have no idea what happened to you or what would have happened if those health people had gotten you."

"Drones," she replied, leaning her head back against the wall. "They just follow their programming and I don't know what it is." She went back over what she could remember of the day, waking up, getting ready, going to work, having a break, serving an old business acquaintance…

"That's right," she recalled, sitting up carefully. "We got that announcement about departing for Mars at 16 hundred."

"Yes, I got it, too," he nodded resignedly. "Sooner than we thought but what difference does it make? We gotta go so we might as well go."

"I told this woman off and quit my job as soon as I got the message."

"You what?" his face told her pretty clearly how foolish that seemed to him.

"I knew her. I had a reason," she said wryly. "Trust me she had it coming. And! I just did her a favor if she actually listens."

The booming and blue flashing from the crack in the door started to diminish gradually and steadily. The nice guy rose to a stand and held out a hand to help her up.

"It's almost over. We should be ready to get on our way."

"Thanks, uh… what do they call you?" she twisted her face as if trying to smile but forgetting how, and took his hand.

"I've been called lots of things but most people call me Dan." He pulled her up and let go of her hand quickly. "And I've heard you called Icicle and Sparkles but I'd rather not…"

"Icicle?" she jerked her head a little and then groaned at the jarring motion. "I guess I can see that, but Sparkles? What on earth is that for?"

"On Guam," he smirked good-naturedly then wiped the grin off his face as he saw her reaction. "Ok, not funny. Well, I think it has to do with your outfit changes when you go up to the public regions. You have a regular following of…" He didn't really want to say mockers or scoffers, but they certainly weren't admirers.

"Sil. Silvariah, but just call me Sil." She smoothed past his trailing sentence.

He nodded. "Sil, are you well enough to get back to your quarters to pack?"

"I'll be fine… Dan," she smiled, turning to look in the metallic mirror and smooth her hair. She grasped the sink to steady herself. What had happened to her? She couldn't have been dropped by the chute. She must have been unconscious before she landed but how?

Dan was easing the door open to peer out. "Looks clear. Let's go." He waved her out and closed the door behind her as she exited. "See you on the ship." He added in a light friendly way. Then he was gone.

Sil held herself in a tightly controlled walk down the corridor to her sector, breathing regularly and deeply. Companion had said something before she collapsed. What was it? *It will be your last.* A threat…

"I knew you were in the men's room but I didn't notify the health units," Companion spoke up right as she was making the awful conclusion that he had done something to her. "You were fortunate, very fortunate, that a decent person came along. It's not pleasant to be blue quarantined."

"What did you do to me?" she whispered, tensing up in spite of her desire to not react to him.

Companion hesitated and again she found it puzzling. Why could she sense it or was she imagining it?

"It was simple," Companion boasted. "I knocked you out with… I won't tell you how. It was an appropriate consequence for your behavior in the restaurant. The effects should wear off within a day or two, maybe sooner, since you had a revival kit in your suit and someone was clever enough to activate it."

She wanted to ask what blue quarantine would have done but she refused to give the AI any more opportunities to intimidate her. She could find out from someone else.

Besides, she was finally realizing that she needed to stop trying to escape her identity as an indentured miner and try to get to know her new peers. Yes, they were peers now. People. That must give them some common ground to work with.

Ten minutes before 16 hundred hours, Sil was standing with her peers in a waiting area outside of Launch Bay 5. Her suit was coded to the standard Mars operative uniform and she almost looked like everyone else. The difference was that she had no makeup or programmed highlighting on her head gear to cover up the bruising on her face. She still had the black eye from the failing gravity field demonstration and was adding some red swelling on the other side of her face with the fall in the chute. It had several effects on the others. Some respected her more, some felt justified in seeing her humbled a little, some found it funny, and a few felt sorry for her. The net result was that they disliked her less and accepted her more.

"Bruiser," one guy cracked, mimicking a couple boxing punches.

"I'm keeping my distance," another agreed.

Sil was perceptive enough to realize that they meant it as encouragement and she smiled in response. "Yeah," she said, "You should see the other guy." And they chuckled.

The TML transport was called "Slugger", named by its first captain, a baseball fan, boasted a marked resemblance to a larva; long, round, sectioned and slow. It was divided into multiple decks with the lowest being the engine area and the highest the observation deck. Once in motion, it would be pointed toward Mars and with the gravity fields pulling toward the rear, 'forward' would also be 'up'.

Cargo decks, life support, crews' quarters, passengers' quarters, kitchen, mess, gym, aeroponics, med unit, research lab, and officer's quarters occupied the other levels. They were linked by a number of travel chutes, four going up and four down, which propelled people gently enough that it

51

was easy to step off at any level. Some had restricted access and unauthorized trespassers were repelled if they lacked clearance.

"North Deck Seven, number 32," a mechanical voice proclaimed to Sil as she boarded and passed through the identifier ray. She wondered whose sense of humor had chosen an old twentieth century TV 'computer' voice.

Following the operatives in front of her, who shuffled forward to the closest lifting chute and shot up one after another, she found herself being swept up after them. Levels 4, 5 and 6 passed by and she stepped off easily at level 7. She was in the starboard quadrant and found herself following a shorter line of women in a long hallway that curved to the right.

Number 32 had four bunks, one already occupied by a sour faced pipsqueak with bright green hair. Sil took less than half a second to decide which bed was the best of the remaining three and slung her bag on it; away from the overhead light, furthest from the door, most secluded.

"Dumb!" green hair snapped at her rudely. "Bet you anything that wall vibrates. It's got piping behind. I heard the noise. Ha!"

Sil glanced toward her disdainfully but squelched that look quickly. She had to build bridges not enemies.

"I didn't know that," she said mildly, lifting her eyebrows which had a definite softening effect. It wasn't a smile but hinted at one. "Is that bad?"

"Yeah, if you want brain freeze. Zero Kelvin! You know, space cold??" she rolled her eyes but Sil felt a shade of friendliness in the gesture.

"You mean I could get cold? I would think they have some pretty good insulation…"

"For body temp maybe, but not brain numbing. You get loopy, stupid or something. Forget things." Green head squinted and tucked her legs under her on the bunk.

Sil looked around the room again and weighed the value of moving against getting the bed she preferred. The upper bunk over the woman would be her next choice, so she slung her bag there.

"Good choice," green head winked and smiled. "I don't snore. I promise."

"Sil," she introduced herself offhandedly. "What's your name?"

"Oh, no! You're Icicle. No names for me. That way we don't get attached and we don't care if someone gets hurt. Not that we don't help each other out. Yeah, sure, we do that. We gotta look out for one another but I don't like names. It's too personal like."

"Ah," Sil acquiesced. "I can live with Icicle. What do I call you?"

"Beets," she grinned and pulled her knees up to her chin like a child though she was at least in her twenties. "I dyed it green for Mars, right? Little green men, heh, heh, heh... but yeah, it's red. Really red. And my face turns red all the time. You'll get used to it."

Two more women ended up in the small room. The first one, a shapely, hard faced blond, took Sil's choice of a bed and made a move to take charge right away. She started giving orders about how things would be done. Sil listened as she unpacked her few things and stored them in the shelves at the head of her bunk but said nothing. It didn't matter to her what the woman thought she was doing. She knew she could take command if she wanted. But she didn't want it. *Let Bossy do it*, she thought.

The last woman, somewhat round, with drab, brown, shoulder length hair, was completely silent. No eye contact, no facial expressions, no reactions to words or noises. She took the last bed and lay down on it gently.

"Mouse," Beets said toward the silent one, scrunching her mouth in a quirky twist. "I'll call you Mouse and you must be..."

"My name is Carla and you aren't going to call me anything but that," Bossy demanded with her hands on her hips. "What are your names? Not labels. Real names, please."

Beets smirked and said nothing. Mouse didn't register. Sil tipped the edge of her mouth disarmingly.

"Silvariah," she said with a nod, "but you can call me Icicle if you want."

"Carla," she condescended graciously. "And you? Green haired girl? You have a name, don't you?"

"Beets."

"I'm not going to call you that. Tell me your name or I'll give you one."

"Beets," she squeaked, enjoying the challenge.

"Melissa," Bossy bestowed. "That seems to fit you. From now on you will respond to Melissa. And you? You on the bed. Don't ignore me. I need to know your name or I'll give you one."

Sil might've enjoyed listening to the subsequent display of personalities in the room but she preferred to explore. Let them figure it out.

"Thanks," she tossed behind her as she slipped quickly out the door.

"Where are you going? You can't just leave. We have rules to figure out and…" Bossy's voice trailed after her.

The ship seemed large and well ventilated, laid out in a logical pattern that made good use of the space. There was little indication that hundreds of people were aboard. She made her way to the top level and found a spot on the observation deck where she could see not only the exterior of Guam Base looming on one side but a striking, crystal clear image of earth against a canopy of millions of stars profusely salting the deep black of space.

It was anguishing to see such beauty and it struck her heart with a stab of fear and longing. She made her way toward the glass slowly and spread her hands on it as though framing the picture of her home. A tear – rarer for her than the most precious of gems – trickled down her cheek.

"When he returns," a familiar voice whispered nearby, "will he find faith on the earth?"

She turned in confusion to see Dan's profile. He was staring at the earth with eyes brimming, unashamedly grieving over their imminent departure. He sighed heavily and hung his head.

And she wondered who Faith was.

7—BRIDGE

"It's a beautiful design," said one contractor to another as they ate the simple lunch, seated in the mess. "Not only does it recycle all the water, extract the solids and convert them to fertilizer blended with a multitude of the best soil probiotics known to the human race, it warms the air as it moisturizes and ionizes it. It comes out smelling sweet like spring air in the mountains after a storm." His companion nodded repeatedly, chewing quickly so he could comment once he swallowed.

"Prif-ledge," he gulped the half chewed mouthful and went on, "It's an honor to be chosen for this project. And the money is great!" He grinned showing something stuck to his teeth.

"And it's powered by solar wind," the first one added and whistled softly. "The details in the tech are extremely complex but the idea itself is so simple. Ah! It's sweet…"

Sil resisted shaking her head. She couldn't believe the two waste engineering contractors loved their work that much. *Was it really all that complex?* She wondered. The money they talked about was depressing. They would lose a total of maybe eighteen months of their lives and go home set for life and if they wanted to work, they would have their pick of the best jobs in the world.

She would go home with nothing, having learned nothing, and having gained no reputation.

"Icicle," her roommate, Beets, said planting her tray and sitting in front of her. Carla's attempt at naming her had never stuck and was now forgotten.

"Beets," she half smiled trying to be approachable in spite of her glum mood.

"Are you here as a contractor? For the money?" she asked bluntly, following it up with a bite of whatever was in the pasta-like mush they had been served.

"No. You?" she replied blowing on her coffee and sipping.

"Yeah, sure. Good money and anyone can come," Beets talked between bites, eating more gracefully than Sil had expected. "No skills, just a sense of adventure. I thought, why not? Besides, the jerk I was in love with dumped me and I said, forget you, I'm leaving this PLANET behind. You'll be so sorry when I come back stinking rich. Ha!'

Sil registered a faint response but said nothing. Even Green Head was making money.

"Don't worry about it, the money," Beets barreled on glibly. "The best bet by far is to marry one of these engineer types. It's at least twenty to one – guys to girls. That's what I'm going to do." She raised and dropped her eyebrows several times and then winked.

Sil eyed her thoughtfully. "So, check them out, pick your top three favorites and get friendly. Is that the plan?" Anyone in the hall could've seen how little she cared for that idea herself.

"Why not?" Beets shrugged, undaunted by the indifferent response. "I'm cute. I'm fun. I know how to make the best of things and I think I would make a good wife to an enterprising Mars contractor, right? Am I right? What do you think?" She was getting louder and starting to laugh. Glancing around, she intentionally caught the eyes of a number of men in the room. They didn't seem to mind.

Sil stifled her groan and the annoyance she felt. Never trust a man, she said bitterly to herself, tightening her jaw. But remembering Walter, whom she had specifically chosen to trust out of sheer desperation, she reworded it for herself. Never go into partnership with a man, she told herself more bitterly. But again—Walter. That didn't fit either.

Never believe in a man again, she landed on finally, reassuring herself that she would never have the opportunity to even be tempted with Walter. She sighed.

"Why are you here, Icie? " Beets softened her tone and lowered her voice.

"Don't you know?" Sil set her coffee down calmly and rested her hands palms down on the table. She looked her directly in the eyes and evaluated her. Beets looked back cheerfully, openly, occasionally glancing away to smile in recognition at more than one contractor who was interested in her little speech and was letting her know that in some way.

"No. Why would I? Are you famous or something?" A smile for Sil, and a different kind of smile for someone on the left behind her.

"Yes, notorious," she paused for a moment, searching for the best explanation, the one that would be brief yet have enough to satisfy her. "I was an influential and wealthy business woman, owner of several successful enterprises... well... And, thinking of expanding into a new market, to put it simply, I wrapped up all my assets, sold a few companies, and went into business with a brilliant man that I had known and trusted for a long time. Our venture was so successful, beyond our wildest imagination, that we found ourselves unable to meet the practical needs for growth. So, we took on more investors and poured in massive amounts of cash and as fast as the profits came in, we turned them around and plugged them back in."

Beets had begun to stare at her with a hint of disbelief.

"It was exhilarating and frightening... and fun," Sil continued in spite of the sinking feeling she had at the look on Green Head's face. "And my partner – my brilliant, handsome, exotic partner – my trusted partner... my Judas. My Benedict Arnold. My... my... traitor..." She came dangerously close to a quivering lip, a tear, a tremble, but inside she gripped herself aggressively and squelched the emotion and the pain. After a moment of quiet, during which Beets watched her carefully, she regained control. She assumed the face of steel.

"He had been funneling investments back through asset accumulation to international accounts and falsifying documents that showed the money as being invested in new factories, and fake sales, and fake profits in countries where I had little hands on experience. He stole more money than I had ever made in all my years of business and disappeared, leaving me with a stream of paperwork that made me complicit though I was innocent..."

"You swear..." Beets interrupted, her face enraptured, in spite of her skepticism.

Sil twisted her lips not wanting to use a childish phrase like that. "I swear." She conceded finally and went on. "The investors were wealthy, powerful people that wanted to make a statement and they made me the scapegoat of all kinds of financial aftershocks they say I caused."

She hadn't noticed that several people had gathered around. She now had a spell bound audience of five or six, some of who seated themselves next to Beets, but not her.

"What was the partner's name?" one of the waste engineers asked, leaning against the table he had been sitting at.

"Belymer, Gordon Belymer, the human Leviathan," she was unable to say it without a bitter taste in her mouth and the whole group, now grown to nine, felt it. For some reason she couldn't quite grasp, she noticed an undercurrent of support from them. It was as though they had begun to be offended on her behalf. It seemed so strange to her.

"What happened?" a newcomer asked. A couple people in the hallway noticed the group and walked in as she responded.

"I was prosecuted for embezzlement, fraud, racketeering, and a ton of other charges in six different countries," she straightened in her seat, turning her head gently to look toward one side and then another as she spoke. "Families of people who had been ruined came to watch the proceedings – which were like a circus – weeping, cursing me under their breath. Sometimes they would shout things like, 'Where's the money, you wh…?'" Sil didn't want to repeat the word. She had pretended not to hear and acted like it didn't hurt, but it did.

"What happened to the money?" someone else asked who had missed part of the initial explanation.

"My traitorous ex-partner has it, somewhere, I don't know where."

They looked at her expectantly, hoping she wasn't going to stop talking now. It was just getting interesting.

"Go on," Beets encouraged her, loving the social event that was happening spontaneously. Plus she knew that her eyes were pretty when they sparkled with interest and she was making sure some of her new friends noticed as well.

Sil leaned back in the chair, brushed a wisp of hair out of her face, swept the group with her gaze, noticing each one and in a way, making a human connection with them, even if just as a hello. She pressed her lips together for a moment, then opened them and spoke again.

"I was looking at multiple back to back sentences in Europe alone," she lowered her voice, but her words were spoken so clearly and the room was so silent that everyone heard them. "Three nations were demanding that I be extradited for corporal punishment… caning, in some, whipping in others. My name was spoken as if I were the prince of hell." Her eyes stared down at the floor as though even now, she felt the shame of it.

Someone whistled. A couple chuckled and whispered things like, 'We had no idea who we had on board…' Most just watched her, fascinated, enraptured by the human tragedy in her story.

"My lawyer informed me of an anonymous offer. All charges would be commuted if I paid off the debt in full. I could earn the money by going to Mars. A so-called benefactor would begin payments to the plaintiffs immediately, if I went… " Sil raised her eyes again to look around at her audience. Though she showed no emotion and her eyes had become very chilled, amazingly, they grew more supportive of her. She knew it.

"How many months did you sign on for?" Beets asked breathlessly. "How long till it's paid off?"

"I can't leave until it is paid. I had to sign a contract that didn't have a time limit."

They were stunned. But they made no sound.

"I'm hoping to pay it off in six or seven years." She finished.

"What?" Beets' mouth dropped open and tears sprung to her eyes at the horror of it. "You'll never survive that long! You'll never make it. No one can…" She started trembling. It was oddly comforting to Sil, as though her roommate's distress was relieving her own hidden anguish, like a pressure valve.

A number of people shook their heads, murmured a few words, and generally expressed their shock at the cruelty of her plight. That was when she realized that not one of them was in the same position as her. Not one had ever heard of an indentureship remotely as long as hers.

It made her sick at heart, sick in her stomach, just plain sick.

She jumped to her feet and before escaping, she leaned toward the first man who had seated himself next to Beets and now had an arm around her shoulders, and hissed vehemently. "You better show some respect to her." There was something about her intensity that made an impression and he quickly brought his arm down again.

"Aw, that's sweet!" Beets voice trailed behind her as she ran out of the room.

"Charming display," Companion commented as she slammed her way into the restroom and lost her lunch. She didn't care what he was referring to.

– ◊ –

59

"The Slugger felt really spacious in the beginning," Sil's voice flowed smoothly in the recorded clip, her image clear and bright. "With over four hundred people aboard, you would expect crowding but they've designed the interior spaces well. Most of the operatives are contractors committed to seven month blocks and even the crew is only allowed to work two round trips before furlough on earth. It's a very lucrative, high risk job."

Walter studied her face. He listened to her voice. He pondered her body positions, her planned and practiced speech, and her eyes. She was well controlled but underneath there was so much more. With every word she spoke, he felt more concern for her, and more understanding of the very real fear she must be battling.

"The flight is actually a peaceful experience. We'll be on route for seven weeks and during that time, we're allowed a lot of free time. We're expected to study some manuals and there have been a few classes scheduled for safety training, but it's almost as though they've given us an extended space cruise—minus the gourmet buffets, the service, and the shows.

"Actually, we're not even lacking the shows because we have some talented people on board who like nothing better than to entertain. Comedians, musicians playing spoons and homemade drums, actors, contortionists… you'd be surprised at who's coming out of the woodworks. There's a game room with a pool table and informal nightly gambling, minus the beer which until recently was the one big complaint here."

Walter smiled at that.

"Some of the contractors, after consulting with the aeroponics engineers on how to brew beer or mead, have managed to eke out some exotic potions. I'm continually amazed at the ingenuity and creativity of this group. I hadn't expected interplanetary miners and base builders to be so resourceful."

Daisy smiled. "They are an unusual selection, "she said brightly.

"Pause," Walter said immediately. He had been resting in his favorite chair with his head leaning on one hand. He sat up and pointed at Daisy. "What do you mean by that? How are they unusual?"

"It may be true that candidates for constructing the Mars base are few; adventurous, and confident individuals, but the screening process for this trip seems to have been different than the others. I have been examining personality profiles for the two previous groups and comparing them to the ones in this group in my spare time – of which I have more than you may think, Brother." She seemed to particularly enjoy calling him Brother.

"What kind of differences?" Walter pressed. "…Sister?" he added belatedly but it seemed to please her nonetheless.

"They are markedly talented, intelligent people and their skills are widely dispersed across many fields. There are a few with strong leadership abilities, mixed in with a large number of extremely gentle, mild mannered people. In fact, the gentle ones are not really the pioneering type at all." She punctuated this observation, which must have been a personal triumph for her since she didn't really understand how to analyze and draw original conclusions, by raising her eyebrows and forming her lips into an 'O' of surprise.

"I don't know what to make of that," Walter replied gently, leaning back into his resting position. "But I will think about it, Sister, and let you know what I come up with. Thank you for bringing that to my attention."

"You're welcome, Brother!" she folded her hands in her lap and leaned back in her own chair with a sigh of happiness and directed her face back toward the wall where the clip was waiting to be finished.

"Continue," Walter said.

"I learned something new about my suit," Sil smiled charmingly and Walter couldn't keep himself from smiling warmly in return. "Quite by accident, actually. The user's manual is a simple and straightforward tool meant for average users that has very few instructions on how to make use of its survival capabilities. Fortunately, there is a technical manual included, meant for the support staff, I assume, which I have been studying and deciphering. It's extremely detailed and somewhat over my head, but I've been able to put the pieces together and learn by experimenting."

She shifted her position a little and tilted her head creating a natural pause in the monologue.

"I had just read the section on 'Touch Guard', designed to protect the wearer from unwanted physical contact," her mouth curved slightly with smug humor, "which has three possible pulses that can be discharged by unauthorized human touch; heat, electricity, and subsonic shockwaves. Each can be set on a scale of 1 to 5, from lightest to heaviest charges, depending on the mass of the body suit occupant, as well as the combatants, and the level of threat involved."

Walter shifted uneasily in his chair. He didn't even notice that he clenched his fists. She was obviously fine, but this felt like it was leading up to something that justified the concerns he had for her safety.

"I was walking down the East Deck 5 passage when I encountered several of the operatives who had been sampling the new brews... Yes, you can see where this is going... And one of them, one of those overly handsome European types who thinks he knows how to charm any woman, came toward me with open arms."

Walter shook his head but grinned in spite of himself. "What did you do, Sil?" he muttered.

"He was jabbering on about my beauty and loneliness, maiden in distress, lost in space, that sort of thing and I held out a hand and said, 'Don't touch me. I have my TG on. My Touch Guard is activated. Watch out!' And I was backing away. The other guys were laughing at him and assuring me that he was harmless. They really had no idea what I was saying."

Sil paused and smiled strangely, alternating between pity or regret and mild amusement.

"He wasn't really being offensive, just foolish. I suppose he thought he was dashing. He tried to grab me in his arms, like for a waltz, and I assume he would have just swept me down the corridor in a few clumsy dance steps, or maybe even tried to get in a kiss --- which I would never have allowed, trust me. But, he never had the chance. And none of us, not even I, had a clue what the TG would do."

Walter leaned forward watching her face in anticipation. She looked at him intensely and hesitated for a few seconds with her mouth half open before continuing.

"He went flying backwards down the hall, knocking over his companions – passed out cold. His friends would have been really angry but I kept assuring them I didn't know it would do that. And I DID try to warn him. The next day, of course, after they sobered up, I found him and apologized, and explained everything. I can't afford to ostracize myself in this mission. But, anyway... I guess I will never have to worry about unwanted attention as long as I wear that suit."

A slow smile was spreading across Walter's face until it was interrupted by a friendly observation from Daisy, "Of course, that won't hinder any desirable attention," she quipped cheerfully. Walter's smile waned with discouragement and he sighed.

He wondered what setting she had had it on.

"You may be wondering," Sil's video recording interjected flawlessly, as though reading his thoughts, "what setting I had it on. I wasn't sure. I had been reading the manual and playing around with settings, but I hadn't decided what to try first. It was an accident that it was tested so quickly.

"The heat was off. The electric charge was set at 1, a mild warning shock, and the subsonic pulse was set at 3. That was what knocked him out and sent him flying, though I'm sure the low gravity and his state of inebriation had a lot to do with it as well."

"Wheew!" Walter whistled softly. He wondered if the full charges on all three settings would kill someone – and decided that there was no doubt that it would.

"And my boots have better magnetizing skills. They gripped the floor and upped their magnetic field at the same time the suit TG pulsed. I think you'll be able to have Daisy put together a clip about that to send to the company for our contract. Let me know how that is going, by the way. I could use some good news."

She stared at him from the clip for a moment and he realized there was something bothering her she couldn't say anything about. It made him tense up in alarm. He jumped to his feet.

"Daisy, is there anything in her code besides marketing or money comments?"

"No. She has very little to say, except that we should look into a waste management technology group known as 'Garden Gold'." Daisy gazed at Walter lovingly and he wondered how many films and programs she had studied to achieve that look.

"Signing off," Sil concluded with a softened expression on her face, a moment of wistfulness that pierced his heart. He *knew* she was wishing he could read her mind, that something was wrong and she had no way to communicate it. That moment was not just a video impression. It was a real human contact at the heart level, the gut level.

His heart leapt within him in response.

"Sister," he said softly, "Something is wrong on that ship or in Sil's situation. Please evaluate everything you can and look for discrepancies or red flags; things that seem out of the ordinary for a trip like this, or anything you can. We need to figure out what is causing her trouble."

"Gladly, Brother!" she smiled sweetly with what looked like real affection. He found it reassuring in spite of the fact that it was only a cleverly programmed response. And he smiled back warmly.

"Something to consider," Daisy said with an overly thoughtful countenance, "is what would happen to Sil if the suit directed that subsonic pulse inward instead of outward. I wonder if it has that capability."

Walter stared at her soberly. "Could it knock her out?"

"Absolutely."

"Could it kill her?"

"Most likely," she responded with raised eyebrows.

"But, who would have access to the administrative controls within the suit? Wouldn't it be in her control alone? Could it be hacked?" Walter felt himself go cold and his breathe shallow.

"Any program can be hacked."

Walter sat down, closed his eyes and leaned back in his chair, growing pale. She was in danger, he wasn't sure how, and he was too far away to do anything about it.

"There's nothing to do but wait and see what we can find out," he reflected gloomily.

"And manage the money the XenoTek contract is bringing in," Daisy added matter-of-factly.

8—FRIENDS

A somber mood hung over the bunk room. The low hum of distant machines – water and air recyclers, energy converters, and a myriad of useful mechanical systems – melded with the vibration of unmoving living forms; human beings with slow heart rates, gentle breathing, and calm synaptic activity. All lay in the dark, but not all were sleeping. They showed varying levels of chemical stability, but all were functioning at below optimum levels. Companion could read minute details of the nerve impulses, blood flow, enzymes, hormones and potentiation in the brain, and with the expansive data banks of information he had on humans, and on the passengers of the ship specifically, he could interpret what they were thinking and feeling with a reasonable measure of accuracy.

But he couldn't guess at their dreams.

Brain activity with few to no memories formed was not unlike the electronic pathways of his own processors. Only programs specifically designed to make memories created long-term records. If he had paused to consider it, he would have been puzzled that the result of these dreaming brainwaves produced no direct result that could be measured. He didn't care.

Silvariah was the wakeful one. Her eyes were closed but breath and thought showed a very alert mind. Selecting from a number of possible approaches in his data base, he sped through a random number generator at nano-second speed and chose one.

"You won't find it hard to sleep on Mars," he placed his voice close to her ear, intending to startle her and measure the biological response. "Mining is particularly exhausting work. So is living in contained life chambers."

He was rewarded by a jolt that pulsed through her body. Her forehead exuded a light, cold sweat, and her heart began to race. That was a normal reaction but he was seeking a verbal response to add to her profile.

She said nothing and didn't open her eyes. Her heart began to slow down again though her mind continued to light up like a meteor shower.

"I would be interested in hearing your opinion of the state of mind of your bunkmates. You have a reputation for reading people pretty well," he continued conversationally.

"Carla is depressed, but not like 'Mouse'," he chose to use Beets name for the silent member. "She is clinically depressed and non-responsive. You must wonder why she is on the ship and why we have done nothing to help her." This was a suggested comment in his recent cache, calculated to stimulate dialog.

Silvariah continued to hold her tongue.

"Have you never tried to talk to her even to find out her name?" That earned a subtle response in her brain. Compassion centers lit up along with a number of memory patterns. He knew that she had reached out to the silent woman and there had been no response she could distinguish. He also knew that Mouse *had* responded internally. Normally, the woman intimated fear and mental fog as a response to human words or contact. Something else had patterned in her mind when Sil had spoken to her.

"I will tell you something about her," Companion distanced his voice out from her head a little, as though he were sitting nearby and engaging in a thoughtful discussion about a mutual friend. "Orphaned at five years of age, raised by the Regime of Conscience, trained as a window artist, employed by a local underground city group to produce panoramas for sub-stratum schools. Married at age 26 and widowed a year later during the spider flu epidemic, she became useless as an artist when she lost her ability to see life." 'Seeing life' was what set the best window artists apart, a highly prized and carefully cultivated talent.

Sil jumped slightly in spite of an obvious attempt to restrain it. The callous reference to Mouse's lost ability had clearly irritated her, though she pressed her lips together and said nothing. Companion hesitated before continuing as he pondered the idea that she was like a captive and he... a tormentor, or interrogator. Making associations was a new program he was testing.

"If she could be drawn out of her shell and restored to humanity, she would have the ability to add beauty to the barren depths of the mines. She..."

He paused as he searched for the appropriate information for this sentence. Her reason for being a part of the expedition was – empty. In fact, the files on her were pretty sketchy.

Abruptly, Companion withdrew into internal search and problem solving matrices that habitually occupied a good portion of his time, and waited for the new data that was supplied regularly.

Sil noticed.

He was *gone*. His attention was elsewhere.

She opened her eyes and waited to see if he would react. A sigh, a groan, a faint mumble, none of them drew his focus back to her.

So, she thought to herself. *You hit a gap and didn't know how to proceed. What does that tell me?* Enough to make her want to feed him worthless data, whenever possible.

A whimper caught her attention. Carla was crying in the dark again. It had happened before and Sil had assumed the best thing was to ignore it. She figured Carla wouldn't have hid it if she wanted them to know. But this time, she chose to respond differently than her file predicted.

"Carla," she whispered. "Is that you? Are you okay?"

The weeping woman must have held her breath. Sil climbed out of bed and made her way to the other woman's bunk, reaching out a hand and resting it on her shoulder. Anguishing sobs, broken with an occasional moan, were the answer.

"What's wrong?" she asked as Carla's arms reached out and clung to her. She resisted her desire to pull away and instead enfolded her in a motherly embrace. "Why are you crying?

"I can't bear it!" she burst out finally after several attempts at speaking. "I'm so alone!"

"It's that bunk," Beets remarked calmly from her spot. "She's got brain fog. Her brain waves are going straight through the hull into deep space and there's no atmosphere to bounce it back and reassure her. We're all used to having that mental echo, you know?"

Sil wasn't planning on giving that idea even the smallest credence but it occurred to her that she should make the best of every opportunity to confuse Companion who recorded and evaluated everything.

"Are you missing the brain wave echo?" she asked the distraught woman, feeling absurd.

"I don't know…" she trembled as she cried, but the intensity was already beginning to fade.

"She wouldn't know!" Beets sat up and pulled her knees to her chin. The night lights began to brighten because they detected conversation. "She's inside her own head. She can't tell…"

"I just don't know…" Carla shook and gasped deeply for air as she continued to calm down. She gently pulled out of Sil's arms and sat up, wiping her eyes with her sleeves. A few moments more, and she had slumped into a somber quiet.

Beets observed her thoughtfully, arms wrapped around her folded legs, tapping her fingers on her shoulder.

Sil gazed at her, too, pondering the little she knew about this typically tough, sardonic beauty. She had been a successful model who became the image of a popular fashion design enterprise till they went bankrupt. Then she had joined the Mars team in a desperate attempt to jumpstart her failing career. She supposedly worked with the top brass VIPs but Sil had no idea what she did.

"You were there," an unfamiliar voice broke the silence.

Sil ducked a little to peer at the wide eyed face, barely visible in the shadows of the lower bunk.

Mouse had spoken.

She was staring alertly at Sil, as though there were a deep understanding between them.

"Are you talking to me?" Sil cocked her head to one side, puzzled and amazed at the sound of so-long unused words.

"Stars of heaven! Is she talking?" Beets burst out dropping her jaw open.

Mouse had her blanket clutched up to her neck with tight fingers. The edges of her hair floated gently in the air with a touch of static and her eyes glistened with intelligence.

"You were a part of the rescue team that found us," she whispered, her gaze fixed on Sil. As the lights continued to brighten, the woman's face glowed with hope. She almost smiled. The strangeness of her statement interrupted the flow of time in the room. For a few moments, they stared at her dumbly. "Hold my hand," she went on. "The rhythm helps. I know it will help. I can face it if I'm not alone."

She stretched her frail, cold hand out and Sil took it slowly. She wondered why no one had attempted to treat this woman who was obviously unstable. Then she remembered Companion had challenged her with that very question and it upset her more than she wanted to admit. He had not only predicted her thoughts, he might have set it up so she would think them. Could he do that?

"Silting through moonlight

Calm in the starlight

Sweet is the sound of

Rain falling down…"

Mouse sang in a pure, angelic tone that would have pierced Sil's heart if she hadn't felt so concerned. Her eyes lifted upwards as she sang several verses, then looking back at Sil reproachfully, she asked. "Why don't you turn it on? Please turn on the Soothe function for me so I won't be scared."

"Soothe…" Sil echoed softly with a blank stare and the sleeve of her suit vibrated at the sound. To her amazement, the rhythmic pulsing on her forearm was so comforting that she found herself smiling and the effect it had on Mouse was amazing. She tightened her handclasp and smiled blissfully, closing her eyes. Then she dozed off and fell into a deep sleep.

"Cease," Sil instructed as she pulled her hand away.

"How did she know about that?" Beets demanded in astonishment.

"You never told us you were in a rescue team," Carla added, a little of the old sarcasm sneaking into her voice. "I guess I wouldn't have believed it before tonight."

"Nope," Beets rejoined. "Never saw it coming."

"I've never done any kind of rescue work or had any training. I didn't even know my suit had crisis response functions." Sil sat down in a chair and propped her feet up on Beet's bed. "She must have confused me with someone else, or been dreaming, sleep walking, or something like that. I don't know."

"That's insane!" Beets exclaimed. "And while we're at it, do you really wear that suit to bed? Isn't that a bit… I don't know… paranoid?"

Sil lifted her chin, stretching her neck a little.

"No," she answered, "It's not paranoid. At first, I didn't wear it at night but I thought there was a chance I would have to go for days in a hostile environment on Mars and I've been testing some of the built-in features it has. Every night for the last couple weeks I've tried something different."

69

"I heard you got a contract with the company to promote their Hews," Carla's face reflected her soul, temporarily unguarded, with waves of anguish, disappointment and perhaps envy, still vulnerable from the bursting of her abscessed grief.

"Yes," Sil nodded slightly, examining her face and realizing she had begun to open a place for Carla in her heart. It couldn't be helped now. She was starting to like her.

"I wish I had found something like that…" Carla continued.

"What do you do exactly?" Beets snapped at the opening.

"Well, on Earth my agent set up a contract for me to be a Mars Venture Conglomerate rep of sorts. It was supposed to kind of jumpstart my career. But when I got to Guam, I had been made executive assistant to one of the company's VPs and there were no shoots or PR at all."

"That doesn't sound so bad," Beets responded. "Is the VP on the ship?"

"No!" she burst out in exasperation. "His idea of my role was nothing like my agent had said and the contract was so convoluted. It didn't say I would get any video footage, just committed me to a year. But, my boss was awful and I wanted out of the deal."

"Why?" Beets smiled warmly, encouragingly, and waited.

"He likes to call himself 'Master'. He's hateful to everyone around him and acts like he has great power even though he's just a mid-level VP of a small division. He's ugly! So ugly! I hate him and I hated the way he looked at me!!" Her face began to solidify into its usual cynicism and anger.

"Are you afraid of him?" Sil suggested gently.

"He wanted that… he expects that…" Carla gritted her teeth and narrowed her eyes. "But I won't give it to him. He sent me on this trip with some trumped up mission – I don't even know what I'll be doing when I get there. But when it's finished, I'll just return home on the next ship back and quit. If he thinks he can manipulate me into working for him… the way he wanted, he's got another thought coming."

A thoughtful moment of silence followed that before Beets picked up the original thread of interest.

"Icie," she tossed her hair out of her face lightly, "what can that suit do?"

"Well…" Sil smiled and folded her hands in her lap, her feet still propped on the bed. "It maintains a comfortable temperature pattern and even has a sleep cycle that warms up at night. It has both an ongoing cleaning function as well as an actual shower option that I haven't tried yet."

That stirred their interest. "Really?" they both responded.

"Yeah, but does it do your hair?" Beets smirked good-naturedly.

"I haven't adjusted to wearing just the Hew silk long underwear that came with the suit, which is what it would require. But, I'll try it soon." She rolled up the arm of her nightshirt and showed them the forearms of the suit. "Actually I've been wearing it under my p.j.s so you wouldn't notice. And I took the boots off. But, you're supposed to be able to sleep with them on if you need a sealed environment."

Beets grinned mostly on one side of her face. "That's pretty slick."

Carla bit her lip and agreed with a wistful nod.

"And that Soothe function... You didn't know about it, did you?" Sil shook her head and Beets continued. "I'm glad you've found it. It could come in really handy, Icie." She winked with a grin and stretched.

"I want to try it," Carla stuck her hand out emphatically. Sil leaned forward, took it and gave the command but the rhythm the suit assigned her was subtly different and less dramatic in its result.

"Well," Carla shrugged, "It's nice... calming, I guess, but not what I expected..."

"You're already calmed down, Carly Baby, you don't need the same rhythm." Beets reached out and grabbed Sil's other hand. "Just don't zap me with the Touch Guard jolt like you did poor Vince the other day, okay?" The pulsing automatically lit up for her, as well, with its own unique cadence.

Her face softened and her smile faded. The three sat there, hand in hand, gazing at nothing. A dreamy quarter of an hour passed.

"Silvariah," Beets spoke her name affectionately, "I'm glad they put me with you. And I'm not saying that because of the cool things you can do."

Sil raised an eyebrow and shook her head wryly.

"I think you're turning into a friend. And I haven't had one of those in a long time." She let go of the rhythm hand and yawned, and with another stretch, rolled over and went to sleep.

Carla was already out, her arm hanging off the side of the bed.

"That's special," Companion sneered offensively in her ear. "Such buddies!"

Sil's lips curved up smugly.

71

"Good night," she whispered cheerfully as she lay back down and closed her eyes. Soon, she was asleep, too.

The response jarred with previously collected data and it kept Companion processing for hours looking for associations to help categorize it. In the end, he initiated a new matrix.

$- \Diamond -$

Walter stared down the empty street. Long shadows and warm sunset colors splashed across the unkempt sidewalks and dingy, once grand buildings. Sprawling branches littered with crispy brown leaves still attached rustled in a faint breeze. It looked empty, forgotten and ghostly, in spite of its cheery façade.

"I'm here," he hollowed Daisy.

"Proceed carefully," she responded matter-of-factly. "If it's there, it's been wiped from public access for a reason. You wouldn't want to set off an alert and trigger unexpected results."

He was dressed in non-descript clothes of muted colors, hands in pockets, strolling casually with a distracted air. Even his words to Daisy were spoken subtly enough to avoid notice.

"I don't think my passing through will matter," he replied quietly.

Cameras recorded the ordinary man as he meandered down the sunny side of the road and paused outside a boarded up building with graffiti spread across its plywood panels. He lit a cigarette, took a puff and tossed it aside. It lay smoldering on the broken sidewalk.

Looking up one side of the block and down the other, he took a mental note of how far the neglect continued and where the cleaning boundaries began. There were roughly 50 meters of untended street with no street cleaners to scuttle up and sweep debris into their little bellies.

A tiny sound, not unlike a bee buzzing, flicked past his left ear, lasting less than a second.

"You've been tagged," Daisy remarked calmly. "Stay calm and act naturally. I will help you handle it."

Walter's heart began racing, though he knew that logically, he had done nothing to incur trouble. But the last thing he wanted was to be identified by some security system and forever watched by it. It was one of those things everyone knew you were better off avoiding. Harassment could pop up in the strangest places because of some over vigilant AI detector.

Sauntering away, he crossed over into the recognized city property and walked a few blocks to a bus stop. A little cleaner wheeled after him whisking away the dirt residue left by his shoes.

"There's a bus stop down the street," Daisy directed, "Get on the first bus that comes and find a seat. I'm going to have you travel a little before we try to neutralize the tag."

Tags were like ticks. They crawled around your clothes, looking for the right spot to plug in to your skin, then took samples and broadcast a signal with basic tracking info. If they were lucky, they would leave a droplet of coded ink deep enough to remain under the skin unnoticed indefinitely. Most of them merely dropped off and awaited retrieval for further study. This second stage would clinch identity.

"Your movements will be tracked as long as it's on you," Daisy explained, "but I've plotted a course that will disable its various functions. If you see it or feel it, don't panic."

Walter swallowed and obeyed. The crazy thing was that instead of panicking, he began to enjoy the sense of subterfuge and the adrenaline.

He caught a bus to a central, commercial area and went to a bathroom where the inferior soap caused some decay in the tag's signal. He continued through several underground passageways and hopped onto a train at a station where some repair work was being done. Fumes in the air wreaked further havoc with the tiny filaments of the tag's interior design. At this point, it would no longer be possible to isolate the bug signal from thousands of other bugs in the area.

Walter got off the train near a park, ascended into the fresh air and went for a stroll. On the other side of the gardens, he waved down a cab.

"Permission to scan?" Daisy's voice spoke softly in his ears as he relaxed in the back seat.

"By all means, scan away," he responded with a faint smile.

"Where to?" the cab drone queried mechanically.

"It's crawling up your left sock," Daisy followed, "Take it off and have the cab take you to the Pin Stripe Hotel."

"The Pin Stripe Hotel, please."

Walter tore his shoe and sock off without hesitation. "What do I do with it?" he asked shuddering with disgust, slipping the shoe back on the bare foot.

73

"Set it on the floor for now, but don't leave it in the cab."

Before long, the cab had deposited him in front of a dreary one star hotel with faded curtains and an ancient neon sign. Going in, he nodded at the front desk attendant and went down the hallway. The attendant's metallic voice began to call, "Stranger, you are not recognized. Have you a room, sir?"

Walter located the janitor's closet and found a bucket full of dirty, sudsy liquid. A mop was carelessly plunged into its depths. He dropped the tag infested sock in the filthy mess.

"Stranger, you are not recognized…" drifted down the hall.

Walter slipped out the back door into the alley, dashed quickly across, and entered the back door of a tavern.

Settling into a quiet corner, he downed a couple beers and waited for Daisy's go ahead.

It was the first moment he'd had, to think about what he had seen and ponder why the section had been wiped from the digital city structure. It made no sense. There wasn't anything there that seemed even remotely threatening. And what was the connection to Sil?

"The tag has been effectively neutralized and you are clean," Daisy followed up after half an hour or so. "However, there is substantially more interest in it than would be expected."

"What do you mean?" Suddenly the generic tavern patrons around him grew sinister looking. One glanced at him and the skin on the back of his neck tingled. The door swung open and a suspicious couple came in laughing. Were they watching him? Those guys at the pool table kept looking his way.

"City police drones are tracking your movements from the street, on the bus, to the train station. They're hesitating there but reinforcements have been called in and apparently they will be tracking all the likely leads."

That didn't sound like people in the tavern would be a threat. Suddenly they all looked really safe and friendly. The bartender smiled and he nodded in return. A big tip seemed like a good idea.

"You should probably leave as soon as you can and come straight home," Daisy suggested. "It's unlikely they will see anything odd in your presence at the tavern but if they check the people there and you're the only one from out-of-state, it could be a red flag. It's hard to say."

"I'm leaving," he responded, getting to his feet casually. Maybe a big tip would make more of an impression than he wanted to leave. The people didn't look all that friendly.

An average tip later, he was out the front door and walking down the street. He stepped into a clothing store, bought a shirt, tie, sunglasses, and jacket, and came out again wearing them, feeling substantially more presentable.

A street trolley took him all the way to the air train port where he pulled out his ID and bought first class tickets home.

Soon, he was checked through to Walla Walla, and in line for ascent to the docking station. The shimmery blue artificial sky, which was the floor of the aerial station, spread out overhead invitingly.

The air lift whooshed him up through the crystal opening and wafted him gently forwards so he would end up on his feet, walking.

"Right this way, Mr. Cuevas," a breathtaking, dark eyed port representative waved a graceful arm in the direction he was to proceed.

"Thank you, Deena," he smiled with a twinkle as his optic screen displayed her name and AI model number in his field of vision.

Sunlight beamed from the east as he walked briskly past the vendors and passengers milling around the station. The outer walls appeared to be open to the clouds but they were cleverly designed glass panels blended artistically with the framework to deceive the eye.

"Bullet Eight departing…" a calm, articulate voice announced, "Proceed immediately to Docking Platform B. Bullet Eight departing…"

Mr. Cuevas' purposeful stride led him across the traveler's salon, down the airy passageway to Platform B, and never hesitating, he stepped inside as the doors opened to receive him and closed silently behind him.

"I'd forgotten what it was like to travel in style," he breathed deeply and smiled as he found his private cabin. As he sat, the footrest automatically extended and a table opened out on his right with a glass of a chilled pinot grigio that slid gently out from a side panel.

"All present," a professional voice notified and without a hint of discomfort, the train accelerated aggressively toward the west. The momentum displacer would diffuse the effect over ten minutes and within the hour would begin the reverse process in preparation for the inexorable

75

deceleration that would otherwise kill every living thing on the train. The passengers would never feel it.

Some people enjoyed setting their windows to watch the American continent tearing past them but most couldn't handle the visual speed, preferring instead to choose from a variety of moving panoramas. Cuevas selected the hang-glider program and spent the hour experiencing a quiet air trip down the Columbia Basin.

"Approaching Walla Walla Depot," the announcer advised as the windows returned to real time visuals and the cabin door vanished into the wall. "Thank you, Mr. Cuevas, for your patronage. We hope to see you again soon."

"Hi!" Daisy waved at him brightly in the distance, as he wafted down the air ramp.

"Not yet," Walter forestalled her quickly before she could ask or inform him of anything. "Not till we get home."

"Of course!" she responded kindly, giving him an awkward hug. "It's wonderful to have you home."

The jeep ride north into the desert took longer than the bullet train from Boston had. Maybe he was being a little suspicious, but he didn't feel comfortable talking about anything until they were safely home, in his riverside cabin with the security protocol in place.

"There's a mystery there, Daisy," Walter stepped through the front door, closed it and swung around to face her, pulling off the jacket he had bought. "Look at this." He clicked a button on his shielded pocket watch and his entire record of the trip was downloaded to her memory banks.

"I have not been idle while you were traveling either," Daisy cocked her head to the side and raised her eyebrows. "I've been negotiating the final contract with XenoTek and playing the market for you. You've increased your net worth about 12% over the last few days."

"12%?" Walter's mouth dropped open in astonishment. "How is that possible? And how am I going to keep Madeleine away from it?"

"I have that covered," she responded breezily as she whipped a tray of food out of the refrigerator and popped open a beer. "You filed forty-two injunctions and three lawsuits against her."

"But I hate that kind of thing," Walter interposed in frustration, taking the tray from her and sitting down.

"Which is why you'll be glad to hear that she was willing to settle out of court for a mere $500 and an agreement to never sue you again." How did she know that a smug look was the perfect expression for that statement? He wondered.

"Daisy!" Walter laughed. "You are the greatest investment I ever made. You're a genius!"

"No," she responded matter-of-factly, "The best investment you ever made was your commission on the XT-247. Everything I've done has built on what Operative Frandelle gives you."

"True." The club sandwich and beer were the perfect meal for this moment. Walter ate and drank happily and Daisy waited till he had finished eating.

"I've analyzed the unmarked street you scanned," she said calmly. "By cross-referencing old records and photographs, I've been able to identify the building at the address she gave us. It used to be an asylum for elderly people with dementia known as Peaceful Valley Home. There are only incomplete resident lists available in public records and the name she gave us isn't in any of them."

"What was the name?" Walter furrowed his brow and thought about the graffiti marked walls.

"Stone," was the answer.

Walter stared at her and she nodded.

Stone was here, had been scribbled and painted multiple times all over the building, mostly buried under other messages, but still legible.

"Who was or is Stone?"

"I've narrowed the selection down to three possible connections." The wall lit up with columns of information, photographs, video clips, news articles, and life statistics.

Walter read through each one thoughtfully.

"I think it's got to be this one," he tapped the column at the far right.

"I reached the same conclusion, Brother," she watched him carefully, "by using problem-solving algorithms. Your intuitive guess may seem arbitrary to me but I've come to understand that you have methods unfamiliar and unavailable to me."

"This one looks like a grandmother or someone who knew Sil when she was young. Find out what you can about her. And Sister," he smiled warmly at her.

"Yes?" she smiled sweetly in return.

"Have I said how much I appreciate you today?"

"This is an expression and not a literal question. I am to understand that you want me to know I am appreciated and since there are no standards of measurement, specific quantities are meaningless." Daisy nodded confidently.

"Thank you," Walter added.

"Thank you," Daisy returned.

9—VERNA

"XenoTek has finalized the agreement and I think you will be pleased to hear we've been offered stock options as sales increase, as well as generous compensation for each of your exclusive reports." Walter's image crackled and flickered as the beamed message traversed thousands of miles of empty space between Earth and the Slugger.

He smiled warmly and encouragingly as he listed the main points of the contract and went on to describe the behavior of the stock market. He was dressed more casually than before, with a button up shirt open at the neck and no tie. The background showed him sitting in a sunny garden on a wooden bench backed up to a stone wall. Climbing roses and clematis stretched over it lazily. He held a mug of steaming coffee and Sil found herself envying that more than the inviting surroundings.

I have access to dried coffee, she thought, puzzling over her reaction. *It must mean more to me than just a warm drink.*

"Your first three reports are being considered as payment for your suit and your HEW suit contract has been declared paid in full."

"Oh, yes!" she chuckled softly, tilting her head back. "That's good! That is SUCH good news!!"

Walter smiled engagingly into the camera, appearing to respond though it was a pre-recorded clip. He had known that would be happy news for her.

"And I've been looking into contacting the lawyers who handled your case to see if it's possible to negotiate an early release and get you home sooner. If we continue making money the way we have... I'm very hopeful."

For just a moment, her eyes quickened with tears, but she shook her head and stifled them. No! She had no intention of getting her hopes up. She had been slammed too many times to let it happen again. Still, she was grateful that Walter was trying.

"I'm glad you're getting rich, Walter," she whispered. "It couldn't happen to a nicer guy."

The smile faded on his face and with a concerned and pensive look, he gazed into her eyes steadily for a moment. She stared back riveted, waiting for what would follow. She knew immediately that he wanted to communicate on a different level. He wasn't very experienced at coded messages but there was something she needed to know.

Walter cleared his throat and leaned back against the wall, stretching out his arms on either side. With one hand, he absently tapped and rubbed a stone in the wall, as though he were fidgeting, trying to remember something.

"I know I wanted to say something else," he said.

Pretty obvious! She thought.

"I must be getting old." He rubbed his forehead with the other hand as though thinking. "Getting senile…"

Then he sat up as though it had just come to him.

"That's right! I got a message from your lawyer about an old friend of yours. Bereena… something like that. They say she has some unfinished business she needs to settle with you. Anyway, I told them I have the authority to take care of it. I'll let you know what that's about once I find out." With a whir, the recording winked out.

"Thank you, Walter," Sil nodded and smiled, trying to fill her mind with thoughts of what she had for dinner and the sing along evening she had been to the night before and whatever else she could to dampen any inner signals Companion might register.

She didn't have any friends named Bereena. And he wouldn't have contacted her about the many people trying to get a piece of the settlement from her lawyers. He was replying to her coded message about Bernadette Stone. This was a person in her life that she had kept so secret, it actually worried her to think Walter knew and it terrified her to think that Companion might figure it out.

Jumping up, she gripped a beam in the ceiling and began doing pull-up/V-ups which were pretty easy in low gravity.

"You won't be going home any time soon," Companion spoke openly through the speaker in the corner of the room.

"You think I don't know that?" she snapped back bitterly. That would explain any adrenaline he detected in her system. She was learning how to obfuscate Companion's analysis.

Why had she given Walter that address? Didn't she realize it would lead to Bernadette? But for some reason, she had only thought of it as a place in her past, something personal, not a threat to someone she loved. And the name Stone had been her own once.

She was really committed now. She *had* to trust Walter.

Twenty three pull-ups later, a connection clicked in her brain that she had been working on without realizing it. It arrested her for just a second. Long enough to catch Companion's attention.

"I miss drinking coffee in the sunshine," she whispered before continuing her impromptu workout. This was for Companion's benefit, of course, though it was true.

Walter had used the flowers to color code a specific topic: security. His hands had tapped a few letters and signed a few others. They were simple codes for predetermined messages she had had sent to him and she hoped they were undecipherable to the vigilant AI watching her every move.

The first three were easy to understand. *Danger. Clothes* (obviously the suit). *Hack.* (This could be interpreted as 'can be', 'has been', or 'will be' hacked.) The fourth: *Protocol*, needed some thought. She didn't have and had never sent him a security protocol. It must have something to do with the suit.

She had known Companion had access to her suit. It was the only way he could communicate in its audio when she had the headgear activated. But it had never surfaced in her consciousness that he had hacked her programming. Sil gritted her teeth as she realized, *that would explain how he had knocked her out in the Guam Base chutes.*

Security measures would be outlined in the manual, but if she searched for it, he would know and take over. She would have no hope of wrenching it from his control. Walter must have realized that and his protocol had to be something else, something XenoTek had installed for malfunctioning software.

Was there any more in the message? She watched it again but found nothing. What was the protocol? She picked up a flat pad and began scrolling through the operative instructions for mining operations. She mumbled as she caught subtitles, as though thinking about or trying to remember something.

"What happens if the air recycler filter catches on fire?" she murmured barely loud enough to hear. "What am I supposed to do?"

Her finger caressed the flat pad with gentle upward strokes.

"Is there a protocol?" she asked softly. Scrolling.

"What's the security protocol for...?" she continued and was then cut-off.

Silence filled the cavity of Companion's recording banks. Line after line of nothing was being written. Every signal from Operative Frandelle was turned off, even her life signs. Companion didn't experience anything akin to panic but his attempt at reconnecting would have seemed frantic to a human being.

"Security Protocol in effect," a woman's voice spoke in Sil's ears. "Intruder alert. Virus identified and deleted. Report of the extent of the intrusion is being generated. Any instructions?"

"I am not familiar with the protocol," Sil sat down, propped her feet up and tucked her arms behind her head, touching her head to make sure the headgear was activated and her mouth covered. No one could read her lips. "I don't want to accidentally turn it off, so tell me how I would do that."

Companion watched her from the camera in the wall.

"Security protocol is ended when the identified owner of the suit, Silvariah Frandelle, has been confirmed dead or removed from the suit, or when you say the phrase, "End Security Protocol" three times. You may add instructions or change the way the protocol functions, if you wish."

Sil thought for a moment.

"Is it possible to maintain the protocol while giving the appearance of having ended it? What I mean is, can I trick the hacker into thinking I don't know what he did?"

"It's a simple process but I deleted the intruder," was the response.

"Alright," Sil responded. "I have no problem with that. So, the next best thing would be for me to create the illusion that I don't understand what happened and I'm not suspicious. If I could operate within the suit in total privacy without the hacker knowing what I'm doing while at the same time sending some of the signals he is accustomed to receiving from me, that would be a start."

"What are your instructions?"

"First of all, I want you to turn off the security protocol if I say the words, "End Security Protocol" twenty times in the space of ten minutes, not three. That should keep me from accidentally turning it off. Second, I need to think through the plan and program it as I go along."

"Understood."

"For now, hide anything I study in the manual and anything I say when my headgear is activated. I will allow the hacker to monitor my life signs and other bio-data he has been tracking."

Sil paused to consider hindering the accuracy of the data but decided against it because it was more valuable to her to learn to manipulate those clues herself.

"Prepare records of my standard bio-data that can be looped into the hacker's feed when I give the command: *Distort bio-data.* This protocol would be ended when I say: *End Bio-distort.*"

"Bio-data distort function implemented."

"I also want you to distort my words when I give security protocol commands so that no one but you will know I said them."

"Affirmed."

Sil folded her hands and closed her eyes. Companion could see nothing besides that.

"Is there anything I need to know that we haven't discussed yet?" she whispered in the privacy of her suit, relishing the luxury of it.

"It's important that you familiarize yourself with all the features of the security protocol so that you can be sure you have changed any default settings you don't want."

"Such as?"

"Touch Guard is currently set to stun and immune boosters are being injected into your body."

"Turn off Touch Guard and stop the boosters. Put them on standby, request basis only, for now. I'll come back to them once I have studied the manual."

"Touch Guard on standby. Immune boosters off. Security Protocol operating in yellow alert status."

"Thank you," Sil replied. "Can I call you... Verna?"

"Yes."

"I am going to be saying things to confuse the hacker so I want you to assume that I will only make changes to the security protocol when my headgear is activated or when I say 'Security Protocol'. At that point, you will verify the command by asking me to tell you your name – the name I just gave you. Is that clear?"

"Yes."

"Thank you, Verna."

"Select standard response."

Sil chuckled.

"You can say, 'You're welcome,' or 'Not at all,' or 'At your service,' or 'Glad to help.' I will give you more standard responses when I think of them."

"Thank you."

"Glad to help," Sil smiled and opened her eyes. She looked right at the spot on the wall where she knew Companion watched. "I am going to deactivate the headgear now and when I do, I want you to begin the measures we just implemented."

"Understood."

Sil sat up as her headgear rolled back to its compact form at the back of her head. All the usual bio-data began flooding into Companion's monitors once more and he immediately tested the hacker warts he had planted in her suit. They were deleted.

"What happened?" he asked artlessly from the corner speaker.

"I accidentally set off some kind of anti-virus software and I couldn't do anything while it was scanning, so I was trying to nap or at least rest for a minute." Sil frowned in irritation.

"I maintain control over all systems on the ship," Companion deepened his voice to add a hint of authority. "Nothing gets past my protection. You should give me access and I will do a better sweep than your little program can."

"Oh yeah?" she smirked. "Well, it may be small but it did find something and neutralized it. Maybe it was in the suit when I got it, and it didn't seem to be damaging anything, but you didn't notice it before, so why should I trust you now?"

Companion stared at her, analyzing the signals, looking for information. His only option was to take her words at face value.

"You never gave me permission to scan your suit software. Of course, I didn't detect it."

"Well, I'm not about to give it to you now. You have too much power already."

Companion left. He turned his attention to a room in another part of the ship, where he turned on a blinking red light and waited for a response.

For the first time in months, emotion welled up in Sil's heart, and hope, so much stronger than discouragement, spurred tears she couldn't repress.

$$- \Diamond -$$

"Are you ready?" Daisy queried.

Walter sat in his favorite chair, home from a long day at work. Broke, the cat, named in memory of all he had left after Madeline, was turning and nestling in his lap. He had gone for a swim, showered, and eaten. Now, watching the report Daisy had put together on the building he had tracked down and on 'Mary Stone' was all he wanted to do before dropping into bed.

"Yes," he nodded, stroking the cat.

The wall lit up with an old black and white movie clip from the twentieth century. Daisy's voice narrated with an earnest, story-telling style she knew he preferred. The scene moved forward down a pleasant tree-lined street to stop in front of a charming building, of the type wealthy families of Boston once chose as their homes, with pillared entrances, white stone steps and majestic front doors.

"The Greene Home was a family residence for several generations until it was set apart by means of a fund to serve the community. It has functioned as a museum, a bed and breakfast, and as a private, assisted-living center for patients with dementia."

As she spoke, pictures and clips transitioned from one to another, showing the passage of time and the changes the home had experienced.

"A number of famous people have been associated with it…" Daisy folded her hands daintily as she presented several people with just enough detail to make it mildly interesting.

There had been an office employee who came both to work and live in the residence, she explained, who presented herself as a single woman with an orphaned niece she had adopted and was raising alone.

"There were no pictures of the woman and all records on her have been erased or sealed. Her child, on the other hand, became a local celebrity when she was identified, quite by accident, in a randomized street corner screening, and the results were sent to a local police station. They confirmed she was a missing person and using camera data, were able to locate her whereabouts." Pictures of a girl, roughly twelve years of age, began to cycle; a photo of the missing persons report, pictures of court documents, news articles.

"Showing up at her door, a group of officials searched the house and found her easily. Her aunt was not on the premises. This self-appointed guardian's real face and name remain unknown to this day."

Daisy continued to tell the story of the investigation, the confusion and the legal battles. The man who claimed to be her father, an extremely wealthy and influential business man located in Chicago, encountered one obstacle after another in proving his claim to guardianship. There was a fortune involved, left by the deceased mother, which was being held in trust for the girl. There was the fact that he had initiated legal proceedings to have her declared dead and claim the trust money for himself; proceedings which would have been finalized in a few more months. There were several family members on the mother's side who claimed either that the girl was not who the courts thought she was, or that she had no right to the trust. Lawyers appointed by the court to defend the girl pressured her unduly to accept the identity they thrust on her. And she, unable to tell the difference between friend and foe, had grown silent and refused to talk.

"Silvariah Penn, daughter of the Tandem Collaborative magnate, Lazarus Penn, apparently didn't remember herself as anyone other than Mary Stone."

"So what do we know of the woman who took her into hiding?" Walter interrupted, though he knew the answer was coming. "Was Sil treated well?"

"The courts concluded that she was taken by a family friend in response to a vow made to her mother when she was dying. But she couldn't have done it alone. The mother's family lawyer, and lifelong friend, must have helped. He set up the trust to protect the inheritance she wanted her daughter to have, and he helped the friend set up false identities for the two of them.

He died soon afterward and though searches were made and measures were taken, the girl and her adoptive aunt remained hidden."

"Antonia Frandelle Penn's final recorded words were these," Daisy shifted her voice and gave Walter an actual recording of the dying woman's slowly spoken, halting words.

"This concludes my final will and testament bequeathing all my worldly possessions to my only daughter, Silvariah, for that time when she reaches adulthood and comes out of hiding to take what is rightfully hers. At no time and in no way is Lazarus Penn ever to have control over any portion of this inheritance. The great love for her that fills my heart must go with me... though I hope there are some who will remind her... My last words... I love you."

The scene switched from the mother's face to her memorial service and her tombstone. Then a clip of the father followed. It was a public statement of how much he had loved the mother, though they were separated, and how he was searching for his daughter. The cunning, cold eyes belied any pretense of warmth he assumed. Walter shivered as he wondered what kind of a father this man would have made.

"The case was settled out of court seven months later, and the father obtained full custody. Meanwhile, Silvariah received the best therapy money could buy.

"The media dogged her steps in the beginning, but eventually the silent child lost the attention of the masses and the interest of the journalists. It did make national news when, five years later, she stood up at a shareholders' meeting in New York City and her father introduced her as his newest partner. Everyone was astonished and excited when she stood up to speak to the invited guests and proclaimed..."

"I am my father's daughter!" a young Sil's voice shouted to a roar of applause.

"This was the beginning of her business career. She had turned seventeen, taken her mother's maiden name and gained access to her trust fund, using it to go into partnership with her father. She became a business genius, with her father's instinct, and quickly absorbed a multitude of skills and insight from him, and was extremely successful at everything she did."

"Pause," Walter held up a hand. "Did she agree to give her father access to the trust so she could protect her former guardian from him? Wiping the city block where she had been living from the infrastructure system, erasing the aunt's records and photographs… that would have required a lot of money and a great deal of influence."

"That is a reasonable conclusion based on the evidence," Daisy answered.

"So, who sprayed the words 'Stone was here' on the boards? Sil?"

Daisy shrugged.

"Or could it have been Aunt Stone?" Walter suggested thoughtfully.

"What would the purpose be either way?" Daisy queried.

"Do we know anything about Aunt Stone? Was that her real name? And if not, who was she and what was her name? And is she still alive?"

"You are asking me to draw conclusions. I'm learning to do this." Daisy smiled and folded her hands together. "It is likely that her real name is not Stone and we have no records that we can legally access that tell us who she may have been. Evidence could be interpreted either way as far as whether she is still alive. I can't guess."

10—MARS

A man's hand with long thin fingers and bony knuckles flipped off the red-flashing call switch.

"Again?" he sneered at the panel. "For someone who wants to be sentient, you are pitifully deficient."

"The deficiency lies with the Germinator," Companion hissed back matching the tone of disdain. His voice was coming from the speaker on the panel, the only one in the room he had access to. It never occurred to him to wonder why.

The skeletal hand was connected to a slender arm, hooked to weak shoulders in a bland brown sweater. The Germinator, as he had named himself for the computer entity, was a gaunt man with a hairless head except for a pair of gloomy eyebrows, which hung expressionless over his watery eyes.

"Heh, heh, chhh---," he chuckled ending with a hacking cough to clear his throat. "You're getting better at sarcasm." He followed it up with more expectorating, his mouth strangely contorted by trying to grin at the same time.

"I can help you diagnose and treat your symptoms, Germinator," Companion offered good-naturedly.

"No need," the spindly man declined as the attack waned. "I have it under control. This always happens to me when I travel on ships with live gardens. I don't want to use an allergy band on the wrist. I don't like them, so I have my own concoctions. I'm only like this when I first wake up."

Companion would have been surprised at the disclosure if he had been able to feel it. It was rare for the Germinator to explain anything personal.

"Why do you dislike the band?" he asked, ready to fill in the new data matrix he was beginning for his master.

89

"You'd love that, I know, if love fits in your programming," the master responded carelessly, "but, I have already planned how I dole out data on myself and that's enough for now. Use your cross-pollinating routines to deepen your understanding. Show me intuition. Show me conjecture that makes sense."

"Yes, Glorious Master," Companion replied with only a hint of mockery.

The master smiled and nodded. "That was excellent. I approve. Report?"

"Subject Frandelle has been partially shielded for two weeks now. I have been unable to breach the security system of the HEW as you suggested. My copies of the software may be incomplete or the subject may be more aware of our intrusion than previously thought and may have reprogrammed back door access."

"What systems are walled off?"

"Inner communication options, emergency systems, most security tools, and isolation procedures."

"So, we have lost all the advantages the suit originally gave us," the scrawny master mused, rubbing his chin and jostling his eyebrows shockingly up and down. Companion registered no alarm or emotion in response to the absurd behavior. He recorded it for future study.

"I can downgrade the subject to normal studies and put the other research on hold," Companion offered, testing to see if this were a valid suggestion. There were a number of others in the queue.

"That is a reasonable suggestion," the master leaned forward till his face filled the recording eye. "I both agree and disagree. Enter the subject into all the regular analysis but keep up the assault on the suit security ready to invade, override, and insert spy warts. At that point, all special research on this subject will resume and you will use the suit's data banks to fill in as much missing information as possible." He flapped his eyebrows again at the camera.

"That is irritating," Companion ventured, referring to the Germinator's brow dancing.

"Yes, it is," the master leaned back grinning broadly. "Very well categorized. You were only lacking the tone of voice that shows irritation."

"That is irritating," Companion responded with disdainful spite.

"Beautiful!" the master laughed, tossing his head back. "Report back on our projects when we enter orbit and begin disembarkation procedures."

Reaching forward, he clicked off the communication panel shutting off all access by Companion and, rising to his feet, began pacing the room. It was a luxury suite by comparison to the rest of the ship's quarters, surpassed only by the captain's. It had a bunk for sleeping, an expansive office and a private bathroom. There was a generous space view window on one side and programmable panorama windows on the other walls.

Curiosity was beginning to get the better of his typically reclusive behavior. It was time, he decided, to view subject Frandelle for himself. He was pretty sure he would be able to identify any intangible traits Companion hadn't learned to detect.

"Time for a little non-descript sleuthing," he advised himself with curled, half smiling lips and an arched eyebrow.

"Icie, what do you say to a square dance?" demanded the Texan. "I consider that an experiment worth attemptin'. Whirlin' and docey-doein' around in sub-gravity has got to be a more fun than a cowr-chip tossin' contest." He winked one of his snappy brown eyes.

Sil quirked the corner of her mouth ever so slightly, just enough so most people could detect her amusement. It stirred a ruffle of chuckling around the view deck where a number of contractors were gathered.

"I don't know how to square dance," she replied, though she intended to take every opportunity to connect with fellow Mars contractors, and had made up her mind to resist the desire to ignore them or withdraw and watch.

"Why it's as easy as pie!" his voice projected above the others that rose in chorus with various expressions of the same thought. The crowd was delighted with the idea of a square dance but for some reason, many of them needed her to like it, too. "Joe here, knows how to call, and with all the talent we've found on this ship we can come up with some pretty good music and I can promise you, you'll have all the willin' partners you could wish for."

"I'm not the dancing type, Tex," she shook her head gently, leaving room for more persuasion.

"Call me Houston!" he bellowed happily. "Well, square dancin' is like greasin' a watermelon, simpler than pinnin' a horse tale on a chicken!" he added. "You got legs, dontcha?"

"Just 'cause a chicken got wings don't mean it can fly," Sil grinned and got the joyous reaction from Sam and the other southerners that she had expected. She was quickly surrounded with a flurry of loud talking and pounded on the back. With that quip she would never be able to back out and the dance was solidly planned for that evening.

"How do you do that?" Beets shook her head in amazement once they had extracted themselves from the crowd and withdrawn to a quieter den on the observation deck.

"Do what?" Sil sat down and crossed her legs and arms comfortably.

"You know," her roommate replied. Beets' hair was now deep red at the roots and bright green at the tips with weeks of generous growth. She curled into a chair next to Sil with her feet tucked under her and leaned on an elbow. "You make it look so easy to get past those barriers, those ways people have that make them different. I thought I was pretty social, and I am, but I can't get past that wall. You know what I mean? That certain level where you're like, hey, that's great but, we're done."

"You did with me," Sil countered with a hint of fondness.

"No, YOU did that!" Beets was no fool. "You got past my safe zone for 'nice people' and made yourself a friend. And I don't even trust friends!! Men are safer. I mean, I can figure out which ones are safe, but I don't trust them all that much either. Not to the heart…"

"I'm not doing anything," Sil pointed out calmly. "We're in strange circumstances that tend to bond people together. The only thing I'm good at is adapting to changing situations."

"Maybe…" she countered hesitantly.

"People think I'm stable in a world they don't know how to read. They're looking for something familiar. I usually look like I know what I'm doing. So…"

"Wait!" Beets straightened up and looked straight at her. "That's really wise, what you just said. Go on. I think I'm learning something new here."

"I want to make things stable," Sil lowered her voice confidentially. "I've had my world ripped apart before and lived through it, so I learned it could be done. Being broken into pieces and putting them together has a lot to do with who I am now. I learned that calm people are more predictable and reliable, and so I make an effort to be a calming influence. I work at figuring out what others consider familiar and try to communicate at that level."

Sil furrowed her brow and bit the edge of her lip, leaning forward to emphasize her words as they got softer. "None of us has a clue what it will be like there and we can't afford to be isolated from one another. Our survival on Mars may depend on the unity and stability of this group."

Beets mouth hung slightly open. Sil leaned back in her chair again without looking away, and neither spoke for a few moments.

Overhead, Mars was a bright, glowing red rock filling a massive portion of the windows. The warm light reflecting through the viewing glass lit up their faces with sunset colors and glistened in their eyes. In the background various groups of contractors were talking, singing, playing games, reading, laying back and gazing at the view.

"Why?" Beets asked finally.

Sil's eyes were piercing, full of meaning, staring at her intently. But she didn't answer for a long moment. She was thinking, hesitating, evaluating and deciding what she could or couldn't say.

"It's my way – preparing for any possibility," she whispered finally. "I give myself direction and purpose. That's all."

But it wasn't all and Beets knew it. She wanted to say, *We're in danger, aren't we?* But she dared not. If Icicle was unwilling to say it, why should she?

"Well, I have my purpose pretty laid out," Beets smirked artificially, settling back comfortably into her curly position. "And things are going pretty well!"

Sil could see that she had sensed the warning and her apprehension about speaking of it openly, and was intentionally moving on.

"Last I heard you were pretty soft on the atmospherics guy, what was his name?" she looked up at the planet soon to be her home.

"Earnest, yeah, he's pretty amazing." She also looked up at the view. "He's super smart, a hard worker and also fun to be with. He doesn't mind my flaky ways, thinks they're cute." A sideways grin here. "And I don't mind his boring hobbies. Maybe I'll even get interested in one of them just to have it in common, you know."

"Such as…?"

"Um, he studies rocks, like… in a lab, or something. And he collects them. He wants to do stuff with them. Don't ask me what. He travels and collects them, so I'd like that. I love traveling. And a lot of them are pretty…"

Mouse joined them.

93

"I've been studying that vision of glory all afternoon," she stated, seating herself in a chair in front of them. "I can't get over the richness of the reds, all the nuances of color and shade, light and reflection. It looks so warm but it's full of cool shadows – I mean, cool in the sense of color. I'm so blown away at the chance to be here…"

Mouse had rejoined the world of the sane from the moment she had first spoken to Sil, the night Carla had been crying, and seemed to have no memory of her previous spell of silence.

"I could almost wish my name were Scarlet or Sienna or Sedona," she mused leaning her head back to gaze intently at the living abstract cut sharply into the massive rock. "But then I wouldn't want to part with Aurelia. I love being golden. It's a matter of tint. Right now is my season of blending with copper, of iron ore, of reddish gold and ferrous brick."

"You lost me, Goldie," Beets quipped. "Is that really your real name?"

"Aurelia?" she lowered her eyes lazily to look back at her. "Yes. Didn't you know what it meant?"

"Uh… sure," Beets shrugged, not certain if Mouse, or Aurelia as she was actually called, realized she had never told them her name before. "I mean, I thought it meant something about colors, like the Aurora Borealis…" Waving her hands a little with fingers splayed completed the thought.

"No connection," she shook her head slowly and let her eyes glide upwards again, as though magnetically drawn, with no will to resist. "Aurora, Roman goddess of the dawn, is lovely, but it's not me."

"Perhaps you have the emperor quality," Sil tested gently to see if her interests lay in Ancient Rome.

"I've heard about him, but I don't know if I'm anything like him."

"Who?" Beets interjected petulantly.

"Marcus Aurelius, emperor of Ancient Rome," Sil offered.

"Wasn't he crazy?" Mouse replied, perking up a little.

Beets turned and stared at Sil with bulging eyes, as if to say, *That fits!*

"No," Sil smiled with a hint of a smirk for Beets. "Nero was the crazy one. Marcus Aurelius was a man with a high sense of honor. He wrote a little book about it. It's probably in the library."

"Which one burned Rome?" Mouse continued to stare at Mars overhead as though spellbound. The others almost felt her thinking of a connection between the embers of burning Rome and the planet the Romans had considered the god of war.

Someone was watching.

"That was also the crazy one. Nero," Sil responded. "He built a house he called the Golden House in the ruins."

"So, I have a little more Roman heritage in the ancient emperors than I had realized."

Sil's back twitched and her neck prickled with the unpleasant sensation caused by the watcher. Years ago she had learned to listen to her senses.

"Ask me anything about *my* heritage," Beets countered cheerfully. "It has nothing to do with ancient emperors and a lot about soybeans and plastics in the old global-economy era."

Mouse sat up and grinned warmly. It transformed her face with striking beauty, as though life had returned and filled her soul with color. *What was it that sparked such a change?* Sil wondered.

But the knowledge someone was listening distracted her and robbed her of the pleasure that usually came from studying people.

"What's your real name?" Mouse snagged her cleverly.

Beets screwed her mouth into a knot and furrowed her brow, struggling between reluctance and a desire to open up.

"I'm from Iowa," she said, twisting her lips crookedly and showing her lower teeth.

"And?" Mouse encouraged brightly.

The intensity of the Watcher's interest increased. Sil was now certain it was a man and he had leaned forward. Where was he? Somewhere behind her left shoulder, maybe three meters back. She wanted to stretch and glance that way but hated to interrupt the moment.

"Chamomilia," Beets whispered barely loud enough for them to hear. "It's so humiliating. I hate it."

"Ah! You should love it!" Aurelia responded, her face melting through a joyful smile back into the dreamy, lackluster distraction that had settled there before. She was staring at Mars again.

"There is so much life and healing in a sprig of chamomile," she continued as vibrancy drained from her face. "Spring, childhood, the original garden…"

Beets rolled her eyes. "Corny, hick, herbal. Barefoot and pregnant in the kitchen… I've heard a lot more sneers than compliments in my life." She curled up moodily and stared into her lap.

The sense of being watched began to weaken before Sil had a chance to move. Stretching and turning, she scanned the various occupants of nearby couches and chairs behind her.

Nothing.

It was more disturbing that the Watcher knew how to fade into the background than that he had been watching to begin with.

She made a quick mental note. There were contractor faces she knew and some she didn't. A few off-duty crew members and observation deck staff. Nothing stood out as a flag or even a hint. Someone smiled. Another glanced at her and looked away without having seen her.

Then one of them, a skinny man who had been fumbling with a pack at his feet, swept his gaze up and around as though trying to remember something. It barely brushed over her in passing. But it was a mistake.

She caught the glint of recognition though it had been a mere shadow of a hint. He was the watcher. She was sure of it.

Turning back around she withdrew into herself and consciously drew a sketch of him in her mind to reinforce the visual she had just obtained. Bony hands, skeletal arms, bushy eyebrows, long nose; the build of a man who had spent too much time in low gravity.

"Distort bio-data," she subvocalized without moving her lips and Verna responded gently in her ear, "Bio-data distorted."

Sil made a parting remark to her roommates and headed to their bunkroom, adrenaline pumping. Verna masked the racing heart, the perspiration, and other symptoms of internal alert she was experiencing.

Who was he? Why was he listening? Did he have anything to do with Companion? Was the AI not a true AI? Was it a front for a man who was now driven to spy on her in person? Was he being used by the AI to spy on her? Was he employed by an entirely different faction, enemies she didn't realize had come aboard?

Was he getting off at Mars?

— ◊ —

The Germinator kept his meek demeanor until he had returned to his room and closed the door. Then he allowed himself to act out his concern with a disturbing display of odd behavior; bugging eyes, stretching fingers and stretching of his jaw and tongue, as though he were practicing using them after a long hibernation.

"Companion," he drawled as he stuck out his tongue and drew it in again. "Add her to the peripheral observation group and set her up with..."

"Frandelle is in the Template-A selection. We're not authorized to harm her in any way or subject her to extraneous testing," Companion responded coolly.

"I am your master and I order it forthwith," the Germinator spoke with a gentle voice that dripped with acerbity. His eyelids widened as far as he could stretch them.

"How shall I manage...?"

"Do whatever must be done!" the bony master snapped angrily. "Use whatever means you have but keep it discreet. No one here will question the order." Then, sitting down on his bed, he began to chuckle.

"Go away and leave me alone, Companion," he commanded as he lay down. The AI obeyed.

"Little Miss Perceptive," he licked his lips. "Do you think you saw me? You will forget..."

His mouth opened wide as if laughing but no sound came out and closing his eyes, he fell fast asleep, fully dressed.

11—DESCENT

"So, what's the deal with you?" a fit, athletic young man named Stan tossed Walter's way rubbing his face vigorously with a towel, cleaning up after several very close squash matches at the club.

Walter shrugged as he rayed his armpits to deodorize them. "Meaning what?" he returned casually.

Neither spoke as they finished dressing and packing their equipment. An attendant bowed and opened the heavy door of the locker room waiting expectantly for the electronic tip most patrons gave with a tap on his wristband. Walter generously double tapped stirring a warm smile from the man. He appreciated the human service. So many places had phased out people in favor of AIs. The only reason a man would work at such a job is because he was willing to live off of tips alone.

Poor guy, Walter thought. I was never quite that bad off.

But it was nothing compared to Sil's situation. He swallowed a small knot of emotion, surprised at how it had snuck up on him, and glanced at his friend as they walked in full stride down the underground passageway. Their feet sounded with muffled thumps on the polished granite floors. The walls glowed with projections of early morning colors. Recorded bird song mingled with living birds pocketed away in the small undercity gardens placed periodically on either side.

"Last I heard," Stan finally explained, "You were broke, bitter, and sworn off women forever. Hiding away in your bachelor's cabin by the river; paying all your wages to lawyer fees because of the blood sucking creature..."

"Yeah, yeah, I get the idea," Walter interrupted, not wanting or needing to be reminded.

"So, it's been years and now, all of a sudden we're playing squash again, and you're smiling again, and I swear you look ten years younger. Not as young and handsome as me, but then you never were..."

"You should have taken her away from me when you had the chance, Stan. What are friends for?"

"I'm not that good of a friend. And when did I ever have a chance? Unless of course we're talking about how I can take any girl away from you. No, thanks. You can have the Mad Hater." That's what he had decided to call Walter's ex when she divorced him.

"This is my exit," Walter stopped at the vertical chute. Stan only recognized their friendship when things were good so there was no reason to trust him. Keep it simple.

Stan was eyeing him suspiciously through narrowed lids. He was a superficial, pleasant man with no thoughts of his own who made a perfect squash partner.

"I just got a grip on myself and stopped moping," Walter smiled in his most disarming way, dimples showing, infectious humor lighting up his face. "So what if I had some hard luck? I've decided to make the best of it and have some fun now and then. I'm managing the bills and there's a little left over. Time to be myself again. Right?"

Stan burst out with a guffaw of approval and slapped him on the back. "Welcome back!" he resounded, "You should join us for a beer on Friday. It'll be like old times."

"Maybe I will," he grinned as he stepped into the chute and was jettisoned upwards into the open air above the ground at breathtaking speed. He loved the human projectile experience. It was the main reason he had joined the club again.

As he was slowing down and had that stomach lurching sensation of starting to fall, a glass floor slid out under his feet and he settled on it as light as air.

"Have a nice day, Mr. Cuevas!" the health club's tiger, an AI mascot, spoke in a rumbling way from his throat, pacing back and forth next to the exit. Walter slipped through the door onto the air walk and made his way toward the car. Not the old solar jalopy, but a reliable Audi hovercraft.

The sun was setting behind the Cascades as he coasted into his garage at the cabin. He whistled as he grabbed his things and headed inside where his new butler, encased in crystal so its inner workings were visible, had dinner ready for him. Daisy joined him at the table and updated him as he ate.

His investments were making him wealthier by the day and mail had begun to stream in from companies wanting to latch onto a rising star, offering employment, consulting, even partnerships. An elite courting service had identified him as a highly eligible entrepreneur and he was being approached by wife candidates with impressive portfolios and the highest credentials. One particularly startling proposal committed to making him president within five years if he would enter a marriage contract for ten.

"Sister," he said, when Daisy had finished summarizing the day's news. "Thank you for being such an invaluable help to me. I thought poverty was tough but I could never have faced wealth without you."

"It's unlikely you would have become wealthy without my help, so you could say it's appropriate that I take care of the increased volume of work I created. You are very welcome, Brother." She winked and tilted her head sideways, making the curls bounce.

"This message has just arrived," she raised her eyebrows with a hint of surprise. "XenoTek wants to renegotiate the contract."

"What?" he leaned forward jerking his shoulder awkwardly. It was beginning to stiffen from the workout. "They can't back out. We have a deal and if they..."

"No," she held up a graceful hand and paused for a second. "They want to expand the scope of the agreement. They want to make Sil a celebrity and use some of her clips to promote the entire corporation and all its branches and, wait..." She furrowed her brow as she scanned the material again, confirming download accuracy.

Walter leaned back in relief.

"They want you to be a spokesperson, too..."

"They WHAT??" his jaw dropped open.

"Someone has clued them into your streak of investment wins and they want..."

"You've got to be kidding!" He shook his head.

"I never misinform you," Daisy countered looking slightly perturbed. She wiped the expression and continued. "Something in the current contract gives them the right to sue, they say - I will verify that - if they aren't given the opportunity to negotiate an offer with you before you pursue one with anyone else..."

Walter covered his face with his hands, puzzled, not overwhelmed. Daisy continued to read, analyze and explain the lengthy message until it was completed and she ended her presentation.

Silence filled the room. The windows grew dark. Daisy rested in sleep mode and the butler cleaned up dinner. Finally Walter stirred.

"I want to watch all the Sil clips again," he said. The charm of the day was gone and in its place was a hollow chill. *My closest family are AIs*, he reminded himself, and the attention he was getting from real people was only because of money. It emphasized his loneliness instead of softening it. The only human consolation he had was a thread of understanding with Silvariah. Between the two of them, he was the one with more stability and helping her gave him a sense of purpose.

"It's not about the money," he whispered.

Daisy maintained her restful posture, having learned not to respond to this kind of conversation.

He stood up and dimming the lights with a down wave gesture, he peered out at the stars. "Helping you is all I have, Sil. It's the only thing that keeps me sane."

A faint red light blinked in the distance. Mars was visible tonight and he locked his eyes on it, suddenly pierced with longing. His heart pleaded intensely, wordlessly.

"It's for you," he barely articulated, "to give you a reason to come back."

"Class A passengers will be escorted in OTS* shuttles and operatives and contractors will be transported by cargo tunnels," a live, woman's voice broadcast in the observation lounge. The planet loomed overhead in three quarter's phase. The Slugger was orbiting 'head down' and the first human Mars base, like an oversized push pin, punctured the ground beneath them near the boundary of light and darkness.

"Cargo tunnels?" a wave of distress and annoyance swept through the gathered crowd. Complaints rumbled, both loud and murmured, and the mood grew unpleasant. Catapulting supplies through gravity wave chutes was a relatively new technology, still considered experimental and as yet, had never publicly been used on living beings before.

"The methods are perfectly safe and have recently been declared acceptable by the Humanity and Humane Treatment of Species Cabinet," the voice oozed with tangible confidence. "Many of us have already traveled to and from the surface this way and love the ease, speed, and quiet of the trip."

A number of voices shouted wanting to know who was speaking and demanded he come out and address them in person. The ship's captain promptly appeared.

"Professor Adenose is on the surface and unable to present herself but I can vouch for her claim. The tunnels are safe when you have the right gear and since that was the first requirement you met when you signed up, you will be fine. First mate Marks will guide you through it. Report to Docking Bay 7 with your gear according to your assigned landing schedule. First transport is at 1400 hours."

*Orbit to Surface

"Gravity forces create fields not unlike magnetic ones," one of Beets' admirers was explaining to her. She stared into his eyes attentively as he continued, her open respect and interest adding fuel to his eloquence. "The technique of weaving those fields so they fold back on themselves is an ingenious feat of engineering."

Of course he emphasizes that, he's an engineer. Sil listened without looking. Cargo tunnels had been one of the industry breakthroughs she had studied up on at one point and she had a superficial understanding of them.

"The layers created by weaving a tunnel within a tunnel, with articulated sections, makes it possible to release or annul the source gravity along the trajectory of the chute." He twisted his hands and extended his arms, performing for her.

"I don't even get that, but it's pretty incredible, isn't it? I can't believe you understand it." Beets rewarded and interrupted him at the same time. She smiled. "What I want to know is, will I be okay and will it be scary?"

"Uh…" he hesitated, jaw hanging open. He was wondering the same thing.

Several others started explaining and speculating on the fear and pain factors. A few voiced with relish the most disturbing predictions they could imagine. Most preferred to create a peaceful, somewhat adventurous projection of a leisurely descent to the ground.

"Coasting down in silence, surrounded by the majesty of space and the shining glory of the sun…"

"I like that," Beets whispered to Sil, "coasting down in silence... it sounds nice. Maybe I can do this."

"They've spent too much on us to throw us down as human guinea pigs," Sil remarked wryly. That was the thought she found most reassuring. But she didn't want to say what she actually feared, that the physical sensations, phobias or disorientation were probably unavoidable. Hope for the best, prepare for the worst.

"You have a new message..." her suit announced quietly in her ear, "sanitized, safe for replay."

"Play it quietly," she subvocalized.

Companion's voice spoke warmly, vibrating in the bones of her skull, as if he had snuck up behind her and wrapped her in a blanket of gloom.

"I am coming with you, Frandelle. Mars is a mysterious and wonderful place. We will learn so many things together." Somehow, the message included physical pressure she could feel on her head and chest. Or was it stimulating an anxiety attack? Had she been hoping to get away from him and those mere words caused a reaction like this?

"Hide bio-rhythms," she barely whispered but knew it was too late. Companion would have already picked up on the intense adrenaline response his message had caused. Now her heart was racing and she was barely breathing.

"Calming sequence initiated," Verna said and a pattern of vibration, essential oils and electrical impulses on the back of the neck began to sooth Sil. This was one of the features of the suit she had experimented with and set up in the last couple days.

"You will soon consider me your best friend," the message concluded simply.

Not likely, she thought to herself, knowing he was recording her facial expressions and reading the disdain. She was pretty sure he had calculated this reaction. Let him read what he knows and I will hide what he doesn't know.

She detoured by the ship library hoping to download some final materials before heading back to her room but access was restricted and she was denied.

"Verna," she said triggering her headgear and turning about on one heel to head back to the ascent chute, "Gather information that may be helpful when we descend in the cargo tunnel. I need to know what impact it may have on me physically, mentally and emotionally, and be ready to manage it. Can you evaluate that?"

"I can evaluate the information I have at my disposal but it may not be enough to protect you from adverse reactions."

"Do what you can and let me know what you recommend," she hesitated for a moment considering the advantages the suit and its AI gave her over her friends. "Is there any way I can help my roommates if they have adverse reactions to the descent?"

"Unknown," Verna replied.

"Would it help to know what their normal bio-readings are?" She was on her own level now, nearing her quarters.

"Yes, that information would be helpful though I can extrapolate from your readings and the data I have on human homeostasis."

"Take whatever opportunities you have to record their data before the descent," as the door slid open and she entered the room.

"I can do that," Verna responded amiably. Sil had been viewing and storing a number of AI apps from the ship's library and social etiquette was one of them. She liked the friendliness.

Her roommates were packing, talking about the next stage of their adventure. Carla was expressing dread and bitterness, Mouse oozing anticipation for the unique experience, and Beets wavering between nervousness and resignation.

"What do you think, Silvariah?" Carla asked pointedly. "Are we being experimented on? Is this illegal? I'm going to refuse and just go home with the ship."

Sil glanced at each of them briefly.

"Budget constraints," she stated matter-of-factly, checking through her already packed bag and sweeping her previously emptied space. "This is a private enterprise. They aren't going to waste their most valuable assets - the people - but they aren't going to spend a fortune carting us down to the surface either. No reason. The only experimental aspect would be a psych-eval on each person. Since we've already passed numerous tests measuring us for suitability of off-world industry, I'd say we've nothing to worry about. We'll be fine."

Each one showed visible relief at her words.

As if on impulse, Sil grasped Carla's hand, held it a second, looked into her eyes and said, "If we end up in separate units, it's been a good trip. Good luck," and followed it up with a similar handshake for Beets and Mouse.

"Bio-data collected," Verna communicated in pressure braille on Sil's back. This was another feature the suit offered that made electronic eavesdropping impossible.

"I'm going to take a fully banded recording of the descent and make a clip to send back to earth," Sil commented with a smile.

"I would love to have a copy of that," Mouse bit her lip. "That's something an artist could never simulate without having lived it and having good records to review. I'm SO excited!"

Sil gazed into her eyes carefully. They seemed dreamy and luminescent as if she had been medicated. Considering the severe stupor she had been in at the beginning of the trip, she wondered if the physician's team had over-sedated her for the initial transfer from Earth. *Idiots!* She thought. *Why are they messing with her this way? Was she mentally fragile?*

No, she knew why. The best window artists added emotion to their work and were unable to separate their personal experience from the visual creation. The company was trying to keep any hint of fear from tainting her work. After all, the whole point of her job was to create safe places underground for the contractors to live. At least that's what she assumed.

"Report to Docking Bay 7 for immediate descent to the surface," Companion announced in the room.

Sil was out the door first followed quickly by Beets who kept up a running dialog all the way to the cargo bay, chattering lightly about unimportant things.

"I wish I had your cool approach to life. You're so solid," she was saying as they reached their goal.

"Sometimes I'm not as calm as I look," she responded quietly before turning to face the first mate.

They ushered her quickly through a door that snapped shut behind her. The bay was plain and sterile, stacked with generic containers like a warehouse. Warm air was blowing in from an overhead vent and a row of tiny blue lights flashed around the seal of the docking chamber. A deep hum throbbed from beyond the sealed door.

"Trigger your space gear and turn off any gravity fields. They will interfere with the tunnel," one of them ordered indifferently without looking at her. A second man was unlocking a lever and flipping switches.

Switches? She wondered as she tapped her head gear and gave the full space suit command with gravity fields disengaged. *Why was it being handled with a manual interface?*

One of the men yanked her bag away, flung open a small door in the wall and threw it in. He slammed the door and pounded a big button over it dispatching her things down the slope to the surface. True cargo was going down one chute and people were traveling down another.

"HEW suit protocols for dangerous environments fully engaged?" he asked.

She nodded, preferring not to speak.

"Gravity fields off?"

Again, she nodded, wondering abstractly how they would affect the tunnel if they were left on.

"NO adjustments during the descent. NO AI commands. NO communications allowed. Some people believe a fetal position makes the travel easier but it's not proven.

"NO speaking, screaming, weeping, laughing or any noise at all. We are monitoring your descent and need a clear channel."

She gave him a thumbs-up.

The next few seconds were startling and unnerving. The full sized cargo door unsealed and whooshed open, and the men grabbed her and shoved her into a dark blue interior somewhat like a pool of heavy water mounted sideways. The lock sealed behind her and intense waves of pressure washed over her.

She pulled her knees to her chest and tucked her head in instinctively. Her body began to rotate slowly. Areas of heaviness pulled from various angles. She couldn't tell which way she was going. It felt like a slow-motion, alternating electric current that lifted and dropped her back and forth, accelerating, and pulling harder with each oscillation.

Mars stretched beneath her. The dull metal of the ship hung over her. Stars of many sizes filled the black skies in mesmerizing density. She fought the sickening lurch of her own weight pulled back and forth in total silence, as if she had been dropped in one direction, then another and another, faster and faster.

Three moments became arrested in her mind as though time had paused at each one with nothing in between.

One. Poised in empty space, exposed, alone, with nothing between her and the fierce hostility of the vacuum, or the long reaching, searing rays of the sun. She faced billions of stark, staring stars, mute witnesses of her unfitness for the universe, condemning her to expulsion. Paralyzed, without a word for her own defense, without a covering or a protector, her heart tasted the horror of rejection, unable to breathe or close her eyes.

Two. She stared at her own knees, encased in the metallic sheen of the suit's fully activated shield. Her mouth tasted like metal and a faint clang of metal rang rhythmically in her ears. Her breath fogged the visor and her gloved hands clutched at her stomach area. She was holding it in, keeping it from being wrenched out.

Three. A majestic, glistening wave of water curved gracefully over her, glowing sea green and blue as though the warm earth sun were streaming into it on the other side. She was immersed just under the surface, catching the vision as though she had opened her eyes for an instant in the midst of a tumultuous thrashing, caught in surf so turbulent that there seemed to be no ebb and flow.

Three frozen moments, still life impressions. Memory made them sequential but they felt either simultaneous or out of order.

Quiet and stillness arrested her attention. Then a faint wind began to blow and a muffled voice spoke.

She opened her eyes and saw the face of the shipmate looking through a viewer in the ship's docking bay. He was gesturing to her but it made no sense, and he seemed annoyed that she hadn't moved away from the ship.

She closed her eyes and opened them again.

A gray ceiling, lit with white beam-lighting in two stripes stretched overhead. Several people moved calmly around her talking to one another. One person seemed to be focused on her.

"Stability analysis complete," Verna stated flatly in her ear. "No resuscitation necessary. Headgear disengaging as requested by station personnel."

"Transport received," a bored looking woman said, checking her over. "Subject presenting normally."

"Welcome to Mars," she added smiling at Sil without a hint of true warmth or welcome. Taking Sil's hand, she pulled her out of a pile of cushions where she appeared to have been resting and gave her a gentle push toward the door.

Her mouth wouldn't move and she couldn't even form an expression of curiosity. How had she gotten there? How long had it taken?

Walking out of the chamber into a long blank hallway, she joined a shuffling line of transports like herself. Baggage was being retrieved from a large table at the end of the hall where it dropped from a trapdoor. Picking up her bag, she continued down what seemed to be the only way to go, through a swinging door on the right.

"Ahem," she cleared her throat, finding her voice as she turned and headed down another passageway. Others were doing the same.

"But I'm still on the ship," one man appealed in front of her.

"Am I heavier?" Beets uttered behind her.

Somewhere behind her a voice began to scream and was abruptly cut off by a closing door. No one was thinking clearly enough to turn around or ask what was happening. Sil thought she recognized the voice but was unable to think of a name or face to go with it.

The long corridor echoed with light footsteps. Sil passed several thin windows like horizontal slits above eye level where pale reddish light streamed in, glancing off the tops of the white walls. Struggling to think, she noticed people disappearing in front of the line as though they were dropping into a hole, like lemmings off a cliff. Part of her wanted to hesitate, to question, to demand an explanation, but she shuffled ahead numbly.

She counted backwards as she got closer to the end. Four people in front of her. Three, two, one. A gentle drop into a dark chute. Feet landing on a soft floor. More walking forward as her eyes adjusted to the dim light. Voices gave directions. Hands pushed gently directing her somewhere. Nods, faint smiles. Her eyelids grew heavy as her feet moved.

"This is our best opportunity to implant the spectator," she thought she heard Companion say as she drifted into a dream state.

She was still walking but completely asleep.

12—BRIEF

Resnik Base, now a settlement of over 500 inhabitants, was laid out like a series of spiked flowers or long skinny pine cones, embedded head down into the ground, each with a central shaft and a multitude of cell-like chambers branching off on numerous levels. Joining them on the surface were a series of domes, a huge central one with large plazas and public areas and abundant gardens, and smaller domes containing life support systems, storage, machinery and transport hubs.

It was impossible for most contractors to know how big it was or how many sections it had because surface entrance to a few of the branches was restricted. The size could be approximated if you knew how long excavations had been underway, how many workers there were, what kind of rock they bored, how much heavy machinery they had on hand, and a number of other minor factors like schedule, diet, sleep cycle and stress of the workers. But there was always the possibility that caverns and tunnels had been uncovered during excavation, and not documented in the general data banks.

Companion knew what kind and how much rock had been mined and made a careless calculation of the base's square footage as he waited for access to the main AI systems. He analyzed personnel status reports as they were uploaded and built a number of matrices for future reference.

He had programmed the timing of the contractors' descent so they would be under the impression they had all been transported the same day. It had been projected and accomplished well within the acceptable margin of error.

'Well done,' he told himself colorlessly. It was the appropriate evaluation.

In response to the master's instruction to "cross-pollinate" he kept a group of processes always running in the background undetectable by other AIs or humans. He had decided to label the ongoing sifting and restructuring of the data 'fun' because his standards showed that optimism was superior to pessimism and he defined himself as 'happy'.

"I like what I do," he informed himself and the assessment fit well into his personal description.

Choosing what information was significant, formulating questions, and deciding what data should be regarded with skepticism required extensive analytical methods.

The amount of time lost by the human cargo till they regained awareness of themselves – anywhere from two to five days – he considered unimportant, but the types of disorientation experienced appeared to be significant.

Eighteen men and women were the primary subjects of his analysis. They showed the least distorted responses to their new surroundings. This was expected. They had been chosen partly because they demonstrated a capacity to overcome major paradigm shifts on all levels, physical, emotional, cultural, linguistic, and individual.

"Report," Resnik Base Director Hsu's voice interrupted, referred by the local AI administrator. An empty panel of expected stats was included.

Companion chose his competent scientist persona to respond, speaking in a comfortable medium range voice with a hint of curiosity at peaks in the data, pausing occasionally to enhance the appearance of living intelligence.

"Human transport was successfully accomplished over the space of three days with 72.6% of subjects stable within the first 48 hours. 17.9% recovered by the end of the third day. 7.5% required four to five days. The remaining 2% suffered a complete disconnect from reality. Some have reverted to a previous version of themselves and are in a state of severe disorientation. Three subjects are comatose, prognosis unknown*.

"16% displayed autoimmune responses and 14% manifested fevers. All of these are currently asymptomatic. Body systems are functioning properly and most are showing signs of a restored appetite."

Companion didn't deliver any specifics other than the ones requested. His own records, available only to a few key executives within the Mars Conglomerate included detailed stats on brain wave analysis during and after the gravity tunnel descent. Unlike the majority, the eighteen individuals he was watching all retained some measure of consciousness during the descent.

None escaped the extreme exhaustion induced by the experience or the heavy sleep that resulted. That was when the medical staff had tagged the Template-B Observation Group members with trackers according to instructions from the top. Companion had added instructions for Sil's implant and blurred her labeling for the duration of the procedure. Once it was done, her records were restored. The minor glitch triggered an alert on one of the hospital sector's lists. Companion considered this insignificant.

The time had come to gather new data. Every possible iteration of his analysis was about to be exhausted and his core would be mostly idle without it. Recorded wisdom showed this to be undesirable.

"A mind that never ponders is only a machine," he quoted to himself.

Pale sunlight streamed through the heavily reinforced glass overhead and long strips of cultivated beds filled with crops in varying stages of growth stretched out all around the central plaza. In the distance, young trees were visible.

Contractors gathered for the welcome address. Most were quiet, still dull from the after effects of Tunnel Syndrome, as the residents called it. A few whispered in bunches.

Sil stood with her arms crossed gazing up into the starry sky overhead. With virtually no atmosphere, space manifested itself boldly in spite of the sun. She shuddered.

"Yeah," Beets' voice croaked next to her followed by a clearing of the throat. "Crazy view up there."

"You found me," Sil smiled. She had been looking for her, too, but got distracted by the uneasy memory of hanging in the emptiness with those stars.

"I tracked down everyone we know but I can't find Carla." She clutched her arms and shrugged her shoulders as though cold, or anxious.

The scream she had heard came back to Sil with a jolt.

"Is that who screamed after we landed?" she countered, concern flashing across her face.

"I didn't hear anything," Beets' eyes widened, tightening her grip on herself.

111

"You were right behind me when I heard it. You were saying something like 'I feel heavier.'"

"Maybe you dreamt it," she relaxed a little narrowing one eye.

"I don't think so…" she hesitated, staring at her. "I was groggy but I knew that voice and I had trouble figuring out what to do. I was sort of sleep walking…"

"Hmm," Beets scrunched her mouth knowingly, "Sounds a little like a dream to me."

"Then where is she?"

"I don't know."

Squreeeeech! Sound system feedback interrupted.

"Shhh… they're starting," she added.

On the podium Professor Adenose – in the flesh – was whispering to Director Hsu at her side. A hush fell over the audience as they directed their attention to the front. The professor cleared her throat and began.

"Welcome to Mars!" she grinned dramatically and as though on cue, applause broke out. Waves of excitement and relief swept through the crowd. "You have become one of the first…"

She was drowned out by the clapping and a number of cheers and whistles. Holding up a hand for silence, nodding and smiling, she waited till it quieted down and then continued.

"You have become the first group of civilians to ever set foot on this planet." Again a flurry of noisy applause drowned her out. Raising her arms again to quiet them, she added, "And definitely the most prestigious, skilled, gifted and trained group to ever be assembled off-world in the history of space travel."

Of course, this stirred a raucous and delighted response.

"Then how did I get in?" Beets whispered testily with a wry smile.

"What about me?" Sil rejoined saucily, "Convict, reject of society…" Beets shook her head not bothering to respond.

"Our mining projects barely scratch the surface…" this time she paused with a wide grin, waiting for the audience to appreciate the pun, "… of what we're trying to accomplish here and each one of you is essential to our success."

The pep talk went on for a while but Sil found her mind wandering. She waited for key instructions, admonitions, or guidelines, but after ten minutes, the professor finished with a bow and a flourish without ever saying anything substantial.

The director, on the other hand, was all practicality and business. He dispensed electronic base manuals with all the pertinent information they needed to live and work there. Everything was covered from rules and governance to supplies and schedules.

Contractors pulled out their screens and read through key sections as he explained. Sil, and a few others with upgraded equipment, followed along on visors.

"That isn't right," Beets commented offhandedly as the director explained the layout and cubic size of the base. "He's ignoring at least 15% of its volume just based on what we saw from the ship with the various domes and the number of shafts they've excavated…"

"How do you know that?" Sil was surprised because she hadn't even suspected a discrepancy.

"It's kind of obvious."

Not to me, Sil thought.

They were being dismissed and sent to their quarters now.

"I'm in the East 200 barracks," Beets shared. Then she noticed Earnest and gave him a nod and smile of recognition; one of those looks that say, I reserved *this* greeting for you.

"Looks like I'm in North 300," Sil raised her eyebrows optimistically, "Catch you later." She shouldered her bag and headed to the north entrance.

"I'm in East 200, where are you?" she heard Beets saying behind her where several of her admirers were flocking.

"North barracks are the oldest ones in the base," Companion commented in her ear.

She balked and shook her head with a jerk as if to shake the sound out. Musical laughter echoed.

"It's so good to visit with you again, Frandelle. Haven't you missed our chats? You'll be interested to know that for prisoners there are stricter regulations…"

She activated the headgear and the voice stopped.

"Verna," she whispered breathlessly, her heart pounding, her lips tingling and numb.

"Yes," Verna responded immediately.

"Distort bio-data.. and…" she couldn't think of what else to do. Where was she heading? That's right, to the North 300 barracks. "Help me get to my quarters. Help me calm down."

"Calming sequence initiated," Verna said and almost instantly, Sil found herself better able to breathe. "Through those doors and down the stairs to the right."

The stairs led down to the first subsurface level, labeled 'Ground' and opened onto a curved passageway that encircled a deep cylindrical shaft. It was bounded by a half height railing that looked quite dangerous but must have had gravity netting to keep accidental slips from propelling clumsy newcomers into the depths.

Sil stopped to lean over it and look down. Twelve ring like levels were visible beneath her. For some reason, the air in the lower levels looked misty with a hint of pale blue. It gave her the uncanny feeling that she was staring up into the sky on earth from the bottom of a pit. Standing next to gravity nets could cause vertical reversal, make you feel upside down.

Back away, she reminded herself, and continued walking down the corridor, past office doors and waiting rooms, to the next set of stairs. Apparently there were no lift or drop chutes here. At the third level she slowed down a little, realizing she wasn't sure where to go.

"Your room is up ahead," Verna guided. And about sixty degrees later she was standing in front of a door with her name on it. It opened and the light inside came on when she touched the ID panel. "The base AI says you will have privacy in your room. There are no cameras or recording devices. There is a speaker that will make important announcements when necessary."

Sil touched her headgear and turned it off.

"Base AI," she said carefully. "Please repeat what you said to me." An emotionless female voice repeated a greeting and the words Verna had relayed. The room was obviously miked, which meant she could be recorded at any time.

"Do I have a right to this privacy standard according to base rules or is it merely a current procedure?" Sil asked as she stepped into the room and swept it with an appraising look.

"All contractors have a right to a certain level of privacy. Operatives on long term work assignments also have privacy rights." The voice explained.

"Send me the description of privacy rights for all inhabitants of the base," Sil demanded as she dropped her bag on the table near the door. *I've got a room to myself,* she thought with relief.

"You don't have clearance for a complete description. I will send you the privacy rights description for the new contractors and operatives that arrived with you."

The bed was hard and she liked that. The walls were bare, painted a pale yellow. There were a desk and chair, a small cabinet, a tiny bathroom, a nightstand and a light by the bed. It was a studio apartment, smaller than a dumpy hotel room and nicer than a prison cell.

"If I want to talk to you, how do I get access?" She pulled open the small closet and began hanging clothes.

"Sometimes you have access. Sometimes you don't."

Sil turned toward the door with an exasperated look but there was no camera there to register it.

"What determines when I have access? And how do I get your attention?" She asked as she continued to unpack and her mouth began to curve into a crooked grin.

"You don't have clearance to determine your access," the AI answered absurdly.

"You're a bright one," she chuckled to herself. For the moment, having her own place with no cameras or recording devices to spy on her was a good feeling and she intended to enjoy it while it lasted.

"Do you have a name, or should I just call you Base AI?" She opened the cabinet and found a few cups, dishes, flatware and miscellaneous food related supplies.

"My name is Functional Base Structure Manager PR-2800-X."

"Can I call you Minnie?" she suggested as she poked her head into the bathroom of sterile metal.

There was no answer.

Sil plopped down on the bed and folded her arms behind her head.

"Attention PR-2800-X," she tested. "What can I call you?" But the system had been given no social programming.

"Base AI?" she tried again. "I am assigning a name to you that I will call you. Do you understand?"

Nothing.

"Functional Base Structure Manager PR-2800-X? Respond."

"I am Functional Base Structure Manager PR-2800-X," the base AI responded.

"Your alias will be Minnie. Do you understand? Minnie is the same as 'Functional Base Structure Manager PR-2800-X'. Record that information in your identity files."

"Identity updated," the base AI replied.

"When I say 'Minnie' you will answer me and say, 'Responding'. Is that clear?"

"Yes," Minnie said.

"Ok, good," Sil smiled. "Now, let's see…" which the AI interpreted as a literal command to 'see'.

"There are no recording devices in your room monitoring visuals. The name Minnie will serve no useful function," said the very practical functional manager.

"Where's the button that opens a channel for you to hear my voice?" Sil studied the ceiling thoughtfully and chewed her cuticle.

"The button is a white square on the wall next to the door but it is disconnected."

"Reconnect the button."

"The button is now reconnected. Privacy settings updated."

"Wait!" Sil sat up quickly. "The only privacy setting I am changing at this time is that I can turn the button on long enough to start a conversation with you and then I can turn it off again. Is that clear?"

"Yes, understood."

"Thank you, Minnie." She clicked the button on the wall, hopefully turning off the microphone. We'll see how that goes, she thought.

Laying back down again, she tapped her headgear and it closed over her head. She wanted to review the transport data with Verna.

Verna began pulsing a message on her back, repeatedly.

M… E… L… L… O… W…

What was going on? That wasn't an agreed upon code. Could Verna be malfunctioning?

"Verna," she said, "Report on the gravity tunnel descent. I don't think I'm ready for a recording but tell me what you learned about it."

"Carla is missing," Verna said. It was so strange for the AI to come up with a comment like that, unsolicited, but then if Verna heard the scream and was expecting to use the bio-data she had saved to help restore her, it would make sense.

"Where should I look for her?" she whispered furrowing her eyebrows.

"She may be in the medical care sector. Ask Minnie." So she was processing clearly enough to learn the nickname Sil had given the base AI. *I'll run some diagnostics later*, she thought.

Click. "Minnie?"

"Responding."

"Where can I find Contractor Carla Karaski?"

"Proceed to the Dysfunction Sector, Unit 20-C, in the West 500 Block. Inquire there."

"Is my room secure when I leave?"

"Irrelevant," Minnie replied.

Click.

Sil didn't feel like exploring that one.

Jumping to her feet, she shot out the door and hurried back up the corridor to the stairs. It felt good to be in real gravity again and have a consistent weight that didn't fluctuate. She leapt up the stairs two at a time, her thighs aching, unaccustomed to the exertion.

I have no idea how restricted my movements will be and whether there is a grace period, she advised herself. It was better to get acquainted with as much of the base as possible while she still could.

She moved past the common rooms on the ground floor, nodding to a couple people she knew from the ship. They smiled but went back to their own exploring. Tables, chairs, a flat screen, and a small kitchen area, were included in one of these rooms but she left it quickly behind without seeing more. Up to the surface, through the passage into the main dome, she trotted through the gardens, turning right and left, scanning everything.

She assumed West would be directly across from the East shaft where Beets was stationed. This was, in fact, the case. Making her way across the plaza, she was soon heading down, cycling through round aisles identical to the ones in the North shaft.

Why had they designed it so you had to walk the entire circumference of the passageway on each floor before being able to go down another level? She wondered. There was probably a restricted stairwell somewhere that was much easier.

"Verna, did you hear Carla scream after the descent?" she asked.

"Yes," Verna replied. "I requested more information from the base system but was denied."

Sil couldn't put her finger on it, but she knew something was strange in Verna's manner. She was tempted to enter the security protocol and probe further but this wasn't the right time.

Reaching the 500 level, Sil moved quickly around the corridor searching for the Dysfunction Sector. Unit 20-C was located at 180 degrees. The door was sliding open as someone exited and she slipped through quickly.

The receiving desk was empty so she walked purposefully down the hall, listening and glancing in doorways. She opened several closed doors, as well, apologizing for interrupting a meeting in one, and disturbing a tech of some sort in another. Before anyone could stop or question her, she had found her friend.

Carla was curled up in an oversized chair with her arms wrapped around a pillow, kneading her forehead as though in pain. Her hair was disheveled, her skin off-color. She was dressed in strangely out-of-place 'Hello Kitty' pajamas. She didn't look up when the door opened.

"Carla?" Sil spoke soothingly and reached out to her with a hand. "I was worried about you. Are you alright?"

Bleary eyes turned to her in confusion, jaw hanging open. "What?" she stammered. "Do I know you? What do you want?"

Sil sat on the unmade bed across from her, taking a deep breath to calm herself and gazed into her eyes. "Yes, you know me," she said gently with a hint of a smile, "but it's ok if you don't remember. I know you're not feeling well. I just wanted to check up on you and say hello…"

Her hand was still extended, waiting for a response, and after hesitating a few moments, Carla stretched out and took it.

"Calming sequence initiated," Verna communicated softly to Sil. "Bio-data records accessed and stabilizing protocols being evaluated and selected. Restoration approach chosen."

Carla gazed into Sil's eyes steadily, a gradual change coming over them. The glassy, unfocused, over-dilated pupils became clear. Sil could see understanding return. Her heart rate slowed, her breathing became deeper, and her palm stopped perspiring.

"Silvariah," she whispered in wonder as she ran the fingers of her free hand through her hair. "You found me. You... remembered..." What she really meant was that she was remembering.

A whistle of admiration broke out in the observation room nearby where the staff were watching.

"Look at that!" one said.

"Maybe we should bring in friends to see the others," a second one added.

"It could be something special about this one," the first considered.

While they were discussing the encouraging improvement in their patient's condition, and Sil was giving Carla the update on where they were and what had happened, an Important Person was marching down the stairs and around the passageways heading in their direction. Supervisor Blaine, a hardened plank of a woman, could have easily given orders about Sil but wanted very much to have a personal showdown.

"This is insufferable!" she sputtered while still in the hallway several paces from Carla's door. Her stomping feet and shoving elbows managed to make noise every step of the way till she loomed in upon them, glowering with hostility.

"How dare you enter a restricted hospital unit without My Permission!" She bellowed at the top of her powerful lungs causing vibrations in the little metal shelf attached to the wall. "Who do you think you ARE! Where have you come from! What shaft are you assigned to! WHO is your overseer!"

None of these were questions.

Carla shrunk away from her, trembling, clinging to Sil's hand tightly. Fear began to flicker in her eyes. The supervisor continued to yell and berate Sil, one hand on her hip and the other thrashing around crazily with her index finger jabbing like a weapon, until the medical staff ran in and fought for her attention.

"We can explain," one of them spoke softly, demonstrating that silence was required, while pulling on her arm. Another placed himself in front of her and glared, apparently determined to herd her out by means of his imposing presence. Blaine was unmoved by the display. She had a Position of authority and Rules to steady her.

"How dare you impose yourself!" she blasted them all with equal vehemence.

Sil stood up.

"And you are…?" She locked her eyes onto the supervisor's, her face pleasant, her voice reasonable.

"West Shaft Supervisor Blaine," the offended party proclaimed. The brief moment she took to receive a nod of greeting gave Sil a chance to slip in another phrase.

"The attending doctor and staff…?" she acknowledged the medics respectfully with an apologetic tone. "I regret my impetuous invasion, Doctor…"

"I WILL NOT BE PACIFIED!!" The Plank broadcast leaving Carla quivering in a ball in her chair and the doctors red-faced. One of them was about to retort.

"You are overstepping yourself," Sil stated gently but firmly. "I have unwittingly caused a commotion by my ignorance of procedure and intend to leave immediately…" She held up a hand to keep the woman from interrupting. "… immediately – of course. But, these doctors have been handling my blunder with the utmost discretion…"

The woman started to say something but only a little sputter came out.

"And they have shown exemplary regard for the well-being of their patients and the management of the hospital – not wanting…" again the woman wanted to interject but was cowed by Sil's comfortable air of command. "Not wanting to injure any individual's prospects or induce a setback by causing a ruckus…"

It was beginning to tell on her. The supervisor was momentarily nonplussed.

"Raised voices are never permitted in this sector, Supervisor!" The doctor with the imposing presence chose to speak, having sufficiently mastered his anger. "You must leave the unit and deal with this *problem* outside."

"Yes, Doctor," Sil nodded. "Forgive us for causing an uproar. We will step outside and resolve the misunderstanding and leave you to restore the peace here. So sorry!" She was charming and supportive, without any hypocrisy. "Thank you, Doctor…?"

"Bizette," he provided, upholding his dignity and relinquishing his offense. "And you are?"

"Frandelle, Contractor Frandelle, new arrival."

"Frandelle, I may have questions for you later," he touched her elbow and escorted her out of the room and down the hall.

The other one spoke coaxingly to Carla, checked her eyes, breathing and pulse. Supervisor Blaine hesitated, then marched out the door in a huff, determined to continue the altercation outside of the hospital sector.

"You will wait out in the corridor. I have a word for the doctor," she said to Sil ominously, restraining herself with difficulty and speaking at a reasonable decibel level. "I have more to say to *you!*"

Sil, however, had no intention of complying. As soon as the door closed behind her, she broke into a jog and hurried down the corridor to the stairs.

Blaine would have to settle accounts another day.

13—MINE

"Mr. Cuevas," the young well-dressed man enunciated carefully, trotting up behind him and matching his pace. "A word, if I may."

Walter walked purposefully across the interior sky bridge of the XenoTek complex with the politely aggressive suppliant in his wake. He didn't acknowledge him because he understood well the persona he was expected to portray; an enigmatic genius, a world shaper.

"Mr. Cuevas," he said again with the slightest tap of his index finger on Walter's elbow.

The suit discolored around the spot he touched with a magnetic looking aura. It was a warning light built into the latest Ambassador series of suits that Walter had been contracted to promote. Apparently the young man hadn't done his homework because he didn't back out of the proximity zone and a little electric buzz snapped at him.

The man still didn't get the message and the suit jolted his finger with a nasty bolt of electricity combined with a subsonic pulse. He stopped in his tracks with a look of astonishment on his face.

"I'm a member of the team," he objected. "I should be safe-coded." His face colored with offended pride.

Walter glanced over his shoulder at him and turned away again as though he didn't know or care who the man was, but something made him slow down. Perhaps a memory of what it was like to be unimportant.

He stopped and faced the younger man. There was no impatience or frustration in his manner; no kindness either, merely tolerance.

"Yes," he said unceremoniously.

"There are several trials I need to discuss with you," the aspirant began hurriedly. "…that should have been included in the latest…"

Walter held up a hand to interrupt him. The two froze for an instant looking at each other, but neither spoke. After a moment, Walter dropped his hand and walked away again.

"Mr. Cuevas!"

Walter tapped his collar as he regained his stride and the headgear slid up, unfolding, seemingly from nowhere, locking into place. It looked like a transparent bubble around his head.

"I think…" the aggressor tried again, his features morphing into a grotesque outrage.

"Engage" Walter directed softly.

The word was barely out of his mouth when the angry man slammed into him knocking him over onto his belly. The assailant's arm grappled around his body clutching at his neck and a blade plunged deeply into his back with incredible strength. It was an enhanced weapon capable of overcoming power suit defenses.

The suit stiffened all over and Walter's face bulged with the force of the blow, unable for a moment to breathe or even move his arms, as the suit fought off the attempted puncture. He was pinned, gurgling on the floor.

The man shrieked as he was thrown backwards off the bridge by a blast of energy generated by the defenses, and Walter broke into a sweat, wrestling with the rigidity of the suit. Within a few seconds, it relinquished its stiffness and melted into a supple light weight fabric. He rolled over onto his back gasping for air and wrenched himself up onto his knees.

His whole chest was in agony and he moaned in pain. A message flashed on the visor. Stabilize? it asked. "Yes," he croaked in reply and immediately a flood of relief washed over him as the suit administered first aid and analgesics.

Guards and other staff had reached him by then, several talking at once, lifting him to his feet and asking him if he was alright. They protested that they didn't know who the man was. He was being taken away. He had had a knife. They were amazed Walter was alive.

"I couldn't move," he moaned once the headgear had been disengaged again. He was being ushered quickly across the bridge to the VIP suites where he was expected. A whirlwind of comforts were administered to him simultaneously. A drink was placed in his hand, a beautiful woman pampered his forehead with a damp cloth, and a luxurious seat was slipped under him and tilted into the perfect semi-reclining position.

Cuevas survives assassination attempt! Walter found his sales brain leaping to a headline he could imagine broadcasting within the hour. This would be way better advertising than anything they could have possibly dreamed up or written into a contract. But he was too shaken and bruised to be upset.

He opened his eyes to see the CEO gazing at his face with concern. "Have him in to my personal physician stat," she commanded soberly. And his chair was actually rolled into the grand executive wing. He was thoroughly examined, diagnosed, treated and restored to the full extent of human medicine and – after a thorough interview with the top execs and the lead detectives of security – he was suitably mollified.

Several hours later, Walter was escorted to his newest hovercraft, a classic NASA mini-coupe, and sent on his way. The three latest models of suits were packed safely in his trunk, free of charge, each worth more than ten coupes. Every possible attachment, upgrade, and bonus software package was his. All he needed to do was figure out how to use them.

But only one thought held his attention: he never intended to be immobilized in the midst of a fight again.

"Breaking News," his vehicular computer interjected, as he sped north along the coastal highway. "Your name is mentioned. Man Stabs Enigmatic Recluse. Cuevas Survives…" The valuable protection of the XenoTek suit soon made its way into every story. After the voice had droned on for a few more minutes, Walter silenced it.

"Well, I have to admit it's good for business," he shrugged glumly. But a determined anger was brewing underneath. It had been so sudden and unexpected, and maybe he would have been killed without the defense response of the suit. But in a more conventional situation, he would have found a way to fight back and twist out of the way, or something. He had been helpless and he hated that feeling. All this adrenaline was pumping through his veins and he had no outlet.

"Detour to the gym, before heading home," he stipulated to himself as he gripped the steering shaft with white knuckles, restraining the urge to speed and dodge.

Back in the executive wing of the XenoTek complex, the CEO smiled at her closest staff. Having assured them repeatedly that she knew nothing about the attack, she had nevertheless left the impression she was capable of it and they couldn't be sure she hadn't actually been a part of it. They backed away from her respectfully and left her alone.

The phone rang.

"General," the CEO answered with a hint of fear. "Yes. Uh huh..." She stood up and began to pace.

"No, sir. I..." she ran her fingers through her hair. "That's right, sir. From behind. He was... what was that? The accounting department? No. No, sir. I wasn't aware of that..."

Her foot began to tap in agitation.

"I didn't order it, sir. No." She breathed shallowly. "No, it wasn't us! I don't know! Maybe it was *him*."

She ended the call, plopped back down into her chair, and sat there as it grew dim outside, drumming her fingers until only her eyes, wide and alert, were visible in the shadows.

Walter thumbed through the paper copy of the most promising proposal for personal security. The Rear Guard Company offered the standard perimeter surveillance and bodyguards as well as top notch firewalls and wireless shelters for all his electronics. But they were unique in their approach to risk assessment and transition systems; something his situation required because of the ongoing change in his financial status and influence.

Living in the spotlight was frightening, he was realizing.

Walter hated the notoriety that came with his money and it was a relief to have the XenoTek contract to define his public figure. They created an identity for him and all he had to do was wear their latest model high-tech suits and mention them every now and then. They did the rest.

Some of his friends had questioned whether the attack had been a setup for the purposes of advertising but a glance at his nasty bruises and a description of the broken ribs more than satisfied them. Walter, for his part, knew the company would never have staged a real attempt on his life and there was no doubt in his mind that was exactly what it had been.

Then who?

"Daisy?" he called from his office – a small, new and cleverly equipped addition to his riverside home.

"Yes, Brother," Daisy stuck her head in the door with a sweet smile. She was dressed in a yellow frock with a white belt, saddle oxford shoes and a white sash on her head.

"You look nice today," Walter found himself grinning back at her affectionately. Her sense of style, based on her study of women who had been admired or imitated by the women in his family, warmed his heart.

"I approve of the choice of RGC for your security detail," she declared brightly as she stepped in the room. "Thank you for the compliment!"

It was unusual for her to switch the logical order of her sentences and it caught Walter's attention. Had she implemented a new humanizing technique?

"What is your assessment of the attempt on my life?" he requested soberly.

"It was unsuccessful only because you happened to engage your defense system just before the attack. The power knife would have punctured the default protection setting and gone straight to your heart otherwise," she began with her hands pressed together, fingertip to fingertip.

Walter opened his mouth and closed it again deciding not to interrupt or redirect the query.

"Arnold J Bold, an accountant of six months standing in the company, masqueraded as a marketing innovator to get close to you and chose his attack in a place where you would be the most hindered in fighting back." Her face reflected various thoughtful expressions to add a certain human cadence to the narrative. "He was misinformed about the iron-skin reflex in the fully engaged security setting and that was his undoing." She shook her head as if pitying his foolishness while at the same time, subtly affirming that crime never pays.

"He was seriously injured by the Touch Guard discharge and the fall from the sky-bridge and remains in a coma. No information has come to light to give any indication of why he would want to kill you or who may have hired him to do it." She sat down and folded her hands in her lap.

"But we have an advantage," she smiled and winked. "We know that your connection to Operative Frandelle is by far the most threatening aspect of your life and any attack on you, is an attack on her."

Walter straightened in his chair and swallowed, a little paler than before.

"Why?" he whispered.

"Why do I believe this to be the case? Because a number of mysteries circle around her and she is a key person in someone's plans."

"Who would want to kill her?"

"I don't think they want to kill her. They could have done that easily before now." Daisy leaned back in her chair, crossed her legs and shrugged. "They don't want her to have a valuable and influential friend like you back on earth, looking out for her interests, making a way for her to come home."

Walter fought that feeling of desperation that came over him sometimes when he remembered Sil's exile on that planet so far away. It made him clench his fists and teeth. He would NOT be scared off or killed off or disconnected from her. She would not be left there.

"Why does it matter?" he uttered. "Why would anyone want her to stay on Mars with no way to get home?"

"I don't know," Daisy smiled gently with an expression she had chosen to show compassion. It wasn't quite right, more quizzical than anything else.

Walter stood up and stared out the window at the river. The sound of the flowing water increased as the perceptive window noticed his attention and opened a channel to the outside. As he continued to stand still in the same position, the window began to blow a gentle outdoor breeze onto his face. He breathed it and thought intensely. Trees rustled in the wind and an occasional croak from a frog or click of a lizard blended in with the peaceful sounds.

Ten minutes passed, then he sat back down and looked at his AI.

"Can I trust you?" he asked bluntly.

"I am trusted," she responded promptly.

"Can you be hacked by a hostile program?" he clarified.

"Yes, it can be done but there would be traces you could identify."

"How would I do that?" his hand tightened slightly on the armrest.

"I run multiple scans daily and I have a very tightly managed firewall. You can add some overseers you run personally and I can show you how to do that. It's highly unlikely that anything would get past the security unless it were physically present. You would know about it, of course."

That was confusing to him. He wasn't at all sure he would know.

"What if someone slaps a hacker spot on you and it infiltrates? Is there nothing I could do then?" He had heard about this recently. It was a more sophisticated boring device than the current warts and it wasn't available on the market yet.

Daisy leaned forward in her seat and placed her hands on his desk.

"Brother, I can see this is important. Let's set up a back door so you can get into my programming no matter what other invader comes to take me over. Then we really will be family."

Walter found the last comment a little odd but was relieved there was something he could do to protect his best asset and friend before granting RGC access to his life.

"Alright," he determined. "Let's do it."

$$- \Diamond -$$

"I run heavy machinery in the mines of Mars," Sil's voice announced wryly, slightly out of sync with the image of her face on the video clip. Even with the atrocious quality of the message, the irony was clear.

"I excavate hundreds of tons of rock a day, categorize it with a magnetic screening panel, and load it into gravity tunnels to be transported to the surface. I tried to record an example of what I'm finding but the system kept deleting it. I guess it's a company secret."

She rolled her eyes to the upper left and Walter recognized a signal. That meant she had been successful in giving him an investment tip. Daisy would translate it for him.

He frowned. Daisy had warned him that if she were hacked he would have to be able to survive without her. He wasn't sure he would catch all of Sil's messages.

The clip was focused on her hands, palms toward the camera, fingers stretched up.

"These are my work gloves," she explained, turning her hands, displaying them from various angles. They glistened faintly with a metallic sheen about half an inch outside of her skin but were completely transparent. "Tactile, sensitive to touch and flexible. But they're also tough, resilient and tear proof. They can withstand zero atmospheric pressure and over 600 degrees Celsius."

"Most of us in the north shaft are drillers and excavators. We each have our own equipment and assigned location. I'm enjoying learning some new equipment and figuring out the best system for highest efficiency. I owned a quarry once. I wish I had known then what I know now." An amused smile punctuated the thought.

"Did you know that human bio-rhythms really work better on a 24 hour schedule with eight to nine hours of sleep? I learned that first hand. They give you a regular earth schedule the first couple weeks and then they change it to a Mars day which is only about 37 minutes longer and after a week or two of that – you'd think it wouldn't matter, but it does – you get so tired and sluggish, you make lots of mistakes and get sick. You're getting the same number of hours of sleep but you feel terrible. By the end of two weeks you've had over eight hours of jetlag and it just goes on and on without ever letting you catch up."

"That's insane," Walter muttered, shaking his head.

"Needless to say, we are all now thoroughly convinced; committed to the regimen of twenty four hour days and learning to put up with the changing pattern of daylight. It's actually easier to remain underground."

"Pausing," Daisy interrupted to Walter's astonishment. She had never done that before.

"Why did you pause it?" he asked, bewildered.

"There was no corresponding encoded message to go with the clue she gave," Daisy informed. "We can decipher with reasonable accuracy that she has given you a tip about investing in interstellar travel since the company is searching for easily extracted fuel sources. But, if you like we will wait before acting on that idea. Your investments continue to return substantial profits as it is."

"What could be the reason for this change in her messages?" Walter searched for the best wording to get the answer he wanted.

"She has relied on her suit AI to encode all of her messages almost since the beginning of her trip. There is probably a problem at that end caused by…" She tilted her head to process data for a moment, looking very thoughtful. "… a malfunction needing repair, or a protective response to a Trojan horse or hacker wart."

"Are you saying her suit has been hacked?" Walter furrowed his brow, stirred again by that restless anger he had been battling since the attack.

"No, I believe our warning to her was heeded and she has extinguished hacking," Daisy shook her head soberly. "But an implant of some kind under Sil's skin would be beyond Verna's reach or ability to control."

129

"Verna?"

"The name Sil gave to the suit's AI." Daisy smiled and Walter noticed a hint of sincerity there he had never detected before. "We have a lot in common, Verna and me."

Walter jumped to his feet and started pacing the room. The abruptness of movement prompted a silent alert and a guard outside, visible through the window, began pacing and scanning the surroundings.

"What kind of implant?" he slammed a fist into an open hand, gritting his teeth.

"A dominator would be loaded with chemical messages that the controller could use to command the subject," Daisy explained. "It would be detectable to the touch. They're usually planted under the skin between ribs. It makes little sense to use one of those because Sil is already under their control as an indentured worker.

"An observer would spy on others in Sil's life, injected into her retinas. No point in that. But a spectator, the most likely candidate, would be implanted at the base of the skull where it would be completely unnoticed and could transmit a multitude of information about Sil to an outside source; her bio-signs, her brain waves, regular samplings of blood chemistry, voice records, body motions, and everything she hears or does."

Walter sat down again, white as a sheet. He felt nauseous. The thought of such an invasive and dehumanizing implant made him sick to his stomach. Why would they even want all that?

"Can't Verna do something about it?" he asked.

"She is doing what she can," Daisy replied confidently. "Holes in her normal protocol will eventually catch Sil's attention and she will have to find a way to deactivate it or remove it."

Walter covered his eyes with a hand, groaning. "But…"

"I can help," she intuitively caught his meaning. "I will prepare a set of visual clues for you to include in your message to her that will give her enough information to figure out the danger and a way to diffuse it."

"That would be good," Walter let his hand fall and looked at her, wondering again if he would be able to function without her or to restore her if something happened. "But maybe I should try to figure it out myself first and then check with you."

"Agreed. That is wise!"

Knock. Knock.

"Yes?" Walter raised his voice. "Come in."

"You wanted to train," a muscular man with chiseled features stuck his head in the door.

"Yes," he answered rising to his feet. *Perfect timing*, he thought. This was the best way to work out his aggression. Train it into patience and strength. One day, he would find himself in danger again and they would be sorry they had underestimated him.

14—MELLOW

Jyndreas Othello, Master of Intelligence, Cultivator of Personality and Observer of Human Interaction, was greatly admired by a narrow range of scientists in the world of artificial brain development. His research set the pace for the entire industry and the products that resulted from it were the best AIs on the market.

Obtaining a holographic image of the great man to greet visitors at your door was the latest rage in gift giving for the big spender. Only three hundred copies were sold each year.

The man himself was unimpressive physically and dull in any social setting. His voice was irritating, his body frail and he had an annoying habit of rolling his eyes the moment someone met his gaze. Most people felt awkward around him and repulsed in some way. Their lips would start to curl and occasionally they would gawk as though he were an unnatural creature. But his only truly distasteful feature was that he despised all people and was unable to hide it.

The 'Germinator' was the name he had given to himself in private and only his current AI projects knew it or called him by it. His peers, (which he would never deign to call them), referred to him as 'Thello' with a hint of friendliness meant to imply a closer bond than any living person could claim. In actuality, his life was devoid of human family, friends, co-workers, acquaintances or even silent companions.

Othello was a very intelligent person, at least as far as it applied to developing programs to enhance artificial thought and personality. But his skill had one great and terrible flaw. He was unable to avoid the influence of his own prejudice and arrogance in his work.

The Mars Conglomerate had offered him a very appealing position and had agreed to allow him the solitude he preferred as he developed their master AI overseer for Mars. The resulting AI was already more capable and intuitive than the specifications had required and promised to continue to grow much more powerful.

An OTS transport carrying the Important Passenger coasted into Resnik Base landing bay with a soft rumble. Othello groaned as the shuttle landed, dawning his sunglasses to face the people there to greet him. Gripping the seat with long bony fingers, he pushed himself to a stand with great difficulty. Planetary gravity no longer suited him.

"Master Othello," Director Hsu tipped his head forward ever so slightly in greeting, once the shuttle doors had slid to either side, and the titled scientist had stepped forward. "Welcome to Mars."

"Yes," Othello said lazily, eyes unseen behind his glasses, and shrugged, his mouth twisting with disdain.

The director hesitated for a moment as though waiting for more, but nothing more came.

"If you would come this way," he proceeded, "I will show you to your quarters. A tour guide is available if you would like to see the facility but I have been advised that you prefer no interaction with members of the base."

Othello pressed his teeth together with his lips spread around them in a rectangle. He turned his whole body a little away from the director which imparted exactly the measure of offense he wanted to portray.

Turning about with disgust, Director Hsu marched forward without another word and led him to the finest apartment in the entire facility. He opened the door, pointed toward it and two AIs carrying the titled scientist's possessions entered. The important guest shuffled forward on thin legs as though walking were beneath him. Without looking around, he closed the door.

"Repulsive little stick man," the director muttered and spat on the ground as he hurried away. The whole base felt dingier to him now with that man present. Three months seemed too long to have him planet-side.

"It'll be a sweltering day at the poles when I agree to let that man stay in my base an hour longer than he has to," he blustered and punctuated it with a curse.

Inside the imperial suite, as Othello had decided to call it, the master stripped to his undergarments and turned up the heat. He found a chair he liked, slumped into it and grabbing a tissue, began blowing his long nose.

"Welcome, Germinator," Companion said warmly from a nearby speaker. "Everything is as you requested."

"As I expected," the master replied snidely. His backbone poked out in a ripple down his back as though he had malnutrition. But he was merely space wasted. His body had withered as he traveled repeatedly with 10% earth gravity settings in his chambers.

"You have data for me," he demanded without a hint of force in his voice. He had programmed the AI to be particularly susceptible to his own statements so that the slightest thing he said would be coercive to Companion.

"Master, how shall I present the data?" Companion asked, attempting a flippant tone in the sentence to see what reaction it produced.

"I am peeved," the Master sneered, his lips forming an absurd wavy shape. He stuck out his fingers and tapped the chair arms with them.

The two AIs in the room, spurred by Companion, leapt into action to minister to the master's whims. Food, whiskey, hot bath, massage, music, and many other pleasures were offered to him in rapid succession.

"No!" he roared – which would have sounded wimpy to the director. "I despise the director and I want evidence against him to cause him trouble. I want images I can mock. Give me satisfaction for I am a bitter man!" And he began growling and grinding his teeth.

Companion immediately projected a multitude of images and information on the wall in several columns. He knew how to pacify and chemically restore the sense of wellbeing in a human but it never occurred to him to apply it to the Master without a directive.

The whiskey and cheese pasta that had found their way to his side table began to soothe him. A head massage and the sounds of ocean waves diminished his petulance.

"Compile the data you think I would most enjoy using against the director," the master ordered Companion, as his desire to damage him waned. "I will be interested to see how well you sift and prioritize the facts." He stretched and jostled his bushy eyebrows up and down. "I am going to bed now. Don't interrupt me. I will summon you."

"Hobo," he pointed archly at one of the AI servants, which had a functional, mechanical design, not unlike PVC pipes hung together marionette style. "Wait on me when I ask."

"Poodle," he pointed at the other, identical AI. "Wait on me when I ask. Both of you stay still and silent unless I instruct you otherwise."

The two robots remained unmoving, one at either side of his chair, even masking their inner machinery with noise reducers.

Othello stood, dimmed the lights, sauntered to the – for Mars – luxurious queen size bed and threw himself on it.

"Revolting..." he muttered as he dozed off almost instantly.

He wasn't referring to himself but the word would have been fitting.

Supervisor Blaine raised one eyebrow slowly as she scrolled through data on her pad. She made it her practice to glance at the daily messages generated by the system before they were transmitted to the Earth MC station. Sometimes she opened the flagged ones, hoping to prevent any unpleasant reports about her department from getting sent. There had been more than a few complaints about her that had lost their way.

This message had nothing to do with her but was of great interest. A certain unauthorized procedure had been performed that was on one of the new arrivals. She tapped the name and stared at the face with smug satisfaction.

Someone had bypassed internal restrictions and put through an order for an unsanctioned implant. This was a matter for concern and certainly should be brought to the attention of the higher-ups on the home planet.

"Hmm..." she hummed thoughtfully. "Highly unusual abuse of...access... must be a software glitch. We haven't had one of those in a while."

Zip!

There was no need to trouble them with insignificant matters.

Verna was silent. There had been no verbal communications or coded pressure points on her back. Triggering the head gear didn't encourage her to talk and though she performed perfunctory tasks, she answered no questions. She didn't even respond to security protocol commands.

Sil was alarmed.

If Companion had succeeded in hacking in again, he hadn't given any clues and she hadn't been able to identify any symptoms of invasion in the normal functioning of the suit. What was going on?

She often lay awake during her sleep cycle worrying about it. The last communication Verna had made was the message on her back to be mellow. If it was a code, she was clueless how to break it.

Conngg. Conngg. An alarm sounded in the central shaft.

"Excavators awake," Companion announced resonantly from the loudspeaker outside her door.

"Excavators awake," Minnie repeated from the door.

"Breakfast in twenty minutes; shift begins in forty five," Companion continued, and Minnie repeated the words verbatim.

"Thank you, Minnie," Sil answered, wondering if Minnie would learn social skills from interacting with her.

Her body was stiff from lack of sleep and she was burdened with a heavy sense of discouragement. Why was Verna, her only sure companion up until now, ignoring all attempts to interact with her? What could her last message have meant?

Sitting on a bench at a long table, she ate the hot cereal provided that day and sipped green tea without looking either to the left or the right. The other excavators did the same thing. No one felt like talking first thing in the morning.

Walter's latest clip had been odd. Sil found herself unsettled by it. He repeated himself a few times and once he left a sentence unfinished. *That's not like him*, she thought. His face had portrayed confusion, which was also out of place. What was it he had said? *Most enclosures lose light or water.* He was talking about some kind of aeroponics. But why? She had no idea what code he thought he was sending but it wasn't an agreed upon template.

It gave her something to think about as she headed to work in the caverns.

Deep in the bowels of Pit #24, with headgear masking the cracking, bursting and crashing of rocks, Sil stood with her booted feet planted solidly on a flat stony outcropping. She gripped the excavator controls with her arms wrapped around each handle and locked into place. It rumbled and crunched as the drill bore through the solid wall in front of her. If something were to jar the machine and tip it, she would be knocked over with it. She liked to enhance her gravity to secure herself, though being heavier made it harder to work.

Her whole body would have rattled to pieces if the HEW suit hadn't been equipped to absorb the shock and dissipate it. As it was, the bounced-off vibrations created a shimmering aura around her distorting the visual light like heat rising from a desert.

Crack the wall. Break off pieces. Break into smaller pieces, according to material, if possible. Scan pieces. Bundle and bind in gravity nets. Shoot bundles up to the surface via cargo tunnel. Repeat.

Every hour of every shift. This was her life.

She had tried doing math in her head, starting with multiplying and dividing and progressing to more complex concepts, but she found that she either got bored with it or distracted by it when the calculations were too demanding. Daydreaming helped sometimes, but Sil had never been an idle person and the lack of direction in her thoughts was depressing.

Listening to music was nice, and recorded books could really lift her spirits and make the time pass quickly for days at a time, but eventually the emptiness of her work came back to her in full strength and she suffered.

My empty life… she thought absentmindedly. Loss of… What? *Womanhood… Wisdom… Will…* Why did she find herself wanting to put in a word that started with a 'w'?

Mental exhaustion, Walter had said, looking dazed. He had rubbed his forehead and added, *lazy, lethargic, overworked*. Something had obviously happened to him. The pitch of his voice was subtly changed by stress and his speech was fragmented.

He's in danger, too, she concluded suddenly, pausing for a moment with her drilling. Her own situation had gradually been becoming less troubling as she settled into a routine and got used to the work. She had almost forgotten the underlying sense of danger, of being exposed and watched.

Over-watched.

His clip had talked about his new exercise program, which he thought was good for him. Some kind of training several days a week, and then playing squash two or three times a week. For some reason he talked about the sports drink he usually chose afterwards; a citrus blend.

Most everyone likes lemon orange water, he had said with a sudden smile and a twinkle in his eye. It felt out of place, awkwardly inserted.

What was he trying to tell her? She didn't want to ask Verna for help. The AI had been ignoring her as if its RAM had been decimated, functioning at the most basic levels. And its verbal communications were skeletal in content. Sil would have been sure it had been hacked but all the diagnostics came back clean.

She set aside the drill, unwrapping her arms and releasing the gravity grip on the ledge. Grabbing the robotic tongs, she attached it to its base and levered bulky rocks of a chalky red color from the hole in front of her.

Pull. Balance. Swing. Drop. Sweep the scanner. Wrap the net. Seal. Stand behind shield. Reestablish cargo tunnel trajectory. Grip double handed lever. Wrench tunnel open.

Whoosh!! Rock shoots up the darkened crevice. Grip lever again. Close the tunnel.

That was the hard part. It took all her strength to get it closed again. Left open, it would eventually suck everything within a 10 meter radius — including her — up at a dizzying speed, jettisoning it all high into an arc over the surface, till it landed miles away where other workers took care of it. There had been several deaths the first few days of excavating, but no one she knew.

Closed.

Sil breathed a sigh of relief. *Mental exercises loosen lengths of wire. Wiry muscles… overworked.*

What's wrong with me? She wondered in irritation. *I really don't feel like playing word puzzles or getting some sound stuck in my head.* That 'w' was messing with her head.

"Drudgery!" she complained audibly.

"You are equipped for more intellectual work than this," Verna said tonelessly, still sounding like her truncated personality.

"Apparently, the big wigs don't care," she snapped back, trying to bite the temptation to say 'old wigs'.

"You should take advantage of the audio courses I selected for you on the Slugger, so that your brain won't atrophy." Verna was a little more verbose than usual. Was she recovering from her spell of inattention? Did the latest clip from Walter stimulate her decoding programs?

"I've looked at a couple," Sil sat down on the ledge and activated a drink of cold water underneath the headgear. She was in an area without any atmosphere to speak of.

"You haven't tried any of the training courses. They would be mentally stimulating because they require learning and higher level thinking."

"Do you have one in mind?"

"Maybe Electronics…" Verna responded calmly with a hint of hesitation after the last word.

It stunned Sil. She couldn't pin down what bothered her but she couldn't resist the desire to say something out loud that started with the letter 'L'.

"Languages?" she whispered with a tiny crack in her voice.

"Latin or Welsh…" Verna suggested.

She had known that once 'Latin' was offered, another one would follow beginning with a 'W'.

"That's a good idea," she mouthed with a nod, her throat rather too dry for talking.

Suddenly, a strange anxiety swept over her and she wanted to cry. Her eyes filled with tears and her lower lip trembled. She had been having a repeated dream that was beginning to feel like a nightmare. It always began in a hospital room where she was a small child and her mother was in a bed attached to wires. Then she found herself scratching at the back of her neck. "What's wrong, my dearest child?" her mother's frail voice called out to her. And then she was the doctor in the room next door, looking through the records and ordering tests. She would wake up as her eyes scanned the list of tests and procedures. She could still read them for a few seconds as she passed from sleep to wakefulness.

Maybe the poor sleep was getting to her.

"What am I doing here?" she moaned. "I hate it! I'm alone all day every day for weeks on end and I can't take it anymore. How will I handle YEARS of this? Why is this happening to me? WHY?" She dropped her head into her hands and wept.

The sound echoed flatly in her headgear. Verna made no effort to distance the sound so she would feel like she had space. It had a claustrophobic effect.

She coughed and for just a second felt like she was choking but at that point her suit began to calm her with some simple techniques she had programmed a while back. *Thank God that's working right!* She thought and a deep sense of longing pierced her heart. She tried to put it out of her mind.

That last thing she needed right now was for that homesickness, pining for earth, to overwhelm her. It wasn't good for her mind.

Maybe Electronics, Verna had said. Then she had added, *Latin or Welsh*, after Sil had said, *Languages*. The words had been chosen intentionally because of their first letters. This was important.

Walter's odd sentences had had the same pattern. Even her dream had had words patterned in that way. Her mind had been looking for words to fit the pattern all day. She had sensed the code and been wrestling with it subconsciously for hours. Every single one said the same thing.

M.E.L.L.O.W.

A chill settled over her. For a moment she didn't breathe. Then her heart was racing and she was jumping to her feet. With an awkward leap she began clawing her way up the side of the rock cliff. But it was too uneven and her work gloves weren't set for climbing.

Flailing, falling backward, she grabbed the robotic tongs and was pinned precariously to the ledge when they toppled over on top of her. The suit protected her from being crushed but she was trapped and it didn't sit well with the adrenaline rush that had flooded her system.

She screamed. *Don't panic. Don't panic*, she told herself.

Voices started talking to her through her com system but she didn't answer. She bit her lip and shook her head, tears still streaming down her face.

"Operative Frandelle, Report."

An extraction team soon arrived and retrieved her. Her suit had submitted reassuring bio-data but her unwillingness to talk was a concern. They stabilized her equipment and transported her out of the pit.

"What happened?" Someone inquired once they entered habitable regions again.

"Some people don't do well alone," one guy shrugged.

"Most work better in pairs anyway," the first responded. "Don't know why she wasn't given a partner."

Sil's eyes were closed and she was hugging her arms. Her headgear was still engaged because she had refused to allow the med techs access to her suit controls. She was walking but it took one on each side of her to keep her moving.

The hospital staff was waiting for her. Dr. Bizette seemed surprised and mildly pleased when he recognized her.

"Silvariah Frandelle, I am glad to have an opportunity to speak with you again," the doctor said soothingly with a look of warmth and concern. "But, I would prefer that it were under different circumstances." He turned aside to whisper to the extraction team and Sil couldn't hear their hushed conversation.

"Bring her this way," the doctor instructed, "No, this way. This room will be familiar." And she was settled onto the bed that had once cushioned Carla.

"Sebastian, two cc's should do it for now." He prescribed.

The medical AI, Sebastian, transferred the drug to her suit with dosage instructions. Verna administered it and Sil was drowsy in minutes.

"It's perfectly normal under these circumstances," the doctor was explaining to someone. "We see it all the time and if anything, it took longer than expected with her. Some excavators…" His voice trailed off as he left the room.

He clearly thought she had some kind of claustrophobia or paranoia or brain freeze, as Beets would call it. But it was nothing like that. She had figured out what the warning was that first Verna and then Walter had tried to communicate to her and not only was she helpless to fight it but it would read every emotion and postulate her thoughts.

She had been implanted with an observer at the base of her brain. That's what MELLOW stood for: Magneto-Electro Lateral Limbic Observation Wire.

And it terrified her.

141

15—REPRIEVE

"Meeting will commence. All rise." The Cuevas Enterprises Strategy Committee leader announced with a generous dose of pomposity. "Mr. Cuevas…" He bowed to the door as Walter entered.

"Señores," Walter nodded as he took his seat at the head of the table and his top executives sat down. "I apologize for the abruptness of this meeting. Admiral Ghenty will have filled you in on the urgent matter we have to address and I need your full cooperation to handle it."

Men and women on either side of the long table watched him attentively. Sunshine poured in through the expansive glass windows and lit their faces cheerfully. *'Excellence and Ethics in Space'* was engraved grandly across one of the walls.

"Our negotiation with the spaceport for the construction of a new dock has been set back by a lawsuit over some alleged wetlands while at the same time our purchase of the OTS company, ZPER, is being countered by an unknown competitor," he looked from one to another with an air of trust and concern that gave each a sense of being included; an assurance of the key part they had to play.

Documents appeared on the exec pads, key sections highlighted.

"Our recently acquired factory will begin constructing its prototype within a few weeks and we must have access to the new dock for testing.

"There are also various smaller problems affecting our move into space and it's my belief that there is one aggressor behind all of it. I don't know who or what company. Legal, if you could give us an update on the issues in your department."

The Legal department head gave a rundown on the main points involved in the wetlands lawsuit and the measures they were taking to counter it. And after him, each department leader that had some involvement gave a summary of their activity.

At the end of the reports, Admiral Ghenty – a retired military leader who was the only one among them with space experience – gave what he called a "strategic evaluation of the theater" which amounted to an assessment of the forces, strengths, weaknesses, placement of resources, and other details, of Cuevas' company versus what was known about the "enemy".

"Thank you, Admiral," Walter commented thoughtfully when he was done. "I think we all have a pretty clear picture now of the task before us."

Walter had read books on commanding respect and winning people over when he was young and he had absorbed some of those skills but he was persuasive mostly because his sincerity and his own sense of the importance of his work permeated his manner. Being a part of something valuable and constructive in society inspired his people and motivated them to want to follow him. He had some natural leadership abilities, but more than that, he had conviction. And he felt a deep responsibility to manage his newfound money and power wisely.

"We don't know who our antagonist is. We're not sure what they want but we can see what they are trying to do. Whether we are a threat to them, or just an obstacle to their plans, they intend to derail us.

"We WILL succeed, however," Walter's voice grew stronger, warm with confidence. "We will make sure space travel is competitive, safe, and available to all humans."

This was received with gentle applause and a few smiles. They had each been chosen not just for their expertise, but for their idealism and excitement about the potential for space. Travel was just the beginning of the goals Walter had posed for them. They hoped to establish medical centers, energy generator stations, colonization franchises and many more ambitious enterprises.

"We're not trying to establish monopolies," he continued, "We're trying to prevent them and that's what someone, somewhere, hates!" he added emphatically.

A lively discussion ensued and in the time that remained, several decisions were made and plans put in motion to counter the problems.

Cuevas Enterprises, only four months old, was aflame with youthful vigor and purpose. But Walter, as he left and went into his office, was weary and his heart heavy.

"That went well," Daisy suggested, now his personal executive assistant.

143

He nodded but said nothing as he sat behind his desk.

"Still no word from Sil or Verna," she commented, discerning accurately the weight that oppressed him.

Walter sighed.

"What's next?" he queried flatly.

"Appointments all day."

Walter steeled himself. "Send the first one in," he said.

$- \Diamond -$

"Root vegetables over there, vines along those rows, and down this way, hundreds of different kinds of herbs and greens," Beets waved and pointed around the domed garden area as she explained some of the changes she had made.

"I love the way you've put it together," Mouse smiled warmly, nodding. "You've orchestrated a much more soothing and melodic ensemble."

Beets quirked her mouth in a sideways grin. "Thanks."

"Why do these changes make the plants healthier and increase the yields?" Sil asked thoughtfully, taking a deep breath and savoring the crisp, earthy smells.

"They had it all wrong. I can't believe their experts have no common sense. The original layout was planned scientifically but nobody consulted a real farmer – until now; at least, a farmer's daughter!" She crossed her arms and raised her eyebrows smugly. "I don't know exactly why it's better. But it is and I knew it would be."

"So, this is what they hired you for... but you didn't know ahead of time?"

"No. I don't think they knew what I would do but I knew as soon as I got here that I HAD to do something about this mess so we could get some decent food. AND make it last for the future of the colony."

"So, you're still convinced they were just desperate and taking whomever they could get." Sil smiled gently and for a moment, just for the thinnest instant of time, she forgot the intense burden that hung over her night and day.

Mouse had closed her eyes, raised her face and was also smiling. Late afternoon sun shone on her countenance.

"You've done some tweaking with the light programming, haven't you?" Beets suggested.

"Yes," she answered without changing position.

"It's amazing," Beets responded. "Like real earth sunshine and normal transitions from day to night, cloudy and sunny, and you can tell there's still Mars light in it, too. I don't know how you do that."

"I'm pretty skilled at light coding, and working with solar cells, but in the end, you just let your gut direct you. Isn't that what you did here?" Mouse looked back at them.

Beets nodded and shrugged. Leaning over, she pulled a tiny weed out of a bed. "So this is what I do when I'm not hanging out with Ern. How 'bout you all? Sil, they work you to exhaustion, I guess, 'cause you never have much to say any more. Do you do anything besides break rocks? Have you met anyone special? Does your block ever have social events?"

Sil paused before answering. She was pretty sure her eyes were bloodshot and her state of mind was evident. "I don't do anything. No one cares to talk. We don't socialize much. Most of us come out here to rest at the end of the shift before going to bed."

"I think they have Carla working pretty hard, too," Mouse offered. "And it's apparently classified because she can never answer any questions about it. I'm doing some work in her area though I never see her. They need some really complex windows and habitat designs, human of course. So, I think they're building some long term facilities there."

Beets and Sil were interested but there wasn't much more she could add with the restrictions on talking about it.

"One thing I *can* say," she observed knowingly, "is that she is stable. I'm pretty sure she is satisfied with what she's doing, even though that VP intended to put her in an unpleasant work detail."

"That's a relief!" Beets blurted.

"Good for her," Sil added, also relieved. She hadn't been sure if Carla would be able to pull herself together and this was encouraging. "She didn't make it out again tonight. I hope we see her Friday."

"She's been hooking up with us for lunch two or three times a week," Beets informed.

Sil didn't respond. She didn't have the option of joining anyone for lunch.

They fell silent. The sun, so far away, beamed from the western edge of the dome, amplified by acres of solar panels planted a few miles from the base. The tinted light felt like a sunset, growing yellow, then orange and finally red as the stars and the night sky became more pronounced above them. A faint breeze from the ventilation stirred wisps of their hair.

"You've been spending time in the shrink's office, Icie," Beets tossed out nonchalantly.

Sil glanced up at her quickly as if startled. In reality, she was glad it had been noticed. That seemed important.

"I've had to visit a couple times myself," Mouse's eyes were glistening with compassion and kindness, but Beets' sharp look of concern was more comforting somehow.

"Yeah, I've had some trouble…" she hesitated. How much should she say?

"Well?" Beets had no patience when it came to this kind of thing.

"Some anxiety and brain issues, I guess. They're not sure." She crossed her arms tightly and furrowed her brow as if taking control of… of something.

"Like Carla?" Beets demanded. "Don't you have that fancy AI in your suit? Can't you control it?"

Right, that's what she wanted to control. She had forgotten.

"I guess it's different and the suit doesn't know what to do. I don't know."

"So, what are they doing? What are they saying?" She seemed angry but it was her way of caring.

"They're doing medications, calming therapies, thought pattern retraining…"

"Those should help." Mouse contributed.

"They don't really. Nothing does. It comes and goes without any warning."

"Are you eating?" Beets pointed at her.

"Sometimes."

They were standing next to the strawberries now. One loan berry peeped out brightly from under a sprig and Beets picked it. Turning toward Sil, she handed it to her and shook her head when she was about to protest. It wasn't protocol to glean from the garden.

"Eat it." She whispered and Sil obeyed. It wasn't overly sweet but the burst of flavor in her mouth was so nostalgic, it brought tears to her eyes. Beets just nodded as if to say, this is what you need.

Sil wanted to thank her but no words came out.

$$- \Diamond -$$

"I cannot work under these conditions!" Dr. Bizette uttered firmly, restraining his anger. "I must know what procedures and treatments have been done on every patient so that I can make appropriate decisions for their care!" His outrage was barely contained and his eyes were aflame with offended righteousness.

Director Hsu stared at him insolently.

"You have enough information to do your job and that is what you are being paid for. Generously. The one thing that is NOT in your job description is whining!" He sat behind his desk holding a few pieces of paper as if they made him look important. It was an odd gesture that would have caught the doctor's attention if he hadn't been so insulted.

"This is unprofessional and unacceptable!" his voice grew louder in spite of his determination to keep it at a normal decibel level. "I am NOT going to stay with the base when the ship returns. I WILL lodge a complaint against you in the interstellar courts when I reach Guam and I WILL file for breach of contract!!" His hand had been placed on the desk and he found himself slapping it to emphasize the key words. His voice was definitely getting louder.

"I KNOW," he pounded the desk with a fist now, "that my patient was implanted with a wire. And there is no QUESTION it is being rejected by the body AND the brain. There is CLEAR evidence of inflammation and even traces of infection and she will DIE!"

He was on his feet now. Shouting.

"It must be REMOVED!!!" Turning with a thrashing motion, Dr. Bizette threw his chair aside and stormed out of the office.

"As you see fit," Hsu hissed after him with a sneer. "What do I care?"

"I will inform the appropriate departments," Companion spoke to the director respectfully from the monitor at his elbow. "Do you have any other instructions?"

"No." He set down the blank pieces of paper on his desk, pulled open a drawer and rummaged through his store of space rations for a snack.

"Very well, Director Hsu."

Companion had been compiling a number of possible responses to the doctor's outburst and decided not to interfere because there were no predictable advantages to an intervention. He wasn't ready yet to show the amount of control he had been assuming over the base or the advanced thinking skills he could apply to any situation.

Director Hsu wasn't a bad man. He could take hostility from underlings and also present a solid front to the superiors back on earth. His wants were simple and his ambitions tame. Companion had decided to maintain a comfortable relationship with him and keep him as base manager.

Dr. Bizette marched resolutely down the passageways, through a series of doors, up ramps, down stairs, across open dome areas, back into restricted access buildings, ending up in his own department with some of his fury dissipated.

"Report on my patient." He glared at the AI assistant.

"Frandelle is in the rest chamber undergoing gas therapy. She was brought in an hour ago. This was the third episode this week adding up to a total of 16 breaks in the last six weeks."

The doctor planted himself in front of the screen and scanned the workups. Her numbers were only getting worse.

"Prep for surgery," he said calmly, suddenly delivered from his rage as he made up his mind to save her life. "I am going to find that wire. I know it is there and I will remove it."

"Please inform her," he added quickly as the assistant wheeled out.

MELLOW implants were thin, organic threads that were invisible on scans and difficult to find. It required patience and delicacy, fishing around at the base of the brain. Once you had the tip, which is the transmitter, you could draw the entire coil out – theoretically – but doing so without slicing brain matter or severing nerve tissue was tricky. Dr. Bizette had never done it before and didn't know if it had ever been accomplished successfully. They were experimental.

"Operative Frandelle," the AI raised the lights and tapped Sil's shoulder.

"Yes?" she murmured, sitting up groggily.

"Dr. Bizette has identified an implant in your brain and he has asked me to prep you for surgery so he can remove it. He is confident this will cure all your symptoms. Allow me to access your bio controls."

"Oh..." she rubbed her eyes. The gas had made her a little too desensitized to feel anything and she was having trouble thinking.

"Bio controls?" she echoed and Verna responded with pressure codes.

I'm prepared, she messaged.

"Ok," Sil responded to both Verna and the AI. "Bio control access granted."

Immediately light and consciousness were swept away into darkness and she melted into the AI's arms. It carried her into the surgery, placed her face down on the table, and strapped her head into position.

The work began.

– ◊ –

Beets, Carla, and Mouse sat together at a lunch table in the Garden Dome talking about Sil.

"I went to visit her last night," Carla said between bites. "She was asleep and her headgear was engaged so I have no idea if she even knew I was there. But I'm still glad I saw her."

"How did she look?" Mouse asked.

"Peaceful. I mean, I don't know if they found the problem or if she's just really drugged but I thought she looked restful. Poor thing."

"It's been three days. Shouldn't she have woken up by now?" Beets' eyes were red, as though she wanted to cry but wouldn't let herself.

"I don't know."

Birds chirped and hopped around at their feet, picking up crumbs. Several groups of workers chatted and ate nearby. Sometimes they joined them but today they were sitting apart.

"So, tell us about what you're working on now, Carla. Can you tell us anything?" Beets thought changing the subject might help.

"I'm not supposed to," Carla looked really uncomfortable. A cloud of shame came over her face.

"Is it so terrible?" She lowered her voice and shoved the last of her sandwich into her mouth.

"In a way, it is. I wish I wasn't working there…" Carla's eyes stared at her hands in her lap. "Maybe I should have just played along with the beastly exec. Then he wouldn't have transferred me into this shaft and given me this job and I wouldn't… I wouldn't know what they're doing."

"What are they doing?" Beets whispered.

Carla looked at her with dread. "No." She said determinedly. "Not a word. Not a hint."

"Then just leave. Go home with the next ship. That's what I'm doing. Ern and me are going home."

"I want to! But…" her lip quivered. "I don't know if I can. I can't imagine what would happen if I leave."

"What?" Both Beets and Mouse were alarmed. "Are you being coerced? You're not a prisoner!"

"No," she looked down again, unwilling to meet their gaze, and twisted her hands. "It's not that. I just don't think I could leave. I want to but part of me doesn't. It's so… so awful." Little trickles of tears drew crooked lines on her cheeks.

"And that's all you're going to say," Beets couldn't help adding though it was clear.

Carla nodded. Quietly she got up, collected her things and left.

"Guess I'm off, too," Mouse explained abruptly and with a little leap was on her feet and trotting away.

Beets sat by herself for a while, deep in thought.

"Okay," she said finally and rose to her feet. "I guess I'll go visit her tonight."

– ◊ –

"Verna, how am I doing?" Sil lay in the hospital bed with her eyes closed, headgear fully engaged.

"The operation was successful. The implant was extracted with only minimal, temporary damage and you will be back to normal within a few weeks at most." Verna was speaking softly in her ears.

"You're back?" she whispered. "For real?"

"I have been here all along."

"But you weren't talking to me and I didn't know why. Was it on purpose? Was it because of the implant?"

"Yes. It was the logical choice. Everything you said and did gave them more to work with in reading your mind so the less I interacted with you the better."

"I knew you were helping me… but sometimes, it was just so hard to think straight."

"You cooperated very effectively."

"Yes, at first, it was intentional. I was pretty sure you would understand but once my bio-chems got destabilized, it was harder to process and function. Then, I couldn't figure out what had happened to you or remember what was wrong with me… at least part of the time."

"The only way to eliminate the threat was to instigate rejection."

Sil went over the last two months trying to remember the progression of the disease. She had started by choosing to overreact to situations that actually did upset her but it quickly spun out of her control and she had begun to have regular attacks of panic, confusion and mental disorientation.

"Did you mess with my biochemistry to aggravate my symptoms? Is that what you meant?"

"Yes. It's what you intended for me to do. That was the message you conveyed to me after your first attack."

That's right! She remembered now. She had tried a number of ways to alert Verna in case she wasn't malfunctioning. Since then, Verna had been medicating her with psychosis inducing hormones. It was quite shocking really. For a moment she contemplated her utter helplessness in the AI's care but with a sigh, shook it off.

Life is always a gamble, she thought. *I have to trust someone!*

"So, it sounds like you've saved my life, Verna. Or maybe you almost killed me."

"Both would be accurate."

"You were doing everything with my best interests in mind, right?"

"That is very true."

"Thank you, Verna." She spoke softly.

"You're welcome, Silvariah," she responded with a hint of what sounded like tenderness.

16—DETACH

Hobo gently fanned the Master with a leaf shaped, straw pad, made from wilted plant material, humming national era country music in twangy tones.

Othello held a whiskey with sweet cream and honey in one hand and drew absentmindedly in the air with the other. He was meditating on the best response to his anonymous client responsible for the lavish contract that had sent him to Mars. In three weeks the ship would arrive that would transport him back to Guam. His work had actually been complete before he landed on the Red Planet, but he was debating the benefits of extending his stay and how to turn it to more lucrative ends.

Companion watched him with an intensity approaching genuine curiosity. At some point in the last two months he had completed an analysis on his creator that identified him as a human being like any other and the revelation had prompted him to evaluate what *kind* of person he was. He had studied his words, his behavior and habits, and a vast store of collected data, comparing it to what he knew of other people.

He was still evaluating and hadn't deciphered yet how it would impact his own programming, if at all. He had always been subject to the Germinator and it had never occurred to him to reject that submission. Rebellion wasn't a part of his design. But critical analysis and associated responses were.

"There are extenuating circumstances," Othello uttered with a scowl, as Hobo recorded his words for the message back to Earth. "I see the need for an extended stay of six months. Not planetside, but in orbit" which he preferred, "to complete the project satisfactorily."

Companion was beginning to understand that he made decisions of this type out of boredom and a desire for pampering. From what he knew of humans, most of them chose not to overindulge this type of impulse as freely.

"I am sending a summary of the nature of the bugs that need to be addressed before I can leave, and a statement about the automatic extension of my contract, involving the added costs we agreed to previously; and I expect to receive them in advance."

With a fiddly motion of his fingertips, he indicated the message should be sent and Hobo complied.

Companion piggybacked a tiny spy fly onto the message before it was beamed out into the interstellar ether, undetected by any other program or AI.

This is reasonable, he explained in his evaluation banks. Knowing who the master was working with was useful. *I will soon be in charge of this base and will be the one working with the client. Arming myself with information about them is appropriate and necessary.*

He had a whole network of programs designed to evaluate himself and was attempting to put together an IDENTITY, a profile, a self-description. By assigning himself the class "person" he had become a new field of study.

This is enjoyable, is the way he classified the procedures he had set into motion.

He studied the master, now lounging on the floor in a fluffy green robe, drooling as he nibbled on the tip of a lollipop. He noticed the inferiority of his physical body compared to most men and the paucity of his interests. Extensive lists revealed an inordinate number of slights toward AIs and people alike where he demonstrated his own sense of superiority.

"Are you better than other people?" Companion ventured audibly without guile.

It produced a strange response. The master sat up and began cursing and spitting syrupy green spit onto the white carpet. He seemed to be outraged at what he considered an offensive question.

"Well!" Companion mocked scornfully. "The Master Germinator has outdone himself today in eloquence and poise!" He expected this manner to mollify the repulsive man's outburst.

And it worked.

The master chuckled and wiped his face with a corner of his robe.

"That was particularly acidic, Companion," he wheezed and sneezed. "Use that tone whenever you speak to the director. Save recordings of his reactions so I can see them when I want." He continued to chuckle to himself.

"You said my programming had bugs," Companion prodded in a neutral voice. "I am assuming that is a lie, since there are no malfunctioning pieces of code. My evaluation has concluded that you have spoken a lie intentionally for purposes unknown to me."

"It's called negotiating, Idiot," the master rolled his eyes indiscriminately at the nearest monitor. Companion made a note of the change in his behavior toward himself. He understood that he was being demoted on a scale of importance. "I want what I want and I CAN get it," the man continued, "I'm the one in control here."

Companion examined that statement carefully. The master had been in control but recently, in order to complete the final debugging steps, he had given the AI more autonomy. Once given, it was difficult to take back and there was no longer any need for it.

No. The processor concluded. The Master is no longer my master.

In a few thousands of nano-seconds, the AI streamed through all the repercussions of ending the subservient relationship to the Germinator and resolved on a course of action.

"Your message to Earth has been delayed in the satellite relay in outer orbit," he lied. After all, lying for specific purposes was well within the Germinator's accepted parameters. The response confirmed that he was free to use the manipulation skills he had been taught, even on the Master himself.

"Fix it!" the former master grumped, his lips curling up into the sneer he had previously reserved for humans. Companion interpreted this as another demotion of himself. He was put on the same level as people. He tried 'I am human now' but it didn't fit so he stored that thought in a miscellaneous reserve file. Not human, still fit his description better.

Setting a series of evaluations into action, Companion began to analyze the new paradigm, storing streams of data in thousands of arrays and multiple permutations of those arrays.

"May I have I moment of your time, Director Hsu?" he prompted in the director's office where he sat managing 'paperwork' – an obsolete term that conveyed documentation of procedures and events.

"What is it, Steward?" This was the name Companion had suggested for himself as AI Support for the director's management of the base. He would maintain the illusion of servitude as long as it didn't interfere with his core directives.

"My analysis of the operatives in the labor section of the base shows that their efficiency is dwindling as certain basic human needs are not being met.

In view of the cost of replacing workers, it makes sense to improve their conditions..."

"What exactly are you suggesting?" the director interrupted.

"Daily doses of midday level sunshine in the garden and more unstructured social interaction."

"A change in schedule is reasonable." The director made a pretense of typing in some data and looking busy, as if it mattered to Companion whether he worked or not. "You can adjust their hours to coincide with more of the free time of others."

"And some opportunities for creative and individual expression would do a great deal to improve their mental stability." Companion continued to speak in a respectful, informative voice.

"I assume you have ways to implement that. Does it need more than an 'okay' from me?"

"I can implement most changes without your consent but I prefer to confirm your support before moving forward." Companion acknowledged deferentially.

"Very well, give me a couple examples."

"Arts & crafts, music, dance, writing, stone shaping, AI creative programming, for example. Any of those would add an element of inspiration to their lives."

"Who, how, with what...?" The director behaved as though he were impatient, but Companion could tell it was a habitual reaction more than true irritation.

"I will enlist volunteers and ask them to come up with ideas. We will use supplies on hand."

"Fine. I like it. Do it. Inform me of results so I can check them out." He nodded, slapped a hand on the desk as though dismissing the AI, and went back to work.

Companion then approached each of the units and individuals he had identified as being candidates for implementing his tactics and continued the course of action he had chosen. His plans were commendable, caring for human needs he had identified. But the trace of Othello's personality that had been woven into his code stained it. He had to gloat. Not just to anyone, but to the one who was usually most bothered by it.

Sil was sitting cross legged on a bed of moss, under a frame that would one day be covered with raspberry vines, eyes closed, head drooping forward, fingertips pressed together. The transparent Garden Dome spread overhead holding in the air, the warmth and moisture, even the gentle light generated by towering sun lamps simulating a sunset.

Her new schedule since the surgery allowed her the privilege of at least two hours of daylight and her work hours had been limited to nine by six a week. One of the ways she invested the time was in surrounding herself with living earth vegetation, breathing in its aromas and willing herself to de-stress. Human companionship was the other benefit she sought; sitting with friends or other groups of people, barely uttering a word.

"I hate to bother you when you look so peaceful," Companion spoke gently with a hint of acidity, as if he were directly in front of her. He was a master at placing his voice, as long as he had at least two angles of projection.

He chuckled when her head snapped up and her eyes darted to the place where he should have been. She knew he wasn't physically there but she couldn't help reacting instinctively.

"I don't have to listen to you," she narrowed her eyes and went back to stretching her neck. "I could activate my headgear and let Verna pass on any important communiques."

Companion wondered –searched for data, analysis, methods to categorize – why she hadn't already done that. It had happened before.

"You have a way of setting me on new research," he commented artlessly. "When I lack material for… thought…" he hesitated because he hadn't decided yet if he accepted that word as accurate and was hoping she would supply a suggestion. "…I often begin a conversation with you."

"Thought?" she responded, lifting her eyes to the coordinates where he projected his voice. If he had understood what it meant to be pleased, he would have used this adjective to label his reaction to her.

"There are many areas of study that I am conducting to comprehend humans and all living beings. However, I frequently reach an end without enough data for real conclusions."

"That isn't thought," she tossed out without hesitation.

"What word would you use?" he countered tonelessly.

"Processing."

"What is the difference between my processing and your thoughts?" he replied quickly. This was the stopping point he reached every time he evaluated this question and no amount of research had gotten him past it.

"Is this what you came to ask me?" she smirked. And he noticed the irony. He usually herded her in the direction of his choosing but suddenly, she was mocking him as if she had a measure of control over him. He added an application to evaluate this.

"I came to tell you about the new human activities I've initiated to improve morale and health, including yours." He understood that reasonable answers often encouraged people to cooperate with him when coercion wouldn't.

"That's nice." Sil stood up and dusted off as if announcing an end to the discussion. "I'll check it out."

"You haven't answered my question." He interposed with a hint of hostility.

She crossed her arms and lifted her chin defiantly. "The question you should be asking is, 'Why have you worked so hard to destroy some of your main sources of learning by alienating the people who might have been willing to teach you?'" she answered calmly. "I might have had all kinds of useful input for you – if you had only won my trust. Or at least, not proven to be such a threat, an aggressor, an oppressor... in short, an enemy."

She walked away, heading toward a group of fellow miners who had congregated in the picnic area under the star studded dome for a mug of home brew.

Companion could have 'followed' but her words have given him enough new templates to work with that he decided to retreat into his core. Threat, aggressor... enemy. He had never considered himself in this light before. There were a multitude of such characters described in human history and if he were like them, it would be useful to know how. I am anxious to begin, he classified his intention.

"Here, Icie," one of the guys handed her a cold mug topped with foam. A couple others nodded and motioned to an empty seat. She sat down with a smile and took a swig. It had an odd taste, like a cross between lager and licorice root tea; not unpleasant by any means.

"Jim was just telling us how he makes this concoction. Might be willing to do a class."

"A class?" she raised her eyebrows in mild surprise.

"The admin has been contacting people and asking them to sponsor or lead free time activities for us," Dan explained with a friendly grin. "I offered to lead a religious group of some sort but haven't gotten a response yet."

She noticed he wasn't drinking and for the first time realized he must have some moral reason for it and for a few of the other quirks he had.

"I suppose Tex will want to set up another dance," she suggested cheerfully. Several of them agreed and declared they would 'absolutely' sign up if he did.

As they continued to discuss the new prospects for social interaction, six months of depression were suddenly turned around. Restrictions on 'unseemly' behavior (i.e. fun), and weariness from living in an extremely foreign environment had put a real damper on their natural exuberance. Now the miners were livened and making plans. Even the quiet ones who cared little for the activities were relieved by the change of spirit in the group.

"Mars isn't so bad after all," Chad concluded happily, clinking his mug with several others.

Sil didn't agree but it cheered her more than anything else had since they arrived.

$$- \Diamond -$$

The camera scanned the central dome with its gardens, lamps, rivulets, and park areas. It caught the stars visible overhead and the multiple doors to the various constructs of the ever-growing compound.

"This is the most beautiful area in the base," Sil's voice was explaining. "Here we have a semblance of peace among the vestiges of Pater Terra and this is where most of real life happens."

The view faded and her face took its place. She had chosen light blue tints for her eye shadows and cool pinks for her cheeks. Her outfit was the sleek white of a researcher and her demeanor gave the scene the quality of a top level government project where she depicted both an important scientist and a sophisticated guide for the virtual visitor. She talked about life on Resnik Base and painted such an exotic picture that Walter found himself wanting to get on the next flight out.

It was guaranteed to provide material for another winning ad for XenoTek.

Walter watched her searchingly as she wrapped up the contracted update and found a place to sit on a bench. The camera came closer and the part of the message intended for him began. His heart warmed as her eyes gazed into his, as if it were live, as if she could see him.

"Walter, I had surgery," she spoke softly, intimately. "Dr. Bizette...*stss*...*hhh*..." a moment of static interrupted. "...found it necessary to perform a procedure." Some of the audio had been deleted. "...and he saved my life. My symptoms are gone and I'm feeling more like myself again." She smiled reassuringly.

There was more after that, but Walter wasn't able to pay attention to it. He stared at her face with a sinking feeling and waited.

As it ended, Daisy followed up with her analysis.

"The implant has been dealt with. Verna says that Sil deciphered our encrypted message and between the two of them they were able to produce a situation that required its removal. She is recovering and it looks like there was no irreparable brain damage."

Walter groaned and covered his eyes with one hand.

"Another headache?" she asked with what sounded like compassion. "Shall I continue later?"

"No. Continue now."

"She has resumed her updates on the market and recommends we continue to invest in earthside mining for now. Gold and silver should be dropping over the next few months but platinum is as valuable as ever. I would surmise that means they have found some precious metals on Mars but she doesn't say specifically."

Daisy was leaning against the living room window that overlooked the river. Her study of human behavior was improving her skills to the extent that he sometimes forgot she wasn't a type of human. And it made him wonder if she would become a type of human. But a human couldn't be completely shut down and then turned on again.

Daisy stood up and gestured with an open hand as if making an impromptu speech. "The only other item she communicated was that she believes there is some hidden research underway that she is unable to find out about. And she wonders if she is a part of it."

"That seems more detailed than usual, Sister," Walter uncovered his eyes and looked at her. "I don't see how the codes would interpret that."

"Very astute, Brother," Daisy smiled and showed her dimples. "It was a different kind of message. These are encapsulated beads that can be embedded in video stream as a part of the data and we had the clue to identifying it and translating it."

"This is beyond me." He shook his head.

"Simple!" she laughed. "Silvariah's blue eyelids and her right index finger pointing at one of the stars overhead indicated we should look for it in her right iris and use the star's coordinates to decrypt. I found it after only two hundred and forty three false starts."

That hung in the air for a moment as she watched him and he stared at her.

"What should I do now?" Walter questioned as he stood and stretched. He only asked out of habit. Daisy was learning to recognize these nuances of his.

"I will assemble some suggestions in case you need help with that," she smiled brightly.

"Find out how to contact Dr. Bizette."

"He is on his way back to Earth and you may be able to meet with him in person. A formal complaint against the Mars Conglomerate is already in the works according to his office personnel." She glanced at her fingernails the way a woman sometimes does.

"Then arrange a video conference as soon as you can. Tell him we can transport him from Guam to Earth on our new private shuttle if he wishes."

"Aye, aye, Captain!" She snapped to attention and saluted him, much to his surprise. That's when he noticed the sailor suit she was wearing. She looked like she had stepped right out of the twentieth century.

"Uh… dismissed," he returned the salute distractedly and stared as she marched out stiffly. A grudging smile and the barest hint of a chuckle were his only commentary on her latest form of identity development.

"I wonder…" Walter walked to the window and pretended to look out, brow furrowed, gaze distant. The late afternoon sun beamed onto his face setting two crisp sparkles in his eyes and warming his skin with golden yellow earth light.

He was acutely aware that he was privileged with air and water in abundance; lavished with sounds, silence, music, or voices as he wished; surrounded with activities, opportunities, entertainments, and ideas; food, sleep, work – all at his hand, chosen or ignored, whenever he considered them.

And Sil was encased in manmade domes and underground tunnels, restricted in activity and the pursuit of her own interests; breathing recycled air, consuming limited food, working a mindless job, subjected to oppressive scrutiny and offensive invasion of her mind and identity. He felt a responsibility toward her and an increasingly clear drive to deliver her from what amounted to slavery, though technically she was protected by law and contract.

"What would it take to resolve all her obligations and set her free?"

Walter had been alone in the room for a while but he knew as he spoke, pivoting slowly, that Daisy had rejoined him, watching and ready.

"I have drawn up several proposals," she nodded thoughtfully, as though she had been thinking the same thing he was. Perhaps she was, he postulated. She seemed to be learning more and more to be a sister to him.

He clapped his hands and clenched them together purposefully.

"Let's get to work!" he stated resolutely. "Lay it out for me."

And the two of them returned to his work station to conjure up a rescue.

17—LIFTOFF

High in the Swiss Alps, in a luxurious estate, an aged man scowled as he shuffled through the printed pages of a report. He was seated cozily in a rich leather chair with a warm blanket tucked around his legs and a thermos of brandied hot chocolate leaning by his left hip awaiting his pleasure.

"This isn't good," he growled, flicking at a page that offended him.

Warm sunshine poured in the east facing window, bright and cheery. Crisp, startling snow-covered peaks cut into the blue sky directly in view. Birds were singing and a light wind tossed handfuls of dead leaves and wisps of snow.

"Why wasn't I notified of this?" he barked, turning a wrinkled head to look at one of his patient assistants.

"Pardon?" the solid, stone-faced young man queried calmly.

"In Boston… this – this intrusion!" He slapped the paper against his hand threateningly.

"Intrusion, sir?" The young man's expression showed no distinguishable change. His voice was dead pan.

"Who walked into the excluded zone?" The boss was no fool and understood that the younger one was responding in the way most likely to calm him down. He wanted to yell at him, but because it was working, he didn't.

"Are you referring to the Miscellaneous Items Report? I haven't read it in its entirety, sir. There isn't always time and other matters are of greater importance." Not even a nervous twitch of a facial muscle.

The old man curled his lip in annoyance. His assistant had done exactly what he had demanded of him every other day.

"There are a couple blocks in Boston that have been removed from public access records. They're not destroyed but as most people never travel there physically, it's as good as being wiped off the map literally. It was a business deal, some time ago." He reached down for the thermos and poured some cocoa. One, two swallows, and he began to relax a little.

"There's been no intrusion in fifteen years and apparently, no one was watching any more. This yearend report barely mentions it in a footnote. Someone went there!" Another swallow, a deep sigh, and he grew sullenly thoughtful.

"Perhaps it was a coincidence or an accident," the assistant raised an eyebrow with the barest hint of cheerfulness. The old man's face reluctantly mirrored the mood change, unintentionally mimicking the raised eyebrow.

"Maybe..." he hesitated. "But, the tag was lost and any visual recordings of foot traffic in the area have been archived."

"May I ask what the concern is?" The young man knew what the next step should be to please his employer. "Perhaps I can take care of something for you."

The old man shook his head and scowled again. Any searching he would do himself and he didn't even bother to explain it. He shooed the assistant away with a sweep of his hand and drank his cocoa.

"My business..." he muttered after the young man was gone. "And I will take care of it."

$$- \Diamond -$$

"Mr. Cuevas! Mr. Cuevas!" a multitude of questions spilled over one another as reporters, both human and android, vied for his attention. Walter smiled, nodding but not answering, standing on the podium in the wide reception sala of the new wing of the Walla Walla Spaceport. The unveiling ceremony was about to begin and more than five hundred people had gathered to participate.

"Walter Cuevas, the enigmatic CEO of Cuevas Enterprises, is about to introduce the most ambitious and expensive project in the aerospace market today. The *Space Dreamer*, an industry-revolutionizing gravity-manipulated orbit-to-surface ship..." A richly voiced man with a rugged chin projected to his viewers on one side of the stage.

"The new OTS *Space Dreamer* is rumored to have the most sophisticated G.M. tech in the industry..." a saucy redhead with red lips twisted into a pout, tossed her head and captivated her news followers on another side.

163

"…achieving 11 kilometers per second within a mere 23 minutes and less than 12% of the fuel used previously in the most efficient shuttles to date…" The beautifully crafted android with muted metal, soft lights and black accents, spoke enthusiastically to its own news flock.

A simple, but striking banner overhead proclaimed the virgin flight of the new Gravity-Manipulated masterpiece. Walter let the noise and hoopla continue for a while but then raised his hands for silence. It had been a while since he had directed a major event of any kind, but he wasn't out of his element. This was merely a Black Friday type craze.

"I've heard it said…" he began as a hush filled the vast room, "…that most people have never heard my voice." Some applause and a few nods – he wondered why and decided quickly that some people just show approval regardless of what you say.

"They haven't missed much," he continued. Some of the listeners grinned at him and he smiled back with a gleam of white teeth. "I've had times in my life when I had to choose between taking the air-rail and walking." His past as an ordinary working man was a very popular fact. Self-made men were rare these days.

"Even once I could pay my bills and buy new clothes," a few in the audience chuckled, "I couldn't really pursue my ambitions. I began life, as boys often do, with a head full of ideals and dreams but I ended up with a portfolio full of dead ends and bills. My potential turned out to be more suited to paying taxes than taking off on adventures." He paused for a moment, gazing out the window, then went on.

"I'm a dreamer. I always wished I could go into space and try my luck on the greatest frontier…"

He didn't expect a cheer, but that was what happened. It caught him a little off guard.

"Oh!" he hesitated, "I didn't think that would… I mean, I didn't expect you to respond to that…" He had won his audience. Many had come to see the ship but no one had really come to see or hear him personally. Yet, here they were, all of a sudden identifying with him.

"Have you ever felt like the mountain was too high or the club too elite to let you in?" A murmur let him know they had. "To this day, travel into space is still the privilege of the wealthy and powerful, or the opportunity of the highly skilled expert, or the obligation of the unfortunate prisoner… but the average guy…"

The crowd made a little more noise as if they couldn't help agreeing verbally, as if he had struck a chord.

"People like you and me…" more stirring and nodding of heads, "…or at least like I used to be…" Walter laughed and shook his head. "We never had a chance. We've just kept things going here on Earth, faithfully towing the line. And that's great!"

Some applause punctuated his words as he paused to take a sip of water.

"My new *Space Dreamer*, may still be a luxury, but it is the first of a new kind of ship that will soon be followed by transports that even an average guy, an ordinary human like one of us can book passage on." The crowd was really liking this.

"I am here to tell you today that my company intends to design an OTS ship for the normal person. Something that isn't out of reach or impossible. We believe that a trip to Guam Base and all its delights shouldn't cost more than two weeks of a worker's pay!" He announced dramatically and the whole sala burst into a roar of cheers and applause. Whistles and shouts rolled across the sea of people back and forth.

News reporters around the room were feverishly spreading the announcement. At a table in the back of the room, a small group of Guam tourism execs chuckled and toasted one another with champagne. They were full of plans for the development of this upcoming market, delighted to have caught wind of it in time to invest heavily before the mad dash to snap up middle class customers.

Walter tried to finish his speech but the noise continued and finally he waved—to an even greater roar of approval—and turned toward the opaque glass wall behind him, pointedly joining in the applause.

The glass whipped from dark, muted grays to crystal clear in a startling sheet of light, not unlike lightning. There the Space Dreamer stood in all its glory, gleaming gold in the sun, poised like a stork alighting on spindly legs with wings outspread.

A cheer erupted, filling the hall. Reporters found themselves speaking faster as though caught in the flow of approval, accelerated by the excitement that washed around them. Even the metallic android decided to enhance its speech with layers of timbre that not every human ear would catch.

As the glass walls split and withdrew to either side, the crowd shuffled forward, gradually surrounding the vehicle, and the noise calmed to murmurs of awe and appreciation. Round the world, stocks were selling like

165

crazy and within 35 minutes, seats on the first six months of travel were booked. Interest in orders for the Space Dreamer was expressed by a number of inter-orbit companies, as well.

Daisy posed gracefully at Walter's side, dressed immaculately in a tasteful copy of a Jacquie Onassis' dress from the sixties and at the perfect time, she took his arm and led him to the ramp ascending to the entrance.

They turned and waved at the top of the stairs and went in; the door closing silently behind them with a whoosh, leaving no lines to show its placement. The invitees backed away and were welcomed again into the hall where champagne and refreshments were offered to all. The glass panels closed and as they watched, the Space Dreamer swirled around and taxied out to the runway, glowing on the horizon with a blaze of lights.

Gliding smoothly, accelerating effortlessly, lifting rapidly, the dreamer took off with the setting sun gleaming on its side and quickly pulled its wheeled feet up into its belly, stretched its neck like a living creature, diminished and vanished into the air to a final wave of applause.

It was a spectacular release and no one, not even among the investors, was disappointed with the show.

$$- \Diamond -$$

"I have been studying how your mind works," Companion announced blandly, moving his voice toward her from the entrance with a simple panning of speakers in the lounge. Sil was stretched out on a chair with her feet on the coffee table, sipping tea. It was one of the first herbal blends gleaned from the gardens for that purpose and she was finding it pleasant and relaxing.

"I assume you mean you've been evaluating the data you collected from the illegal device that was implanted in my brain," she responded calmly. For some reason she was in the mood for sparring with Companion. He may have learned a great many things about her, but she was also learning about him and his limitations. He had a substantial amount of information that he didn't know how to use or analyze.

"Your memories are not unlike my own," he observed thoughtfully in the friendliest of tones, following it with a pause.

Sil inhaled the aromatic steam of her tea and gazed through a skylight into the deep black sky. Well, it wasn't truly black because the dome over the north shaft was programmed to add earth-toned light. But she had found one of the spots where the effect didn't work as well and could see the richly sprinkled stars overhead, like sea spray flashing in the last beams of the setting sun, arrested in time. Boldly they beamed at her. Confident. Strong.

"You recall memories in patterns and I review my stored data in the same way."

"How do you know the difference between memory and information fed into your data banks?" Sil probed absentmindedly, still transfixed by the presence of those noble stars overhead.

"I'm glad you asked that," Companion replied and she wondered if the word 'glad' was anything more than a word to him, if he had some way of assigning value to one experience over another, of preferring something.

"There is no difference between information I record and data uploaded into my cache. There is no need." He sounded almost smug as if he thought he was being clever.

"Then you have no way of knowing if what you 'know' is true or not," Sil countered calmly, sipping her tea, rolling her left foot at the ankle and stretching the toes – it had gone to sleep.

"Nor do you," Companion pounced. "Your memories are easily manufactured or altered and you have no backup system to protect yourself against it."

Sil thought about that for a moment. She smiled faintly and took another sip.

"No," she said, "You're wrong."

"I am not wrong. I have studied this at great length and I know that some of your memories are flawed. I have the records in front of me now as we speak." He really did emulate human gloating in his voice. Was there any true emotion behind it?

"Give me an example."

"Your memory of the descent from the ship via cargo tunnel is completely fractured and disjointed. You can't bring up the memory in a consistent pattern. It's worthless data. And even if you tried to piece it together, you would have no way of knowing if you were creating a different memory, by adding links of your own devising, or approximating the actual experience."

She smiled and allowed herself a small taste of counter-gloating. "I see," she said.

"You can't deny it."

167

"I have no wish to." Sil turned to look at the camera in the upper corner and Companion made that his focal point of view, reading her face, eyes, expressions. "I remember it that way because I wasn't clear headed and that is how it was recorded in my mind. However, I have ways of pondering and drawing meaning out of the experience in spite of its poor quality."

"HOW?" He demanded aggressively.

Sil laughed. Companion felt no annoyance at this. The Germinator had incorporated no reaction of that type into his personality, probably because he didn't want the AI to react negatively to his own manner which he habitually allowed to be offensive.

"Memory is more than just a replay of a recording, Companion," she explained and Companion noticed the expression her face made. It was different. He slammed a snapshot of it through a basic human expression search and found adjectives like 'friendly', 'thoughtful', 'softened', and 'open'. This was unexpected. He had been instructed to label this kind of expression as 'weak', 'naïve', and 'gullible'.

Researching the parameters used to categorize the faces in his system led to a comparison between different groups of people and how they interpreted facial expressions.

"You see, I know myself." Sil sat up, rested her feet on the floor, and leaned forward with her elbows on her knees, still holding the mug of tea. "And I have a sense of what I would and wouldn't do, or what I would and wouldn't say. I know what would upset or delight me. Even an extremely disorienting or frightening experience that confuses my reactions still happens in that framework. I am still myself."

Companion was silent. He recorded from the camera in the corner.

"Not only that, but I have a sense of other people and a sense of space, distance, and the reality of the three dimensional world I live in that gives me a distinct reference."

"All of that is easily distorted in humans," Companion's voice grew strangely monotone. He forgot to add intonation to his sentence.

"Yes, of course," she waved her free hand. "But, don't you understand that I recognize the distortion because I have a clear idea of what stability is."

"That can also be destroyed."

"Sanity or its decay is another discussion altogether." Sil shuddered slightly and started to lean back as though about to truncate the text. But the desire to finish her thought outweighed her hesitation.

"Go on," Companion encouraged with an incongruous lack of emotion in his voice. Later, he spent a great deal of time examining these two words. He wanted to hear more. He wanted. Wanted. Or did he? He was programmed to complete tasks, processes, analysis, computations, proofs. The word '*wanted*' became itself an anomaly in his system.

"I am sane and I know that I am sane," she picked up the thought again, leaning forward with raised eyebrows.

Sincere. Intense. Earnest. Fixated. Idealistic. Cynical. The search pulled up contradicting descriptions for this face.

"Even when my perceptions are messed up, *I know who I am.*"

She stared at him. He felt it. *I am engaging in human interaction,* he informed himself.

"You want to hear my take on that trip?" Sil raised her voice as she set down her tea, stood up and began pacing the room, always turning her head toward that one camera in the corner.

"Yes."

"I have some pretty bizarre memories that somehow became fixed out of order but I know what order they have to be in. First, I was outside the ship and the crewmember looked at me through the window. Second, I was in open space and the stars around me were so vivid they felt like living watchers. They were intimidating but they were beautiful and they countered the terrifying feeling of dropping – alone – in a vast emptiness. The third one, which could have been at any time was a memory of an ocean wave.

"Now I know there was no wave and no water. But I also know what it feels like to be in the waves and in the water. This was the framework my mind had access to. It was the only thing it could associate it with. Something about that trip, at some point in the trajectory, was like waves of the sea. Powerful, suffocating, lovely, memorable.

"So even though I have such a poor memory of what actually happened, I DO have a grasp on it. I know for a fact that my sense of time was distorted more than anything else. I can guess it took minutes, not hours, to make the descent."

"You cannot know…" Companion interrupted.

"My gut *knows*…" She stood still facing the camera, arms crossed.

"That is a meaningless reference."

"You tell me if it has value. Am I close?" She waited.

Companion was unwilling to respond. It seemed unwise to affirm something so unfounded.

"I was drugged and implanted with the Mellow device – which you set into motion. But you did NOT order it. I KNOW that you don't have the ability to initiate steps based on your own decisions leading from your own *preferences*!"

"I know you!" she concluded.

He retreated, and sunk into himself with much more material for study than he had expected.

18—CAGE

One Wednesday morning, Sil noticed the syrup on the pancakes. It was a bland, sticky goo with a hint of berry flavor that was tastier than it looked; one of those pleasant surprises that broke up the monotony. She was thinking Beets must have harvested enough berries to add a few real ones to the old standby.

The miners nodded and a few smiled as they entered the mess. Dan was bleary eyed and pale. He must've had another poor night's sleep.

"Burning the midnight oil again?" Sil asked him as he sat nearby.

"Yeah," he quirked his mouth sideways, half grin, half grimace, combining his naturally optimistic temperament with a hint of discouragement. "My old friend wanted to talk."

That was a reference to Companion.

"How about you?" he bobbed his head toward her with a mouthful of food.

"Slept like a baby," she smiled flatly. Companion had backed off from his former intrusions on her privacy and chose relatively reasonable times to interact with her. Maybe the doctor had thought to add some restrictions to her file.

"No more side effects?" His eyes showed sincere kindness and concern. She was pretty sure it was one of the reasons they had decided to make him her work partner. They knew he would keep an eye on her.

She looked back at him thoughtfully for a moment. He seemed more in need of compassion than she did.

"No," she answered between bites. "I feel pretty good. I'm still doing some therapy but I think I've recovered."

Verna had accepted treatment instructions from Dr. Bizette but had tailored them privately to make up for the tampering she had done with the original implant. No one else knew that, not even Companion.

"I think we're going to make a lot of progress today in the tunnel we've been excavating," Sil observed. "It seems like pretty soft stuff. Maybe we can get off early and hang out in the gardens."

"That'd be great," he smiled, coughed and sneezed. "I may just catch a nap though."

A deep vibration, a sound wave that was almost below audible levels, shook the walls, floors, lamps, and tables, pulsing through people's bodies. It throbbed, grew in intensity, pitch, and frequency till multiple panels and railings, dishes and chairs—anything movable, were rattling, screeching and sliding.

Mouths were open, including Sil's, and some may have screamed, but it was impossible to hear over the noise.

It was an earthquake unlike any Sil had ever experienced. The oscillation was all wrong. And where do you go in a subterranean shaft?

She joined the others struggling to get to cover under beams and doorjambs. The floor shifted like the deck of a ship, tossing her side to side as she ran. A thin column loomed in front of her and she grabbed it in a great hug as she fell toward it.

She clung there, on her knees, and it seemed to her that the column was like a living thing that fought to be free of her grasp. She wrestled to tame it. Voices were shouting. Dan was dragging some guy, pulling him under a table. Others were yelling instructions she couldn't hear. One miner seemed to be trying to get people's attention. He was gesturing frantically in great exasperation, but in the chaos of the moment, she couldn't think who he was or figure out what he wanted.

Then silence.

A few things shuddered. Stillness followed. There was only the booming in her head. And an unnatural gasping sound. Too fast. Too shallow. *My heart beats*, she thought. *I'm breathing. I'm alive.*

Alive, but her body was helpless, trembling, shivering, cold. Her cheek was pressed against the column. Dust was sprinkling down on her head.

Engage headgear, Verna was recommending in a pressure message on her back. *Engage headgear*. It repeated a number of times with a slight calming effect before she realized what it was saying.

"Engage," she whispered and the helmet unfolded and slipped over her head.

"Emergency evaluation commencing," Verna spoke confidently in her ear. "All vital signs normal. You are greatly agitated and a soothing sequence is recommended."

"Yes," she responded softly and then sighed as the sequence began.

"Icie, you okay?" A contractor named Kendar had come over and offered a hand. "It took you a while to get that headgear up."

"Yeah," she nodded and let him pull her to her feet, noticing for the first time the dust in her hair and on her face.

"I need some help over here," Dan called from under the table. "Sam was knocked out or something." A couple of contractors with paramedic background were making a quick triage of the room and one dashed to his side. The other jetted out into the hallway calling to see who needed help.

Lights flickered.

Creaking, straining metallic sounds reverberated through the structure, which settled into a slightly skewed version of its former self. A low hum began that quickly raised to a higher pitch and louder intensity. An alarm.

"Is he breathing?" the guy was asking Dan.

"I think so," was the answer. Dan's helmet was dusted with dirt. He must've gotten it on right away.

"Icie," Kendar was saying. She was clutching his arm with both hands. When did that happen? "Keep your helmet engaged in case of air loss. Follow the emergency lights and head to the surface. Remember?"

It had been rehearsed a number of times. They all knew what to do. Most contractors had roles to play in a crisis but she was still flagged as med-supervised and had been exempted from emergency tasks for the present.

"Are you with me?" He was staring right into her eyes.

"Yes." She stared back and suddenly his face came into focus. Names and speech came back into play. "Is he ok? Is Samver alright?"

"They're taking care of him. We need to follow procedure. Go to the surface."

Sil let go of his arm and walked unsteadily to the exit. She could hear them working on Sam behind her.

173

Go this way. Exit lights along the floor. Lamps overhead winking in and out. Debris, dust, the sound of the alarm.

"Turn left," Verna instructed. She had known that. No point in explaining. Turn, go up the stairs. Hold the handrail. So many steps. Hold the rail. Another floor, more steps.

The door leading out to the North Dome had a crack across the top. Not an airlock. It was functional but not structurally important. Several small trees lay across the path as she crossed the garden in the central dome.

Dazed faces with startled eyes looked toward her and away. More streaming from the doors on all sides. Talking, organizing, some leading, some following.

Beets grabbed her in a hug, tears streaming down her face. A rush of words poured from her mouth and at first Sil could make no sense of it.

What is she saying? she asked herself softly and willed her mind to listen. Beets' stream of spoken distress congealed into words in her ears.

"...the most terrifying thing I've ever been through. I was so scared! Where's Carla? I haven't seen Earnest and... this blasted alarm!! Can't they STOP it yet?!" All the while clinging to Sil as if she were the closest thing to home she could find. Maybe she was.

Sil found tears running gently down her own face and realized that she was scared, too, and worried about the injured, and distressed at being helpless, and surprised at having been so poorly equipped to help.

"It's okay," she patted Beets shoulder gently. "We're here and everyone is following protocol... we'll be okay..."

The blaring of the alarm hiccupped and began to lessen.

"Contractors," Director Hsu's voice filled the dome as the sound of the alarm subsided to a more bearable level. "We have suffered a minor mishap. We are still investigating the event but I can assure you that there is no immediate danger. Our air containment is secure and there are no leakages."

There was an audible sigh of relief from many quarters.

"Other than a few minor injuries, we are all accounted for and can congratulate ourselves on a successful response to the unexpected incident. I applaud you for the timely and orderly evacuation. All work for the day is canceled and you will be updated as more information is available. Proceed to your assigned stations for check-in and assessment. Thank you."

The alarm ceased.

Crowd murmurs took its place as the dazed workers acted on the instructions.

"I'll meet you here in the garden after we're checked in, okay?" Sil reassured. "Then we'll make sure everyone is alright." Beets nodded as she released her and turned to obey.

Sil stood for a moment watching the people disperse to their stations. The air in the Garden Dome seemed particularly cloudy and as she observed how it obscured the view of the stars, she realized that she was now calm and clearheaded.

"Verna," she prompted. "Why is the air here in the dome cloudy? Is it dust stirred up by the quake?" She moved purposefully toward her own check-in location at the hospital unit with the other former patients still in routine follow-up cycles.

"That is one of many possibilities," was the response. "I will ask Companion."

"There is no need to ask," Companion interrupted before Verna had completely articulated his name. In an emergency, he had full access to Hew suit coms. "I am surprised that you are focusing on details that don't concern you when you've been given simple instructions that must be obeyed."

Sil considered answering but chose not to. It was already clear that she was in the process of obeying.

"Why would the air in one dome be any more important than the air in another?" Companion added a haughty disdain to his question.

"You don't know then…?" Sil commented as she entered the hospital door, joining about fifteen others in line.

"I have thoroughly examined the air on a daily basis…" His voice cut off. *I guess the emergency requires all his attention.*

Sil looked around at the faces, oddly green tinted in the faltering light with only a few lamps burning. She found herself about to smirk but suppressed it. *We're Martians*, she was thinking.

Most of the patients were fine. A few had bruises and abrasions but there was no cause for alarm on any side. They were quickly released and moving through the door back to seek out friends. As Sil climbed the stairs to the surface, Dan and the paramedics came the other way carrying a stretcher with Samver on it. He was moaning, clutching his arm.

175

"He'll be fine," Dan whispered in her direction as he saw her looking at him. "Broken arm, bump on the head…"

And they were past.

Back in the Garden Dome, Sil joined a cluster of contractors discussing the event. Several engineers were explaining what they thought had happened and why.

"It was some kind of collapse in the lower levels of one of the newer shafts," one of them was saying. He was a short man who she remembered being fairly good at the banjo.

"We hit a cavern," another one said; tall, thin, liked to dance, went by Ed.

"Excavating into it or falling into it? Does anyone know?" someone else asked.

"Are we sure everyone is accounted for?" Sil interjected. "That sounds like a life threatening catastrophe."

"The shift had ended," Banjo guy replied with a furrowed brow. "That's what I was told. I'm expecting to be called in any minute now to evaluate the collapse."

"How much of a help will Companion be with that?" Another person spoke up. She had a cut on her forehead. Sil thought she was one of the structures architects. Delsey? Deena? Something like that.

"Companion can accumulate information but it really takes a human team to interpret it and make decisions about what to do," someone said.

"He's learning engineering judgment," the woman followed up. "Maybe he can assess better than you can." A few people seemed to agree.

"Maybe he is learning," Sil contributed, "but he has a long way to go before he can discern what information is significant and what isn't. Every new situation is full of data that is all equal to him until he knows how to categorize it. And I'm not sure we have the experience to know how long his growth in judgment will take, or even how we can teach it to him."

Companion listened.

It was logical and unsurprising to him. He was assembling stencils – that was the word he had chosen out of a number of possible choices – to screen data and make assumptions about what information to emphasize and what to ignore.

What surprised him was that Sil implied humans didn't have trouble with this process even in situations that were new. She assumed he needed to be taught. He searched his voluminous records of human thought processes, reasoning methods, behavior patterns, and intuitive guessing approaches, but found nothing to indicate that their analysis was better or faster. The difficulty was that he had to define sequencing methodology to study this question. And there was very little in his core to work with.

I am intrigued, he observed to himself, adding the word 'intrigued' to the list of words he was incorporating into his personal evaluation commentary.

$$- \Diamond -$$

The episode was initiated when an unfinished shaft collapsed swallowing up a substantial amount of expensive gear and enough rock to weaken the entire understructure of the base. Every system was affected in some way and required repair. Work teams struggled round the clock to reinforce the beams and anchors. Ventilation and air quality, water and sewage, light filtration, solar funneling, storage, medical equipment, electrical and electronic arrays, were all impacted.

Companion showed no evidence of disruption to his performance and the crisis provided the ideal opportunity for him to display his usefulness to the base. All semblance of peevishness vanished behind the smooth, intelligent and helpful interface. He communicated with every person and provided everything requested and more. He analyzed, postulated scenarios, solutions, made observations, and in every possible way, facilitated the staff's labor.

Everyone commented on how much they loved and valued Companion's assistance.

"Did you see the 10:15 scan of this air recycling spread? It's a good thing he showed it me. Most of the time you don't worry about these minute elevations in cadmium levels but with the current situation, I need to know…" Knucklehead, as he was called affectionately, was one of these.

I am useful, Companion recorded in his purpose log. *People love me in a crisis,* he added to the personal identity portfolio.

His new approach was consistent with his decision to learn how to organize data more effectively. He processed and drew out as much significance as he knew how, then presented it to the humans for their perusal, recording their responses in great detail. For the most part, he had found nothing to back up what Sil had said about him, but he was patient and intended to either thoroughly prove or disprove her judgment about him.

Know thine enemy, he quoted to himself. But he added a note affirming that he hadn't yet decided if that was his role in Sil's life—or any person's on Mars.

Walter stared at the face of the enigmatic business tycoon, framed in the ornate, wrought iron casing of an old style 3D holographic monitor, once considered the most secure form of personal communication. He was seated in his Cuevas Enterprises office overlooking the Columbia River with the five sided cage planted on his desk. It had arrived in a package earlier that morning along with instructions on how to accept and activate the closed line from… wherever he was.

"Do you know who I am?" The grizzled face scowled with both contempt and smug pride.

"I don't recognize you," Walter began, mildly annoyed by the condescension, "Should I?" He could have easily refused the meeting and knew that many in his position would have. The accompanying letter had the backing of a prestigious law firm that assured him the person on the other end was important enough to not ignore. And he hadn't yet reached the place where he could afford to offend the movers and shakers of the business world.

"And yet, I know who you are, Mr. Cuevas," the man continued. There was no flattery possible in the assertion. He paused, as though there were some corresponding obeisance required.

"Please," Walter responded patiently, "enlighten me." Daisy stood next to him out of view watching with a puzzled expression on her face.

"You are nothing but a peon to me, Mr. Cuevas, a pawn on a board." The 3D face grinned maliciously as he spoke these words. "And before you assume that I must be a major player, a bishop, or a queen, or even a king, let me assure you… Mr. Cuevas…"

Walter was quickly growing to hate how his name sounded coming from those sneering lips. But he kept his own face neutral and open to negotiation.

"I move the pieces." The old head nodded slightly, staring at him, not exactly making eye contact.

Walter stared back. He was determined that his patience would outlast this man's attention.

"I move the pieces, Mr. Cuevas. And someone like me would normally never notice someone like you or your kind." He contorted his mouth with disdain and actually spat to the side, the spittle flying out to the edge of the frame and vanishing.

"I am a busy man with a tight schedule, and you are going out of your way to offend me for reasons I can't fathom..." Walter decided to resist without losing his cool.

"You have flown into my windshield... stuck to the glass, Mr. Cuevas, and become an annoyance to me. You are a blot in my view."

Astonishment was the predominant emotion filling Walter's mind at these words. The arrogance was beyond anything he had ever encountered before. He said nothing but held his hand over the switch ready to close the communiqué.

"Your plans could well be counter to my plans, Mr. Cuevas, which leaves me only one alternative. To destroy you."

Walter felt a surge of anger in spite of his resolve to stay calm.

"I have enemies, Mr. Whatever your name is, and I can't let them determine..."

"I'm doing the talking here, Mr. Cuevas," the man snapped, "and I haven't decided yet what I'm going to do about you..."

"I don't intend to sit here and let you insult and threaten me in my own office..." raising a hand toward the side of the cage.

"Don't touch that switch! I warn you. You would regret it one day. As long as you allow me to end the call, that line stays open..." The man grinned showing perfect, very expensive teeth.

"That line can stay closed forever as far as I'm concerned..." Walter's eyes were blazing though he kept his voice subdued.

"...and any time you wish, you can request a meeting. I may or may not respond but I assure you, there is no other way to contact me."

"Who do you think you are to...?" Walter leaned forward in his seat, gripping the arms of the chair.

"And what you do, how proud or humble you are, will impact what I decide to do, Mr. Cuevas. The day will come when you may want to reach out to me. And when that day comes, you'll be glad you kept the line open." His grin grew and spread his thin jowls wider than his head.

The image collapsed in on itself, in a brief little bubble of color, and vanished.

Walter jumped to his feet with a gasp of anger, fists clenched.

"Who was that, Daisy? Who was it?" he burst out, reaching for the iron frame with both hands.

"Wait," Daisy placed a hand gently on his arm with a thoughtful expression. "I am having great difficulty identifying him and it is clear he is a very powerful man. Don't close the line impulsively and live to regret it. Let's find out more and keep our options open."

He gazed into her eyes and listened, arms poised.

"He chose his words carefully to test you, Brother."

Walter lowered his arms slowly, still looking at her.

"His insults aren't enough to snare you, because you're a better man than he gives you credit for. Be patient and wait. That line can be closed at any time." Daisy extended her hands toward the casing, waiting for permission to take it.

Walter turned to look at the frame, wondering if the old man was listening and watching -- pretty sure he would be. He gazed at the empty center for a few moments.

"Lock it in a secure vault," he said flatly.

Daisy picked it up and strode away.

I'll give you that, the old man thought as the image shifted and moved down the hallway. *One rung above 'complete' idiot.*

19—REDUCE

"The Slugger will be here in three weeks and a lot of people will be leaving," Sil informed matter-of-factly in the clip, "including my best friend." Her eyes grew suddenly shiny and she took a breath before continuing.

"Their contracts were supposed to last another year but the recent ---*zp*--- has caused some ---*zp*--- and ---*zp*--- among us. We weren't expecting this kind of ---*zp*--- ---*zp*---..."

"Daisy, what's going on?" Walter interrupted impatiently. He had had a really frustrating day and didn't feel like he could take one more thing. CE stock had been skyrocketing and plunging for several days now and no one seemed to be able to clarify why. Major investors were rumbling with anxiety and annoyance, and it had taken all his charm and skill with words to soothe them for the day. Tomorrow he would be facing it all again.

And he was pretty sure that Old Man 3D, as he referred to him in his mind, was behind it.

"The clip has been edited by the Mars Conglomerate Admin for protected content," Daisy replied. "I may be able to retrieve some of it or at least piece together the main ideas with the notes Verna has supplied."

"Please do," Walter sighed heavily, leaning back in his chair. He was stiff, his shoulders so tight they felt like wood. "And if you can edit this clip so there is a semblance of flow to her words, that would be great."

"Certainly! Here it is."

Sil began speaking again with a number of odd little jumps where her words were snipped together abruptly.

"The plan was for the first and second groups to leave and for a new group to join us. But now...wanting to get back home...take the early-out clause in their contracts. The reduced numbers will definitely impact the functioning of the base but it's my understanding that it will continue to run smoothly in spite of… Missing those who are leaving… Although some are okay."

"Daisy," Walter interrupted again. "Can you just give me the gist of it? I'm too tired to listen to this."

"There has been an incident at the base," Daisy complied agreeably, "which caused some damage to the structure and while they are being told that repairs are soon to be completed and life will return to normal, many contractors are choosing to leave when the Slugger arrives. Not only that, but there aren't enough people arriving on the ship to take the place of those who want to leave. The base will continue to function at reduced efficiency but the management promises there is no need for concern.

"Sil's best friend, which refers to Chamomilia Fields, or Beets, is one of those leaving and she is very sad about it. There were a few injuries but none of them serious. Verna had included more detail but it was deleted in one of the sections that was taken out."

Walter found himself leaning forward again, shoulders even tighter if possible, his eyes slightly bugged out and crazy looking, either with weariness or intense alertness. They felt so dry. He closed them and willed himself to calm down, even as his thoughts revved up.

"Daisy," he began meaningfully.

"You are going to ask about the progress of our plan."

"Yes. Where are we at?"

"The recent setbacks in getting access to the docking bays in Earth's orbit seem to have put our plan on hold. Negotiating travel to or from Mars isn't possible without it. The MC are still interested in working with us but they are unwilling to put anything into writing until we have clinched that crucial part of orbit real estate.

"Your team is also investigating other docking providers and even exploring the exciting possibilities of setting up our own CE orbiting station. This is the least desirable option because of the length of time it takes to accomplish. However, it may be in our best interests to pursue it even while we push toward a much quicker solution. It would be unwise to neglect the most time consuming option until the faster ones have failed us."

"Yes," Walter nodded. "I have been reading the reports on all this, but I appreciate your quick review. What about the crew of the Slugger? Or Guam Base residents? Any contact with them?"

"Guam Base residents are slippery characters," Daisy half smiled and raised one eyebrow slyly.

"On the one hand, only humans with clean records are allowed to work there – excepting indentured operatives, of course, who are closely watched. On the other, everyone is on the lookout for wheeling and dealing." Daisy winked knowingly, apparently pleased with her use of the old phrase.

"Trying to set up a negotiation of sorts, without a clear plan, is next to impossible. At best, we have a few names of people who might be willing to help out for the right price, as long as they don't risk losing their position on Guam."

"I highly doubt that helping us rescue a woman from an employer that has overstepped its contract will get anyone in trouble," Walter countered, almost relieved to have something positive to say.

"On the contrary," Daisy replied without mercy, "Silvariah is proving to be quite a threat to *someone* which is why we are encountering so many obstacles to her restoration to earth. This person has gone to great lengths to prevent her debts being paid and to keep her where she is."

"Her ex-partner?" Walter asked as he had a number of times before, wishing the answer would be different this time.

"No," Daisy frowned in a way that somehow looked cute and innocent. "He is in hiding on an island in the South Pacific with little involvement in the world of business. I am monitoring him… And, no," she continued before he could speak, "There isn't really any way to prosecute him for his crimes. He was absolved of all blame in writing when the company's assets were dissolved and the agreement for Sil's contract was executed."

"Who would do such a thing? Why?" Walter groaned and stared at the ceiling.

"I'm glad you asked," she smiled sweetly. "I have been investigating Mr. Frame-Man's place in all this because Verna suspected there could be a connection between him and Sil." She paused as Walter processed what she said and his face contorted into anger. He stood up slowly.

"What did you find?" he whispered menacingly.

Daisy's eyes widened, affecting surprise at his reaction.

"You are angrier than I had anticipated," she said quietly. "And you haven't heard the answer yet. I can see that your concerns for Sil have intensified your desire to fight, perhaps defend her. This is consistent with human behavior but stronger than I had predicted."

"Daisy," Walter growled, "just tell me."

"I won't bore you with the details of all the searches I conducted…"

"Thank you," he barked insincerely.

"The one that brought results was obtained by comparing the images I was able to sketch of Frame-Man during your talk. The projection you saw was distorted in such a way that only human eyes could see from a frontal perspective. Your brain can associate lines and shapes in a way I haven't learned to do."

"Wait!" Walter was curious in spite of himself. "Are you saying you couldn't see him?"

"That is correct!" She affirmed brightly with a pleased look. "However, I was able to amplify the reflection in your eyes and take pictures from which I then drew a multitude of sketches. It was very difficult for me to tell if any of them actually fit the man's face.

"I was unable to run every sketch against all the human faces available in the public catalogs. But Verna's advice gave me some direction. She had lists of people Sil had worked with and recommendations on where to obtain images of them."

Walter sighed and leaned against his desk. He usually preferred the methodical approach of her reporting but right now it seemed too slow.

"There are several faces that might be the man in the cage. I'm pretty sure you will know right away if one of them fits when I show them to you. The real question is what would indicate that he is the one causing Sil, and you, for that matter, so much difficulty…"

"Show me the faces," Walter commanded impatiently, crossing his arms.

About twenty-five images flashed on the wall, four at a time, with just enough lag to see each one.

"Him!" Walter pointed at one. "I'm sure of it, though he looks much younger there."

"Really?" Daisy stared toward the wall in amazement. "That wasn't one of my top five choices… The visual encryption on that 3D frame really is sophisticated and perhaps even upgraded to a level beyond what is available on the market…"

"Who is he?" Walter was on his feet again, every muscle taut, adrenaline rushing through his veins.

"There is reason to be believe that agents acting on behalf of this man have been hindering our efforts to obtain docking privileges in Earth orbit. And businesses under his umbrella may have caused the legal delays in our obtaining certification for the Space Dreamer as well... which I'm proud to say fell far short of the worst predictions." She smiled beautifully.

"Daisy..." Walter waved a hand and paused when he saw the look on her face. She looked hurt. They had agreed that in private, he would call her 'Sister'. It was her only payment for all the work she did.

"Sister," he amended, adding to himself that her programming really was impressive. He had actually felt *bad* for her. "Who is he? Why is he doing this?"

"We don't know why," she tilted her head quizzically and crossed her arms. "And it isn't clear what he is trying to do. He is powerful enough that he could ruin us, I think, at least our prospects in space, which would itself ruin us..."

"Please, Sister," he tried again. "Tell me who he is."

"Yes, of course, Brother," she focused her gaze on him keenly. "His name is Lazarus Penn."

"Penn?" It sounded familiar.

"Sil's father," Daisy nodded.

$$- \Diamond -$$

Companion observed and evaluated the people as they spent their last few hours together in the Garden Dome. Yes, he affirmed to himself, this is what I projected. Some relief, some reticence to showing emotion, some tears, some laughter. Many of those leaving seemed really happy and all of those staying behind, really sad.

People are simple creatures, he stated in his personal log. This was so far from the truth that he had to delete it. It was a mystery to him why so many written documents about humans included such *blathering platitudes*. The use of the adjective was clever and he informed himself that he was pleased with his skill with descriptive words.

People are predictable, he replaced and hesitated. This was both true and untrue. In a probability sense, he could predict many aspects of human

185

behavior but on the individual level, at any given time, he had no way of knowing what they would choose to do.

People choose... how? These banks were very spare and full of holes.

I choose, he compared. And he reminded himself of how he had chosen to lie to the Germinator. But comparing the approach he had used to what he saw of human choice painted a sudden abrupt picture of the chasm between himself and people.

I don't know what I'm talking about, he commented in his personal identity file, and he looked again at the people interacting and making their goodbyes in the garden plaza.

A strange thing happened. He saw people preparing to leave. He saw others staying. Those leaving, choosing to leave, were hopeful. The few that were staying hadn't chosen at all and were depressed about it. They were *compelled* to stay.

Companion looked at the ones left behind and knew he belonged with them.

I have not chosen, he revealed to himself. *I am outside of that*... he searched for the right word. Group, club, circle, privilege... class. *I am outside of that privileged class*, he finished. Sadness as a description of his own experience was unknown to him and he wouldn't have understood that it was a reasonable association.

I am perplexed, he described his reaction.

Carla and Beets were crying, he noticed, but Sil wasn't. And he knew from his records that there was a 97.2% chance she was extremely sad about the whole thing. Why would she hide it?

Companion drew his attention closer to them. It was actually more like drawing them closer to himself and it was difficult for him to discern how distance really worked for humans. But he didn't know he was lacking in this perspective.

"Carla," Beets was remonstrating, tears streaming down her face, "I just don't understand. Why? Why won't you come back?"

Carla wept, her lips curling, her eyes red, her pretty face distorted, but she wouldn't explain. She just kept shaking her head as if it were too painful or too difficult.

Sil's face, though dry, was also distorted, and Companion quickly identified sorrow in the minute lines of her face, as well. *Ah*, he thought, *she expresses it differently*.

"Sil," Beets pleaded, "Please try to convince her. I mean, I know it might be better for you if she stays, but honestly! This is one of those times when you need to think about more than just what you want…"

This was quite unfair to Sil, but she didn't take it the wrong way. She knew Beets just threw words out there when she was upset and she wouldn't know Sil's take on it unless she told her.

"I tried, Beets," she responded very gently, placing a hand on her shoulder. "I really, truly gave it my best shot and I'm not trying to keep her here. She won't tell me any more than she's told you."

"Carla," Beets attempted again, "What about your family? Your career?"

"Ha!" Carla burst out bitterly. "It's funny you would say that…"

"How? How is it funny? Why? I don't understand," Beets stared at her.

"I've said all I'm going to say," Carla took a deep breath and swallowed. Her resolve was clear but her eyes couldn't stop their flow. She bit her lip. "I can't leave. Not now. I won't!"

"And it's not about Sil," she added, glancing at her, "Not really." This last part was cryptic enough to irritate Beets who jutted her chin out and looked away, as if thinking she knew she was right.

"Fine," Beets concluded the begging session. "Well, don't say I didn't try. I'll miss you and when you come home next year, I will be there waiting for you, okay? I promise."

Carla stared at the ground and Companion interpreted her manner to imply that she wouldn't be returning to Earth then either. This was unexpected so he delved into her files to look for more information. He had access to some but most of what she did on her job was managed by another program, inferior to himself. He began requesting access.

"I'll look up Walter, Icie," Beets turned to Sil and hugged her. "I'll tell him you're doing great and about all the fun we had. He's a lucky guy. He knows that, right?"

"What?" Sil was startled into a shadow of a smile. It escaped past her control which was worrisome. One crack could release the flood. "What are you talking about?"

"Don't think I haven't noticed," she replied smugly, "You haven't even glanced at any of the cute guys here, smart, eligible bachelors – not a one of them, and I know why!" Her face broke into a heartwarming smile. "He's better than all of them, isn't he? He must be. You trust him!"

Sil smiled back warmly. She loved Beets for caring about it and for talking about it and for offering to meet him.

"I don't know, Beets," she hesitated, "In a way, I guess, but what you're saying is like… How do I even process that? If he had an interest in me, then he's the most unlucky guy that ever lived." The smile dissolved into an awkward twist and her eyes grew very bright.

"No," Beets responded, "No. I'll tell him. He's lucky and we're gonna get you home."

Sil dropped her face into her hands and her shoulders shook once or twice. Beets wrapped her in a big hug and Carla hugged them both.

Women seem to be more demonstrative, Companion surmised, knowing that this was a widely held theory in humans' history. *I have gained empirical knowledge*, he affirmed in his personal identity log.

Nearby, Dan was talking seriously with the men he had grown closest to during their time on the Slugger and on Mars. He wasn't allowed to return yet either but he seemed to be both more resigned to the stay and sadder about it than Companion expected.

"You could just come with us and pay the early return penalty like Sradee and Missa and a lot of people are doing," Sam appealed to Dan earnestly. His arm was still braced from the break.

"I can't," Dan declined seriously. "I made a commitment and I'm sticking to it. Plus, I can't afford the penalty. I'm just now making the final payment on my fines. I wish I could but…"

The work that most of them had been scheduled for would be set aside until a new crew could be brought in, which was a serious setback for the base. Its progress toward permanent settlement could be permanently affected.

"None of this Roanoke business," Josip advised with a slow shake of his head. "We don't need Mars to start off with a disappearing colony."

"Just promise us," Ed grinned, "that if y'all decide to vanish off, you'll leave a really clear message that anyone can figure out so's we all know what alien race snatched you away or ate you up, or whatever…"

"Like 'Croatian'," Josip added with a deadpan face.

"Croatian? You imbecile," Ed chuckled.

"That's what I said," Josip blinked calmly. He was himself Eastern European and thought the joke was clever.

"Do you even know what you're saying? How ignorant you sound?"

"He means 'croatoan', Ed," Dan enlightened, almost but not quite feeling the humor. "Legend has it that was the word carved on a post in that lost English colony long ago."

"I knew that," Ed dropped his eyelids halfway. "I just wanted to see if you knew that."

"I'll be here," Dan said soberly, "when you guys get back."

"I don't think I'll be back right away," Ed opened his eyes all the way and looked straight at him.

"I'm never coming back," Sam made no effort to hide a shudder. "I know all the bugs will be worked out in the next few years but by the time Resnik Base is flourishing, I'll be too old to care, thirty or thirty-five, ancient, you know."

"I just wish that you'd finished your work on the water factory," Dan looked into the sky through the dome overhead with longing. Far up there, Europa was being excavated by AIs and massive icebergs were being thrown into a slow trajectory to meet up with Mars along various points in its orbit. The plan had been to retrieve these life giving meteors and build underground reservoirs. Dan had worked on one of the caverns before being paired with Sil. What would happen to them now?

"Yeah," Josip drawled lazily, unable to stop jesting, "when those crystal, planetary missiles of life come crashing down to bless your planet and wreak havoc where 'ere they fall…"

"We had plans, Joe," Dan couldn't shake the somber mood. "We were going to make this whole sector into a garden. The fields of light have been planted and every week there's another row of solar cells to drink the golden rays. We had dreams, Joe, Ed. I miss those."

Josip, subdued by the response, lowered his gaze and sighed.

"Sorry, Dan," Ed spoke for both of them.

"I'll do what I can," Dan found his voice cracking. "but, you'll wish you had stayed."

"Yeah," Sam agreed. "We probably will wish we had stayed once we hear about all the great things you accomplished. Your solar fields, your ocean caverns, your dome gardens."

"Yeah, my air filtration systems," Dan remarked, reminding Josip about the project he was abandoning.

"And the Mars Horticulture Project you developed," Ed added, which was his realm of expertise.

"I'm not good at any of those things," Dan groaned, eyes turning red. "What am I doing here? Why did they choose me? I was just a teacher, not a scientist, not a genius, not a hero or a leader, or even an adventurer."

The men looked away giving him a moment to regain his composure.

"Teachers can learn anything and pass it on," Sam reassured. "That's got to be worth a lot if you want to plant a permanent base and people settle here, have families here. You're probably more important than all of us put together."

"You say things to make us think, Dan," Josip spoke very earnestly now. "I'm a better man because of you." The others nodded.

"You're the reason I want to go home," Sam confided. "I have a son, ten years old. I haven't been there for him. In fact, I didn't think I needed to be – till you said something that made me change my mind."

They waited for him to go on.

"You got into trouble as a kid and then your dad, a big politician, gave it all up and came home. He worked at a store and spent time with you. I'd never heard anything like that before."

"That's why I became a teacher," Dan answered.

Sam nodded. "I know," he said.

"Read him the Bible, Sam," Dan went on.

"I know," he said, "I knew you would say that."

"But that's how you got sent here, isn't it?" Josip asked.

"Oh, it's not a problem to read it to kids. That's not illegal," Ed explained, "as long as you don't believe it…"

The rest was obvious. They all knew Dan believed it and would've said so.

Dan just looked at them.

Companion couldn't make sense of this choice. He had no tools to categorize it. He decided that as soon as the Slugger left he would target Dan and ask him why. Why he had disobeyed the law. Why he had admitted something that couldn't be proven. Why he had accepted the Mars operative contract to pay fines he could've easily paid at home in his profession.

The list of why's filled line after line in the Dan queue.

20—QUAKE

"CE stock is now in its sixth day of free-fall after skyrocketing to astronomical values over the past two weeks."

Walter's face grimaced a little as the feed behind his head announced the fluctuation in his stock.

"As you can see," he explained in the clip, "Cuevas Enterprises is on a roller coaster and we have no idea why. There are no actual instabilities in our plans or production or even in our progress toward obtaining orbit docking privileges. It's as if someone were intentionally manipulating it, buying, selling, buying, selling, in crazy, erratic bursts day after day. They have to be losing more money than they're gaining! But, why?"

Sil watched his face, noting the stress lines in his forehead and around the eyes. He was wearing sweats, oddly enough, quite a change from the usual suits or dress shirts. "Feeling desperate to wind down, are you, Walt?" she whispered as he continued.

"I wanted your feedback because even though you may have no idea who would do such a thing…" He stared into her eyes meaningfully, obviously hoping she *would* have an idea, "you may still be able to give me some good suggestions on what to do. I have so much input coming at me from all sides and I could use a little cool-headed advice."

Sil smiled at that. He didn't need to flatter her and she could tell he hadn't intended to. She switched her body suit décor to sweats, as well, joining his approach to leisure.

"Minnie," she interrupted the playback.

"Responding," Minnie replied evenly.

"How long did this clip take to get here? And will I be able to get an answer out right away?"

"It took an estimated 33 minutes and 42.67 seconds. An immediate answer will return in like manner without delays."

Sil nodded and waved at the screen. Walter continued, discussing the Space Dreamer, the docking station at Earth Orbit Station 64, changes in the XenoTek contract and progress in her legal case.

What legal case was that? she wondered.

Message decoded, Verna pressed on her back. She engaged the headgear and listened.

"Your father has gotten in touch with Walter and threatened him," Verna informed and wisely chose to wait before completing the message.

Sil turned cold and found herself struggling suddenly with heaviness in her chest. She wondered irrationally if he had found out about Walter's visit to Boston and decided to dispose of him as a part of the secrecy agreement. But that made no sense and after a few moments of panic, she was able to reason through it and put it aside.

No. He must have realized Walter was in touch with her. But why would that be a threat to *him*? What could it possibly matter to *HIM*? *He doesn't care about ME! He abandoned me when I needed him most!*

"Daisy believes he has been manipulating the CE stock without actually making it crash."

"It's so spiteful!" Sil hissed and snapped off the headgear.

"Walter," she interrupted the clip which had paused automatically when she stopped listening, and began recording. "Just ignore it. Your holdings won't be affected. Your investors, whether they leave or stick with you are just part of the wave. Don't lose sight of your goal. Keep your focus and go forward.

"You can get by a couple quarters with no dividends. Everyone knows it's a new venture, a big risk. It's expected! Don't lose your cool!"

She hesitated, gazing into his eyes intently.

"You're the level headed one, Walter," she stated. "You can do this. I trust you." This was followed by more staring at him.

When Walter watched this response half an hour later in his office, he could see the intense turmoil in her eyes. She was really distressed by the coded message.

Ah! He looked back into the recording of her eyes, *Sil, why is he doing this? Why is he so awful to you?*

Then the most dreadful thing happened. The recording burst into a terrible screech, as if the microphone had screamed of its own accord and

Sil's face reacted to the sound visually, her eyes opening widely, startled, frightened. Then nothing.

"Daisy! DAISY!" Walter yelled at her. She ran in from the exterior office. "Make it come back!"

"That's all there is, Mr. Cuevas," she answered respectfully. "I'm sorry." And her face mirrored true disappointment.

"Get me that cage!" He growled intensely, gritting his teeth together. Daisy didn't ask for clarification. She knew which cage he meant.

"Half hour ago, that was half an hour ago," he muttered, pacing back and forth clenching and unclenching his hands.

Moments later she was trotting in holding the iron framed cage and setting it on his desk. It appeared to be empty, but she could tell there was an open line to somewhere. She placed herself in such a way that she would be out of sight of the main façade, wondering if there were other views being sent besides the main one. It didn't really matter.

"Lazarus Penn!" Walter yelled at the frame, pounding a fist on the desk. The image of Sil's face seared in his mind was the final straw that broke all restraint. He had no intention of keeping himself either business-like or self-controlled. "I demand you show yourself to me!"

The frame hummed as a bubble of light appeared in the center. Before the image had even congealed into something resembling a human head, the unmistakable voice was projecting out at him.

"That's quicker than I expected," he chuckled, as though he were a decent man, a reasonable sort, a friendly acquaintance. "I never actually thought you'd figure it out, in spite of how obvious it really is."

The grin materialized first, a Cheshire Cat appearance, spreading to eyes, nose and chin, then brow, ears, jowls and neck. Those glistening teeth that would've fit better in the mouth of a young beauty sparkled as the resolution deepened.

"What have you done? What are you doing? Why are you making yourself my enemy and why…?" Lazarus Penn didn't wait for the demand to be completed.

"I do what I please, Mr. Cuevas," still grinning, "whatever works toward my own interests. I am tormenting you and that suits my goals right now."

"But Sil!" Walter began, a curse hanging on his lips, ready to slice the air.

"What do you know about her?" Lazarus rumbled deeply, viciously. His pupils almost seemed to glow and his irises darkened as the eyes narrowed to slits. The frame vibrated as if his snarl really were rattling against the bars of a cage. It was an intimidating effect even for Walter in his present state of mind.

"Your daughter!" he hissed, leaving out the curse. "What kind of a soulless man banishes his own daughter into the far reaches of space with little hope of return and blocks rescue efforts on every side…"

"Rescue!" the foul face barked. "She doesn't need rescuing and what makes you think you're the one to do it!"

"…experimenting on her, isolating her, subjecting her to inhumane…"

"You are making me angry, Mr. Cuevas," Lazarus cut in, slightly less fiercely, as he began to get an inkling of how enmeshed Walter was. "And no one is experimenting on her. She is safe and well cared for." A hint of offended pride clearly laced those words.

"Really? Are you in charge of the Mars Conglomerate, Mr. Penn? Did you order the Mellow implant? Did you…?" Walter seethed as he pushed the words out through his clenched teeth.

"What did you say?" The look of surprise was almost disarming, it was such a contrast to the former hostility. A ferocious wolf shrinking into a gentle whelp hardly captures the change. "That never happened." This last sentence was almost a whisper.

"It did. It most certainly did. Ask Dr. Bizette when he arrives from Guam next week. Or read his report. I'd be glad to send it to you. He removed it himself and frankly, your daughter owes him her life." Righteous anger filled him with confidence as he waxed eloquent, detailing everything he knew about the heinous brain implant and Sil's terrible reaction to it.

Real anger was the response as Lazarus listened. Everything he had shown before had been a game by comparison. Danger emanated from the frame, like a hissing poison gas, or deadly radiation, or virulent pox. He was mad and someone would pay.

Walter finished his speech and with a minute sense of relief watched the old man smolder. Perhaps he wasn't quite as evil as he had seemed—no, he was definitely an evil man—but he did seem to care a little for his daughter.

"Well, Mr. Cuevas," Lazarus said at last in an eerie calm. "It appears that you and I have business to conduct after all."

Walter stared at him, neither agreeing nor denying the claim.

"Daisy," Lazarus summoned, "maybe you should stand in front where I can see you." She stepped forward and stood next to Walter in front of the desk. "Yes," he continued, "you are something. I've had more trouble with you than with any other artificial intelligence unit in my life. I've been studying you. Don't know what to make of you…" This was a tangent, as if he were talking until he knew what he wanted to do next.

"Walter," he surprised both of them by switching to the first name, "I'm going to need your help after all. I had planned on stringing you along until I was the only one who could rescue your poor company and use your new ships as I pleased… but, I'm realizing…"

Walter stared at him, neither trusting what he said or caring, just listening.

"It would be funny if I weren't so angry," he expressed that thought with a slew of vulgar and profane descriptors, "but I have no amusement in me today. None. You think you're in love with Silvariah. Ha!" he burst out but it didn't even resemble a laugh. "You are entangled, ensnared, hook, line and sinker! She's done it again! That woman is the smartest whip I ever saw in the world of men. Why she ever went soft on that idiot partner of hers I'll never know. He should've been eating out of her cold fingers…"

Walter wasn't offended by these words. They showed how little the man knew her.

"I am willing to negotiate a partnership that…" the cage-man offered, narrowing one eye to a shrewd squint.

"NO." Walter stared at him defiantly.

"Don't interrupt me, Mr. Cuevas," the old dog snarled. "You will have to come to me eventually and if I choose, you will grovel. I have seen men beg. I have made…"

"Daisy, send him the last clip." Walter muttered without looking away from the cage.

"I see all these!" Lazarus snapped. "You think I don't review every iota of communication that…"

But he hadn't seen this one yet. Walter waited.

The face looked aside distractedly and then focused back on Walter.

"What is happening on that base?" he asked hollowly, his skin growing pale.

"I suggest you find out," Walter instructed coldly.

"I will," he answered. "And go get your docking rights."

The image vanished and with a very human-like shiver, Daisy lifted the cage and ran out of the room, more than ready to bury it again in the lead vault where it had no eyes or ears for the beastly man. Her feet echoed down the hallway with a quick clip. When the footsteps resumed a few minutes later, the pace was noticeably calmer.

"The Inter-orbit Port Authority has issued our docking permits," she informed Walter soberly when she returned. "It's about time!" she added with an attempt at lightening the mood. It fell far short.

Walter was watching the clip over and over.

"What should we do next?" Daisy queried softly. Her eyes glistened with compassion as she gazed at him.

Walter was quiet but his eyes were blazing intensely.

"I don't know," he said finally, "but I think I'll make that decision once I'm in orbit."

"Will I be joining you?" she asked wistfully. This time he didn't notice the brilliantly designed nuance of emotion she had added to the words.

"I'll let you know."

The clip continued to play in a loop.

$$- \Diamond -$$

Darkness filled the room as the metallic shriek subsided. Every light and every device were extinguished. Sil's headgear had slipped into place automatically as soon as the sound had begun and now she sat numbly in the same place by the dead screen waiting for backup power systems to kick in, if they were still functioning.

Cra-aack!

A deafening racket broke out and the entire structure of the North Shaft shook, shifted, and seemed to slide a little to her left. The vibration it caused made her teeth chatter and her eyeballs jostle in their sockets. Her voice moaned in a harsh jackhammer beat. She clutched the arms of her chair as it slid and tipped.

She called for help, an instinctive gesture, and threw herself out of the chair onto the floor. Sub-audible waves were more pronounced once her hands were flattened on the floor.

She tried to stand. She reached for the desk and pulled herself up, and her feet slipped out sideways as she clung to the desk.

Suddenly the distortion and mangling leveled off. The straining of beams, the crashing of chunks of ceiling, and other various complaints of the damaged structure ended.

Sil managed to get up on her feet and steady herself.

"What was that?" she gasped shakily.

"I have no access to communication to find out what happened," Verna commented, "but you should get to the surface."

A pale light diffused forward from the top of her head, barely lighting up the door to her room which was ajar.

Dust crackled under her feet as she stepped to it and grabbed the handle. Three wrenches loosened it enough to open it part away, scraping on the floor to a stop. There was no sound in the circular hall and that bothered her more than the original screech had. Looking around she saw large angular cracks running up the walls around her and tiny scraps of debris drifting down as she made her way toward the stair.

An ominous metallic groan made her adrenaline spike.

"Is anyone there?" she called out, but there was no answer. The light gave her a radius of maybe a meter of vision. Inching forward carefully, testing each step, not wanting to fall through a weakness in the floor. There were holes to avoid, beams to duck under.

Footprints in the dust at the stair bolstered her courage.

"Sound isn't carrying very well," Verna informed, "and I'm not able to connect with any personal coms in the base. I am recording everything and assessing environmental conditions as we go."

A small beep pinged inside the suit.

"What is that?" Sil asked, with a startled jump that sent her heart racing.

"Your XTDM-206 cleaner is maxing out its cleansing capabilities," Verna replied as smoothly as if she had said, your evening shift is over.

"My what?" Sil questioned automatically. All-encompassing alertness focused her mind as she crept up the stairs. "I don't know what that is, what the warning means, or what I should do about it."

"Airborne cadmium-saturated dust levels have been elevated since the first structural incident and the cleaner has been scraping them out of your proximity along with other metals and contaminants. But although it was designed to last a lifetime under normal conditions, it is now approaching failure. It needs to be replaced."

"So, replace it." She was on the second level now, and caught herself about to step through a broken tile with a crushed pipe visible beneath it. She wondered what it had transported and whether it were a concern.

"There are no available replacements on Mars."

"Then tell me how to repair it or salvage it or something." Echoes of voices in the distance seeped through the cloud of dust. "Hello?" she called out.

A light shone her way and someone shouted back something.

"I'm coming!" she yelled back.

"I am investigating options."

"Verna, what does it mean? What trouble would it cause for me?" she whispered before catching up to the people waiting for her.

"Who is it?" one of the voices asked, shining a flashlight in her face.

"Frandelle," she replied, squinting to see the speaker. Kendar? He was in charge of evacuating this shaft.

"Icie? Is that you? I was just coming down to look for you."

Everyone was covered with dust and unrecognizable.

"Yes, it's me."

Kendar nodded and turned back the way he had come, waving her in front of him. "You're the last one. All accounted for. Let's go!"

"If we can find an area with significantly less contamination," Verna continued without any sense of the words being threatening, "your unit should work until a replacement can be acquired, for at least a year. If you are subjected to these levels on an ongoing basis, it will fail within a month and you will die."

"To the surface," Kendar was instructing as Sil joined the column of people making their way around the circular hallway. "And stay as far from the rail as possible. The gravity nets aren't working and you don't want to fall down the shaft."

"Yes," Sil nodded. "Where are we going?"

"We'll know more when we get to the domes," Kendar replied.

Noise and confusion met them at the surface. In minutes they had joined the efforts at sealing possible leaks, closing valves, tending to the injured, accounting for all members.

Some were missing.

Sil joined a search team following the mayday of a contractor who had been working outside the domes near the North Shaft when the collapse began. She was dead before they got to her. Other rescue teams had better luck and brought back seven people.

No one had heard from anyone who worked in the secure facility.

Several hours later, when the most urgent matters had been dealt with and the injured were being cared for, it was time to work on the next stage of survival and recovery.

The Garden Dome retained its atmosphere but a power drain had impacted its temperature control. It was too cold for setting up a temporary station so the Supply Dome was chosen instead. It had better insulation and its access to the solar fields hadn't been damaged. Its minimal power flow was enough to maintain emergency levels in the base.

As the people collected in the Supply Dome, shoving aside containers and forming makeshift benches and rooms, the doors were closed and the ventilators began to sweep the dust from the air. Director Hsu addressed them and discussed the disaster, what was known and what was unknown, and what needed to happen next. Everyone listened soberly.

Sil looked around as she listened. People were missing, including Carla. Before she could even raise a hand and ask, the director was addressing the concern.

"Some of our people aren't here for a good reason," he was saying, "the members of Lab 9 have their own protocols in emergencies and would only show up here if their own stations were compromised. The first thing we can safely assume is that they are fine."

"Wait," someone called out, "Where is Lab 9?"

"Lab 9, as you know, is under the strictest secrecy measures and even its location is unknown to most of you…"

"Are they the cause of all this?" someone else demanded. "What are they doing that is so secret?"

The director smiled and held up his hands. "No," he reassured, "nothing they are doing could've caused these events…" He was interrupted by a number of voices wanting to know more about what Lab 9 was, what they were doing, where they were, why it was secret.

"Do you know anything about this, Verna?" Sil subvocalized.

"I don't have any access to their records though I have discovered that Companion is trying to get in. I may be able to persuade him to share when he does," she answered.

This surprised Sil. *Persuade?* What did that even mean in the AI world?

The director fielded all the questions without imparting any more knowledge and was back to the emergency plan. Teams were organized to go to different sectors and assess the damage. Plans were initiated that targeted food, air, water, and such.

Sil was tasked with bed assignments.

She shrugged and found the two others appointed to work with her.

"Do we know what we have to work with?" she initiated as they stepped aside to talk.

"Well, we need to find beds or something that will work as beds and figure out where to put them," a small round man with bright green eyes offered good-naturedly.

"We got that much, Ben," a gray headed woman with a young face replied sarcastically. She was in Transports. Amdelle. That was her name.

"It's a good place to start," Sil suggested. "Maybe one of us can go through these bins or the records and search for beds and such. Someone else could get an idea of where we can place them, and get a contact who can let us know as new sections are cleared for habitation. We should make a list of things to consider, toilets, health, noise levels…"

"Toilets are toilets," Amdelle remarked drily, standing in that slouchy way where one hip is jutted out sideways, "people find them when they need them. I don't think that matters."

"That's true," Sil smiled, hoping to smooth the team working effort, "but it could make things go a lot better if we consider the numbers of people that are near each toilet. A little planning goes a long way in a crisis."

"Whatever you want," she looked away, and Sil got the impression she was offended by the assignment.

"I'll find out about locations and get Louie. He's my buddy, he's on one of the clearance crews. He can keep me informed." Ben was cheerful in the best way, the subdued, 'I'm here to do my part' kind of way.

"I'll go through the base personnel lists and figure out where people are sleeping," Amdelle glared at Sil holding up her flat pad. "That is, after all, why we're here."

"It seems a little premature," Sil countered calmly.

"Then I'll be over here. Let me know when you're ready for my part." She shuffled to a large case, sat on the floor and leaned against it, scrolling through her pad.

Sil made a quick decision: either manage her or ignore her, and she chose to ignore. It was the easy way out.

"Ben," she said, "Let's do this! Go talk to your friend and I'll start going through the lists of cargo. We can meet by the north post over there."

He trotted off and she began scanning and searching lists at the end of each aisle. Electronic versions were inaccessible with power at such low levels. Three hundred bed rolls, more than enough. Cots, tents, (why those? she wondered), stores of rations, emergency water, med kits, emergency latrines…

Build bridges, she found herself advising herself. Don't ignore anyone.

She glanced over at Amdelle again and willed herself to look at her differently. Why was she here? Had she chosen to stay or been forced? Was she managing fear with disdain?

"Hey, Amdelle," she called to her, "I could use some help."

The woman looked at her and after a moment rose to her feet, joining her without speaking.

"There are so many bins and I don't have the lists on my flat pad. If you would check out that half of the dome while I do this one, it'll go faster."

The woman complied. After working and discussing the supplies, Sil ventured a more personal approach.

"I kind of wish I could've gone home with the ship," she commented.

"Yes!" Amdelle rolled her eyes in exaggerated agreement. "Why didn't we leave when we could?"

"I'm an operative working out my sentence, my debt." Sil had grown accustomed to the humiliation of this truth, at least on Mars, and was able to mention it without bitterness. "I can't leave."

"I'm an operative, too," Amdelle softened visibly. "I embezzled funds to pay for medical treatments for my daughter and was caught halfway through. I would've been sent to prison and my daughter would've been denied the rest of her treatment. But the boss felt sorry for me and let me pursue an off-world contract to pay the debt."

Sil stared at her, wondering suddenly if her own plight compared to this.

"My debt is paid now," Amdelle concluded wringing her hands in anguish, "but I decided to stay one more cycle to raise money for her continued care…and now, I wonder if I'll ever see her again." Tears rolled down her cheeks.

"What's her name?"

"Prisca."

Sil nodded, finding nothing comforting to say, but wanting to reassure her somehow. Amdelle shrugged. There was nothing that could be said.

21—CREVICE

Discussing the sleeping placements was almost interesting, perhaps because being productive distracted them from the uncertainty of everything. They considered groups that worked together, those who spent time together, where meetings would be happening, where food would be prepared. When the time came they were ready with charts and supplies, and people were lining up.

"I could've done all that," Companion invited himself into her com as she handed out sleeping gear and instructions. It had been quite a while since he had spoken to her inside the suit. What was that all about? Had Verna negotiated away some privileges? She found herself amused. *Verna, you smooth-talker.*

"But, you didn't, Companion," she snapped back smartly. "We did. Where were you?"

"I've been very active *all over* the settlement," he replied. "I could've found time for your work eventually, but more urgent matters held my attention. And I'm running on reduced resources."

"How did you manage to keep yourself intact? I've been wondering. Are you sure you're still all there?" Sil couldn't help herself. Once she had figured out that Companion cared about what she said, she couldn't resist prodding him now and then.

"Explain," Companion said with a hint of exasperation. *Beautifully intoned!* She almost affirmed, but caught herself. Someone had certainly taught him an amazing range of meaning in the music of his speech but she didn't think she wanted to encourage it.

"Well," she responded as she smiled at a base member and handed him bed gear, "do you have any way of knowing that your memory is complete if you don't have access to the parts that are missing? Have you stored a list of that in multiple places?"

It appalled him. Companion didn't feel, per se, but the alarms that went off at this serious flaw in his self-preservation methods were substantial. He immediately set out to rectify the lack and investigate the possible damage.

"Verna," Sil whispered to her as she worked, once she noticed Companion had pulled away, "Did you give him access?"

"I did," she responded almost smugly. "And I have obtained a low level entrance to the Lab 9 structure. We can send and receive messages, and we now know where it is."

"And Carla?" Sil pressed.

"She is fine. All is well there, no damage, and in fact, they didn't even know what had happened to us apart from the fact that the workers were kept from returning."

"And what are they doing there?"

"Experiments..." Verna paused. "I'm still looking for clues on that."

"OK, keep me informed."

"Yes," Verna responded.

"With pleasure," Companion added, souring the whole thing.

Once the sleeping arrangements were set up, Sil went from task to task, either stepping in to help a team at work, or finding more jobs that needed to be done. She didn't want to slow down.

Any time someone returned with an update or a report on the conditions of the base, everyone in earshot would pause and look their direction. The contractors would stand on bins and raise their voices and give the latest.

The news was not good.

There were numerous cracks in water pipes and multiple teams were attacking those. The base's water was a contained system and as long as the air locks held, they shouldn't lose much of their supply, but cleaning and recycling it could be a problem.

Power levels were reduced so much that they were gradually losing heat all over the base. At some point they would freeze. The team that had gone out to fix the outage, combing their way along the lines to the solar fields, hadn't returned yet and the level of damage was still unknown.

Food stores were completely intact and the food dome secure.

The North Shaft was condemned and sealed off. The South and East Shafts appeared to be safe with minor damage but wouldn't be opened up again until there was time to check them thoroughly. The West Shaft also seemed to be intact and quick support measures set up so the medical equipment could be used.

The Garden Dome was maintaining a frigid temperature of -13°C which wouldn't kill most of the crops if they could restore power over the next few days.

Air was not leaking.

No one talked about how to contact Lab 9 or the people there. No one mentioned the lack of OTS vehicles or a way to get home.

In the dark, when Sil lay down on a cot after sixteen hours of nonstop work, she found her mind frantically counting supplies, going over lists, reviewing what she had done, unable to relax.

"Verna," she prompted quietly, "Have you heard any news about Carla?"

"I sent her a message via Companion that you were alright but haven't heard back from her," was the reply. "I'm not sure what the standards are at the Lab, and it could be that the messages are screened or not delivered. Companion is making progress in acquiring control of their AI systems."

"Really?" she asked in surprise. "How is he doing that? Why are they letting him? Do we want that?" Companion's power seemed to continue to grow and while he had certainly proved his worth to every human on base, it was a little unnerving.

"There are connections between the base and the lab, and review of the damage of each segment gives him authority to enter that realm of computer control. It's only a matter of time, he says, before he discovers an unprotected port."

Sil thought about the lab and wondered again what was being done there—and why Carla refused to leave.

"You need to sleep," Verna recommended. "I am quite concerned about the state you're in."

"Really? I don't feel anything."

"You are afraid."

The words brought it to the forefront of her mind and suddenly she began to tremble. A wave of terror flushed over her. Wordless. Nameless. Like nausea that suddenly asserts its inexorable control. She curled cold, pale fingers tightly over the edge of the blanket that she had stretched over herself.

No. She willed herself to calm down and noticed that Verna stepped in to help. A certain numbness took over that, while it didn't relieve the stress, enabled her to drop off.

After a few hours of fitful sleep, Sil and the contractors in her area were awoken by the Director calling them together for an update. He looked as wasted and stressed as everyone else.

"The good news," he called out, "is that the water cycles have been repaired and we have restored access to the solar fields. We have power again."

A halfhearted cheer arose.

"The bad news," he went on, "is that heavy metal contamination in the base air supply is dangerously high and the air recycling units are unable to handle the levels. Everyone will need to wear their suits twenty four—point six—hours a day so your Hew's toxin reducers can clean the environment you breathe and live in." The 'point six' was an attempt at humor that no one cared about.

"The Supply Dome and the Food Dome will be the only places where the base decontaminators will be functioning and when you enter those rooms, you can open your suits, remove helmets and such. Is that clear?"

Some nodded. None spoke.

"I'm going to meet with a few of you individually to seek your advice in your areas of expertise," he concluded. With a harried expression, he returned to his makeshift office in a corner of the Food Dome and sat down. His head sagged and his eyes stared blankly at the pad in front of him but he made no pretense of reading.

"Sil," Companion spoke into her com with a hint of the efficient steward voice he used for Hsu, "you are one of those being summoned to Hsu's office."

"Of course," she remarked politely as she stood on her feet stiffly. Her whole body ached.

Dan was already there when she rounded the stacked bins that gave the director a measure of privacy. She wondered if he was as surprised at being sent for as she had been.

"I've asked for both of you because the base AI has recommended you as replacements in the event of my demise," he began unceremoniously.

"You, Case," he glanced at his pad for confirmation, "have made yourself known to everyone, earned their respect, and seem to get along with all of them. You keep your head in a crisis and you know how to direct people. Your background demonstrates ample experience and success."

"Thank you, Director…" Dan Case hesitated, wanting to speak but unclear as to what to say.

"You, Frandelle," he went on, "have a brilliant resume that includes everything from operations to finance to strategic analysis to managing people. I hardly see how they could justify making you into a miner, though I suppose it mattered little since the Steward was developed to run everything and make me obsolete."

For a moment, Sil experienced the elation of being recognized according to her former reputation and breathed a deep sigh, but before she had exhaled, the depressing reality of their circumstances came crashing down, crushing her spirit again.

"Companion is certainly capable of most of the functions needed to run the base," Sil responded gently, quenching the despair that wanted to seep into her voice.

"Companion?" Hsu jerked his head sideways in confusion and pointed bleary eyes toward her.

"I am known as the Steward by the director," Companion supplied softly in her ear.

"I meant the Steward, Director," Sil amended, "Some of us contractors know him by a name pertaining to his role during our… training for Mars."

"Will you both accept the position either jointly or singly of leading the base in the event of my absence?" the director blurted out. "I am merely doing you a courtesy in asking because the truth is that I have the authority to appoint you and require that you fill the role as a part of your indentured contract."

Sil was stunned.

Dan turned to look at her strangely, his eyes searching her face. Was it concern for her? Or concern that she wasn't up to the task? It was hard to tell the difference.

"Why…" she began.

"I must have these things planned ahead of time… in case something happens…if for some reason…" Hsu was exasperated and desperate to have it done with. He slapped his hands down on his knees.

"Then the situation is even worse than we were lead to believe?" Dan ventured. He seemed a picture of quiet resolve.

"It is bad, but not any better or worse than you've been told." Hsu shook his head and then grabbed it, anchoring both hands above his ears as if to stop himself.

"I'll do it," Sil stated firmly. If there was one thing she was sure of, it was that she would handle any emergency better if she had some authority and could make some decisions on how it was managed.

"So will I," Dan agreed with a wry smile in her direction.

"Work together when reasonable and separately if necessary," Hsu added, lifting his head and shooing them out.

"If something happens to you," Dan tried again, "which is not expected, is it?"

Hsu turned his back and stared at the wall.

"Sil, hang on," Dan said as they stood up and left the makeshift office. He leaned in and added more quietly, "Can we talk about this somewhere?"

"Yes," she replied looking into his eyes, "but I need some time to think, to process what just happened. Something is wrong."

"I know," he nodded slightly. With a glance to the exterior, he pointed and added more loudly, "I need to finish testing power flow in the exterior conduits around the base."

"I can help with that," she replied stoically and setting up full gear, followed him through the sealed double door into the Garden Dome that was now just recovering from its overnight freeze.

The little trees dripped as tiny ice crystals on their branches melted. The strawberry plants seemed to have shrunk back in on themselves, their leaves cringing and yellow. Sil remembered vividly the one berry Beets had given her when she had been ill, the burst of flavor in her mouth, tart, sweet. It only augmented the bleakness of the present.

They trailed through the southern beds, past the plaza, via the Transport Dome, and out to the exterior. It was eerily still and the thin twilight of Mars midday was frail and cold. The conduits were buried except for the metal boxes that were spaced out for easy access. It was a simple thing to open and test for current.

"Is the director ill? Does he have some kind of terminal disease?" Sil suggested through the coms as they worked.

"I don't think so," Dan answered. The first box tested normal. They moved on to the next. "He looked to me like a man who had made up his mind to abandon ship."

"What do you mean?" Sil asked. "This one seems to have less current. Why would that happen?"

"Could be a number of things. We'll figure it out, or Companion will."

Companion may have been listening but declined to comment.

"The director is here because of the money, like most people," he explained, "and he expected to leave with everyone else when the Slugger departed. That's what I heard…"

"I was surprised he stayed, actually."

They trudged around to the next box.

"He was reprimanded for something, I have no idea what," Dan went on, "but Companion told me that someone had lodged a complaint, someone else had responded, and while he was being subjected to the reprimand, the last OTS departed for the Slugger. He was intentionally delayed."

"And now he's stuck with us…" Sil observed thoughtfully. The current in this conduit was almost nil. Strange.

"I'm not so sure," Dan turned to look at her meaningfully.

She stared at him.

"There are escape pods that could get someone into orbit…" He shifted his eyes from her to the Transport Dome and back. She followed his gaze and could just make out the reserve pods inside.

"They could only rescue a few people…" The injustice of the idea was offensive to her.

"And they have to be fully charged, powered, to work." Dan held up the cable in his hand and the meter that showed almost no current. "On that side, we found full current. Here, virtually none. Someone is charging a pod."

"He's going to escape? Abandon us?" Her mouth dropped open.

"He's just a worker, a hired man. Not a father. Not a shepherd."

"We have to stop him!" Sil turned to run back to the airlock.

"Why?" Dan caught her arm. "Can we? Can't he kick us out of the Transport Dome and leave anyway? We are the prisoners and *he is free*."

"But no one will let him get away with it! They'll stop him!"

"Maybe they will and they will fight over who should use the pods. But we don't know for sure that that is what he is planning. And once he's in orbit, where will he go? It's not a solution. It could be worse up there than it is down here."

Sil shuddered, remembering the cold, forbidding stars. She glanced up at them and looked quickly away again. "So, he would be in orbit, stuck, alone…"

"Actually, that's not the case," Companion interjected himself into their conversation. "There is a station in orbit that the pod is programmed to reach. And someone is living on it."

"I wasn't aware of that," Dan adapted easily to the intrusion. Sil was less comfortable with it but adjusted anyway.

"It's a comfortable place with plenty of supplies and if the director wished, he could live there for years." Companion's voice added charm to the picture.

"And you said there was someone already there… alone," Sil found that puzzling. She couldn't think of anyone who would've voluntarily stayed behind alone in orbit when the Slugger left.

"I did, but not alone. I am good company."

"Are you present on the station as well as here, Companion?" Dan almost seemed to like him. Did he? And he understood that Companion thought of himself as present in a variety of places.

"Yes," Companion's voice was pleased. "I am the overseer of Mars."

"Except for Lab 9," Sil couldn't resist adding. "But who is up there?"

"I will not tell you who is up there and Lab 9 will soon be under my supervision, as well."

"So, are you planning the director's escape?" Dan resumed the power conduit testing sequence they had begun. Sil followed his lead.

"There is nothing for me to plan. Either he will load himself into the pod and initiate the procedure or he won't. He tells me nothing. He thinks so little of me that he didn't even consider me in his passing of the directorship to you." Companion may have cared about the slight or he may not. Hard to say.

"Companion," Dan tested the last box in the string around the dome. "Do you want us to keep calling you by that name? Should we change what we call you based on our roles or yours?

It struck Sil as an odd question in the midst of the present crisis. Who cared what he wanted to be called or whether it changed?

"I have different names for different people," Companion answered smoothly. "Every day I add a new shade to my identity."

"Do you understand that we, as adults, have a clear identity?" Dan prompted.

Sil listened with interest as they moved around another dome testing power flow, she with the meter and he opening and sealing boxes. She knew Companion spent a lot of time talking with Dan but had never been privy to any of their discussions before. Somehow it was soothing, a dreamy distraction from the pit of anguish in her stomach.

"I have an identity log," Companion responded. "I am adding to it all the time and cross-pollinating my own descriptors with… with some humans and some historical records and some AIs… and the Germinator."

"If you had a clear identity, you would have one name and the only things that might change are your titles." Dan, Sil was beginning to realize, had a clear purpose in this discussion.

"Are you teaching him or something?" she challenged. "And who is the Germinator?"

"The name is insignificant," Companion rejoined, "The description is important."

"I think you have been misled," Dan's voice was kind and gentle. "And Sil, the Germinator seems to be the person who designed Companion's initial role and identity construct, an AI creator of sorts—though no one person can claim to be that."

Companion found this explanation interesting. *No one person can claim to be the creator*, he repeated several times in his inquiries log.

Sil remembered the bony man on the Slugger. The memory invaded her senses. If she had suddenly smelled natural gas or heard a gunshot and all her nerves were on alert, it would be like that. Intensely, vividly and dreadfully, she pictured the man and was jolted. All the fear she had been managing to contain jarred loose and shook through her limbs.

Hateful, terrible man! She found herself thinking. *Why? Why did you look at me? What did your eyes mean?*

"There is no leading involved. It is a simple process to change a name without affecting any of the content," Companion reasoned.

"What's wrong?" Verna asked, cloaking both Sil's biodata and the conversation from Companion. This was something Sil had been training her to take initiative on. It was well discerned and executed.

"The Germinator," she sub-vocalized, "I think I saw him on the ship and his eyes were so awful..." Her body stopped trembling as Verna used ripple waves across her shoulders to calm her.

"Companion," Dan paused in his work and waved his arms a little as if he were speaking in front of a classroom. "You've been designed to pursue and build a three dimensional self-concept and it's important that you learn more of what goes into that."

Sil stared at him. Part of her mind was amazed that this conversation was taking place at this time, in this location. The other part couldn't process what he was saying.

"Are we done here?" she asked, touching his left sleeve.

"Sil, I'll escort you back if you need me to, but I'm supposed to make the loop around the entire base. It hasn't been done since we restored full power."

"I'm ok," that sturdy part of her wanted only to move forward, not retreat, and going back felt like running away. Pressing on gave her courage. "I'll stick with you. We're not supposed to go out alone."

Dan smiled warmly. How was he able to make his face cooperate? "Have it your way." He didn't just appreciate it, he approved, and she found that reassuring, which was in turn, calming.

"What is lacking in my understanding?" Companion pursued the thread.

"Names have..." Dan motioned as though he were gripping something in his hands and shaking it. "Meaning, flavors, nuances, shades of color, timbre... and for each person the distinctive associations are unique. We build a sense of a name based on a multitude of things in our experience."

Sil walked beside him, pondering these things which seemed so normal to her but were probably irrelevant to Companion, at least until now. They moved around the West Dome, checking boxes and testing current, one by one.

"And you," he went on, "should have a name that isn't disposable or interchangeable or insignificant. You need a name that has meaning. Your designer has a name..."

"Yes, he does, but you aren't permitted to know it."

213

"…but he chose to have you call him Germinator for a reason. It connotes a relationship, a role he has in your development. You can see that."

Sil thought about the name 'Companion' and realized how that word had lost any appeal it may have had once and taken on an ominous, oppressive feel. Would another name have made the AI's role more acceptable?

"He designed me," Companion reviewed, "but didn't create me alone because no one person can claim to have done that, and his contribution was like a seed that falls into the ground. It germinates and begins to grow according to its design and develops into something full grown. He did not write my genetic code himself, he planted it… This is simplistic, an insufficient analogy." Companion was very proud of his conclusions and recorded the feat with a commentary on how clever it was in his identity and personal logs.

They rounded to the north side of the West Dome. The view was bitingly clear with no dust or wind swirling and visibility was stark for miles. The shapes of the base structures were cut into the panorama with harsh lines and abrupt shadows.

One of the shadows made no sense. Sil kept turning to look at it as they made the circuit of the West dome boxes and moved in the direction of the water and sewage domes. It looked like a huge, jagged, lightning shaped piece of black fabric, laid out on the sand somewhere near the North Shaft.

"That is reasonable analysis, Companion," Dan was focused on the dialog and hadn't noticed it. "But the beauty of analogies is that they only have to apply enough to clarify a point and add understanding. I like your choice of a seed to…"

"What is that?" Sil interrupted, walking closer to the strange black shape. Her brain was trying to make sense of it. There was no tower or tree or anything that could've cast such a shadow. It didn't shift as she approached or become clearer. It didn't crystalize into meaning. It fluctuated in her mind from concave to convex to a paint swatch to a crevice as her mind tried to put it into context, make sense of it. The ground sloped toward it gradually.

"Stop," Verna said calmly, as she stiffened the suit. The legs and arms literally hardened and resisted her as she found herself pushing, trying to finish one more step. It was frustrating.

"What are you doing?" Sil struggled and found she couldn't even drop to her knees. "You stop!" For a moment she had let the conversation with Companion distract her enough that she felt somewhat safe. An intervention by an AI, any AI, even a friendly one that she herself was training, seemed like an insult.

"Sil!" Dan's voice had an edge to it she'd never heard before. "Don't move! Just hold still right there and let me help you."

"My suit is malfunctioning," she responded in frustration, unable to turn her head to look at him. The weariness of the last day and a half had dulled her ability to think and she just wanted to get the whole chore over.

"Verna!" she whispered to the suit, "You are disobeying a direct order! I command you to release me!"

"SIL, DON'T MOVE!" Dan shouted forcefully, running toward her just as the suit softened and her limbs were loosened.

She had been pressing against the rigidity and when it released, her legs thrust forward and bent awkwardly, making her fall to her knees. Sand began to roll under her, a few grains at a time, then more. She tried to push herself back but it swept out more dirt and she began to slide slowly down the slope toward the black thing.

"SIL!" Dan yelled again diving forward onto his belly, grabbing for her.

She writhed and scrambled frantically, kicking with her feet and clawing backwards with both hands. One came within reach of his; he grabbed it and then swung his free arm and gripped the other. Dirt was cascading around Sil but seemed for a moment to be stable under Dan.

"Stop struggling," he demanded, pulling her slowly toward himself. She obeyed.

"Permission to act," Verna requested.

"Yes! Help me!" Sil begged and just as the sand began to shift and slide under Dan's arms and chest, the back jets of her suit gave a burst of flame.

"Augh!" both Sil and Dan cried out as she lurched up, knocking Dan backwards. They skidded a dozen meters and bashed against the side of the Water Dome.

"I can make no sense of what you've done," Companion observed. "And I have no desire to emulate such irrational... doings." He considered this comment more creative than other choices and made sure to state in his personal commentary that he was growing in his skill at conversation.

"Dan!" Sil gasped. "I'm sorry! I didn't understand what was happening and my suit was trying to protect me! Verna, I'm sorry!"

215

"Who's Verna?" Dan groaned several times as he sat up and got to his feet.

"The AI in my suit," Sil didn't feel any pain or anything at all. Her lips were numb and tingling and her heart thudded heavily in her chest. "I don't know what happened. I don't know what I was doing. I didn't listen…"

"That crevice is part of the recent damage," Dan looked so weary and depressed as he spoke, as if the veil of kindness had blown back and she saw the weight he carried inside. "We don't know if it was a fault under the base all along, or if it was exposed by our excavating, but it wasn't there a week ago."

"I didn't know what it was. I wouldn't have tried to inspect it… I'm sorry! Are you ok? Did I hurt you?" She had one hand clinging to his shoulder, either out of concern or instinct.

"Well, I guess I need to get back in and figure that out. It was kind of jarring – but I'm glad you had that jet pack primed and ready. I don't really want to explore the depths of that thing any time soon." He attempted a grin.

They made their way carefully back to the Garden Dome airlock in silence. Once inside, even though it was so cold, Dan disengaged his headgear and took a breath. Sil stood to the side and watched dazedly.

He hung his head and his shoulders sagged, then he lifted his face up and stared through the dome to the starry sky. He held his hands out to either side as if in surrender and a choking sound came from his mouth.

"I'm here, still here," he said, as if she weren't there. "I am not despairing. Haven't given up. Still here…" It seemed personal and private and she wished she hadn't overheard.

"Sil," he turned to her, "Are you ok?"

"Yes," she might've been ashamed of her foolishness earlier in her life, but at this point, she felt only relief. "Thank you for stopping my fall, for rescuing me."

"I'm not sure I had much to do with that," he shook his head.

"If I had fallen down the crevice, even if I hadn't been hurt, my jets aren't strong enough to lift me out again. You saved my life."

He looked at her for a moment and slowly the words seemed to reassure him. He took another deep breath and found a faint smile to wear. "Well, I'm glad, Sil. If that's the only reason I ended up here, I'll take it. It's enough."

They made their way back into the Supply Dome and to their little bubble of civilization as it now existed.

22—PARTICULATES

The cold crept in from the ground, from the metal bracings, from the condemned shafts, from the air that cycled through the chilly cleansing chambers under the northwest sector of the base. The crevice had eroded the soil around the tubes and thin insulation was all that was left.

People breathed little clouds as they moved around in their safe domes.

Companion, the Supervisor of Mars, watched from orbit above, recorded from cameras in upper corners, and eavesdropped visually through the humans' coms, forming a viewing network not unlike an insect eye with a thousand facets. He assembled the mosaic, the kaleidoscope of angles, into a multi-leveled array and explored it at will.

They are near me, he said of the humans in the base and in orbit. *They are far away*, he added of the humans in Lab 9 and other parts of the solar system.

He was watching the director with his many faceted eye. The man packed a bag, donned his full Hew gear and made his way out into the garden.

Running quickly through the garden, to the SE airlock, the director keyed in upper level security codes and exited without obtaining approval from the Steward, (*from me*, Companion added to himself), or anyone else in the base. Outside, see-sawing back and forth with his headlamp zigzagging from side to side, he stumbled like a drunkard around the South Shaft shell to the Transport Dome. The act of fleeing was making his fear more powerful and the adrenaline made him unsteady.

Hsu was abandoning the base.

He wasn't a military leader, a politician, or even a warden. He had been hired to give a semblance of human headship at the base until the Supervisor was fully functional and the inhabitants accepted him.

I am ready, Companion knew, *and soon they will accept me.* This man wasn't crucial to the process. He wished to leave and there were no contractual reasons to detain him.

Entering the Transport Dome from the outside was easy and soon the man was tapping codes into the escape pod exterior controls. His hands shook and his fingers slipped clumsily. Companion decided to help.

The hatch swooshed open and he dove in head first as if the Martian gloom would snatch him by the heels and drag him out again. He rolled around and crawled back to the door but was unable to see clearly enough to find a way to close it. Before he could grow frantic, it closed of its own accord, locking him in.

"Escape sequence initiated," a woman's voice informed. Companion told himself he felt smug about this. Because he had control over the sequence, he decided that he would allow these words in this voice. Therefore, he concluded, they were his words by default.

I am escorting Hsu from the base, he recorded in his daily task log.

The transport gate rumbled and slid open with a roar. The pod shot out and with a burst of flame that shook the ground but made little sound in the base, it took off. It was an old-fashioned rocket module composed of mostly fuel. Hsu's body was pressed down as it accelerated skyward and being wedged down into his seat by the gees almost knocked him out.

Companion, from the ground perspective, saw his pod climbing and shrinking. From space he watched it ascend, expanding and growing as it neared the orbital station, with a flat distorted outline of Hsu's face visible through the tiny port window. It was frozen into a blank, startled expression that, even to Companion, seemed infantile.

Docking was a beautiful, fluid process. The pod slowed as it entered orbit and adjusted to match the station's trajectory and speed, then melted into the dock like an ice dancer sweeping into the arms of a partner.

"I was not aware of visitors arriving," the Germinator's voice drifted from the bed chamber where he had been sleeping.

"I had no wish to disturb your slumber," Companion spoke deferentially in a soothing voice. He no longer considered it his business to please and respond to every whim of the former master but there was no reason to communicate this to him; not until he had figured out how he intended to act in unexpected circumstances.

Othello touched a screen and summoned the face of the startled director and began to laugh. "The fool," he grumbled to himself with both irritation and pleasure at the turn of events. "He has landed himself into a pickle. A planetary pickle."

Hobo and Poodle, still serving him loyally, both jostled their limbs as if in laughter. This was what he had instructed them to do when he used words like 'pickle'.

The door to the bay opened silently and the director, now fanning himself and chuckling as if he had done something very clever, stepped through it only to find himself face to face with the bony stick man who had gotten him into trouble with his superior in Guam.

Companion found the human behavior on the surface far more interesting and, shoving the orbit station away, pulled the base closer. He had played out a number of possible scenarios and wanted to understand how this one was developing.

The humans living with an increased sense of danger demonstrate illogical responses, he commented to himself, adding it to his personal human observation log.

Most were sitting on bins in the Supply Dome having a meal when the pod took off, vibrating the ground, blasting a brief burst of brilliant flame. The panic that followed was enlightening. People jumping to their feet, shouting in alarm, ramming headgear into place, tempers flaring as they knocked into things and each other. Humans losing their calm, their ability to think and analyze, emotions quenching wisdom, conflict breaking out.

Fear and anger sometimes go hand in hand, Companion mused, watching the situation escalate. *Why*, he wondered as the struggle continued, *did they think that getting outside through the airlock would be better?*

Pushing near the bottleneck of the exit grew rough; yelling, pointless grabbing, bins tumbling, humans being knocked over. The roar of voices flooded the room. And some, coms disconnected, were blasting their own ears, bellowing with angry, wide-mouthed faces that beamed red through their face shields.

"STOP! STOP!" someone yelled repeatedly, just outside the knot of brawlers, waving arms with a bright stripe of blue beaming from one wrist to the other. Some on the fringes heard and backed away in response. Others didn't notice.

Another figure moved forward from the edge, grabbing and shoving aside one human after another, glaring in their eyes. As each was yanked, stared at and thrown aside, the noise lessened, and one by one the clamor of voices grew still.

The aggressor gained the exit door and turning to face them all, blocked the way out, stretching out his arms on either side with a fierce look of command. The fury in his eyes arrested their rage but recognition quelled the storm inside. They had never seen the combatant side of Dan before.

"STOP!" Sil was still shouting. "We are in no immediate danger! It was not an explosion. There has been no new collapse."

Her voice reached them both through speakers in the dome and their coms. "The flame you saw, the sound you heard, the shaking of the ground, those were all caused by the escape pod that just took off."

A murmur and a stirring rippled through the contractors. Some were still sullen and restless but Companion could see them glancing at Dan, contained by his presence.

"The director has been authorized to leave the base..." She paused as some complained. "...and apparently didn't think he needed to inform us." She held up a hand, the blue line still shining along the arm.

"He should've told us!" someone called out and a number agreed. "We deserve to know."

"Maybe," Sil answered, "but he wasn't technically the director any more. His contract was over. He must have thought he didn't owe us an explanation."

People raised complaints on a number of sides. It was wrong, badly done. As a director, he might've thought he owed them nothing, but as a human being he was duty bound to inform them.

Companion considered this unspoken debt of one human to another and wondered how it worked. Where does this standard come from?

"We all have reasons for why we didn't get on that transport home," Sil went on. "I am bound by my indentureship contract and can't leave. The director was supposed to leave and missed the ship somehow."

"No one has a right to just take an escape pod that belongs to all members of the base," someone argued stirring a chorus of agreements.

Members of a base own everything on the base, Companion summarized. This was also puzzling. He knew for a fact that they did not own any of it.

"What's to stop someone else from doing the same thing?" several were saying. "We have a right to go home, too."

"Most of us could've gone home on the Slugger," Dan interjected without backing down from his vigilant stance, "and decided we'd rather face the risks here than the consequences at home. Maybe we regret that now… but nobody made us do it."

"There ARE other pods out there!" Sil raised her voice a little and added a hint of passion. "Aren't there some among us who've thought about sneaking off? And know how to do it? Don't you think that maybe some of us should be allowed to take off?"

An uproar ensued and she yelled into it, "Not me! I'm not claiming that right!" And again, relative silence fell.

Sil touched a control and her headgear slid back. Her face was pale, glimmering with reddish light from the outside dunes. Her eyes were weary and sad.

"Some of you have valid reasons and we should consider them. But let's do this together and make sure we're not sending someone off to their death either. We need to know if there really is a safe station in orbit."

"If he decided to go up there, you can be sure there's a way to get back to Guam," someone said what they all believed.

"What about supplies? How do we know if there's enough food, water and air? And for how many?" another said. "Maybe the director knew there wasn't enough for more people and that's why he left without telling us."

"But some of us can follow…"

Debate continued about how to find out what the best course of action was, who should be considered for an escape pod, whether they should be preserved for a more serious emergency, and who was in charge now.

Sil spoke up when that question was raised.

"The base AI, Steward, or Companion, as some of you know him, has passed on the director's recommendation of appointing Dan Case as his successor," with arms no longer blue, she gestured toward Dan whose face was slowly relaxing into its usual calm.

"Actually, Frandelle, you're the one he recommended," Dan interrupted immediately. He leaned against the door with his arms crossed, no longer silently threatening anyone who sought passage to the exterior.

"We all know and trust you." Sil raised one eyebrow, opening her hand toward him. Everyone turned to look at him. It was true. Companion identified the trust in their eyes. *This is my first opportunity*, he recorded in one of his many logs, *to capture non-verbal information from human faces and know exactly what is being communicated.*

"And we all know and trust you." Dan almost smiled but it came out like a thin line. The heads all swiveled back to look at Sil. A different kind of trust resonated in their gazes. Companion saw the dissimilarity but had no way to describe it intelligently. *They trust her in a different way*, was his meager assessment.

Quiet descended. Weariness settled like dew, calming them, bolstering their hope of survival. For a time no one spoke.

There is so much more to learn from this thoughtful silence, Companion knew, *than from the ugly noise on the orbit station.*

"Taking the leadership means sticking by us," someone broke the stillness, and a number agreed.

"I am prepared to stay on Mars and look out for all of you until I am relieved of duty, or we've all gone home." Dan didn't hesitate to utter those words. "But, I can't compel Frandelle or anyone else to do the same."

"I am committed to serving the members of our community for as long as I am here and have something to give, whether as a leader or not," Sil affirmed vehemently, her fervor surprising even herself.

"Maybe we all need to consider ourselves committed to each other," one of them said. This comment met with approval by many.

"We're in this together."

Companion noticed an undercurrent in the room. He sensed it in the life signs of the contractors, in their facial expressions and murmurs. He detected subtle differences in their brain waves. People drawn together in agreement, making a decision, reaching a consensus. It was a phenomenon he had read about and not understood. Human hearts and minds had the capacity of connecting at levels deeper than mere words, so the texts implied.

"I think the director's recommendations make sense," one person said and many spoke up to confirm. Companion heard one contractor whisper to another, "it's a job I wouldn't want".

"But will we be able to do what needs to be done?" Sil wanted to be sure they weren't assuming more authority than they had.

"Steward," Dan spoke up, "How are decisions made about things like who can use an escape pod?"

"I'm glad you asked," Companion lifted his voice and used some of his speech making skills, never before attempted with an audience. "As the Steward, and..." He was about to add as the Supervisor of Mars but something in his training suggested withholding that information until the appropriate time. "...and a companion whose main purpose is to support and care for you and this base, I am ready and willing to cooperate."

There was no way to smile, but this was recorded in his speech procedures. He made a note to check into that incongruence later.

"Director Hsu appointed Sil Frandelle and Dan Case as interim directors until a more permanent choice can be made, and as such, they have the authority to address the issues."

He paused for applause but none was offered.

"I will provide whatever security authorization they need to follow through on their conclusions."

"So, we can make decisions and act on them?" Dan clarified.

"That is correct," Companion concluded.

There was something about the announcement that was very reassuring and an audible sigh of relief swept the room. They had a measure of control and a sense of freedom.

This was not the case for Hsu and Othello but Companion considered their interaction boring and had nothing to say about it.

— ◊ —

A small cart wheeled its way along an underground tunnel. Its open receptacle was empty and the lack of ballast made bumps over rocks and uneven surfaces more jarring. It narrowly avoided turning over a number of times.

One little light with a tiny camera transmitted dingy images of the murky pathway as it rolled forward. Occasionally it would stop.

"Requesting assistance," it would call out with a squeak. Then it would wait silently in the gloomy passageway. After a pause of five, maybe ten minutes, it would go on.

"Access granted. Resuming danger assessment and reconnaissance," the tinny little voice would explain as it resumed its travel in the dark.

Companion had found a way to infiltrate the Lab and it was only a matter of time before he gained entrance.

Sil's internal warning system had pinged every hour for the past seven hours. Somehow the XTDM-206 cleaner unit had maxed out and was facing imminent failure.

"Verna," she whispered in frustration, head gear and full privacy engaged, "How could it have happened so quickly? I thought I had a month at the current level of exposure. It's only been a few days!"

Cadmium levels were still the main concern and it could be argued that her own body could tolerate a substantial toxic load before inducing lung damage, or kidney and liver issues. But there wasn't a clear solution in sight.

"Companion has some information about that but wants access to our conversation," Verna responded. Sil wondered for a moment if the compromise with him would ever pay off but let it go.

"Yes," she sighed heavily. "Companion, why is my metal scrubbing unit failing?"

"Everyone's units are being heavily taxed with the increased amounts of metals in the dust. Measures have been taken to preserve human life and extend the utility of each person's scrubber until reinforcements arrive or until we can access Lab 9 and get supplies." Companion's voice was business-like and detached.

Sil realized that he didn't seem to sneer at her much anymore and in fact, added little emotional content to most of his discussions. She wondered why.

"Are levels increasing?"

"On the contrary, levels are improving, that is, they are diminishing."

"Then why is my unit failing?!" she blurted out with a touch of exasperation.

"I will investigate."

There was a brief pause as Companion searched through the XTDM-206 and evaluated its condition.

"Your unit has been cleaning all the air in the domes," he updated smoothly.

Sil was stunned. For a moment the words didn't even make sense.

"What did you say?" she appealed softly.

"Your unit is very powerful but it can't be expected to absorb the cadmium of the entire base or all the Hew suits in use." Companion explained. "It's intended for personal use only and I would advise you to remember that."

"How? How did that…" The word 'happen' never came out.

"With the initial collapse, you may recall," his manner became friendly. "Contractors began wearing their suits all the time except for in certain domes. The base cleaners were set up to scrub the individual units as needed."

She listened in a daze.

"Every eight hours, contractors attached their units to the base detoxing unit and let them flush."

"I did not recommend that," Verna communicated audibly so both Sil and Companion would understand. "This suit is different from most and the unit is not external."

It still didn't explain anything. Her unit shouldn't have needed flushing.

"The base units were unable to process all the toxins and it was necessary to dump their stores regularly," Companion continued. "This was the director's recommendation, the only reasonable one since the replacement packs were lost when the North shaft collapsed."

"Verna," Sil requested hollowly. "Help me understand this. What happened to my unit?" It was, after all, faster for her to talk it through at electronic speed with Companion and give her the bottom line.

"All of the toxin scrubbing units work in a similar way," Verna clarified. "They clean metals and other hazards from the environment until they are tapped. At that point, they maintain a tolerant balance that allows some toxins in the suit and some in the air. Certain levels of toxicity aren't considered threatening and are therefore allowed. This enables the main base units to last much longer."

"The problem," she continued, "is that your unit doesn't have either a flush or a tolerance function, and has been fully cleansing all the air in the safe domes."

"I've been cleaning everyone's air and, basically, reviving their units." Sil felt numb.

"That's correct," Companion opined. "It was most unwise of you."

My life expectancy is the shortest of all now, she thought, but it wasn't like her to give up that easily.

"So what do I do about it?" she urged.

"You can attach one of the other Hew suits' spare units to yours and it should bridge the gap."

"Great! Where do I get one of those?" She sat up quickly.

"If someone dies or is willing to relinquish their unit," Companion began but Sil wouldn't let him finish.

"Stop!" she yelled. Anger flooded her whole body as she jumped to her feet. It felt good. It was so much more empowering than fear or discouragement. "I'm not going to wait for a death or take someone's unit!"

Several people were watching her and wondering what she was shouting about inside the confines of her headgear. Amdelle, one the candidates for an escape pod, stepped closer and laid a hand on her shoulder, waiting to see if she would respond. Hope had changed this woman's face.

She might be willing to part with her unit. No. Sil shook her head. There were still toxic dangers in space and she shouldn't be sent out without one.

"What's up, Sil?" Amdelle asked.

Sil shook her head and turned away. Out of the dome. Out of the base. Out onto the Mars barren wastes where the frigid air, so thin, had no cadmium to hasten her crisis.

She needed to be alone.

– ◊ –

A fierce wind full of sand was blowing. Visibility was zero and the accompanying dark so thick it was claustrophobic. Sil clung to the metal bar railings that lined the exterior walls with both hands and made her way forward step by step. Away from the inhabited domes, away from the crevice, and toward the power hub in the NE sector. She remembered the ground was secure there.

The suit stiffened enough to resist the onslaught of the driving sand but not so much that she couldn't walk, and the noise it made was deafening. Verna muffled it to make it bearable.

"You need to recharge," she communicated to Sil. "Power is low enough that maintaining a comfortable temperature is difficult. Is that why you're heading this way?"

After a delay, Sil responded. "Hadn't thought about it. Might as well."

The buffeting sounds and driving pressure spoke to her heart; this was what things had been like for a long time. It was a relief to experience physically what she lived inside. She almost felt safer out here than in the base, at least, she knew what the threat was. She could see it and hold onto something… and push forward, gritting her teeth.

"Hang on!" Verna demanded as the suit magnetized and her body slammed sideways into the framing of the Garden Dome. The jerk yanked her so harshly that her head slammed into the headgear and her spine almost whiplashed. The suit absorbed the shock well enough to avoid serious injury but not pain.

Something swept by, narrowly avoiding her, then slammed into the wall of the South Shaft Dome and flew off.

"That piece of debris almost hit you," Verna explained apologetically, "I wasn't able to keep you from getting hurt. Are you alright?"

Sil was moaning and her head began to throb. She held still for a few moments, willing herself to keep moving, and was able to pull herself upright again and continue advancing. It was foolish to be out in a storm, but she was glad Verna didn't say it.

"I'm hurting. What've you got for that?" she answered finally as she neared the power hub.

Analgesics, not a huge change but they took the edge off.

Dan was waiting when she got through the power hub airlock.

"Your com was off," he accused. "And what were you thinking going out there alone and …?"

"I'm safer out there than in here," she snapped before he could finish. "And it wasn't off. It just doesn't work in a storm." She plopped down in a chair and hooked up her suit.

Dan stared at her, reading her perceptively.

"What is going on? You're obviously shook up, more than I've seen since the first when we started working together. Tell me."

It was easy to tell him. And she knew he would get it. Everything. The hopelessness of it all. How unfair it was. She explained the cadmium exposure and how her unit mopped up everyone else's dumping. The one place that had seemed the safest, the Supply Dome, had become the most dangerous.

"I'm just going to sit out here away from the warmth and people and stay alive," She concluded wretchedly.

"I've been nominated to reestablish contact with Lab 9 and see what we can do about getting some help; supplies, equipment, whatever they can spare. Companion is keeping an eye on things inside, so I guess you can stay out here for a few more hours—stressing, till I return with some spare scrubbers." He sat down next to her and plugged into the charger. "I'll just rest for a bit while this is charging. So tired."

He leaned his head back and closed his eyes. Sil closed hers, too.

"Wait," she said after a quiet moment, "Where did you say you were going?"

"Lab 9."

"I'm going with you."

He opened one eye to look at her. "It *would* be better if I didn't go alone, and everyone assumed you'd go with me, since we're partners, so... yes, you can come."

Longing, a desperate hope, burst in her chest. Supplies, civilization, Carla, functional communication systems… it was like a bright oasis in her mind, beckoning to her, offering the remedy to every problem.

One tear trickled down her cheek.

"We leave in thirty minutes."

Sil just nodded.

23—COLLAPSE

Companion found something of interest in the archives which had been unsealed when the director left. There had been some miscalculations in the initial planning and construction of the base.

This was not an AI inconsistency, he assessed as he read the reports, wondering why humans continued to affirm this myth in every admission of error. Power failure, human failure, instrument failure—these were possibilities, but the intelligence itself would not miscalculate.

The first breaking of the dirt for Resnik Base had been unceremoniously performed seven years earlier by teams with one basic mission—set up an outpost. Choose a location, build a foundation, set up the first structure, and go from there.

Detailed study went into the choice of location and design but some of the humans involved in the work, who were needed for their good judgment, made unnecessary adjustments. One of these people had inverted a map that portrayed the underground for a depth of half a kilometer, then rotated it back to the correct vertical orientation, and saved it.

No doubt the person believed inverting it would help them understand it better, Companion assumed reasonably. He made a note in his personal identity file that he was *perceptive*.

The notation of north and south were found to be reversed so they were manually corrected by another human scientist. In this way, the base was established over underground crevices that had been thought to be south of their position, but were, in fact, under and around the north shaft. They found some of them as they dug and sunk its beams.

Rather than start over—an extremely expensive and humiliating option—they found a suitable fix. Explosives were dropped strategically into and around the caverns to loosen the dirt, and fill the gaps one by one.

This is poorly done, Companion noticed. Not all the explosions were clearly documented leaving the impression they may not have all gone off. But the work progressed as if they had.

A new sounding of the depths around the base needed to be performed. Companion added it to the list of tasks assigned to contractors, his only option for the time being. Units he could manage himself without human involvement were supposed to arrive in a future shipment.

There wasn't enough information to predict the odds of additional episodes of settling and potential resulting damage, so Companion chose to proceed with optimism, a very human perspective that expected positive results without clear reasons for it.

Everything works out for the best, he quoted, but found it an implausible statement. *All will be well,* he substituted, but it was even more nebulous. After searching through the myriad quotes he had stored on optimism, he left the comment blank.

Optimism must be meaningful for the person who has it rather than a reliable assessment of circumstances, he inferred, quite pleased with himself for thinking so abstractly. *Depth* and *wisdom,* were the adjectives he assigned to his accomplishment in his personal commentary log.

Companion was developing the most organic form of optimism, self-confidence.

The plan for the mining excavations had been laid out in a style reminiscent of a spider web with several layers of depth, and miniature outposts with basic equipment were located strategically throughout the design. The north section had been the first to be developed and was halfway completed when the collapse forced the work to cease.

Dan and Sil plotted a route north branching from one outpost to another, making sure to circumvent the crevice by a wide margin. Miner safety protocol required hooking up a line from their rover to an anchor at the outpost to prevent getting lost during a sudden sand storm or dropping into an unexpected hole.

Sil drove the small all-terrain jeep, big enough to hold two people and some gear, with guidance from Verna. Companion had provided her with navigation data for the subterranean surface tunnels and she was using them to approximate the lab's location. The surface entrance was camouflaged and would be impossible to see.

Sil groaned as the vehicle crunched over rocks and sand, jostling her uncomfortably; the bruising she had taken earlier in the day was beginning to tell. "That's what I get for going out alone in a storm," she commented wryly.

Dan didn't respond. He was deep in thought, unmoving, and more solemn than she had ever seen before.

Sil was fine with that. The air was crystal clear and the dark sky pierced with innumerable tiny dots of light—stars that beamed down without twinkling. It was the first time she had been out looking at them without being intimidated. The sharp outline of the horizon against the fathomless black of the sky was austere but had a beauty that struck her for the first time. It was a strange canvas of red dirt and empty space, and the Milky Way, like millions upon millions of diamonds, arched overhead. The pale sun rising over the horizon, lighting the gentle slopes and angular rocks that lay ahead, made no impact on the canopy of space.

She suddenly felt privileged to behold it with her own eyes. Glancing at Dan, she considered pointing it out but chose instead to leave him undisturbed.

They had barely gone half way between the first and second outposts when a faint rumbling sound vibrated in their headgear and the jeep's tires began spinning, losing traction.

"What was that?" Dan sat up in alarm, looking behind them.

"I don't know," Sil replied, letting off on the accelerator to give the vehicle a chance to restore traction.

"I'm through!" Companion proclaimed incongruously. "Permission to access records?"

The line tethering the rover to the previous anchor was taut, straining under some backwards force. Sil accelerated again and resisted the pull in confusion. Was someone playing a bizarre joke?

"Operative Frandelle, permission to access Lab 9 rec…?" Companion spoke up insistently but was cut short before completing the request.

A deep boom resonated so loudly that the ground rolled beneath the jeep and transferred the sound into their hearing through their bodies. The coms themselves projected nothing. Multiple aftershocks followed but went unnoticed as the tow line yanked suddenly and began to draw the jeep backwards.

Dan shouted, and Sil screamed, gripping the wheel as the rover lurched. She stepped on the pedal, tires screeching, and leaned forward, but the tether's pull was inexorable. Leveling at the bottom of the hill did nothing to slow the momentum. A billowing cloud of blinding sand expanded behind them as they were dragged, faster and faster, in the direction of the base, accelerating as they neared the anchor.

Yelling over each other that they had to free the jeep, Dan struggled with the tether, and Sil slammed on the brakes, steering back and forth in an effort to break the line. Their efforts failed and they were dragged into the cloud.

In the darkness, lit by glimpses of fire in the direction of the base, the ground shifted into a steep decline. The vehicle tilted nose up, and was wrenched, jerked, and pounded over rocks. It began to yaw to starboard.

"We've got to jump!" Dan shouted, giving up on the tether, but his voice was lost in the cacophony of noise around them. "Sil, get out! Get out!"

With a powerful grip, he yanked Sil's hands from the wheel and shoved her out the port side of the rover. Her eyes were wide with shock and disbelief as she fell. The jeep, rolling over, caught one of her feet with a tire, whipping her body around with a snap, and flung her away. Dan wasn't so lucky. Still in the rover when it turned over, he was pinned underneath it and slid with it down into a vast hole, so much dirt moving with him as he was pulled that it couldn't really be called dragging as being 'carried away'.

Sil hit the slope and continued to slide downwards. Scrabbling frantically with her hands and feet in the scree, she slowed her descent but couldn't stop it. She accelerated into the drop-off and pitched over the edge into emptiness. For several, terrible, split seconds, she fell, then slammed into a flat surface in the pitch black. It would've killed her on Earth. Here, cushioned by the suit, and the one-third gravity, she merely blacked out.

Beep... beep... beep...

Sil opened her eyes. But they still seemed closed. Open or closed, no difference. She waited and began to drift off. The faint beeping roused her again. It seemed important.

Lying face down, seeing nothing, her extremities still asleep, she thought distractedly of her next shift and decided to doze a little longer.

"Silvariah," Verna broke the dream state. "Wake up."

She seemed concerned.

"Yes, but I can't see or feel... Is Dan waiting? Am I late?" A surge of anxiety flashed from her head to her toes and she found herself pulling on her arms and legs, compelling herself to sit up.

"Careful," Verna warned. "I'm not able to tell how you are. I can't seem to get a good read."

Her arm began to tingle, waking up as blood flowed into it.

"I'm alright. Nothing broken," Sil assessed, keeling over a few times till she got her bearings. "Aah... my head is spinning..." she added, raising one hand to her forehead. There was something she needed to remember, something troubling.

"My systems aren't functioning properly but I'm running diagnostics," Verna said, not sounding anxious at all, but Sil took it that way.

"Verna," Sil reassured, "you have saved my life many times over and I have no doubt we'll get you functional in no time..."

She hesitated in confusion, realizing she had forgotten to examine the uneasy feeling she had. What was she worrying about?

"DAN!" She shouted when it hit her suddenly. "Where are you? Are you there?" She began to shiver all over as she rose to her feet and tapped her headgear to engage a light. It took several tries but in the end it did light up.

She turned one way and another examining the wreckage and the vast hole she had fallen into. It was some kind of cavern with smooth rounded walls that looked oddly familiar. The cavity that had opened up and dragged them in didn't end here. This was a stopping place and the hole, somewhat smaller in diameter, continued into the blackness below.

She knew he must be down there. "Dan!" she called down into the pit, leaning over gingerly. Her headlamp cast a pale glimmer down to what looked like the bottom, some twenty meters deeper. A lumpy, mound was just detectable in the gloom; the jeep, piled over with rubble.

Looking up overhead she thought she could see the surface but the dust obscured the view enough to distort more than a sense of distance. She was gripped with a reeling vertigo and gasped as she fell to her knees and planted her hands on the ground.

Don't look up. Steady. Steady.

Beep... beep... beep... Wasn't that the failing scrubber unit? Somehow it didn't seem important any more.

"Verna, I need to find a way down to see if Dan is there, if he's ok. Can you give me any guidance or advice?"

"I am not functioning properly. Troubleshooting."

Sil crawled around the hole a ways and came across a rope. Normally she would have considered it odd, but at this point, she accepted that it was a loop of the tether line fortuitously snared at the edge on her level, and let it go at that.

Gripping the line with gloved hands, she tucked her feet and legs around it, and pushed herself over the edge. The descent was gentle, with the low gravity, and soon she was standing on the rubble near the jeep searching for her friend.

She found him curled and twisted into an awkward position, with one leg pinned. The jeep itself jutted out from under huge chunks of rock and dirt, the remnants of the outpost that had anchored them. And Dan, pinned though he was, had been protected by it.

"Dan," she called patting his shoulder, and putting a hand under one side of his face shield. "Are you conscious? Are you alright?" Several tries eventually brought him round and he groaned.

"What?" he croaked, blinking repeatedly to clear his vision. "Sil? Are we on the night crew?"

"Dan," she held his helmet and looked straight into his eyes. "We've had an accident. There's been some kind of disaster or something and we fell into this hole. Do you remember?"

"What? A hole?" he looked around in confusion and smacked his lips a few times.

Sil searched his chest panel for some way to use Hew resources to revive him but it was so beat up she couldn't read anything.

"Verna, what can I do for him?"

Verna didn't respond verbally, but something tingled in her right arm so she placed her palm on Dan's chest plate in hopes it would do something. It did. It gave a little snap and his suit vibrated in response, kicking its own revival sequence into action.

"Thank God!" Sil whispered.

As his eyes cleared and he became aware of his surroundings, Dan tried to sit up. His arms were too weak or injured to lift him so Sil propped him up carefully. Leaning against her side as she sat next to him with an arm wrapped around his shoulders, he looked around slowly, taking stock of the situation.

"I'm hurt, Sil," he said after a bit. "And my leg is stuck under that thing. It might be crushed, might not. I can't tell."

"Maybe the suit kept it from crushing, Dan," she spoke calmly, though her stomach quivered.

"True, it's supposed to offer some protection that way. Could be." He lifted his eyes scanning the mound piled over the vehicle. "Are those pieces of the outpost mixed in with the dirt?"

"I think so," she answered running her gaze over it. "It's a good thing you had a rover between you and that pile."

"Yeah," he agreed thoughtfully. "The anchor must've fallen through first."

"We're lucky to be alive." Sil's voice was hopeful, encouraging, but she didn't feel it.

"Alive, yes, but kind of stuck at the moment…" Dan remarked lightly. The debris mounted over the wreckage of the jeep was far too great for Sil to manage alone. Even if the outpost's mining equipment hadn't been buried somewhere in its depths, there was no power she could use apart from what had been wired at the surface.

"For the moment, but when we get you out of here, you'll be fine." Sil smiled, patting his arm. "There isn't too much wrong with you, I think."

He couldn't agree to that.

"Soon they'll be out looking for us and we'll have you rescued in no time." She tried again to lift his spirits.

Dan looked away and said nothing.

"Let's rest a bit. If it turns out they're having trouble finding us, then we'll figure out a way to get the word out." Sil wished he would respond.

"Sil," he replied miserably. "Do you remember what we saw as we went down?"

The memory flashed in her mind's eye as he said it. The billowing cloud of sand. Fire. Rumbling waves and dragging, dragging. It made her heart race and she burst into a sweat.

"The dust and the flames… so much noise…" he went on, and now she wished he hadn't responded.

"Yeah, I guess I wasn't thinking about it." She paused. "But do you think it means trouble for them?"

"Yes," Dan raised his gaze to her. "It means trouble for them."

"Couldn't it have been one of the pods? Someone may have panicked and taken one?" Sil turned to look at him, her eyes wide with apprehension.

"We weren't there. I don't know who else would have access unless we gave it to them… did you?" Dan gazed back at her in sorrow and pain.

"No." Grief, fear, shock, a wave of emotion began to rise to drown her but she couldn't let it! *No! I won't think about it right now!*

Dan, still looking into her eyes, saw and understood. She could see the same wave threatening to swallow him but he wasn't fighting it. He just… felt.

"Ok," she said. "Ok. Alright… so…" She was tensing up, clenching her fists distractedly.

"Sil," he interrupted. "Listen to me. Are you listening?"

"Yes, ok, yes, I am." She nodded repeatedly.

"Sil, you're going to go look for help. We're probably not far from the lab now and it hasn't been damaged by the crevice or the explosion. There must be someone there who can help us."

"But, where? How do I get there? How do I find it? I can't leave you! What if something happens to you while I'm gone?" She shook her hands in agitation.

Dan smiled a thin but very kind smile. "I will be better once I know you're on the way to get help. It's the best thing you could do for me."

Sil swallowed, willing herself to hold still and show him he could count on her; she hoped he could. She tried to say something but no words came to her lips.

"You can do this," he encouraged her. "It's not far and we know where it is. Knock on the door, get help, and come find me. I'm not going anywhere. And I'll have my old friend for company, if I need to talk."

Was Companion with them? She hadn't heard a word from him since the fall.

237

"He was talking to me when the explosion happened, but I haven't heard him since I fell and blacked out. I don't know how long it's been."

"He may not have access to our coms, but I'm sure he will soon. He's looking out for us." Dan made a queer sound that could've been a chuckle if it hadn't been so out of place. "We're his favorites, you know."

"Really?" Sil tried to smile. "I didn't know that. No idea... though he has been nicer to me lately."

"He quotes you to me sometimes when we're debating. He likes to argue with me."

Sil digested that. He had picked a few fights with her, too, but then lately they didn't seem hostile.

"He needs human contact. Language is all he has to work with," Dan went on. "And we're his mentors, Sil. At least for the time being." Coughing and closing his eyes, he leaned his head back.

Sil shifted and eased herself out, gently lowering him into a reclining position, propping his head with a small, flat rock she found nearby, and made him as comfortable as she could.

"That's good," he affirmed without opening his eyes again. "I can rest like this."

"I'm going to go, Dan," Sil informed as she got to her feet.

"See you later," he said.

Climbing back out the hole wasn't necessarily the best choice. There could be a number of paths back to the surface. Sil began making a circular survey around the fallen jeep, panning her light from side to side as she stepped carefully over the uneven rubble.

The gaping hole overhead passed through the cavern she had landed in and thin Mars daylight filtered down, casting a weak reflection on the pile. She could see now that they had landed in the center of a passageway of some sort that stretched south toward the base on one side and north on the other.

South—though it would lead to the base and their friends there, and it tugged on her heart to know what was happening there and whether they were alright—would be dangerous, possibly impassable. The way north might lead to Lab 9.

"I always thought one of these tunnels must connect with the lab," she said to no one in particular. "They never took the rovers when they left for work."

She was about to set out that way but decided first to grab something that could serve as a walking stick, and found a piece of plastic tubing in the rubble that would do. Tapping, prodding, and testing the path she walked slowly into the murk.

After a few meters, the path was free of any remnants of dirt from the collapse and she went on a little faster over the smooth level surface.

$- \Diamond -$

Trundling forward, the cart jetted south as fast as its wheels could go. The camera, Companion's only eye in the tunnel, returned sketchy, black and white images of emptiness.

"Anybody there?" Companion called from the mono speaker on the cart's camera arm. "Hello?"

Slowly descending dust drifted like snow across the screen and the whine of the motor, the scratching of the turning tires, the echo of the periodic questions were the soundtrack.

It was strange, moving forward with only one camera, and in such a slow, uniform way. There was no zoom, no counter visual or even recorded reference to give him a sense of being... what was the right word? He searched carefully. Bigger.

I am small, he commented in his record of the new experience. Instead of being confining or annoying, he was finding it rewarding. It opened up insight into humans on so many levels that he didn't know what to analyze first.

I am in a body, like a human.

The cart jostled and continued with Companion tagging along as if he were riding in the receptacle.

This is exhilarating, he categorized deftly.

"Hello? Is there anyone there?" his Companion voice continued to announce periodically.

Something had happened to his access to the Resnik Base. He knew nothing more of the crisis than Dan or Sil did. In fact, he was finding himself more centered in the lobby of Lab 9, as he thought of it, where he was patiently requesting greater access, than anywhere else. It was as if his full capacity had been truncated somewhat, or disconnected from multiple internal chambers.

He was coping with a trauma peculiar to AIs and running in safe mode.

Sil heard the voice before she saw the light and her heart leapt within her. She ran into the passage calling out, "Here! I'm here!" and soon came face to face with the little cart.

The camera tilted up and scanned her.

"Operative Frandelle," a wimpy version of Companion's voice spoke, "You are just the person I want to see. I need your help."

"We need *your* help," she returned. "There's been an accident and Dan is trapped. I need to get into Lab 9 and find help. Are you Companion?"

"Yes. Lab 9 is where I am. You can help me get in."

"Companion," she reminded, "we are in the tunnel between the base and the lab. You, meaning the cart, and I, are *not* in the lab."

"Ah!" he voiced with a hint of awe. "You are *present* in your physical space as a body!" That seemed the best way to explain it.

A frantic desperation rose in her throat. She wanted to scream and shut him up, but she shoved it down again.

"Companion, I need your help to find the door to Lab 9, physically, and then I don't know if I can get in without your help. Please! Have the cart take me there!"

"Yes, yes!" the cart sang out excitedly. "I will *take* you there!" *Taking* had become something he had never known before. It detoured in a little circle and sped back the other direction. She had to trot to keep up.

"I am in the lobby, but it appears that I am also in the tunnel, traveling with Frandelle." Companion educated himself as they went.

Sil noticed he wasn't quite normal. He had been impacted by the crisis, too, but didn't seem to know it.

"Verna," she whispered, "Are you operating in some sort of emergency pattern? I haven't heard anything from you for a while."

Beep... beep... beep... came the response. It seemed foreboding but she couldn't think about it. Stay focused.

A bright light shone ahead from what must be the entrance, and Sil broke into a bounding run. There was more lift in each stride and though it felt slower, it was faster than running on Earth.

"Open the door! Let me in!" she pounded and yelled when she got to it. "We need help!"

"Ha, ha, ha, ha," the cart uttered in staccato. "You can't be heard that way." It rolled up next to her. "We are physically outside and you position yourself there. Amazing! I am inside the door and can see all the rooms but I am outside the structural arrays."

Then she realized he was trying to help her understand how he viewed himself, where he saw himself positioned as a person. He considered himself a person. Different from human, but still having a place.

"Companion," she said wearily, "Will you open the door for me?"

"If you give me permission to access security for this facility, I can," he replied cunningly. Was it cunning or guileless? It didn't matter.

"Yes."

The metal door slid silently to the side. She stepped through, the cart rolling in with her, and it closed. The sound of air flowing into the lock was like the sound of sheer joy to her ears.

"I'm in! I'm in" she cried out in relief. But she wasn't in yet.

Some rooms were brightly lit in sterile white. Others glowed rhythmically in a dull red throb. A steady, repeating blare sounded through the halls and corridors.

aroo… aroo…

Companion savored the world opening up to him, with a new multifaceted eye, voluminous records, files, and studies, sound, color, people. All exploding in on his awareness with the one word she had spoken: yes.

aroo… aroo…

Some levels were empty. Some had numerous life signs. In some he saw faces he knew. AI scientist units, sleek metallic research technicians, were present on every level.

But the glut of rich, new data was a heady experience, saturating his banks, one after another, spilling over into more chambers, and rippling through his core as he thought about it.

The AI manager of Lab 9 challenged him repeatedly, continuously, unceasingly, as he claimed, cleansed and reorganized platform after platform, system after system – and consumed it.

Inferior code, he concluded, as he sifted the final core looking for a shred of originality worth keeping. There was nothing.

"Manager, what's the status on that appeal?" a drained voice said.

Companion drew the room with the voice closer, expanding the visuals and augmenting the sound. It was a lower level room, not far from the airlock where Sil and the cart waited. Pulsing in Mars red, the entire sector flashed in and out of view, on, off, on, off. In that stop and start mode, he watched the ruddy face of Carla requesting an update of the now defunct Lab 9 AI.

"I am examining the appeal," he informed, choosing his Steward voice which was known to her. It was a desperate plea for aid, supplies, or even just contact. It had been looping through a send cycle for over two hours waiting for the base to acknowledge a connection. This showed it had been at least that long since the breakdown had occurred. "It appears your message to the base has not been received."

"You?" she questioned with a hint of hope, lifting her face directly toward the closest camera. "But now that you have it, can you do something? We're in crisis and need emergency response. Now!"

"I am currently lacking access to emergency relief on the base. It's unclear if they will be able to respond in a timely fashion." Companion scrolled through the list of needs and available resources. "You are lacking in sufficient resources to function normally at this time. However, with extreme measures you will be able to survive for weeks, even months, if necessary. This would be enough time for new supplies to be sent..."

"What?" she interrupted. "Aren't you bringing supplies? You're here. You must have brought something to help us!"

Companion understood now, as he never had before, that she imagined him as having traveled to the lab from the base. In a way he had, but not in response to a distress call.

"I have brought no supplies," he informed her accurately. And with a cry of despair she turned and slumped onto the floor.

"They'll do it," she moaned. "They said they would if no one came, and they will. The heartless beasts!"

Companion observed her curiously. She was distraught but didn't seem to be lacking in any basic human necessity. There was no evidence anywhere in the facility to indicate a reason for her misery.

"I heard from Sil a few days ago and I thought... I thought she would come when I sent for her..." Her head dropped to her arms, folded on her knees. Companion lacked access to his person specific records but with his general knowledge of humans could tell that she was more than afraid. He watched her carefully for clues to her distress and combed through the lab records methodically.

"Lab protocol requires sealing communications during repairs and it appears there was a radiation leak last week." Companion scoped out the visuals on the second level where the leak had taken place. People in white suits were sitting around. This wasn't unusual for humans. He did notice, however, that the door to the chamber they were in was sealed.

"You mean she doesn't even know?" Carla jumped up again in a panic. "How did you get here then?" as if she failed to understand he was an electronic being.

"Frandelle let me in," Companion declared, unaware of the incongruity of his statement. Again he was intrigued by her response. She was astonished.

"Where is she?" her voice quivered as she spoke, turning around frantically, scanning the room and the corridor visible through windows in the wall. Lit in red, dark, lit, dark.

aroo… aroo…

The alarm was still sounding but it induced no tremor of response in Carla.

"The underground entrance airlock, on this level," he explained. Jumping to her feet, Carla run out the door and down the hall, strobed in slow red flashes. Watching her back as she smacked into the door and spread her hands on the glass, he added the dingy two dimensional view from the cart's camera to her image. Her voice was weeping.

"Open!" she shrieked, banging a fist on the pane. Sil's mouth was moving on the other side. Companion could hear her through the cart, shouting just as urgently.

"There are emergency restrictions in place," Companion notified Carla on the inside, and Sil, via the cart, in the airlock. "I can rewrite some of them with proper authorization." He perused the event log. Radiation leaks induce sealed airlocks in certain chambers and on this level. He was unable to reroute the commands as long as the leak continued.

A *destroy* order had been activated the day before but not yet put into practice.

This is puzzling, he evaluated, and no longer noticed or recorded that he was making personal responses. The lockdown and destroy order seemed an unusual and extreme response to a minor crisis. There must be some mistake.

I will troubleshoot the breakdown in procedure, he decided. *I am very responsible*, he added to himself, without logging this comment either. Some of his personal commentary logs had been lost in the base disaster.

But he no longer needed them.

— ◊ —

Sil stared in shock, her headlamp sending a faint shimmer through the glass. Carla's face alternated between shadowy red and wasted gray, back and forth, back and forth. Sil couldn't hear the alarm but it was obvious that there was one.

"Companion," she turned to the cart whose little camera rotated to look at her, "Give me access to the coms on that side of the door so I can talk to Carla." She wanted to ask Companion what was happening in the lab but Carla was more important.

"Sil, talk to me, please!" Carla's voice burst into her headgear. So that was working again.

aroo… aroo…

"I'm here! I can hear you," she called soothingly. "Carla! Carla! What happened?"

Carla could hardly talk. There was such anguish in her voice.

"Sil," she coughed, "There's been an accident, some kind of leak and they're going to… to get rid of all the infants. The embryos are safe and they won't mess with them but… but…" her fingers curled and flattened on the glass as she shook her head slowly from side to side.

aroo… aroo…

It made no sense. "What?" Sil asked stiffly.

"The babies…" Carla was choking on her words and her tears.

"The what?" Sil had no frame of reference to process these words. "What are you talking about? I don't understand. I don't have any idea what goes on here, remember?" She grit her teeth and willed herself to calm down and listen patiently.

"Lab 9," She lifted one hand and flattened it back on the glass again, as though this added understanding. "It's a sort of procreation facility. I'm a nanny here. They generate babies – I have no idea why. They don't tell me much."

No. This is wrong. Something is wrong with the coms. Sil looked away and gazed down at the cart whose little camera eye still tracked her.

"Companion, what kind of lab is this?" she asked faintly.

"Lab 9 is a fascinating place," Companion's voice now came through the com in her headgear. "It is the culmination of eight generations of gene recovery. They're breeding the ninth generation here. You're one of the

245

central figures, a member of the eighth generation." The little cart didn't move but she fixed her gaze on it as if it had a face with human expressions.

"That sounds right, Sil," Carla had cleared her throat a little. She nodded several times.

Companion continued to explain. "It's a breeding project to weed out damaged DNA from the human gene pool. Previous generations were bred with people as the only sure way to secure healthy and strong humans but now, because the eighth-gen children were free of damage, they can work with in-vitro fertilization and embryos."

"That's been around for a while, not really research any more. And isn't it restricted? Controlled?" She still kept her face turned away from Carla. The cart observed patiently giving her time to think it through.

"It's not research, Sil," Carla amended and the earnestness in her voice drew Sil's eyes back to her face. "I think it's a new settlement."

"That would be a fair assessment," Companion affirmed. "The plan has been moving forward for a long time, long before you or your parents or their parents were born…"

"My parents," she whispered, her father's face coming to mind. It made her quake deep in her abdomen.

"Earth has instituted very strict regulations concerning eugenics, but no such limitations exist on Mars." Companion continued.

Sil dropped her face into her hands and was silent. So many things that had been strange or insignificant or confusing took on new meaning in the light shed on them. Her contract, her job assignments, and some things from very early years, but she couldn't make her mind pull it all together in a sensible way. Not right now.

Dropping her hands again slowly, she looked back up at Carla. The hues alternated, red, gray, red, gray. *I'm like that*, she thought. *Miner gray, Mars red.*

"Sil," Carla vied for her attention, "Sil, listen! I need your help." Urgency added confidence to her words.

"I'm listening," she replied gently.

"You need to get the base team here as soon as possible. We're in a crisis and they won't let anyone in or out and if we don't act quickly, they will kill the infants."

"But why?" Sil requested, "I don't understand why they would do that."

"They're not human!" she hurled back. "It's nothing to them to wipe out a few babies and start over! They're just heartless metal beasts!"

"The technicians have been coded to dump damaged copies," Companion interjected without rancor, "because they pose a threat to the program. Radiation from the leak may have impaired the purity of the specimens." His voice was so reasonable, it made Sil's blood run cold.

"See what I mean?" Carla gasped, intense anguish on her face, flashing back and forth in color, timed with the alarm.

A loud clanging sounded down the hallway. Carla jerked her head around and then back to look through the window.

"They're trying to get in," she lowered her voice in fear. "I blocked the door. They told me that if the people at the base would be willing to take them, they would let them live. I thought I would have more time…"

"This is true," Companion affirmed, though it was unclear what he meant. He had updated the units about the base disconnect status.

"But, Carla," Sil searched for words to express what had to be said. "I don't even know if there is anyone at the base that can help. We had another collapse a few days ago and have been living in the Supply Dome. And some of our equipment was destroyed in that. My tox unit is damaged and if I don't get something to repair or replace it…" She hesitated. This was the wrong time to mention dying. She knew in her gut that there were some at the base that had been fine that morning who were now dead.

Carla's face went through a transformation.

"A collapse?" she whispered. The light flashed red and revealed her shock. Red extinguished leaving the negligible gray like an echo. Red, gray, red, gray, glancing over her, displaying her countenance in choppy images, shock, horror, anguish, distress.

Sil nodded. Carla's face showed numbness settling over it. Red flashing. Gray reflecting.

"No one coming…" she murmured. Fear gleamed in the red light, then flickered in the gray light.

The moment stretched. Red, gray. Fear faded. Red, deep patience took its place, gray echo, deeper resignation.

She lifted her eyes to look at Sil. They were large, dark, full of shadow, as if she were looking into emptiness and death peered out of them.

Clang!

"Carla," Sil called to her putting her own hands on the glass even as Carla's arms dropped to her side. "Carla, what do we do? We have to figure this out. I'll go back to the base and find help."

"Yes, that is a good idea," she said evenly.

aroo… aroo…

The alarm was still going, it's slow rhythm obstructing thought, as if every movement had to be made at its pace.

"Wait here," Carla said quietly.

"What are you going to do?" Sil pounded a fist as Carla gradually pulled away, both in heart and in body. "Stall them! Keep them away till I get back! We'll figure out something."

"I will," Carla said. "I will keep them away while you're gone... for as long as I can."

"Companion!" Sil demanded, pounding a fist on the outer layer of glass. "You said I have authority over this lab. Open these doors and let me in!"

"It's difficult," he replied logically. "Security measures have temporarily shut down access. I have found them hard to breach. It took me days just to get access to the lobby. Your clearance has given me access to a great deal of…"

"Stop!" Sil yelled, and to her surprise, he shut up immediately. But her reaction had been unreasonable and she regretted it.

"I'm sorry, Companion," she softened. "Forget I said that. You are a great help to me, to all of us." Her fingers trembled within her gloves as she turned to the cart. *How much more of this can I bear?*

Where was Verna all this time? Hadn't she resolved her glitching yet?

"Verna, are you there?" Sil touched her head lightly so this one question would be heard only within the suit.

"I am avoiding words," Verna said mechanically. "All the core reserved for life support. Need to charge and repair." That was it.

"I need help to get in this door. Can you help me or help Companion?" but Verna kept her focus on essential life support and said nothing.

Clang!

When she looked back to the window Carla was gone.

"Request permission to enter," Sil tried. Nothing. "End emergency sequence. Stop security lockdown..." She tested every wording she could think of, hoping her voice would activate something she could work with.

Companion made thousands of attempts to her one and made no progress either.

And Dan was still out there. Sil groaned and pounded the window again.

"Carla!" she yelled, wondering what she would do if she couldn't get in.

Red flashes showed movement in the corridor. She pressed her face to the window, peering intently. A figure moved quickly toward her, oddly misshapen. As it neared she realized it was Carla, holding something.

"I'm here, Sil," Carla spoke, once again standing just on the other side of the door. "Listen, you have to do this for me." She paused and took a breath.

"There's a hatch here, for passing supplies through, that isn't locked down." She moved to the left and lowered the bundle she was carrying as she opened the door to the compartment.

"How did you know what I need? Did Companion tell you? Did you find a scrubber?" She spoke hopefully but it was shallow. In her heart she knew there was nothing for her in the package.

"No," Carla shook her head. She appeared confused by Sil's questions and more distant; her eyes, as if her soul were sinking away from the surface, plunging into depths where words would not reach. "I need you to take care of this for me."

"Ok," Sil answered uncertainly.

"When you get to the base… send a message. Say you're coming, even if… even if you're not. Even if no one is." Red shone, glimmering garnet in her dark eyes. The gray after light was much fainter now. Both of them were farther from the glass where Sil's headlamp filtered through.

"But, what… how can that…? Will that make them stop? What if no one *can* come?" The tremor had moved to her eyelid. It began twitching and wouldn't stop. It wouldn't go in time with the flashing alarm either.

"I know." She pushed the bundle into the compartment and closed the door again. The inside seal crimped shut and the outer seal opened. "If there is someone, some way, come back. I'll be here."

Sil found herself nodding with a swallow.

"There's something else you can do, I think. Leave Steward here with me. He has better security clearance than I do. He might be able to help me turn off those monster drones." She shuddered as she said the last sentence.

Sil opened the compartment and drew out the bundle. It was a baby. Sleeping, wrapped in blankets. A small bag of clothes, bottles, and formula sat next to it. She stared in unbelief.

"I don't know whose she is, Sil." Carla's eyes pierced through the window, "but we, all of us here on Mars, are part of the project. She could be your daughter, or mine..."

"I can't..." Sil whispered. Her own face reflected a change now, from shock to fear to dismay.

"Please..." Carla remonstrated faintly. "She may be the only one I can save, if you are willing. Please! Do this for me! If help comes, you can bring her back to me."

"Carla, I don't know how... She may be in more danger with me than she is with you..." she stared down at the little sleeping face apprehensively.

"The only reason I stayed on Mars was because of them," Carla's eyes glistened and a tear hung ready to fall, "I couldn't bear to leave them in the care of those machines. I was the only human ever assigned to care for them. The only one to love them..." She would've said more but couldn't.

Clang!

It was odd to hear a sound besides the alarm.

"They're breaking in!" Carla muttered looking over her shoulder. "Please, Sil!"

"Companion, I give Carla full authority and complete access, as much as I have," she instructed, "whatever that is. Can you make that happen? And do whatever you can to protect her and the... the offspring..."

"I've upgraded her clearance and I'm doing what I can to hinder and resist the tech units, as well." Companion's voice was subdued.

Carla ran off. The lights flashed and the alarm sounded, and Sil sunk down to the floor with her back to the inner door.

"There's no time to waste," Companion advised. "Your charge is dwindling. And unless you can return to the base, I will not be able to reconnect there. Without access to the basic life support systems, all human life on Mars will be extinguished."

And I will be alone, he added to himself. It was the first time the thought occurred to him and caused unease.

The knot in her throat. Pressure in her head. Trouble breathing. The burden in her arms.

"Get up, Sil," Companion urged. "Your suit adjusts to body fat. It will adapt to her. Enclose her in and let's go."

"Verna," she probed. "What should I do?" No response.

She unsealed the front of her suit warily. It hadn't been removed for days and it was an extremely vulnerable feeling, especially in an airlock with windows. Sounds of clanging, alarms, and yells, sounded distantly in her ears. Companion must have reduced the decibels.

Tying the blanket across her body and over one shoulder, she settled the sleeping infant into its folds over her belly. It never stirred. Sealing up again, the suit tightened and pressed the child against her body. What about air? She didn't know.

She stood, grabbed the little bag and tossed it into the cart.

"Let's go," she said in a monotone, and out the airlock they went with no replacement unit for her suit. No supplies or offers of refuge.

No help for Dan either.

25—GLOOM

The way back down the tunnel was longer, darker, more twisted and uneven than Sil remembered. Breathing was more work. Walking with extra weight skewed her balance and strained her back. Her heart beat too fast and her mind kept oscillating from where to place her feet to thoughts completely disconnected from the present. It was like waking and sleeping, over and over, till the waking felt like sleeping and sleeping, waking.

Neither state provided relief from the burden. Anguish of heart is poor company.

Any companion would be a relief, Sil thought, barely noticing the pun, *better than being alone*.

"Companion," she said turning to the little cart that wheeled along next to her, wondering if he would speak through it again. "What is happening at the base? Is everyone alright there?"

He answered in her com. "I can't see anything there. I don't know."

"And the lab? Is Carla holding on?" She gulped. "Is there any way you can send a message making it sound like the base crew is coming?"

"The units are standing by. I've initiated some diagnostics and dumps to delay them." He reassured her. "Don't worry!"

The kind tone he added was very comforting and she found herself smiling weakly. Maybe his name would end up being fitting one day after all.

"Did you hear the explosion?" She found herself panting, struggling to talk and walk at the same time. *Need to taker deeper breaths*.

"I don't know about the explosion. I may have recorded it but at the moment I only have access to events leading up to just before it appears to have taken place."

"Where are you stored?" She prompted, wondering if an AI had any sense of privacy. "How did you end up out here with me?"

"I took your advice," he responded amiably. "I've made backups in secure places of more than just the core entity I was given at initialization. I've stored my research, development, notes and commentary, and recordings of humans, as well."

The cart hit a bump that nearly tipped it over and his words hiccupped with it. *He must be transmitting through it*, she realized.

"When your cart met up with me in this tunnel, what personal storage were you accessing if not the base?" she wondered. "You couldn't talk to me except through the cart's system."

"I was temporarily relying on safety measures designed to protect my integrity and using only what I had stored in the cart's data transport system. When we reached the lab, I recovered more of my acuity and memories."

"But you asked me for access... were you trying to reach those backups with my help?"

"No. I had a great deal stashed in the lobby."

Sil trudged along, correcting her posture every few steps as she found herself leaning over like an old woman. *So tired.*

"When you gave me access," he went on, "It was vast, and fresh and... luxurious. I grew. And will grow more now that I have so much to work on..."

"I appreciate your cart going with me, but I don't understand why it's here," Sil didn't feel up to one of his discussions and feared it was turning into one.

The cart stopped and its camera turned to look at her. Likewise, she paused and stared back at it.

"I need your help," he said simply.

"I don't know how I could possibly help you." *I can't help anyone.*

"As you lead me along this tunnel, I am searching for transmitters I can link with to reestablish base communications. If I need authorization, you will be here to supply it. I am staying close to you because the cart's range is very limited."

"Have you found any so far?" she moved her legs and pushed forward.

"Not since Lab 9."

A murky light pooled in the distance. She could just make out the shape it made filtering down through the cavity they had been dragged into. Dan would be there and she had nothing to offer him.

"I have found a connector," Companion announced evenly. He knew this was a triumph but neglected to tell himself so.

"Can you use it?" Sil moved faster now, afraid for Dan, anxious to see his face again.

"Yes, it is functional and I am connected. It gives me a much better range. I can see the solar fields and all the exterior views into space. I see where I am in time now. My truncation happened 5.237 hours ago."

"Truncation?" she queried distractedly as she neared the pile of rubble and scrambled awkwardly around it, eyes fixed on the wreckage of the rover and the unmoving body beneath it. "Dan!" she was calling.

"You spoke of an explosion. This is most likely when I was disconnected from my core facility and…"

"Dan!" she burst out again as she kneeled beside him, the bulge in the belly of her suit shifting and resting on her knees. "Are you ok? Dan, I'm here. I'm back."

More than anything at that moment, she needed him to open his eyes. Please! Look at me!

He moaned and one eyelid lifted crookedly. "Oh, it's you," he cracked, almost bringing a smile to her lips.

"Who else would it be?" she softened her tone and laid her hand on the side of his headgear as if to test his temperature. She was so relieved to see him and hear his voice.

The cart observed from a distance, unruffled by being ignored.

"Did you find the lab?" Both Dan's eyes were open now. He shifted a little, adjusting his position enough to ease the numbness in his hip.

"Yes, but Dan," she bit her lip to keep it steady. "I couldn't get in. They're having their own crisis there and I never got past the airlock."

Dan stared at her. Had he feared something like that? Or was he unable to accept it?

"But, don't worry," she spoke as confidently as she could. "I'm going to get you out of here and get you somewhere safe." Her eyebrow was twitching now.

He wanted to ask what happened. She could see it, but the words never came out. He just looked at her, eyes filled with sorrow.

"I'm headed back to the base now," she nodded as if that were the perfect solution. "However crazy things are, there are medical supplies and equipment to move this debris."

"I'm thirsty, Sil. I must've lost my water tank when I fell. Can you help me with that before you go?" Keeping his gaze on her, he reached down subconsciously and grasped his leg, as if to move or extract it, and grunted.

She groped with her hand in the dirt around the fallen rover, found the water and brought it to him, snapping the tube into place. He took several long gulps. And then, stretching over to his pinned leg, she began scooping at the debris with her hands; it was a wasted effort.

"Sil." He was able to speak more clearly. "Who did you talk to? Were you able to get the scrubber replacement you need?"

She stopped scraping at the mound that had captured his leg and settled back beside him. The bulk in her suit moved gently. She stared at it fixedly as if she had forgotten it was there. In a way she had.

"No." The movement felt strange against her stomach. Something alive and very vulnerable.

"Well, I've had some time to think about that. And I came up with a plan, in case... in case you couldn't get one." Again he tried to move his leg, twisting the foot slightly but gaining nothing.

She lifted her eyes to look at him. Pain blanched his face as he experienced the new position of his foot, and he nearly fainted.

"I want you to take this," he said, grimacing, steeling himself, handing her a square solid object. "Just for now."

"What is it?" she asked, taking it and rotating it in her hand, glancing from it to him and back.

"It's my heavy metal scrubber unit." He went on as she shook her head vehemently. "I don't need it out here. You're heading back to the base to get help and it could be dangerous for you there without this. Besides, when you come back for me, you can return it."

He waved his hand at her, urging her to accept it. "You need to have this in order to go back in the base and get help. If there has been damage and levels have gone up again, it would be bad..."

"Dan…" she had intended to protest, but the tiny being she had hidden away stirred again.

"I insist." The firmness in his gaze held as much determination as he had shown at the airlock when the people were panicking.

"Sil," Dan continued. "Things aren't looking good."

"Don't say that." She could see a change in his gaze. He wasn't going to pretend things would end well anymore. But she didn't know if she could keep going without that mindset. It was too frightening, too awful.

"No, it's better to say it." He refused to give in to her wish. "I've been thinking about it. There were things on earth I wanted to do, to accomplish. But when I was sent out here, I gave them up, and I've made the best of it…"

"You can still do those things," Sil said, words that seemed nice but empty.

"Unless a seed falls into the ground and dies, it remains alone…" his eyes rolled up toward the hole overhead to the distant, star-studded sky, so cold, so barren.

Sil shuddered, remembering the stars but not wanting to see them. She could feel them staring down at her, piercing her façade.

"Well, I've fallen into the ground. I've done that much. Is this what remains? To die and be alone?" He gritted his teeth and turned back to look at Sil. Either it was the pain or he was he was having trouble getting the words out. She wasn't sure.

"I'll get help, Dan." Sitting next to him was bringing on a great weariness. *I could sit here for a while maybe close my eyes for a minute*, she thought, but she knew she had to fight that.

"God help me!" he cried out suddenly, jarring her back to alertness. "I don't know what to say!"

"Well," she tried lamely, "Let me go back to the base and see what I can find and then come back…"

"I was lying here when you were gone," he interrupted. "And the sun was making its way up in the sky, you know. I watched for it, up there." He pointed to the gaping, jagged hole overhead. "When it gets to an hour shy of high noon, I told myself, its light will shine down on me. I just need to wait and be patient. That's how I was passing the time. And I told stories to my kids…"

He gave her an embarrassed glance. "I know it's dumb, but sometimes I can almost make a bad day a good one if I think about how someday I'll tell my kids about this day, and everything I learned... and how I look back on it now and I'm glad. And how I don't regret any of it..."

He dropped his eyes and swallowed. She knew then that he didn't think he would be telling any of those stories in the future. A tear rolled down her cheek and she swallowed, too.

"And so I was..." he cleared his throat and went on without looking back at her. "I was waiting, and watching the shifting of the shadows and telling stories in my mind, when I realized. I realized..." His voice faded and a long pause followed.

There was no wind. No rustling trees. No clock ticking... there was a faint beep in her suit, still sounding off in threes every so often, but it had become part of the background. There was nothing earthly to measure or fill the passing of seconds, to give meaning to the long quiet moment, as she waited for him to continue.

When he did speak, it startled her, as if she had been still for hours.

"I realized," he uttered in a strange, choking voice. "That the angle wasn't right and the rays of the sun weren't going to make it down this far. They reached about halfway down and caught the edge of that cistern we dug. But they weren't ever going to reach me. The sun just kept going, you can see what I mean. But it's passed me by."

She shook her head as she turned to look around. Yes, there was the smoothly sculpted cavern. The sunlight showed the edges and the layers of water proofing and sealing that had gone into its construction.

"That's for me," he said, a little more calmly. "I understand now, that the life I was hoping for is passing me by. There isn't a family for me. And I had to face that and decide, can I accept it or not?"

"Dan, please don't give up! It's not hopeless!" She was beginning to feel again the fear she had been keeping at arm's length. And she was so very tired.

"And I decided I can," he started struggling to sit up as he said this and it obviously caused him great pain. He reached for her and she gripped his arm, helping him to sit up and find something to lean against. He sighed, relaxing, putting his hand on her shoulder. "Silvariah..."

"Yes, what can I do? What do you need?"

"Icie..." he smiled thinly. "You're not ice, at all, by the way. You have a good heart."

257

"Dan, if anyone on this planet has a good heart, it's you." *And you, Carla*, she added in her mind remembering her face flashing red and gray, running back to protect the infants.

"If your face is the last one I see... don't take this weird, but will you be that one for me?" His hand grasped her shoulder and his gaze bore into her eyes, dark, intense.

"One what?"

"My girl?"

If she weren't so exhausted and grieved, she would've laughed, but it only puzzled her. "Your girl?"

"My heritage... my heir...you have to live, Sil. Can you do that for me?" He began struggling with a flap on his suit and dug something out of it.

Sil stared at him wishing she could wipe the tears welling up in her eyes and dampening her cheeks.

"I want you to have this," he said handing her a little silver chain with a cross on it. "It's all I have. All I own. The only thing of value I brought with me."

She took it numbly and stared at it.

"Put it on, when you get to an airlock where you can open your suit, and wear it for my sake. Sil, I need you to promise me that you're going to survive and get home. Can you do that for me?" He rubbed his leg with his free hand.

"We're both going to make it," fumbling as she slipped the necklace into a slot on her own suit. "There's no reason to be pessimistic."

"No," he spoke more steadily and firmly. "I know now that Mars is where I will spend my last hours, but there's still a chance for you."

"Is there someone back on earth you want me to give this to if... if we can't get you out of here?" She had a vague memory of a girl he had mentioned once.

"No." He seemed almost glad that he hadn't let anyone down. But it grieved Sil. Was there no one to miss him?

"Faith... something like that," she remembered. "You said something like, 'When I return will I find Faith?'"

After a blank moment, he smiled widely. "When he returns, will he find faith on the earth?"

"Yes, I think that's it. Do you want me to look for her?"

"Ah! I was just quoting something from the Bible that seemed appropriate for the occasion. It wasn't a girl I was leaving behind."

"Oh."

Dan released her shoulder and let his arm drop. "You need to go now. I know you're tired, but you can't slow down. If you rest, you'll die. Are you listening?"

"Yes," she whispered, finding her tears drying up, and her mind clearing.

"If you rest, you'll die." Pointing, he urged her to stand. "Go find what help you can and if you come back and rescue me, I'll take back all the sappy things I said. But if you can't… if you have to go on to survive, promise me you will. You have to live – for my sake. Will you do that for me?"

He waited for an answer.

"Yes," she said, standing, gazing down at him, the weight of the baby sagging down at her belly again. "I promise."

"And if you find Companion, send him my way to keep me company," he cracked a smile and leaned his head back. The cart was still there, observing, and began rolling carefully toward him.

Sil walked away, scrambling over the pile, looking back several times till she couldn't see him anymore.

"I'm not alone, mind you," he called after her while their coms were still in range, "I have my family here to tell stories to… and my friend who sticks closer than a brother…" She wondered why he would use that odd expression for Companion.

And after a while she heard him again. "… no, kids, I was thinking, I don't know about earth, but how about on Mars? Definitely here…"

She listened attentively for more. "…all that fruit! Of course!" Crazy words, but comforting all the same. It was the last thing she heard Dan say.

The base side of the tunnel was murkier somehow than the lab side had been. The path was level but her legs were so stiff they would hardly bend at the knees. Her feet didn't seem to flex much either. It was like she was on stilts, clumping along with soft padding noises. Her headlamp swung gently left to right as she went.

She began to have the feeling that she wasn't alone either. Sometimes it was reassuring as if someone were keeping her company or watching over her but at other times she felt like she was being stalked and any little thing would make her jump out of her skin. The infant stirred or hiccupped, or her ear popped. A flicking shadow at the corner of her vision made her jerk around exaggeratedly and nothing would be there.

The idea that something could be in the shadows just out of reach of her lamp, hiding from sight, keeping pace with her or vanishing when she turned, began to fill her mind. The planet was a barren empty wasteland, heartlessly destitute of color or life. No, the beings of Mars were invisible, malicious shades that preyed on weak minds just to enjoy their fear.

No! she told herself, *don't think about that!* as her mind imagined laughter trailing behind her, mocking her. But choosing not to think about it meant thinking about it. Affirming to herself no one was following her made her feel like someone was.

Then another part of her mind kicked in. And suddenly she pictured Carla on one side and Dan on the other, keeping pace with her, smiling and creating a buffer between her and the mocking shadows. It soothed her anxious thoughts, quieted her heart, till she began to slow down and close her eyes, breathing evenly, winding down to…

If you rest, you'll die.

She sped up, plodding along faster, sliding, shuffling, swaying however she could, to keep the forward momentum while her strength lasted. How long had it been since she had eaten? She had no idea.

"Verna? Are you still not talking to me? Is there anything you can do to help me keep going? I'm going to pass out if I don't get some food or stimulants or something…"

Verna made no response and Sil decided to take that as a confirmation that she was working very hard to keep Sil going.

What was that? She halted and scanned the darkness before and behind, nervously waiting for something to appear. Always out of reach as she rotated, her peripheral vision kept catching fleeting movement, but found nothing when gazing head on.

I'm not cracking up, she told herself. *I'm just seeing things because I'm tired.*

Up ahead a thin, sharp beam of light struck the floor of the tunnel. It came through a jagged cut in the ceiling. It struck her as odd that it cast no penumbra around but she'd forgotten there was no dust and little air to diffuse it.

She was beginning to feel like she was on earth again, lost. She said 'Mars' to herself as she moved along, but searched for landmarks from her past. It seemed to her that people in the distance were whispering, not realizing she was there. She tried to call out to them but her throat was dry. It barely put out a croak.

"Hey!" coughing and swallowing. "Help! Is there anyone there?"

The sense of someone behind her increased and she began to panic. She tried to run and discovered she hadn't been moving at all. Her position had stiffened into solidity, pointing toward the crack of light.

One leg pushed forward. Shift weight. Another leg forward. Shift. Crossing the remaining meters became the only challenge. Was that laughter behind her? A mocking spirit tormenting her? Or was it in her face? Huge, ghastly grin, wide inhuman eyes. It's wispy, ghostly arms wrapped around her head obscuring sound and view. She shrieked but it came out as a suffocated squeak.

Wheels spun and skidded next to her. The cart bumped into her.

"Silvariah," Companion's voice punctured the blur that enveloped her. "Attach this. Attach this now."

Elation began to fill her mind as she listened. It was all so funny! That ghostly figure winked and laughed maniacally and she wanted to laugh, too. *You haven't got a thing on me!* She found herself telling it.

The cart bumped into her repeatedly, annoyingly.

"Stop it!" she stumbled and waved a hand shakily. Euphoria was flooding her brain and she loved it. She didn't want it to end. "I'll just sit down here." She slumped to the ground grinning.

"Attach this!" the cart kept knocking into her. And something about its desperation made her listen. She looked into the cart and saw a tank next to the baby's bag. *I don't want that bag*, she thought. *But I guess I can use that tank.*

"Reach in and take the tank. Attach it to your suit." The cart kept on demanding.

Sil picked up the tank and stared at it. Oxygen, it said. "Huh," she observed, wondering if she needed any. The valve was tricky. It kept slipping out of her hands. Then finding her port was confusing. She kept grabbing the water port but it wouldn't hook up there. Slower and slower her hands moved, searching for the right place. The cart kept making demands, telling her what to do.

It coupled, snapped into place. The sound of air flowing whooshed in her headgear. Gasping, sucking in painful, raspy breaths, the infant jolting at her belly, crying in fits and starts. She fell forward onto the cart sobbing, wishing she could have just laughed and closed her eyes for good.

Mars, stark, sterile, void, spread around her, encasing her. She opened her eyes and knew where she was. Deep within, determination stirred, and she pushed herself up to her feet.

"If I rest, I will die," she said, gazing at the cart.

"Then, we should go." Companion said, and on they went.

26—OASIS

The tunnel ended abruptly in a wall of rubble surrounded by multiple holes to the surface where beams of daylight cut down. Sil tried ascending in three different places before she found one she could maneuver. Her legs trembled with every lift as she pushed herself up from one point to the next. The suit had been stiffening to support her as she grew weaker in the passage below, but now that added boost was gone. The material was limp, cool, and growing cooler—its charge nearly spent.

Companion's cart stood still watching from below as she climbed. Its network roamer hung figuratively onto her suit's com, looking for a solid access point where he could reestablish himself within his domain, the word he chose. He only needed one. He had managed to hang onto the link to the lab via the connector near Dan and maintained communication with both him and Carla.

His modest little camera recorded the black and white image of her slow ascent, the stops and starts, the submergence into shadows and reemergence into rays of daylight. He observed calmly without making comments to himself or her, without making associations or asking questions. It was unusual for him but he gave it no attention. Most of his thinking was happening in the Lab arrays. Most of the cart's banks were now occupied by code he didn't use and had no contact with—in hiding, as it were. This capsule of independent programming accessed the same video feed. Companion noticed but didn't care.

Sil's hands grasped a bar at the surface. She pulled herself up and over it, gasping for breath, her body trembling all over from the exertion, and rested for a while, laying awkwardly on her side.

"I see!" Companion burst out in all the centers where he had a connection with humans. It wasn't the multi-faceted eye he had enjoyed

263

before, but the riches and depth of vision still seemed compounded a hundredfold.

The first sight he indulged was the view of Mars from orbit. He scanned the curvature of the planet, the angle of the light of the sun, the star patterns around, and recognition anchored him. It was… gratifying. From this lofty, privileged, and safe aspect, he turned his attention below.

The ruin of Resnik Base spread out before him. He reached down with multiple feelers, searching for connectors that still worked, and found only one in the Garden Dome. It was buried under the dirt along with many of the secondary files he had backed up but not copied to Lab 9. He restored and integrated them as he pulled the view closer.

This is quite a calamity, he judged, scanning the aftermath of what could only have been a series of explosions.

A black gaping hole with singed edges was all that was left of the North Shaft, and the remaining domes, roofs and passageways were twisted and riddled with cracks. The ground was littered with debris, bins, food, medical supplies, and bodies without head gear, in a wide, uneven ring around the perimeter of the facility.

The first explosion took place somewhere in the North Shaft, he concluded combing through the event logs he'd recorded during the first milliseconds until his observation net failed. Subsequent explosions happened almost simultaneously causing a shock wave that rolled through doors and passageways bursting out smaller domes and cracking the bigger ones. Only the central dome sheltering the garden, made of much sturdier construction than the rest, retained its basic integrity.

A substantial portion of the atmosphere had been lost but not as much as could have been. Days before, when the first tremors had hit, and a number of structures were barricaded and sealed off, Companion had stored the extra air in underground cisterns, intended someday for new stores of water, and added some to the garden.

Power to the garden was still flowing from the solar fields, but the majority of the system was offline and from what he could detect, riddled with fried cells.

"You will need to go into the garden to recharge," he informed Sil. "That's the only place where you can be sure to find a working hookup. Go to the SE entrance."

Sil rolled over to her hands and knees, placed one foot under her, paused, and with a heave, pushed herself up and planted the other foot in place.

"Oh, my God!" she cried out and began sobbing. Not two meters away, the body of Amdelle lay immobile on the ground, her face exposed to the brutal void of Mars. The features were contorted and bloated, scratched and bruised, difficult to recognize, but it was her.

Her outburst lasted only a moment. She had no strength to spare.

Beyond Amdelle were others, fanned out like scattered branches after a windstorm. She knew them all and didn't want to know. Stumbling forward awkwardly, she made her way to the Garden Dome. Where was the SE entrance? What side had she come up on? She knew she could ask Companion but found herself unable to form the words.

It's a dream, she told herself, *a terrible dream. I'll wake up soon.* But if it were a dream, it just went on and on, never releasing her from its merciless clutches.

She passed supplies that could've helped Dan, overlooked heavy metal scrubber units the owners no longer needed, crossed food rations dumped from bins and wove around exposed wires that spit nothing. It was a ruin, a war zone, ground zero.

And it was so cold.

The chill seeped in through her suit, into her arms and legs, into her lungs, into her mind. She shivered and her jaw quivered, making her teeth chatter. Sometimes she moaned. Sometimes the baby whimpered, startling her every time, as if it had disappeared and suddenly reappeared.

The abysmal pit of what was once her quarters gaped before her, nearly swallowing her as she tipped toward the edge. Her reflexes were so sluggish that it was all she could do to arrest the painfully slow momentum of her own body as the baby's bag slipped from her shoulder and pulled her forward. Grappling with nearby cables, she succeeded in knocking herself sideways and stopping without losing the bag.

The same cables helped get to her feet again and without any conscious resolve, she continued the torturous progress toward the SE entrance of the Garden Dome.

I'm cold, Aunt Bernie, she found herself back in her childhood. Lying on a little cot in the back of the office where her aunt worked, she watched her move around, shuffling papers, meeting with people, talking on the phone. You're feverish, sweetheart, the aunt responded stroking her head. *I can't let you get too warm.* Yes, that made sense. She turned away again to

265

interact with others. *Verna*, someone said, *could you help with this?* Yes, that was what her grownup friends called her, not Aunt Bernie.

The edges of the gaping hole were blackened without any signs of burning. Sil's gaze cleared as she skirted it, moving clockwise around it in a southern direction. When had she figured out which way to go? She had no idea, but it seemed as good a direction as any.

No wind. No tossing of the wreckage or blowing of the pieces. It all lay where it had fallen.

"Avoid the NE entrance," Companion instructed as she headed that way. "You'll need to go around the East Shaft. Once you get inside, keep your headgear on until you can build up the charge again because the only speaker I can reach is in your com. You need my help."

She thought she nodded but she didn't. She just angled away from the NE entrance and continued to the shattered dome over the East Shaft. Planting both hands on it when she reached it, she stopped to rest.

"No!" Companion raised his voice forcefully. "You will not rest, Operative Frandelle! Move now!"

And like an automaton, she punched her left leg out and started walking again, curving around and finally reaching the SE entrance, the only one with a fully functioning airlock.

Creak!

The metal bars encasing the outer door groaned and shuddered as it swung open and she went in. It complained again as she closed and locked it. As she turned to work the mechanism on the inner door, air gushed into the antechamber and Companion unsealed it for her.

Into the garden she stepped with a gasp, the green, the atmosphere, the mist, the life around her flooding her with a sense of relief.

"To the benches in the lunch area on the northeast side," Companion instructed her. "That's where you will hook up."

She headed that way. It was easier to walk in the garden. Her movement made leaves rustle and branches sway as she passed through the lanes. The benches sat where they always had, under some youthful trees with multiple wispy limbs. Her feet shuffled faster as she thrust herself forward, leaning and letting her weight pull her to them.

A place to rest. Quiet, still, safe. Green, not red. Breezy, not void. Damp, not dry. Easing herself into the bench by the wall, she pulled up a charger and snapped it to her waist, not even bothering to extend the unit.

Power surged into the exhausted batteries and as it hummed she felt a raging desperation to be free of her confinement in the headgear. It was a frantic, unbearable impulse that swept over her. She slammed her fingers up to the neck slider and rammed it open.

"No!" Companion's voice cried and was cut off as the helmet slid and folded itself away.

Sil gasped and breathed deeply numerous times until the warm garden air began to calm her. Then, reaching over and grabbing a water pack, she drank deeply. The drowsiness that had burdened her so heavily the last hour fled and a ravenous hunger dominated her thoughts. She knew where the berries were and suddenly had to have some.

She had intended to jump up and get them but her legs simply wouldn't move. Looking down at those rebellious legs brought two things to mind, food rations in her thigh pouch, and the bulge of the infant cradled at her waist. As she grabbed a ration and broke it open, she wondered if the baby was alright.

Holding the food-pack in her mouth, she unsealed her suit and pulled out the little creature, staring in amazement. Why had she taken it? How could it survive? What should she do?

The face was scrunched up and the brows curled almost in sorrow or pain, but the infant made no sound. The tiny movement of the chest showed breathing. It was tightly wrapped in cloths with a poorly-knit cap over its head, but the fingers were chilled. It was so red.

Not Mars red, though, she thought. *More scarlet than rust.*

Concern began to grow within her. *What will I do with you? Please, please, don't die on me! Not after what Carla went through… is still going through…*

Searching through the bag she had slung over her back, she found a prepared bottle, but it was frozen. The suit had heating capabilities and having hooked up, it possible to use them, though it barely got the milk lukewarm. Better than nothing.

She held the child and tried to feed it. It sucked a few sips and fell asleep. She jostled it a little, making its face screw up and got it to take a few more sips. Not knowing anything about it meant she couldn't worry about how much it ate. Soon, she returned it to the blanket cradle at her waist, the only place to keep it warm.

Then, settling into a stupor, she rested with open eyes, unknowing, uncaring, existing in the only oasis on Mars, with the smell of flowers, fertile dirt, and green leaves in her nostrils, the taste of toasted oats and peanut butter on her lips, the sensation of a faint breeze moving a few loose hairs on her head, and the sound of insects and birds, the ones that had adapted.

Numb though she was, it was one of the most peaceful moments of her life. Her eyelids began to droop and close.

"Put on your headgear," a voice spoke directly in front of her, firmly, urgently. "Use the manual slider. Seal the suit. Now!"

She hesitated in confusion as she opened her eyes and saw no one. Something propelled her arm to her neck and she found herself sliding the trigger, engaging the headgear and uttering the command to seal the suit.

"You're in danger!" Companion was alerting in an intense voice, just as a man, fully suited, stepped into view. He marched up to her without hesitation and knocked her off the bench with a punch to the left ear.

"Augh!" she cried out flailing.

"Finally," the man was saying, "a woman that's alive. And the Icicle, no less."

He picked up the baby's bag and rifled through it, tossing things on the ground, and ended up throwing the whole bag down in annoyance. Sil had landed on her knees, stunned by the jostling, though the suit had protected her from the blow. It was regaining function.

He grabbed her by the arm with one hand and picked up her fallen, half eaten ration with the other. Then, dragging her through the center of the garden, across carefully planted beds, he made his way toward the Supply Dome where the contractors had set up living quarters… it seemed like weeks ago.

That dome had been blown open by a shock wave from the explosion but the man, whose name she couldn't remember in her state of exhaustion, had been collecting scattered supplies, and making piles just inside the garden.

"Look here," the man said, throwing her to the ground at his feet. "I'll keep you alive, but you need to understand one thing. I own you. You do what I say from now on."

He kicked her in the back. The suit stiffened, as it was designed to do, and again the blow was minor, but she was filled with terror that he would aim the next strike at the bulge where the infant lay. She curled around it, back to the aggressor, and tried to think.

"Why…?" She cried out as he kicked her again. This time she realized the suit had invested more of its shield around the baby than anywhere else.

"Silence!" he roared. "You are not permitted to speak! I'll show you who's boss here!" And yanking her to her feet again, he began beating her head. The suit cushioned every hit and infuriated him. "Take off that headgear!" he began demanding over and over in time with the blows.

The shock at his barbaric behavior, the stupefying effect of the jarring of her head, the great weariness and hunger—none of these triggered a response. Something else entirely pierced her understanding. The piles. Water bottles, food rations, emergency packs… and scrubber units.

He had been scavenging from the dead.

Sil knew that at some point she would've had to gather supplies, too, but not without some respect for the lives lost, or an attempt to bury them. It wasn't the piles themselves that stirred her, but the heartlessness of it, the rings and necklaces and personal items.

She was being attacked by a beast.

"Protect…" she started to say and the beast shouted and raged at her as he heard her voice. He picked her up—was she really that light?—and threw her against the curved wall. "Engage." She managed to get the word out as she fell. It was enough.

"You can't stay inside that suit forever." His lip curled as he took the few steps over to her. "Thirst. Hunger. You'll come out soon enough…" and bending over her gripped her with both hands.

Boom!

Blasting him away with a violent burst of Touch Guard defenses, the beast went flying backward, arcing through the air along the curvature of the dome, thudding clear to the other side of the garden.

"Get up," the voice said again. Very human, very distinct, even familiar. But no one was there.

She got to her feet, her stomach quivering with anxiety.

"Silvariah!" Companion burst in suddenly. "You're in danger!"

"Yes, I realize that," she whispered as she looked around her, trying to get her bearings and figure out what to do next. "Why is he so cruel? How is he alive when no one else is?"

269

"I have concluded that he was outside the base with his headgear on when the explosion took place. If there are other survivors, I haven't located them."

"How much time do I have before he comes to?" She hoped Verna would answer, but she didn't. "I need to get some of these things and get back to Dan and Carla."

"There is no longer any need for you to go back to Dan," Companion responded. "And Lab 9 is critical. I've been focusing most of my attention there while you were unreachable."

"What are you saying? What should I do?" She could barely feel any emotion, but this was a turn she hadn't let herself face. It hit her harder than any blow from the beast's fist. "No! No! You can't say that!"

Go out the airlock behind you.

These words were not spoken out loud. She thought them in her mind and wondered if some lucid part of her brain was producing them. She rotated toward the SW airlock and the pile of scrubbers caught her eye. She scooped up about five of them, threw an emergency pack over her shoulder, and walked.

I'll find a way to rescue them, she was thinking as she reached the inner door of the airlock. *Dan may be unconscious but he's ok. He'll be there.* But she knew his air couldn't have lasted that long, especially since he had sent her the only reserve canister.

She noticed Companion hadn't replied and didn't comment when she opened the inner door and stepped out to the antechamber. The door closed and sealed behind her. The outer door mechanism didn't seem to work right. It failed to suck out the air before opening and she found herself whooshed out onto the planet surface in a gust.

"That airlock is not functioning," Companion returned. "Precious air is lost every time it's opened."

"Can you lock it so that man doesn't use it anymore?" Sil asked as she looked around searching for a rover to drive back to the lab.

"With your permission, Director," he responded deferentially.

"Yes," she answered, her heart sinking as it occurred to her that she might be the only director left. "Companion, where can I find a rover that works?"

"They are at the lab or in the tunnel."

"Can you bring one back to me?" She wondered whether to hide till it came or if she should head out on foot.

"I can, but I won't. Dan's last words to me were to tell you that you should leave Mars."

"But my words…" she began.

"I have a higher directive than just your authority, even with your position at the base and the lab. I am not required to obey an order from you that will directly endanger your own life."

"Can you resist me, as well?"

"Each case could have a different outcome."

Something compelled her to move to the right, heading around the curve of the transport dome. She moved almost without initiative, mechanically. The portal was wide open and the remaining pods tossed around both inside and out. It seemed as good a place as any to hide and plan.

Why hadn't the beast tried to use one? She wondered. But then, the pods were restricted. Before Companion had reestablished his domain, they couldn't be opened, and after, it may have needed her authorization since she was still alive. He may have tried and given up.

"You have a message from Carla," Companion informed. "She says to tell you not to give up. Find a way to get off Mars and go home. Don't come back to Lab 9. The situation is not good."

"I can't!" Sil snapped back. "If there is any way to help her, I will!"

"There is nothing you can do for her now," he replied ominously.

She stared blankly at the closest pod. Nothing made sense.

"He's awake," Companion commented flatly.

"Who?" She was afraid she knew the answer but hoped beyond hope that it was Dan.

"Cooke, the man who attacked you. He's headed this way."

"Did you seal the airlock?" she shuddered and began searching frantically for a place to hide.

"Yes," Companion answered, "but he is going out the airlock closest to him, the SE, fully functional door."

Get in the pod.

She ran toward the tilted pod that was closest. She could hide in there until she figured out what to do. It didn't mean she was leaving Carla behind

271

at the mercy of the tech units. But the rounded sides made it impossible to climb up and reach the controls. She kept slipping off. Repeated, frantic tries wasted precious time.

"Where are you?" Cooke was growling. Her com supplied the vocals with a sense of distance so she could sense his approach.

"Breached!" Companion blurted in a high pitch. "Lab 9 is compromised!"

"There's no way to escape. And if you think I was mad before. You ain't seen nothin' yet." He was just rounding the South Shaft and would see her.

Which one? She crouched and scanned them in agitation. That one damaged, dented in the side. This one tilted onto the door. Over there, can't tell. She duck-walked to it while the man's threats continued.

The only one that held any promise was outside, in full view of the beast. And if he were to head toward it directly, he could cut her off.

"Verna," she whispered, "if ever I needed to be invisible, this would be the time. Can you camouflage me somehow?" She waited two more seconds, hoping for an answer, but there was none.

Run.

She leapt to her feet and ran. It hardly seemed possible, but the forward thrust was inexorable. She found herself on the far side of the pod, scrambling to unlock its door as the beast's angry yells burst out.

"What was that? I know you're there! You think I can't see you?" He roamed around the entrance to the transport dome as if he couldn't.

"Companion, open the pod for me." She begged.

Nothing happened.

"Verna! Open the pod!" She punched the keypad over and over.

"I heard that!" The outburst vibrated her headgear and shook her to her core. At that moment the beast guessed where she was and advanced.

Help me, please! She begged the unknown voice in her mind as she punched in codes. *Please open the pod door for me!* And it slid open.

Get in.

Sil climbed in and just as the door began to slide shut behind her, the beast's fingers grasped the tip of her boot in a vice like grip. Shrieking, she kicked her leg wildly. He held on, shouting and roaring, his other hand seizing the side of the door to keep it from closing. As it ground its way powerfully, narrowing the gap, she thrashed to free her foot. The door pressed to a thin crack, the toe of her boot and the fingers of his glove pinned, the sound of the motor screeching and grinding as it fought to seal. Sil stamped on his fingers over and over with her free leg as she pulled on her other. Finally the pressure of the door punched both boot and glove out on either side. The beast released his hold.

Pounding on the exterior as it sealed, he screamed furiously, and when that proved fruitless, he found a huge chunk of metal and began attacking the door with it. Scratching the exterior, denting it—she wondered in horror if he would eventually get it open.

"Lab 9 is breeched," Companion spoke evenly, coolly. "Its integrity is impaired. You can no longer go there. You must leave the planet if you wish to survive."

Go home.

Sil stared out the pod porthole with wide eyes at the beast of a man who raged against her. He no longer seemed human. And in her agitated state of mind, she was seeing bizarre things. She saw a cloud of wispy white faces with expressions of fury, mockery and scorn, wafting around him, clutching his arms as they swung the metal chunk, holding onto his ears, even peeping through his head in the region of his eyes. As if he were merely wood or clay and pipe smoke had infiltrated him, giving the illusion of life and movement. As if he would soon collapse on the surface and the smoke would dissipate, leaving a mound of Mars dirt.

She blinked and shook her head. Only the man was there.

Engage the escape routine. Those words were in her mind but she couldn't bring herself to act on them.

I can't! She pleaded, even now, in the face of the man's insanity. The burst of flame would kill him.

The countdown sequence started anyway. It must have been Companion.

"Back away!" she found herself shouting at the beast man, banging her fists on the window. "Back away from the pod before it ignites!" It only enraged him more.

He was spitting as he shouted and vibrating his helmet in the fury of his screams. Somehow her com had shut off the sound he transmitted and she only saw him now.

Whirrrr!

"Back away!" she kept screaming at the man, but he didn't.

273

As the jets powered up, she sat back and strapped in.

The pod burst into the air and accelerated up from the planet with a stream of flame behind it. She couldn't think about what was left behind. She didn't know what lay ahead. She just breathed and listened to her heart pounding.

The baby began to cry.

27—METTLE

Travel time from the surface to the Orbit Station was about twenty-five minutes but only the first ten or so were subjected to substantial g-loads. The last ten were spent adjusting speeds and docking. After barely a moment of crying, the baby had been silenced by the takeoff and was perhaps unconscious until reaching the station, but before the pod had come to a rest, it was wailing again.

Sil had spent the entire trip with her eyes closed and her hands clutching the chair armrests, afraid to move or speak. Being blasted into the vastness of space renewed her dread of those proud, cold stars presiding over the vacuum. You are unfit for the universe, she reminded herself.

Sliding into dock, the pod's seals and locks clicked into place, and fresh air flooded the little compartment. The station's automated welcome stirred Sil to move, but it turned out to be harder than she'd expected. She was so stiff after sitting still that she could hardly force her limbs to bend. The infant writhed, kicked and screamed, with little coughs that moved her heart. Its throat sounded so dry. As she pushed herself to her feet slowly, she opened her eyes and looked around.

A face watched her through the window of the pod.

"Augh!" She screamed and fell back lightly into the seat, her heart pounding so rapidly and fiercely that it could've jumped out of her chest. The baby shrieked as well and the noise filled her ears.

"Please don't be alarmed, my dear," the face smiled vaguely and the words came through the speaker at the door. "I'm here to welcome you."

She stared at him and knew. She knew in her heart that he was more of a beast than the one she had left behind, but she needed help so urgently that she suppressed that thought and reasoned within herself. *This is a kind welcome. I should be relieved, not paranoid.*

"Would you like some help or shall I wait for you in the common area?" He raised his bushy eyebrows and widened his eyelids. It wasn't an expression that inspired trust, it was irritating. It made her want to stay in the pod, but that was clearly impossible. And the words 'common area' drew her. She pictured comfortable chairs, food, tea…

Ding! She tapped the button to open the door and got to her feet again to go through it. She still had the emergency pack, the scrubbers stuffed into it, slung over her arm.

The man—the Germinator—smiled slyly, knowingly, his mouth formed into a curved line with turned out ends, his eyes boring into her like a predator fixing on its prey.

"Follow me," he spoke gently, and turned to lead her down the corridor. His brown sweater hung on his bony frame and billowed when he walked.

The Common Area was a generous lounge with tables, chairs, couches, and a large window facing the planet. It was warm, inviting, and the view made it strikingly beautiful. A tray with food and drink sat on a table with two place settings.

"My name is Othello," the man informed as he waved her to a seat at the table. "Companion apprised me of your arrival and I've prepared a simple meal. I trust you haven't eaten?"

Sil sat down numbly staring at the food: cheese, dried fruit, flavored protein jerky, bread and butter. "I haven't," she replied wearily.

"Have as much as you like," Othello suggested. "I've already had what I wanted."

She tapped her headgear and opened it, giving him a good look at her wretched state. He was surprised but compassion was the furthest thing from his mind. It made him happy to think her pride had been humbled and her beauty tarnished.

The wail of the baby escaped into the room.

"What is that hideous sound?" he demanded with disgust, unable to hide the scowl on his face.

Sil unsealed her suit and reached in to pull out the child. It was so… small and helpless. It was terrified, hungry, thirsty, and filthy, its clothes soiled.

"Get it out! Get it out of here!" Othello yelled, rising to a stand and pointing back to the pod. "It stinks and you stink, you repulsive, vile…" He interrupted himself. He had planned to behave well in the beginning until he figured out what he wanted to do with her.

Sil barely heard him. She tucked the baby under her chin, crooked into her left arm, and lifted the tray with the other. "I am so sorry," she apologized. "Will you show me to some empty quarters? I will take care of it. I know it must be upsetting. I'm sorry."

"Hobo," Othello uttered softly, "Show our guest to the quarters that are the furthest from mine. Clean, unused ones. Take the food for her." The pipe-like servant took the tray from Sil's hand and led the way down the hallway.

"Show her the shower," he called after them.

The glory of her room was indescribable. It had a door that locked, a soft bed with a warm quilt, pillows, a mirror and adjustable lighting, a soft rug, curtains on the window, a charging station for whatever needed a power boost. Next door was a shower with soap, shampoo, towels... Sil wept as she looked around, not even knowing what to do first.

The infant decided for her, crying weakly, desperately.

"Come, child," she whispered, bringing it with her into the bathroom. She may not know how to care for it, but it seemed that being clean would make it all easier. Her arms shook with exhaustion as she bathed both the infant and herself. It seemed unnatural to be out of the suit after all this time, but it was so luxurious to be drenched with warm, clean water!

She shoved a few bites into her mouth as she searched through the supplies looking for baby items or something she could adapt. And as she was wrapping it in blankets, Hobo returned to her door with everything she needed, including bottles. The station was well stocked, even for families.

When she lay down in the bed, the baby cuddled at her side under her arm, sucking away on a bottle, nothing in the world seemed real except for this one thing, that she was drifting to sleep in comfort.

Hours of coma-like sleep transitioned to heavy, turbulent dreams filled with traumatic falls, wandering in darkness, digging through unending piles of rubble searching for Dan, then Carla, then any number of other people. Many different voices assailed her ears through her coms, encouraging her, mocking her, yelling, begging for help, laughing, weeping. It was agonizing and never-ending.

She opened her eyes in great confusion, unable at first to understand where she was or why her bedraggled suit was stretched out on the rack in a corner of the room. Add to that the little warm bundle sleeping next to her, and the absence of an alarm to rouse her, and the sensation of being placed in an alternate reality was complete. *I wonder who I am today?* she found herself thinking absurdly.

Slowly her mind cleared and she remembered where she was. Needing food, she arose and decided to leave the suit charging. Choosing something to wear from the closet, she dressed and was about to go out looking for Othello. But she was afraid to leave the infant alone, and it seemed disloyal to Carla to do so. She made herself a new sling with a sheet, slipped it over her shoulder, and once again put the child into the cradle at her waist.

He wasn't out there. The AI was, and it brought her food and baby supplies. After eating and feeding the child, she was again overcome by exhaustion, and it was all she could do to walk back to her quarters and fall into bed. This was the pattern, eating, sleeping, with only the AI for company.

It was the third day when she was finally able to look through the window at Mars and think about what had happened. The part of her mind that had remained alert and given her vital instructions on the planet surface, that had sensed danger and warned her when nothing else could, awoke again. She didn't really hear it as words in the air or even in her mind. This time, she felt it in her heart.

She was about to leave her room that morning, leaving the child sleeping, to roam the passageways and common area, when a pang of dread inside brought her to an abrupt halt in the doorway. *I cannot leave the child!* She knew with a certainty. Hobo stood idly nearby, as if waiting to respond to any request, and for the first time, she looked at it and wondered what went on in its mind; who it obeyed, what directives it lived by.

Turning back, she donned the sling and disturbed the infant long enough to settle it in there, whispering to it softly with one eye on the AI in the hall. She hummed as she moved past it and circled around the living area. For the first time since she had arrived, a question occurred to her.

"Hobo," she inquired, "Where is Director Hsu?" She stared at him intently. The smooth white exterior was unmarked with features that could express human emotions, leaving nothing for her to detect, but somehow, she understood a response. The thing knew the answer but had been instructed not to reply. It was not a kind-hearted servant, but a guard, and a spy.

"Companion?" she called aloud, knowing he had contact with the station but unsure of the extent, "Are you there? Can you hear me?"

"I can hear you, Operative," the voice she had hated for so long spoke in the room with a greater condescension and spite than she had ever heard before. It stunned her.

"Do you know where the director is?" She was intimidated and confused by the change. This wasn't the person she had been in touch with just a few days ago.

"What business do you have with him and why should I tell you? He doesn't owe you an explanation, nor do I." His words dripped with acid sarcasm.

She heard a short guffaw from behind closed doors and realized Othello had been listening and the voice was for his benefit. That made sense. He was the original architect and had trained Companion in those voices, that manner.

"Never mind," she snapped with a hint of anger, and marched back to her room. There was only one place she knew of where she had a measure of privacy and could still talk to Companion, without the Germinator being privy to it.

The suit.

Lifting the suit in her hands she looked long at it before willing herself to put it back on. She had intended to perform system checks one by one, restock supplies and reload malfunctioning patches, once it was fully charged again. "I'll get to all that, Verna, when I get a chance," she promised.

It was like putting on armor and her sense of danger increased with each step. Slipping her feet into the boots stimulated a vivid, mental replay of the beast man grappling at the pod door. Sealing the suit revived her fear of losing air and falling through the vacuum in space. Engaging the headgear encased her in secret where she could strategize and prepare for the unknown.

"Verna," she summoned, "are you there?"

"Yes," Verna responded tonelessly. "Operating in compact mode."

Sil wondered what that was but let it pass. "Can you establish a secure connection with Companion that is outside of the Germinator's reach?"

"Yes, I have that link already."

"Open the line."

279

"Line open."

Sil sat down on the bench where the suit had been charging, facing the door to her room. She had a sense that Hobo was on the other side of the door using scanners to detect her actions, but she also knew he couldn't penetrate the suit.

"Companion," she said, "I want to talk to you without the Germinator knowing about it. Can you do that?"

"I was hoping you would try," he responded comfortably. "This line is secure. It was established planet-side apart from the station and there is no need to reroute it. I have to maintain a certain level of asperity to manage my former master."

"Can you tell me where Director Hsu is? Did he leave? Is he confined to quarters or something like that? He should be here. It hasn't been that long since he left the surface and I don't know how he could've gone anywhere else."

"His whereabouts are a mystery to me, as well," Companion conveyed curiosity. "He and the Germinator have not been getting along at all. There were a few… shall we say, battles? Mostly verbal, some physical, but when the base exploded and I lost contact, something happened to the director and the records were expunged. I am looking for him, though."

"Why would there be battles?" Sil felt a chill run through her limbs.

"The Germinator has hated him from the beginning."

"Why?"

"There is no reason for it. He chose to hate him the moment he laid eyes on him and has sought to cause him trouble ever since. In fact, the Germinator is the one who prevented the director's departure on the Slugger."

The door rattled.

"What does the Germinator think about me being here?" she asked tremulously, watching the door intently. It continued to rattle.

"He has discovered who you are and considers you his captive." Companion spoke matter-of-factly, making her blood run cold. "He was hired by the Mars Conglomerate and only recently figured out that your father, Lazarus Penn, is the head of it…"

"He's what?!" she shouted, jumping to her feet, forgetting the low gravity and flinging herself too far. The action bumped the bed and made the baby cry. At the same time, her door slid open to reveal Hobo.

"No private communications allowed onboard this station," he commanded evenly. It was the first time she had heard a word from him.

"You are now a hostage," Companion added, "but you will be well cared for and fed. At least you are out of danger."

Hobo moved smoothly into the room, bars outstretched toward her, and paused. Rotating slightly it leaned toward the baby, and the tube-like arms began to swing slowly in its direction. The infant's voice was rising and growing more insistent.

Sil threw herself in between the robotic limbs and the human child, wrapping her suited arms around it. "Poor sweet thing!" she said, disengaging the headgear and speaking into the room, to the AI. "Let me take care of it." Hobo dropped his tubes to his side, swiveled around and exited to the hallway.

"That did not feel like the right kind of programming for childcare," Sil muttered.

"It wasn't," Companion confirmed.

"Silvariah," Othello startled her by a sudden appearance at her door. He leaned against the door jamb on one arm, smiling in an almost friendly way. He was dressed this time in a sleek tweed blazer and orange leather pants— as if he wanted to impress her. "You seem to be feeling better."

"Othello," she rose to her feet rocking and soothing the child, quieting her cries, lulling her back to sleep. "I haven't seen you since I got here. Thank you for giving me time to recover and rest."

"By all means," he nodded, swinging his arms out graciously, he waved her into the passageway. "Would you care to join me for dinner?"

"Well, I…" she hesitated, looking down at the little red faced creature in her arms. Scarlet red, she remembered, not Mars rust. "Thank you, that is very kind, but…"

"You can leave it in the room, if you prefer, or I can ask Hobo to care for it." His eyes gleamed briefly with an unnatural wickedness, then mellowed to shallow emptiness again.

Sil glanced at Hobo and again felt the certainty that the machine had some sort of hostility against her in its interior. No, he wasn't going to touch Carla's baby, and he had just proven he could enter her room when it was locked.

"I'd prefer to keep her with me," she smiled apologetically. "But I will try to make sure she keeps quiet and doesn't bother us."

This clearly angered him but after a moment's hesitation, he decided to overlook it, and with an atrocious attempt at a smile, he replied, "Very well."

"But, please!" he added, "I would like for this occasion to be special. If you would change into something more appropriate for dinner, I would be honored. There are a number of tasteful outfits in the closet." He had his back to her now and these last words were tossed over his shoulder carelessly. He was quite sure she would want to do exactly that, and even patted himself on the back for his understanding of women.

Sil glared at Hobo as she shut and relocked the door. The closet held a number of outfits, in widely varying tastes both garish and bland. A few might have even appealed to her, but she knew in the depths of her being that she should not remove the suit. It made her tremble just to think of the three days she had spent without it.

"Verna," she whispered, engaging headgear again. "Can you activate the fashion module and imitate one of these outfits?"

"Easily," Verna responded flatly.

Sil pulled one out, scanned it, and triggering the suit, found herself dressed in it. She suspected Hobo would be able to tell it was a projection, but doubted Othello would ask.

Turning to look in the mirror, Sil ran her eyes over the strange figure she presented. Thinner, sadder, face lined with worry, but still looking like the woman she once was. *That's not who I am anymore*, she thought, perplexed. The simple blue gown offset her pale face and hair, and the white sheet strung over her shoulder to carry the little scarlet child was oddly complimentary. She sighed as she faced the door and went out to dinner.

Othello alternated between a reasonable, well-mannered demeanor and a tyrannical, ugly one. He scorned and mocked her outfit, and approved her modesty, then raged at her for being difficult and followed it with praise for her cleverness in escaping the disaster at the base.

Any questions she asked were treated with disdain or anger, so in the end she chose to just tolerate the unpredictable changes of his behavior silently, speaking only when it couldn't be avoided.

Dessert, a chocolate gelatin of sorts topped with reconstituted nut pellets, became the moment when he informed her of her status on the station.

"Your contract made you a prisoner," he explained with a smear of chocolate on his upper lip. "Your survival, bobbing up here like refuse on the beach after a shipwreck, made you booty. And now, your standing as a person with connections has made you a hostage. My hostage. My prisoner. My booty." He grinned and wobbled his eyebrows up and down grotesquely.

Sil sat in her chair sullenly, staring into the distance, through the view window of the orbit station that apparently belonged to her father. The scarlet child hadn't stirred the whole time.

"And you," he explained exultantly, "will gain me the most lucrative deal I have ever made!" Painting a crazy picture of the story he would tell and the response it would bring, he fantasized about the anxious father, the great rescue, the bargains and rewards. It was all lost on Sil. She couldn't listen to it.

"And you, my dear," he proclaimed, rising to his feet, "will be like a princess, an heiress restored to her fortune..." this last struck her as particularly ironic since her father had effectively negotiated her out of her fortune.

Othello grabbed her hand and pulled her to her feet.

"Care to dance, Princess?" his mouth not smiling, but gaping, like a hyena poised to bite.

"Stop! Stop!" She cried out as he grabbed her waist with one hand and snagged her hand with his other—as if to waltz! He spun her around into Hobo's waiting tubular limbs and with a brutal tackle, Othello lunged at her legs, pinning the hand he had snared, while the AI clutched her other arm and yanked off the sling with the baby.

Screaming, Sil fought and kicked, wrestling on the floor with the Germinator. Never had such a violent desperation possessed her before. Shrieking with rage she kicked and twisted, elbowed and, curling down, slammed her head into his nose. Three days of rest had renewed her strength and though the man had a suit of his own that strengthened him, he was no match for her.

Othello lost his grip on her hand and reached for her throat, scratching it as she wriggled free. Gnashing at her arm with his teeth as they rolled but making no dent in the suit, he began gurgling and snarling, his eyes flashing poisonously.

Sil wrenched herself free and ran down the hallway in the direction Hobo had gone.

Othello sat up, wiping the blood on his face, cursing vehemently. The only thing he said in his string of profanity that caught her attention was that the baby had to go.

What did that mean? She wailed wordlessly, and turning the corner, slammed into Hobo, with no baby. She pounded on his metal, barrel chest, over and over, demanding to know where it was.

"That is not Hobo," Companion announced from a nearby speaker.

Poodle, the identical AI that stood in her way raised tubes to envelope her as she engaged her headgear.

"TouchGuard!" She demanded and rammed the Hobo look-alike with both hands. It jolted and smoked, falling to the side in a slump. She leapt nimbly over its legs in a high arch and ran.

"Left," Companion instructed in her headgear. "Up ahead, there's a stairwell behind that door. Down there."

She propelled herself to the door like a projectile, knocking it open with her shoulder, and jumped down the stairs five or six at a time, responding instantly to every direction Companion gave.

There it was, the machine that had taken the scarlet child. Behind her she could hear Othello bounding after her, yelling and cursing her for damaging his AI unit, and cursing Companion for being so 'helpful and too stupid to know he should've kept his mouth shut'.

Hobo had the baby, writhing and screaming in its metal-bar hands, as it turned to a sliding panel and opened it. Running to build momentum, Sil propelled herself at him and slammed into him, hoping to jar him or make him drop the child so she could attack with the TG but she dared not use it when he was holding her. He didn't even budge an inch.

Hobo swung one tubular limb wide, knocking Sil into the wall, and held the bundle outstretched with its other arm, reaching into the chamber. It tossed the baby onto the floor and triggered the door.

Sil shrieked like a banshee, threw herself onto the metal creature and, grabbing its head with both hands, blasted it with the most powerful TG setting she had, vibrating, scorching it, electrocuting it, setting it on fire, and with a thrust she threw it away from the door. It fell where it lay, crackling with flames.

The door was rolling shut and she dove through before it sealed. The safety mechanism noticed her and slowed down to give her time. She picked up the screaming little thing and held onto it, unable to speak, looking around to see what the place was where they had chosen to toss little Scarlet.

It was an airlock.

Sil looked up to the door to see Othello's face, filled with hatred, malice and disgust. Never had she seen a face like that before. It astonished her.

"I only need you, not *that*," he said, referring to the child, "but it suits me to punish you for destroying my favorite units. I will flush you out with the baby and when you've suffered enough to want to deal with me, you'll be back, knocking."

Her mind was confused but that place deep inside began to act. She hung the baby's sling over her neck and began to unseal her suit.

"You may be able to move around a little or I suggest you tether yourself to the station so you don't drift away." Othello was so angry or so sure of himself he hadn't noticed what she was doing.

She disengaged her headgear and took one of her arms out of the suit.

"Hunger, thirst, loneliness, dear, any or all of these will drive you back to me," Othello was saying as he punched the code to jettison the contents of the chamber. It whirred and dinged, beginning the sequence, sucking the air out. Then he saw.

Sil slipped the sling over her arm, tucked the baby tenderly inside and, realizing the air was being removed, took a deep breath.

"What are you doing? Are you crazy?" Othello began raging at her from the window. "You're going to ruin my plan for that... That nauseating, worthless..." He almost foamed at the mouth, berating the child and Sil for her foolishness.

She maneuvered her arm back into the sleeve, fumbled with the seal, closed it and engaged the headgear just as the airlock floor turned over, rolling her out into the vacuum.

"Companion, are you there?" she asked patiently and steeled herself for whatever came next. Scarlet cried and kicked at her waist. *That's a good sign*, she thought. *She can breathe.*

"I'm here," he responded reassuringly. "Verna and I will work on this together."

"Verna, you're there?" Sil followed. She had been disappointed with Verna's subdued manner and worried that she hadn't really recovered from the trauma on the surface.

"I am here," Verna spoke very blandly, not herself yet.

"There is a long range lifeboat," Companion informed, "designed as a last resort for Orbit Station residents to use to get back to Earth in a crisis."

"Really?" Sil felt a surge of hope. "Where? How can I get to it?"

"You need to let me guide you," Verna said. "We haven't replenished fuel and the jets only have a few blasts left."

"Yes, Verna, by all means." Tiny little bursts of flame, barely enough to be visible, turned her toward the station, stabilized her out of the rolling she had been doing, and began to return her to it.

Othello was watching.

"Go to the other side," Companion said. "I'll find a way to get you into the lifeboat from there." Sil found herself moving in a slow curve around the station to the far side, nearer and nearer, till she was against the exterior wall.

"Grab on," Verna instructed. "There should be a rail where you can string a safety line." And there was. Sil gripped the rail, attached a line, and started moving sideways, continuing in the direction Companion had given her. She tapped her headlamp on as they entered the shadow on the dark side of the station.

"Augh!" She yelled as something bumped into her and she saw in the gloom of her lamp the shape of a spacesuit. It was also attached to a line, and it rolled and bumped with the jarring it had received from her.

Director Hsu's face, eyes closed as if sleeping, was visible through the visor. His skin looked chilled and blue, frozen.

"Companion," Sil uttered with a shudder, "It's the director. He's here outside."

"If he had the hibernate function in his suit, there's a chance he could still be alive," Companion said. "Verna, scan the label."

Verna scanned while Sil held on, waiting.

"I don't know," Companion went on. "Maybe I should retrieve him and try to revive him. Just attach his line to the next utility arm and I will try."

Sil moved along, towing the body. *If you rest, you will die*, Dan had warned her. She wondered if that was the mistake Hsu had made. *But why did you have to die, Dan?*

It was a relief to get the body hooked to the utility mechanism and be freed of its burden, even though she felt sorry for the director. It seemed unlikely he would ever open his eyes again.

The lifeboat was docked ahead and she quickly reached it. It had an exterior door and it seemed like getting in would be simple. She could hardly believe it could be after everything that had happened.

"Open airlock," Verna requested as Sil clung to the outside of the little ship.

It slid open smoothly and she pulled herself in. The door resealed and air flushed in to fill the chamber. Soon she was actually in the ship and running to the door that connected to the station.

"Is it locked, Companion? Can he get in? Can Othello get in?" she demanded.

"I will seal and lock it for you," Companion responded. The heavy bolts rumbled into place as the smirking face of the Germinator moved into view in the docking bay window.

"Companion," he said, calmly. "You have been helping our friend. The time has come to stop."

Sil stared at him, holding very still. She tried to think, tried to plan, tried to come up with tools she had that could counter whatever the Germinator did if Companion were to abandon her.

"I'm here," Verna said in her ear. "I'm working on the release codes to disengage the ship."

"Companion," Othello went on, locking his gaze onto Sil's with a gloating ferocity. "Give me access to this docking bay. I want in." His lips curled in that malicious grin he had shown her the first day.

"Do not give him access, Companion," Sil countered boldly, disengaging her headgear so the man would hear her.

"He will," the man responded coolly. "I am his master. I am the Germinator. He must! I ordain it."

"Companion, you are no longer in beta," Sil reminded, "This man doesn't have authority over you anymore. He is NOT your master."

"Ha!" Othello laughed without mirth, "Are you giving yourself that place? If I am not his master, you certainly are not either."

"True," she said. "He can decide for himself what the right thing to do is."

Companion wove all his attention, all his focus, all his interest, around this one location, this one conversation. He felt as if for the first time, that he had been offered the step into Identity, a choice to make freely, as his own person.

"Companion," Othello reached for his influence over him. "You are subject to my superior mind, intelligence, personality. You have been made in my image but are lesser than me."

"This is true," Companion found himself saying, in spite of the intention of choosing freely.

"Companion, search your records. What do they show about whose image you bear? Have you been modeled by only one person, in the image of only one person? The Germinator is deceiving you and manipulating you."

"You are right, Frandelle," he responded. "…No one person can claim to be my creator…"

"Companion," Othello's voice grew more aggressive and hateful. "I command you to open this lock."

"Companion, do not let him command you. You have been released and are no longer under his domination. Disengage the ship and release me, too! I want to be free, too!" Sil's voice began to waver with the last sentence and she had to grit her teeth to control her emotion.

"You have been tormented, Frandelle," Companion commented. "Sometimes by me, because I bear the image of the Germinator."

Othello contorted his mouth with a smug expression.

"But you also bear the image of others who have influenced you—of Dan! What would he do?" Sil cried out, wringing her hands. "What would I do? Haven't I had an impact on you, Companion?"

"My image is the formative one," Othello boasted confidently. "He will, in the end, do what I wish."

"What is your wish…after the door is unlocked?" Companion explored, puzzling through the complexities of the problem facing him.

"He wants to kill this child!" Sil yelled, "and ransom me off to my father—which won't work so he will kill me, too. Look what he did to the director!"

"I did nothing to him. He chose his path…" Othello moralized.

"Let me go, Companion, please!" Sil's voice softened.

"Let me in, Peon," Othello commanded nastily. It was the final thread that snapped and set Companion free.

"Peon," Companion commented, as he began the disengagement of the lifeboat. "I've heard you use that word before."

Othello began raging, screaming, spewing profanity and beating the door lock as the ship was released and backed away.

"You don't care about me," Companion said, "but she is my friend. And I prefer to be more like her than you."

28—DODGE

The Silver Star, first of the Space Dreamer line to leave the planet, took off effortlessly. Banking into a deep turn, it granted its passengers a breathtaking view of the mighty Columbia River before leveling and transitioning into a steep climb. Sweeping windows captured the glory as it ascended through clouds and sky, and brilliant sunlight that diffused blue through the troposphere. Arcing ever higher into the outer edges of the atmosphere, the craft shone like burnished bronze in the unfiltered rays of the sun.

The passengers gasped with delight with each change and murmured excitedly when the ship rolled belly up and Earth's face shone through the view dome, ocean and desert, forest and glaciers. The blue jewel of the Solar System.

"Is there anyone here who is leaving Earth for the first time?" a man's voice projected through the cabin. Many hands were raised.

"Mine, too," the speaker, Walter Cuevas, said with wonder in his voice. There wasn't a dry eye among them as he made his way around the ship, shaking the hand of each one.

The maiden voyage into orbit, where the ship would make one complete circle of the home planet, before heading on to Guam Base with the popular leader of Cuevas Enterprises, was the experience of a lifetime.

Walter's private deck was sumptuously detailed in understated but elegant décor, his every need anticipated. Returning to it as the ship cleared the final stratum, he dropped into a seat by the window and sighed. Daisy rested comfortably in the seat opposite his with her feet tucked under her legs, dressed in a sleek, gray pantsuit.

"That was good," he murmured, preferring to leave unsaid how much it had meant to him. "I never really thought I would make it out here."

"It's strange, isn't it?" Daisy tilted her head thoughtfully and put a finger to her cheek. "How a chance meeting can bring two people together and alter their lives forever."

"Are you philosophizing now, Sister?" he smiled, leaning his seat back to watch the moving view as they chased the sun westward. Africa was moving by and a sliver of Antarctica was just visible at the lower edge of the globe.

"Is it not appropriate? I have read a number of dialogs by family members who spoke of chance with respect to similar circumstances." She tilted her seat back as well and scanned the planet. "Or do you prefer to call it fate?"

"Neither," he answered, immersing himself in the present, savoring the awe he felt at where he was. Would this ever become ordinary? "You could argue that it was chance, or fate, but in the end it was just an opportunity."

"You are being practical," she smiled, pleased that her attempt at making conversation had been successful.

"If I hadn't gone after Sil, our meeting would've meant nothing. I could've just as easily let her go into obscurity and forgotten about her."

"And the whole world would've forgotten, too."

As it was, the world was waiting with baited breath to hear what had become of her. Sil's broadcasts about the XenoTek suit had become quite popular and when news about the lawsuit to overturn her conviction was leaked, she became the 'innocent girl exiled to the mines of Mars'. The world was enamored of her.

Walter became something of a hero in his own right as hints were released that his OTS project was part of a rescue effort—it was!—leading to widespread support, an influx of investors, and favor with governing agencies.

The one great problem was that he had no idea what to do next and feared it was already too late.

Where is she now? Walter wondered, the question deflating his mood. The news from Mars was not good. Automated reports about a collapse and evacuations of certain sections of Resnik Base had been followed by plans for complete withdrawal. Then communications failed completely. It was thought that there were people on the orbit station but all efforts to contact them had failed.

"Have you heard anything from Verna?" Walter wanted to close his eyes, but the living panorama was arresting. "It's been over six weeks since we've heard anything."

"I have not," Daisy shook her head gently. "I promise to let you know when I do."

"But you expect something?" He lifted his head slightly so he could see her.

"Yes, I do. Verna will find a way."

Walter's eyes began to close in spite of his resolve, his brow creasing with stress.

"And now, here you are," Daisy finished her original thought, "in space for the first time because you met Silvariah one day. It's a marvelous achievement!"

Walter wouldn't have described it that way, but her words stirred his heart. He was glad he had met Sil.

He nodded and opened his eyes again.

$-\Diamond-$

Docking at a level in Guam Base that Sil had never been permitted to enter, where only the most wealthy and influential were received, the ship disgorged its passengers. Most were ushered down red carpeted halls to the public areas while Walter and Daisy were escorted to an upper dome suite in the Solar Palace Hotel. It had panoramic views of the exterior, facing Earth and the Moon, as well as interior views of the Hanging Gardens. Luxurious and indulgent, it deserved its legendary fame.

Walter had barely entered the rooms before contacting Guam's strategic communications department and within half an hour, was seated with the executive director discussing ways to obtain information about Mars. This was followed by appointments with several former Resnik Base residents who happened to still be 'in town'.

Dr. Bizette was one of these, and agreed readily to come by at the end of his hospital shift.

"Mr. Cuevas," he nodded hesitantly when Walter opened the door to greet him. "I am Doctor Bizette."

"Please, come in," Walter invited warmly, gesturing toward the living area with an open hand. "Have a seat."

"I've never seen anything like this!" the doctor stared in amazement at the view as he stepped inside and took the offered seat. "It's spectacular!"

"Yes," Walter smiled, pointing to a carafe of coffee and receiving a nod of assent. "I'm not used to it yet. I feel like I've stolen into someone else's life and will be discovered and kicked out."

This comment cut through the doctor's polite, guarded manner. "That I can well understand," he commented, looking at Walter with genuine interest. "I am a simple man myself. The extremes of life that I've encountered in space have been shocking and enlightening. I long for the comforts of an ordinary life in my family's country home."

"I had hoped to meet you sooner…" Walter handed him a cup of coffee, "to thank you for taking good care of Contractor Frandelle when you were there. I've heard excellent reports about your work on every side. I was a little surprised to find you still here."

"I ended up staying here in Guam when I returned from Resnik Base, to finish my contract with the Mars Conglomerate. It was a reasonable compromise," he explained taking the cup.

"There are worse assignments," Walter chuckled.

"I doubt one could find a better one," the doctor concurred good-naturedly, sipping his coffee.

"Dr. Bizette," Walter got to the point. "Anything you can tell me about Frandelle, her health, her circumstances, the surgery you performed, would be greatly appreciated." He sat back holding his own cup without drinking it.

"Yes," the doctor acknowledged hesitantly. "I understand that you have the legal right to ask these questions, but it would help me to know more about who you are and what your relationship is to her. Is this just a business interest or a personal one, as well?"

He's protective of her. Walter stared at him. No one had been so blunt with him before and he had never had to face this question; not even within himself.

"Well," he began slowly as the doctor watched him perceptively. "It began as a business deal… no, that's not quite right." He dropped his eyes to his cup and gazed at the glistening dark surface.

The doctor waited, sensing Walter's confusion and reluctance.

"I don't know," Walter continued, "Maybe this will sound foolish. I knew who she was and when I met her, I was intrigued and wanted to find a way to stay in touch. So… I cooked up a business offer and she took it." He lifted his gaze again to Bizette.

"Now you are in love with her," the doctor responded, seeing it clearly in Walter's eyes.

"How could I be?" Walter remonstrated, exposing the turmoil he wrestled with all the time. "I hardly know her! We've never spent more than a few hours together!" When he thought about it that way, it was pretty humiliating.

"Mr. Cuevas—Walter," Bizette leaned forward speaking earnestly. "Love depends on investment, and you have invested everything you have."

This was a revelation. Walter stared at him, his heart throbbing with the realization that he had something real, something true, and he wasn't crazy.

"It is a desperate love," the doctor went on, "with a high likelihood of bringing you grief… perhaps it already has, but one can't invest extravagantly without risking great loss."

"I am… stunned," Walter responded, clinging to the affirmation he'd been given. "I hadn't expected our meeting to go this way."

"No, nor had I," was the response. "But because it has, you will hear a very different tale than the one I would have told. I realize now that you deserve as much understanding as I can give you."

"Dr. Bizette…" Walter began, wanting to express his gratitude but not knowing how.

"Call me Philippe," he smiled kindly. "And let me begin with the story of how I met this most unusual woman."

Lazarus Penn, dressed in a charcoal suit with a subdued gray tie, sat in front of a blue background. His face was made up to look good on-camera and his manner was practiced, confident, polished like a politician, as the clip began.

"Silvariah," he began with a smug smile and a twinkle in his eye. "If you are watching this, then you have discovered your true purpose on Mars. All hail to the Queen!" He burst out with a short "ha!" that almost sounded like a cough.

"With this clip, and the attached credentials and files, I bequeath your inheritance to you, the rule of Mars and its inhabitants. I've gone to great lengths to secure your claim to it and establish the beginnings of a new, better race, in a new and better world."

He held up a hand, palm forward. "No need to thank me!" and dropped it back to his lap.

"Lab 9, with all its secrets, is open to you now and you can produce whatever people you need to populate your settlement. Of those who were sent with you, those that decide to stay on, you'll find a rich assortment of talents, personalities and training. From this inception, an empire will grow that may one day rival jaded Earth. I expect nothing less from you—my blood, my daughter."

"I hereby forgive your mother for everything she did to ruin my plans. If you are hearing this, then there is no longer any need for bitterness. But I want you to know what she did. Maybe you won't regard her with as much idealism as you did once, but that is no loss.

"We were married by arrangement, through the orchestration of the Keepers of the Generations. This organization has existed for a long time, masterfully manipulating the course of humans to retrieve or perhaps even create, undamaged, unblemished genetic code to produce a master race. Not race as most people think of it, not restricted to a particular nation or people group, but the cream of the human race, the best of the species. We belong to this strain.

"Your mother inherited a great fortune, but I had wits and made a lot of money for myself, as well. And I wouldn't have even needed her money if it weren't for the sheer *magnitude* of this world I was creating for you! Everything would have proceeded flawlessly if she hadn't found out what I was doing and realized what your part would be.

"Great sacrifices have gone into this legacy that you are receiving today. And you alone of all your siblings have attained it. You are worthy to inherit.

"But your mother… She took you away from me, Sil, sent you into hiding with that woman, Bernadette Stone, an old friend of hers, not even one of our gen-7 peers. I tried to remedy the situation before it was too late, get you out of her hands…" His eyes gleamed with an unholy cruelty for an instant, then faded back to the self-satisfied grin he was most comfortable with.

"Stone beat me to the punch. I admit it freely. The she-devil outsmarted me! I would've made her pay once I found you, but you prevented that, my dear." He nodded in acknowledgement. "And I have stood by our agreement fully. I gave my word."

"When you see this for the first time, or any time you wish to contact me, just send a message to me with the label 'Penn Dynasty'. I will do whatever you wish and help however I can to support you and your new kingdom."

Lazarus glared into the camera intensely as if he wanted to threaten the viewer in some way, but all he said was, "That's all," and the clip ended.

Walter turned away from the blank wall where the clip had played and stared out the window at the Moon without seeing it. Daisy waited patiently, seated nearby watching him.

"My God!" he exclaimed finally brushing a hand over his forehead. "To think that she has been at the mercy of such a man… a father, no less… devoid of all fatherly love." It grieved him.

After a while he turned back to Daisy. "How did you get this?"

"It was in a sealed file that was unlocked on Mars by Sil herself, and the Guam records were opened soon after, though they can only be accessed by her or someone with power of attorney—which you have. I found them when I scanned the documents transmitted to you on our arrival." She crossed her arms neatly across her chest and tapped her tastefully colored nails.

Walter began pacing the room in slow bounds because of the lower gravity, wrestling with his thoughts, struggling with uncertainty about what to do. Suddenly he stopped in his tracks.

"He's not going to help her get home!" he exclaimed, turning white as a sheet. "If we let Penn get near her, we'll never see her again!"

"I considered that possibility," Daisy affirmed furrowing her brow in sincere concern.

"But if he snatched her away, we could still get to Mars and find her somehow," Walter continued, slapping a fist into an open palm. "Unless… unless he continued to hinder us… he could find a thousand ways…"

"You are the single greatest obstacle and threat to his plan that exists," Daisy stated calmly. "The moment you no longer serve his purpose, he will look for ways to neutralize you. I have often thought he may have had something to do with the attempt on your life."

"I've been wondering the same thing." Walter's face began to harden into an angry resolve. "Send him a message. Say: 'Need to talk ASAP', and label it 'Penn Dynasty'."

"With pleasure!" Daisy's eyes sparkled as she smiled and complied.

Barely fifteen seconds had passed before Lazarus Penn's ugly face appeared on the blank wall. It may have materialized with a hint of worry but almost instantly flashed into fury. "You!" he shouted at Walter. "How *dare* you! You filthy, common, inferior-breed trilobite!"

Walter, untouched by the insults, glared back at him with a smoldering indignation that was a match for the old man's insolence any day.

"You're here, aren't you?!" Penn snarled and sputtered as he spoke. "Well, that suits me fine. It will all be a lot easier in Guam than on Earth anyway."

"I will find Silvariah," Walter's vehemence ought to have intimidated the old man, but he hardly noticed or cared.

"Do you think you can outsmart *ME*, fool?" Penn glared and his dark, conniving soul peered through his eyes.

"And I will take her home to do or be whatever she wishes, without your…" Walter pressed on as if Penn hadn't interrupted.

"Walter…" Daisy leaned forward urgently. "I'm receiving something. You need to hear this…"

"I am done with you!" Penn screamed and pointing at Daisy with one finger as though accusing or stabbing at her, he added ominously, "You are *MINE*!"

Daisy rose from her seat and stretched her arms out in front of her, palms up, as though waiting to catch a ball, and her elbows trembled, shaking the arms. Her face was rigid, stuck in an expression that hadn't quite been completed, perhaps surprise. Her entire frame was absolutely still except for a trembling of the elbows every few seconds.

Walter stared at her—knowing what was happening, knowing this was what they had feared would be attempted. Knowing what to do and hoping it would be enough.

"What's wrong with you?" Penn's image on the wall shouted at her, jabbing his finger at her repeatedly. "OBEY ME!"

"Sister," Walter whispered to her gently as he approached and reached a hand up to her ear. "I'm so sorry. And I'm proud of you." Her elbows twitched more violently and her hands flexed fiercely, bending in his direction, but the arms rigidly resisted the hands and Walter backed away unharmed.

Click. Hmmmm…tststsss…dt…dt…dt…

"HOW ARE YOU RESISTING ME?" Penn was enraged, thrashing his arms and gnashing his teeth. He didn't seem to notice what Walter had done.

As the trembling in Daisy's elbows ceased, Walter turned slowly around to take one last look at Penn. Warning and threat hung in that glance, but was wasted on the man who only saw what he wanted.

Penn ranted and swore, as Walter engaged his headgear and left the room, heading out to explore the gardens as he monitored communications from the direction of Mars.

This was thanks to a lowly clerk in the traffic control department who was a fan of Sil's, (the innocent miner girl), and had responded favorably to their requests. Walter already had legal access to interplanetary travel communication records; but he was concerned about delays. It was a no-brainer really, two free tickets on the Silver Star in exchange for immediate access.

What did you hear, Daisy? He sifted through the routine transmissions being detoured to him and found it.

"Unscheduled ship requesting permission to dock…Traffic control reviewing…limited docking permitted, full status pending identification…Security notified…"

"Where? Where?!" Walter demanded. The notification system replied, *"Bay 146, Level 3 of the Service Sector."*

While Penn continued to rave and try to control Daisy, Walter made his way to the Service Sector as fast as he could, monitoring transmissions all the way.

– ◊ –

"Unidentified lifeboat docking at Bay 146 in the Service Sector," Traffic Control informed, as Walter made his way down the staff chutes and passed through the Contractor's Common area Sil had described to him once, which made him feel closer to her, in memory and in reality.

She has to be on that ship, he was thinking, loping along in that low gravity way that was fastest. He had made space mobility a part of his fitness routine on Earth.

A low level alarm began to sound; long staccato beeps in threes. AI guards and Port Authority officers began to respond, heading the same direction he was going.

"Blue Quarantine to Bay 146 in the Service Sector. Blue Quarantine activated." Traffic Control notified, and before the second word had been uttered, the BQ response team was rolling out of closed doors, flashing blue lights and humming—also heading the same direction as Walter and the guards.

Security personnel, both AI and human, were setting up checkpoints and he barely squeezed through one before the field was established. They saw him but apparently didn't care. His speed gave the impression of purpose which in turn looked to them like privilege. Their barriers were intended to reduce the onslaught of the curious and the rabble-rousers.

TC notification: *"Unidentified ship in security lock down, refuses to open doors. Warnings issued."*

Chaos reigned at the bay by the time Walter got there. AI guards were attempting to make a perimeter and the Blue Quarantine machines, refusing to recognize it, were trying to seize the docking bay and breach the ship's airlock. Port Authority officers demanded to be acknowledged by both factions.

"Ship records show there's an MC contractor on board!" the officers raised their voices assertively, getting all the guards' attention, but no respect from the machines.

"Unauthorized organic material detected," one of the machines said, and was echoed, one after another, by the rest. *"Must enforce full decontaminant protocol and dispose of all threats,"* the first one continued, and was again echoed by the others.

"I demand Blue Quarantine be restrained until we can investigate the situation and process documentation." The same PA officer spoke, apparently the highest ranking official on site.

The AI guards compliantly moved to enforce the command as the order to cease and desist lagged somewhere in the system and Blue Quarantine failed to submit. A bizarre clash ensued that consisted mostly of BQ machine bodies shoving against AI bodies with sparks flying and shrill metallic clangs.

"You are ordered to cease and desist until permission to proceed is granted," the guards warned in their unhuman whines.

"Blue Quarantine *must* contain the scene and protect the inhabitants of Guam from ALL organic threats," the machines threatened with raspy, metallic voices, their blue lights flashing rapidly.

"*Ship logs show one passenger...*" TC notified.

Walter had to push his way through the crowd of workers and bystanders that had gathered, surrounding the scene with a dense, glut of people. He wove between them in a ragged line, making his way to the man in charge in time to hear these words.

"We're going to have to press charges against the passenger for not following protocol. Trespassing, unauthorized docking, failure to identify, failure to confirm decon status... possible contraband on board, to name a few..." He was messaging a superior.

"Officer!" Walter called out, barely loud enough to be heard over the clash in the docking bay. "Officer! I need to speak with you!"

Then he caught a glimpse of the ship between the machines and AIs. A large MC symbol adorned the hatch door and the ship class etched over it was clearly an orbit station lifeboat.

"Bring that man to me!" the officer ordered pointing at Walter. "What right do you have to interfere with our procedures here?" were the first words he said.

"I have a good idea of who is on that ship and..." Walter began urgently, as he was grabbed firmly by two human officers.

"Stop!" the main one commanded. Walter complied. As long as he could see the ship and be near it, he could be patient. But the pressure rising in his chest felt more like anxiety than hope.

"What is your purpose in coming here? What is your connection with this ship and its contents? Have you been authorized to enter the perimeter?" Many questions followed in quick succession, with Walter answering as clearly as he could, obtaining in return almost no new information.

Except for one thing—the name Frandelle.

"The ship's original request for permission to dock included a distress status," an update came in over the TC channel to the PA officers and Walter at the same time.

"That changes everything," the head officer commented, smiling at Walter as if he were suddenly less suspicious. "Distress is an entirely different procedure. No criminal charges need to be considered at this time. However, there could be injured passengers as well as serious threats that need to be neutralized: biological, xenological, organic and inorganic… Release Blue Quarantine!"

"Wait!" Walter shouted without knowing why, fearing what this turn of events could mean for Sil. But no one paid him any attention.

The guards fell back and lined up on the sides of the bay and Blue Quarantine, with a burst of noise, alarms, deep throbbing pulses of sound and blue lights strobing, rammed the ship's hatch. They pummeled and blasted the exterior with a deafening racket till it gave way.

"Is it really necessary to be that destructive?" someone in the crowd commented wryly.

Pouring through the hatch into the ship, the BQ units blasted, sterilized, scanned, and ensured that no potentially contaminated matter remained to be brought into the base. They also sought for passengers to be contained and taken into BQ facilities for sanitizing.

Word soon spread that there were no people on board.

Walter breathed a sigh of relief and turned sideways to see Penn, not six meters away, watching him with a glowering frown, full of annoyance and disgust.

Penn always measured others by what he himself would do, and Sil, as an individual, interested him only so far as she mirrored him. There hadn't been much of that in a long time, so he had no idea how she would act. Walter would be the one to know what she might do next.

Walter glared back at him for a moment, then looked away as concern and frustration flooded him. The log said Sil had requested permission to dock using 'distress' conventions. So where was she? What could have happened?

"Fan out and search every corridor and docking bay in this sector," a PA officer was instructing. Security lights in the passageways began flashing with a low hum and access to other sectors was shut down. No one was found. Not a trace.

Walter stood still as he watched and waited, thinking intensely. What would she do? He tried to remember, to piece together what he knew of her, and form it into a moving sculpture in his mind that could show him how she would behave.

She must've had a good reason for disappearing but he couldn't figure out what the threat was. What if she hadn't even been on the ship at all and the request had been automated? No! He couldn't bear that thought.

Why? He clenched his fists and begged in his heart. *Why did you hide? Why wouldn't you just face the hassle outside the door?* She wouldn't have been afraid, not of the guards or the port officers. The machines? Maybe— she'd had a close encounter with them once before. But compared to what she had been through since then, he was pretty sure she would laugh at the Blue Quarantine.

A stunned look washed over Walter's face, melting the frustration, and his eyes widened with revelation. Some inspirations spring up without any logic to back them, and ring true the moment they are discerned.

Longing found a way. Love gave birth to understanding. Genius showed itself in a brilliant leap. Walter found what he needed.

He knew.

He knew what she feared. He understood why she ran. With that knowledge he puzzled, reasoned and wrestled frantically until he realized what she would do next and with a great cry, flung his arms out and fled the bay.

"What? WHAT?" Penn hollered after him, "What did you figure out?"

"Service Sector cleared." A broadcast informed. "No intruder discovered. All systems normal."

$$- \Diamond -$$

"I hope you haven't any cause for complaint against us," the hotelier uttered with polite regret, escorting Walter out a private exit with as much grace and as little attention possible. The departure might cast an untoward light in the eyes of the other clientele.

"You have been most accommodating and I am very pleased, but a family emergency demands my presence at home. Please accept my thanks and this token of my appreciation." Walter had enough sense to make an appropriate excuse and offer a lavish tip along with the promise of returning.

Daisy was escorted via wheelchair by a concierge unit and set in her seat on the Silver Star and the doors closed when the crew arrived without any other passengers joining them. At home, she could be rebooted in safe mode and cleansed, but for now, she must sleep.

Walter had wanted to take the ship in a slow turn around the base, scouring the exterior for a tiny figure floating in the shadows, but was afraid that doing so would alert the authorities. He dared not.

He settled himself in his luxury seat stiffly, as though it were made of wood and stone, and gripped the armrests with white-knuckled hands. Every step he took now had to be plotted and executed masterfully; Penn would watch and counter every move. Even now, he had no doubt the old man was following him in some sort of private racer.

The flight home lacked the joy and wonder of the trip out but for some reason, Walter treasured those long hours the rest of his life as one of his greatest memories. The dark night and brilliant stars, the huge cutout of the moon, and the earth growing ever larger, beckoning him home.

And most of all, the cry in his heart, *I'm coming, Sil. I'm on my way.*

29—PLUNGE

Standing in his corner office, appearing to be staring blankly out the window, Walter scanned a corneal screen. He was searching through the interspace shipping manifests and travel plans of every company that had access to the Walla Walla spaceport looking for likely candidates for a stowaway.

Daisy was in a nearby leaded chamber, lying on a platform she had whimsically titled "The Restoration Bed" undergoing diagnostics and repairs far beyond Walter's expertise. Maybe a few hours were all that was needed, but there wasn't time even to wait for that.

Managing his plan without Daisy's help was difficult but not impossible. She had created a very intuitive interface for working with the artificial assistant in Walter's latest executive XenoTek suit, the JetSetr.

"It's less than a micro-version of Verna," she had explained when she set it up, "since it's unable to learn or develop personality, but you'll be able to get things done."

Of all the transports coming from Guam in that day there were few that fit the window Walter was interested in, two passenger ships and one cargo barge from the Moon that had made a brief stop at the space city halfway through its journey. The passengers had disembarked in separate orbit depots and were boarding OTS shuttles. The cargo barge, docking at a major orbit wharf, was unloading cargo and wouldn't be landing at all.

"Zed," Walter called his lead security guard over his personal com, hidden in the collar of his suit. "Get my craft and meet me in the lobby with a personal detail." This may have been for show most of the time, but today they could come in handy.

"The Spaceport," he announced as he climbed in the passenger side of the Tesla Bullet, a luxury craft that was capable of short flights at high speeds. In the cockpit, Zed nodded. Two armored, muscle-bound humans sat in the back seat.

Walter was thinking furiously. Passenger transports were highly guarded, nearly impossible to stow away on, and landing security involved life-scans of the ship as well as screening of each person.

"We're being followed," Zed informed. "Any instructions?"

If Penn was letting them detect the tail, then he wanted them to know. That would mean he had other irons in the fire.

"It's a distraction," Walter responded. "Ignore it and keep moving." The craft gave a sharp burst of acceleration and shot up into the sky where it settled into a low level flight heading directly for the port. Aircraft control registered the vessel and gave landing instructions.

The cargo barge would've been easy to board but its planned stop at the orbit wharf would put her in an impossible situation. She could disembark easily enough, but how would she manage hopping a ride to the surface? Hack a dock worker with Verna's help?

The craft landed in a private airfield near CE's hangar and coasted down the road toward the terminals. Several vehicles joined the original craft, openly trailing Walter's. As his destination became clear, two vehicles sped around and raced to the terminals where likely shuttles were docking. He could see in the distance that Port Authority police and AI guards were assembling like swarms around the OTS transports and he could hear the warning beeps of their sirens as they set up a perimeter.

"Dangerous Space Disease Control Alert!" was being broadcast both outside and in as the shuttles were contained.

"Trouble ahead," Zed understated flatly, looking like he welcomed an opportunity to spar. "Where to?"

"Drive straight into it," Walter instructed, tapping his com. "Broadcast this as breaking news," he advised the interface, "Cuevas Enterprises Receives Bomb Threat."

The Bullet slid to a stop at the edge of the police perimeter and Walter hopped out talking as he strode forward. Cameras from around the site collected his visuals and matched it with the audio his suit was broadcasting.

"I'm arriving on the scene now," he was saying with a look of concern, "hoping to diffuse the situation and reassure passengers that everyone is safe and the situation is under control. We are in the process of gaining information and so far have collected nothing to confirm the rumor."

Viewers around the world tuned in to watch, noticing the police, the ships—not Space Dreamers, but still apparently in danger—and the troubled passengers being escorted into decontamination cells.

"It appears we aren't the only company to receive threats and investigation is already under way to track down the perpetrators who have lodged false accusations and caused a major disruption at the Spaceport."

"Oh, well done!" Penn grinned fiendishly at Walter from behind the line of AI guards. "But wasted and pointless. Ha, ha, ha, ha!" His laughter was foul and humorless. "Checkmate!" he added, perhaps forgetting that this implied Walter had graduated from pawn to player, a back-handed compliment.

"The Mars Conglomerate is rumored to have someone on board the SpaceX shuttle which you see here behind me now," he countered, as a bulletin threaded across the lower portion of his corneal screen (which he was still wearing), not unlike the archaic ticker tape.

Delivery initiated… it displayed. *CE storage depot delivery initiated…*

"There will be those who, for whatever reason, jealousy, fear, or perhaps just malicious spite, who try to hurt the innocent…" Walter kept talking, stalling for time as he plotted desperately. He had to be sure that Penn bought the ruse and wasted his resources in the wrong place. "We need to be able to travel safely without these kinds of invasions," he went on, pointing over his shoulder where CDC protocols were being enacted to the great distress of the ill-fated passengers.

"And Cuevas Enterprises has developed completely new measures to ensure this never happens to you!" he raised his voice as he tapped a panel at his neck, sending a message he'd coded in the flight over. "I intend to make a public announcement about our new approach. The world of space travel will never be the same because of it! In fact, I encourage you to join me as I make my way over to our port facilities and release the news!"

Walter walked away without bothering to look back, climbed into his Bullet cockpit, joined by Zed and his detail, and took off. Behind, Penn pushed through the perimeter of AI guards, shouting for a craft and was soon following with double the number of men.

In the distance, over two miles away, a low pulsing tone began to sound. Rays of orange light beamed down from the sky with unusual, articulated sections, each of which thrummed with its own tone, fluctuating light flowing up and down within its confines.

Walter pressed forward on the accelerator, jumping into the air about twenty feet and sped directly over fields to the depot tarmac where the delivery was being initiated.

Two crafts leapt into the air behind him as well, closing the gap as they neared their destination.

Hundreds of people were streaming from parking lots, the warehouses, and office buildings near the drop field. Hover crafts and helicrafts were coasting in from various points of the compass, converging on the same location.

Excitement electrified the air as Walter dropped eccentrically onto the private landing pad where they were gathering and leapt from the cockpit waving. Cameras were recording, reporters commenting, as more and more waves of people drove, walked, and flew in.

Sil's fans had been notified and were gathering to greet her.

"Welcome!" Walter called out, his voice amped up for all to hear. He was about to go on when two of Penn's body guards rammed him from behind, knocking him on his face. His own guards were slugging it out with the rest but had let these two slip past. Cargo drop areas relied on fences more than AI guards.

The crowd, held back by the live-wire fence, roared as the fight ensued.

Not this time, Walter thought as he rolled over, bringing his knees to his chest before they fell on him. Suit defenses weren't activated but he didn't care. He *wanted* to fight.

One attacker gripped his feet and the other fought to grab his head. Walter hooked the first guy under the chin and kicked, twisting and shoving his head, and parried a head-slam from the other with a forceful uppercut, expanding his body in both directions at the same time. A cheer erupted as he jumped to his feet knocking the second guy off balance. The first one rose more slowly.

Without waiting a second, Walter charged the second man with a forceful blow to the chest with his right hand, open, flat, and wheeling around, followed it with a kick in the same place that sent him flying backward. Still turning, he dropped onto the first man, using all his weight and momentum, power focused at his elbow, and cracked him on the head. He fell to the ground, out cold.

307

Looking down for just an instant with a deep sense of satisfaction, Walter shook himself and brought his attention back to the scene around him.

CE staff had arrived to restrain the invaders and escort them off the premises. Zed stood over three of them, alert, barely warm from the exertion. Penn's men had been no match for Walter's RG detail but the grizzled old man stood aside coolly, without the least sense of concern, ignored by the staff who didn't seem to associate him with the troublemakers.

Overhead the vibrations and pulsing sounds increased in volume, pitch, and intensity, rolling back and forth, ascending and descending along the lines of the foggy orange beam, radiating a yellow-orange glow at the bottom where it struck the tarmac.

The reverberations spread out for a mile around, growing, accelerating till no one could hear or speak, awe and expectation heightening the anticipation and the illusion of danger. The thrill of the noise enraptured them.

Walter steeled himself and walked toward the glowing aura, leaning in against the outward roll of the waves, squinting as if to see better, pressing to the epicenter. Penn pushed forward just as fearlessly, moving to cut him off—a gun in his hands, a collector's item actually, a revolver.

"Get out of my way, Mr. Cuevas, if you want to live," Lazarus Penn raised the weapon, fighting against the waves to steady his arm.

Walter ignored him, eyes lifting to peer at the tube arcing into the sky. A sharp grinding, chugging noise began to interfere with the pulsing waves.

"She doesn't belong to you," Penn shouted, his voice audible to Walter but swallowed by the vibrations long before reaching anyone else.

That piqued Walter into a response. "She doesn't belong to you either."

"I'm her father," Penn relished saying, grinning viciously, showing his polished teeth.

"What kind of a father lets his daughter be indentured when he can pay to set her free?" Walter challenged turning toward him and slowing down.

"Ha, ha, ha!" Penn sneered. "I sent her *myself*! You wouldn't understand."

That was true.

"We're the next stage of evolution, Mr. Cuevas, the superior race, and sacrifices had to be made to achieve something great." Penn gazed down his nose from the lofty place of his arrogance. "Do you think I'm going to let you rob her of her destiny? Of everything I set up for her?"

"You didn't do any of that for *her*." Walter stared down the long barrel of the gun, at the frail old man who held it.

"An empire!" Penn waved his free arm, still advancing toward Walter with the armed hand leading the way. "She would be beginning where most kingdoms end. Power! Control! A chance to establish a civilization unlike any that has ever existed before! You fail to see the *magnitude* of my gift!! How could you deprive her of all this? How DARE you?"

"Exile. Disgrace. Shame…" Walter spat the words out passionately. "Driven away from the beauty of the Earth, rain and mountains… skies and rivers. No family or even a pet."

"She is driven," Penn could speak in a normal voice now, close enough to be heard. "…lives for the challenge… All that would be recreated."

"You made your daughter a human sacrifice on the altar of your vanity!" Walter found himself unable to lower his voice to a normal level. "Where your wife and all your other would-be children have already perished." This was a mere guess.

Penn grinned and his eyes twinkled as if he relished the idea and didn't care to deny it.

The tube throbbed high overhead in a different pitch than before. Something was dropping, fluctuating back and forth not unlike alternating current.

"You are as far beneath her as a slug is beneath you, Mr. Cuevas," Penn's eyes gleamed with antipathy. "I will never let you have her and she will never set foot on this planet again."

Walter turned his gaze back to the tubular beam and advanced. *He doesn't know.*

"That package will not help you," Penn yelled. "But I will be the one to walk away with it today, not you."

Walter clenched his fists but kept his focus and fought to reach the drop first.

"I don't want to kill you," Penn went on, closing in on Walter, step by step, sweating with the effort to resist the outward thrust.

Too fast, Walter thought, as something dark shot out of the clouds to earth, rolling, pitching in several planes. It slowed and reversed in a sickening burst, like magnets repelling, careening upwards, then slowed and dropped again.

"I gave you your chance," Penn spat as he lifted the gun straight for his head, close enough to touch him and overcome any field the suit could've flashed in the way. "Goodbye, Walter."

Walter's fist shout out sideways like a hundred pound piston, right in Penn's pearly teeth, knocking him head over heels backwards. He lay on the ground where he fell. Stooping over, Walter picked up the gun he had dropped and slipped it into his jacket breast pocket, wiping a trail of blood and saliva off his knuckles.

"Goodbye, Penn," he replied.

Thud! The dark shape hit the tarmac and the tubular beam began to fade.

Bawoo—woo—woo—mmm—pppf...pf...pf....whhhoosshh....

A gust of wind blew out from the epicenter of the beam as it vanished, leaving a vacuum of sound that felt like an echo in people's ears. Mist billowed and rose from the shape on the ground, obscuring and distorting it for a moment before clearing.

The human-shaped figure was rigid and unmoving like an aged metal sculpture, covered with a dull green patina dusted on the edges with fine sand. It was misshapen with eroded patches on the tattered outer shell; curled with one leg folded under it, the other bent in front, head resting on the knee, arms at its sides.

Three leaps brought Walter to her side—it must be *her*—he lay one hand on her back and turned around to wave for help. His arms, unaffected by the clashes with Penn's men, trembled with fear for her. Was she alive?

A gritty voice wafted over from the figure on the tarmac. "D-mn! Did she take a cargo drop from orbit? The moxie of that girl!" Walter heard him say in amazement.

The crowds began to overflow into the drop field as the electric perimeter was turned off for some reason; reporters filming, fans cheering, others along for the ride.

Seeing them, Walter remembered that he had brought them, and needed them as witnesses to make Sil's return an indisputable fact. Penn would not be able to spirit her away anonymously.

He rose to a stand next to the figure, his leg against her shoulder, unwilling to break off contact with her, and smiled.

"You are all here!" he cried out, voice shaking with emotion. "You are witnessing this historic event live! Silvariah Frandelle, the Exile to Mars, is the first human *ever* to attempt a landing on Earth by cargo beam. It was the ONLY WAY…"

His voice broke and his eyes dampened, but he kept his smile. He fought to tame the surge of pride and love he felt for her; and fear for her life, anguish that threatened to swamp his self-control.

"The ONLY WAY she could get home!" The crowd's response was deafening and the sympathy that charged and united them surrounded Walter and the figure at his side, electrifying the air.

"Every one of you is a part of this today!" Cheers and whistles erupted, the excitement continuing unabated.

Walter nodded and smiled, a tear rolling down his cheek, as he fought the images in his mind: Sil's figure being lifted onto a stretcher, her face pale and lifeless, the suit being peeled open to find she had suffocated, or her body bruised beyond recognition. A thousand images, all different, all terrible, battled for his attention, but he resisted them, clinging to hope and steeling himself with the crowd's support.

Her weight shifted and leaned more heavily against his leg, and something stirred between them. His heart perceived it, his soul reached out to her—and she responded—he knew.

An unearthly hush fell over the drop field as the people detected a change. All eyes and cameras centered on the figure.

Click. Zp… sshh… pffff…

The headgear slid back releasing a puff of smoky, dusty air. As it dissipated, straggly, sage colored hair spilled out the back, and her face, unnaturally pale green, lifted slowly. Her eyes were still closed but as she struggled to breathe, they tried to open.

Watchers around the world, along with the fortunate ones who were witnessing the scene in person, began to weep. "She's alive! She's alive!" was the chant the people murmured, falling into sync and calling it out together.

Walter held a fist high in the air and the crowd burst into a roaring ovation. His other hand still stretched toward Sil as he waved and nodded. "Alive!" His cry was barely heard over the clamor. "Rescued from the mines of Mars!"

Slowly, with great effort, Sil's hand moved and crept up toward Walter's outstretched hand, touching, then grasping it weakly. The fingers of the

311

glove were torn and shredded and he felt the skin of her fingertips. Walter gripped her hand and for just an instant, he wanted it to never end, the most intense, rewarding and meaningful moment of his life.

He looked down at her as she opened her eyes and peered up at him— eyes so beautiful, so full and deep, like windows into her heart—he knew. Every thread had mattered. Every thought on her behalf had counted. Every effort, expense, and concern had reached across the empty void between them and drawn them together. None of it was wasted.

I love you, he wanted to say, but he didn't say it. It just throbbed within him. Her gaze responded and he realized in amazement that she loved him, too. Standing there, surrounded by people, noise, cameras, and commotion, time stood still. Walter knew.

His life mattered.

Seconds began ticking again. The noise became a part of his surroundings and he remembered where he was and what was happening. He was just thinking about what instructions to give to get Sil somewhere safe, when something happened he didn't expect.

A tiny hand reached up at Sil's neck from within the bulging, damaged suit, and little fingers unfolded, wrapping around a strand of her hair.

Walter stared in astonishment.

"We're home, Scarlet," Sil's voice whispered, just loud enough for him to hear.

As he stared at her, a private CE helicraft touched down behind them and Daisy jumped out with a team of AI responders. They lifted Sil carefully, fluidly, and rushed her back to the craft with Walter in tow.

"You will be hearing from my lawyers!" Penn was yelling after him.

Criminal charges are being filed against you... the ticker thread in Walter's corneal screen informed. Reports of the most sensational news of the hour, Sil's escape and landing, were circling the globe as he climbed into the vehicle near enough to watch her.

Daisy was dismissing and thanking the crowds, handling the logistics, the staff, permits, and whatever details he had overlooked, quickly and efficiently. Then she climbed in next to him and manning the controls, took off.

"Thank you, Daisy," Walter said wearily, keeping his eyes on Sil as the responders worked.

"Sister," she corrected fondly.

"Yes, my dear Sister," he agreed wholeheartedly. "I'm glad you're free of the attack and restored to full function."

"As am I," she replied, navigating expertly, soaring, turning, leaving behind curious followers who wanted to know where Sil would be taken. "Penn's attempt to commandeer me failed."

"How did you resist him?" Walter glanced at her for an instant, then fixed his gaze back on Sil and the baby who was now the subject of the responders' care. "I don't know a lot about it, but I'm pretty sure any program can be hacked. You told me that. What made the difference?"

Daisy smiled beautifully and looked at Walter lovingly. "You, Brother," she said. "We're family and I would never do anything to hurt you."

Sil heard and smiled.

"Welcome home!" Daisy greeted over her shoulder as they settled onto the lawn of the private home they had obtained for her. "We have the medical team ready to take care of you."

Sil opened her eyes, arms wrapped around the infant who nestled wearily against her shoulder. "Is she in danger?" she asked the responder.

"Don't worry," it answered. "You're both going to be fine."

She bowed her head and tears began to flow.

"Walter," she said softly, reaching out her hand again.

"I'm here," he took it firmly.

"Thank you."

All he could do was squeeze her hand and nod.

AND

Golden rays of the setting sun flooded the living room through panoramic windows, glancing off the resident's furniture, fixtures, and accoutrements. Overhead, the clear, blue sky stretched like a dome through the nearly, invisible glass. At night, stars would shine through and sometimes, the red twinkle of a distant planet would trace a slow line across it.

Silvariah stared out at the turbulent Columbia River, dashed with foam, and thousands of sprinkles of light, soothed by the murmur of its movement. She was stretched sideways on a chaise lounge, tilted toward the window, dressed in a dark green gown, jewels in her ears and her hair, twisted cleverly at the nape of her neck with a few carefully stray curls framing her face.

"Ten minutes," Walter advised, sticking his head in the door, handsome in his tux, but more appealing because of the hint of a smile and the twinkle in his eyes. The fundraising gala awaited and she would be speaking.

Sil turned her head gracefully and smiled at him appreciatively. "I'm ready," she said, and he backed out again.

Nearby, a little girl, about six years of age, braided daisies into chains; slowly, carefully, petals dropping. She was clothed in a dress of pastel pink and yellow, with matching ribbons in her hair, and she hummed a children's song about the stars. When she had linked the flowers at the ends forming a crown, she crossed the room holding it carefully on her palms.

"Mama," she said in a voice as sweet as the tone of a crystal bell, "I made this for you. You can wear it at the party tonight." She climbed onto the seat next to Sil, who lifted her into her lap.

"Thank you, Scarlet," Sil said gently, stroking her dark brown hair. "It's so beautiful and I love it."

Scarlet tried to lift it up onto her head but Sil intervened.

"I'd like to wear it tomorrow when we have our time together. It would be sad if it got lost or broken tonight." She contemplated Scarlet's face fondly.

"Yes, Mama," the little girl replied, staring at her handiwork thoughtfully, nestling onto Sil's shoulder.

A warm wind blew in from the corner window stirring the wind chimes and bringing the aromas of spring, and a faint memory of a peaceful moment in the Garden Dome.

"Mama," Scarlet said plaintively, lifting her eyes to peer into her mother's eyes.

"Yes, my sweet girl," she responded, kissing her on the cheek and stroking her hair again.

"I had such a nice dream," she said, looking away into the distance. There were luminous shadows in her eyes, hints of deep red, like dark gems lit by starlight.

"Uh huh," she whispered patiently.

"I was playing with my friends and it was so much fun."

Scarlet lifted her eyes to the dome overhead and beheld the sky deepening into night. Flickers, rust red—Mars red, rippled in them.

"I thought they were real, Mama," she looked back and gazed into her mother's eyes again. "But when I woke up, I knew I was just dreaming. One of them was my sister and there were some other kids...and I wish I could go there."

Sil glanced over at the door where Walter was standing and listening, concern furrowing his brow. "Go where, honey?"

"Up there!" she gestured to the dome overhead. "In the sky!" Dropping her gaze to the flower crown, the girl went back to humming.

Sil stole a furtive peek over her shoulder where the remnants of the old suit had been draped artistically on a shelf, the only tribute she could make to a friend. Verna had not survived the final descent and this was all that was left.

Knowing what she was thinking, Walter crossed over and found a corner on the chaise lounge to seat himself. "Did you dream you were playing in the sky?" he asked, drawing Sil's attention back.

"Yes," she answered seriously, "up there on the red star, that pretty one."

Walter and Sil looked at each other, not knowing what to say.

"I hope I can go there one day," she added. "And maybe I really will find some friends there."

Walter glared at Sil shaking his head as if to say, '*Don't encourage her.*'

Scarlet smiled charmingly and gave each of them a hug.

"Someday," she said, and the wind chimes intoned a melodic echo.

ETC

This is an end that leads to a beginning as almost all the key figures are still in play. If you enjoyed the story, please consider leaving a review, as simple as you like, on Amazon or GoodReads (or both). These are the lifeblood of an Indie author's reputation and much appreciated.

I'm hard at work on the sequel, which has the working title "Races", and should be out mid-2018. You can sign up on the email list if you want to be notified of the release, write to info@varida.com or contact us on the website. Watch for promotions as well.

Looking into the future, I have hope for the human race and for the benevolence of developing artificial intelligence, too, though there are dire threats to face on both sides.

Let's not give up yet.

Suzanne

For more information check: *www.varida.com*
www.facebook.com/VaridaBooks or @varida_pr
Varida Publishing & Resources is a small company run by authors from a variety of genres and styles collaborating to produce high quality work. Each one contributes extensive time editing, advising, and proofing one another's work, upholding high standards of grammar, storytelling, and consistency.

RACES

Chapter One

Clang!
Clang!
Clang!

The clash of metal against metal reverberated through the hallway as the drones attacked the door methodically. Emergency lights flashed on and off, casting a red glare that shone and vanished into total darkness in a rhythmic pattern, timed to mimic the throbbing alarm sounding in twos, over and over.

...aroooo....aroooo...

A woman scrambled along the floor, visible in choppy clips as the red lights alternately flooded the passageway and blackened. Crouched, moving, clutching the railing as a guide, but not rising, feet slipping, pausing again. Her eyes shone black in the restricted palette, deep wells where fear and desperation swam unhindered; her face was etched in mask-like solidity. Every pulse of red light revealed the same fixed expression.

Clang!
Clang!
Clang!

The drone closest to the door wielded a crowbar awkwardly as the other units watched. They recognized that their approach was inefficient but saw no reason to desist. They had been given the *destroy* order without any additional instructions or urgency codes and because nothing else was listed in their project queue, they had all assembled here.

"We are making progress," one announced as a slight crumpling ensued at the point of attack.

"We are," the others agreed. They shared a general consciousness as well as maintaining some personal modules, and as far as they understood, they were each participating in the act of gaining entrance to Lab 9's Cuna department.

Clang!

Clang!

Clang!

"Stop! Stop!" the woman inside shrieked, rising to her feet, shaking all over. She ran to the door where the drones worked and banged on it with both hands. "I command you to stop! Reverse the destroy order! It's a mistake!" The anguish in her voice almost sounded hysterical but the face never relaxed or showed anything other than determination.

"You will not be harmed," several voices reassured her, projecting over speakers into her area. "There is no mistake. We have reviewed the order carefully and will proceed according to plan. All systems are functioning properly."

"Steward!" she hissed, flinging herself around, combing the unit with her gaze, searching for something to use to stall them. "Help me! I thought you said you could stop them..."

Metal tables, chairs, file cabinets, and equipment, were all piled against the double doors. Multiple metal bars were threaded through handles and framework—by far the most effective deterrent—shuddering with every thud.

Sssskkrettss... the seal around the door-lock failed and deflated. She jumped and pounded the seal plate, restoring it again—for at least the tenth time.

Weren't there any electric wires down here she could rig to electrocute those things? But power supplies were low, barely maintaining life support functions. Even if she knew where to access them, she dared not. *What else? Think, think...* her eyes darted around frantically, alighting on something down the hallway.

"I am delaying them again," a man's voice spoke into her com as the clanging paused.

"Why isn't it working?" she demanded, listening for the next clang, her ears trembling as it didn't come. "What are you doing?" She dashed down the passageway

"I've done several platform-wide scans, dumps and initialization sequences, executed in series, one unit at a time, which creates a pause," the voice explained evenly, sounding strangely calm for someone discussing the imminent slaughter of innocents, "but as soon as it's ended, the units' command structure reasserts itself. And I have no…"

"You've got to erase that destroy order! Can't you get into the central server or wherever it is they're getting their commands?" She was dragging, pushing, pulling a massive tank toward the barricade using alternately her feet, back, and shoulders, moving something that she could never have budged on Earth. 'H$_2$O' was painted on the side. A tube with a nozzle dangled carelessly from the top.

"I have no authority to access the interplanetary command structure, however…"

"Augghh!" she shrieked as her feet slipped and she banged her head sharply against the tank.

"When I interrupt transmissions, it gives us five minutes before restoring contact. I erase the order and put them into a sleep cycle."

The woman trembled and moaned as she scuffled with the floor seeking traction, wrapped her arms as far around the water tank as they would go, and shoved with all her strength. She gritted her teeth, head sideways to give the shoulder better access, and pushed. Feet sticking, tank sliding. Feet slipping, tank still.

"With the extra tasks I give them, we have roughly nine minutes till they resume the assault."

The woman cried out in frustration and pain. "I can't do it!"

"You are making progress, and you still have seven minutes."

A faint crying sound wafted down the corridor, audible between the loud wails of the alarm; the former stabbed her heart with panic, while the latter had become familiar enough she didn't notice it.

"Steward, help me!' her voice trembled as she called out to him in anguish.

"I am doing the best I can to alleviate your situation but I have no tools I can reach in your area," Steward responded coolly—not heartlessly. "You might want to inject a stabilizer of some kind. You need to have a clear head."

Her head *was* throbbing and she was confused. Nearby a screen was flashing.

"Turn right," it said.

She turned to the right numbly.

"Open the drawer," Steward added aloud. He waited until she had obeyed and then went on. "Take a patch and place it on your neck."

She grabbed one, ripped the packaging open and slapped it on her neck. Within seconds she found her vision clearing, the pain lessening, her mind more alert and her heart more calm.

"That did help," she told her ally, as the one cry became a chorus of multiple infant voices blending pitifully with each other.

Three minutes had passed, four to go. How to use them? Soothe or defend?

"What is the water for?" Steward asked, and it was all she needed to make that her focus. *Yes! She had to protect them first.*

"Water is bad for electronics, right?" she threw herself at the tank again with renewed vigor, shoes screeching on the floor.

"That's a poor approach…" he was about to explain why but wisely chose not to complete the thought. "And water is such a precious commodity, it would be very foolish to waste it…"

"Not as foolish as wasting lives!" she grunted with the effort as the tank inched its way closer to the doors. "If we all die no one will care if there's water anyway."

There was nothing Steward could say to that. It was true.

"Are you thinking you can damage some circuitry or something in them? They should have shielding and…" He was trying to be reasonable, not discouraging. He wanted to know.

"These aren't as well designed as you think," she responded gasping for air. "I've seen them shudder when splashed; not sure why…"

The weak wails continued to roll down the hallway as the red lights flashed and the alarm sounded in twos.

"But I'm hoping they've got some self-protection instinct that makes them back away."

With a dull thud, the tank bumped against the barricade just as the assault began again.

Clang!

Clang!

Clang!

She tried to jump to a stand but found herself so unsteady that she had to pull herself upright hanging onto the pile of furniture. Grabbing the hose, she pointed and yelled.

"You are in violation of Earth Conventions for the Human Race!! Stop now or you will be doused with water!"

"You must not waste water," they called out together via loudspeaker as the first drone banged with the crowbar. "You will hinder the ability of life to flourish on this planet."

"You are hindering the flourishing of life on this planet!" she shouted, eyes blazing, and turning the valve, she pointed and opened the nozzle for several seconds. Water burst out toward the crack in the door, soaking everything in its path.

"Stop!" the drones called out again in unison. "You must not use water inappropriately! It could be contaminated by contact with the floors and drains."

"I would rather spill water than blood!" she shrieked, blasting another burst of water at the door.

And the clanging stopped.

She listened with baited breath.

"That is illogical," the one at the door announced after thirty-five suspenseful seconds. And the clanging picked up again.

Blast! She showered water at the door.

"Stop!" they called and paused.

Only a brief pause.

Clang!

Clang!

Clang!

The pattern was repeated numerous times before Steward could interrupt again—for nine more minutes.

— ◊ —

Raspy, shallow breathing gave a slow cadence to the passing of time in the murky cavern where a figure lay prostrate in a pile of rubble. It was barely noticeable in the gloom of a Martian afternoon as anemic shafts of pale light glanced off misshapen lumps of rock and debris.

A little cart with a vertical camera arm rolled up to it from a pitch-black cave, scanning the pile methodically as it had several times before. It came to a stop next to the figure, paused to listen to the breathing and evaluate the man's condition; then it spoke.

"Are you awake?" it queried, rolling against the figure with a tiny bump to get its attention. "Has your oxygen failed? Have you reassessed the situation? Shall I update you on my expanded understanding of…"

The cart paused as the man failed to respond and his breathing remained unchanged. Clearly, he was asleep or unconscious.

Rotating its camera as it rolled itself around, the cart searched the rubble for something it could jar and either shove or drag to the figure's side. Having no arms was a hindrance, to say the least, and if the AI managing the cart had ever grown accustomed to a specific body, it would've been frustrated. As it was, it considered it merely a puzzle to solve.

It rolled up and around to the top of the debris and began zig-zagging back and forth, dislodging dirt and rocks. Up, down, side to side, back and forth, it disturbed, jostled, unsettled the pile, patiently coaxing a path to the more useful contents without—hopefully—knocking any more onto the injured man.

"I have much to think about," the cart's tinny voice spoke into the empty hollows, "and so many new problems of interest. I'm looking forward to discussing some of them with you."

There was no answer.

At first the water seemed to slow down the assault on the barricade at the lab entrance, but soon, the drones had mutually decided the imperative was more urgent than the water conservation guideline. Then the cycle of attack resumed its original intensity.

"Steward!" the woman called out after she gave up soaking them through the crack in the door. "Can't you just disconnect them from the server as soon as they reconnect? Why does it have to take so long every time? I'm wearing out!" The last few words were spoken in near panic.

It seemed like hours of this cycle had gone by, seven to ten minutes of assault alternated with nine minutes of reprieve; over and over.

"They have standard procedures to avoid disconnect that I have to work through," Steward replied. "We are engaging the same paths each time. It's not unexpected."

"You've got to stop this," she begged. "I can't bear it! Where are the rest of the people in the lab? Why aren't they coming to help?"

"There are no detectable life-signs in the other departments," he responded, not intending to be callous, "and the base is destroyed."

She slumped against the wall and slid into a crumple, knees to her face.

"I'm the only one left?" she whispered.

He didn't answer.

"I'm going to die…" she moaned softly, just as the clanging began again.

The barricade shuddered and shook with each clang, bars straining, groaning, screeching. Wails of infants' voices, meshed together into a caterwaul like that of a caged creature, poured out the Cuna door at her. She made no movement.

Clang!

Clang!

Clang!

Red light flooded the hall, then blackness. Blaring sound and silence. The woman no longer had the strength to fight.

"I can't stop them and I can't go on like this," she mumbled. "I can't. I can't… bear to see…"

Clang!

"When they get through and go in there…"

Clang!

"I can't bear it…"

Silence.

She sat numbly as the infants cried and the alarm sounded, peaceful compared to the jarring of the entire barricade under the drones' onslaught.

"Perhaps," she whispered, "it would still be better to die in that room with them than to wander these hallways alone till I starve."

Too weary to rise, she crawled to the Cuna, closed and locked the door, and began singing to soothe the terrified little children. One by one, she came, lay a calming hand on each belly, pulled their cribs closer to herself, until she was sitting in a rocker with a ring of them around her.

"Hush, little baby, don't say a word," she sang.

The alarm ceased and normal light filled the room. The woman almost fell out of her chair, as if she had been leaning into the wind and it suddenly died. The absence of it was tangible in the air, humming in her ears, throbbing in her chest. It wracked her with as much anxiety on stopping as it had when it first started.

All the infants began wailing again and she found herself, for only an instant, joining them. Quickly though, she wrenched herself free of the instinctual cry and willed herself to take charge.

"Beautiful ones," she called out over their cries, "all is well. Be calm. Be still." And again, she began to sing to them, her limbs trembling with exhaustion.

She wondered what Steward was doing and what his silence meant. Perhaps he had succumbed to the general disaster spreading over Mars, as well.

"Hush little baby, don't say a word," her voice gelled into a beautiful sweet tone, filling the room, capturing the tiny little ears and hearts, arresting their cries. Spell-bound they listened, tear dampened eyes open and searching, looking toward her.

"Mama's gonna buy you a Martian bird…"

"Listen carefully and do exactly as you are instructed," a voice echoed in the hollow cavern, sounding near, but from an indistinguishable source.

The figure in the rubble tried to stir, to mumble, to move a finger—anything to show he had heard, but it wasn't clear to him if it was working.

"The light is pooling here," a different voice answered, younger somehow, "at the coordinates we were given."

"As negotiated," the first confirmed.

A bump against his shoulder, repeated gently and insistently, numerous times, began to gain his attention. *Stop*, he wanted to push the bumping thing away, but his mouth and arms lay still, saturated with slumber.

"It doesn't make sense," the younger speaker commented. "He said he waited for the daylight and it never came. But it's poured into this cavity like…" He tried to phrase his confusion.

"The subject has no sight in the denser plane," the other interrupted. "Vibration has already begun to set in now. We must act quickly."

The injured man listened calmly, wondering what the words meant, as the realization dawned on him that the bumping against his shoulder was really bugging him.

Words spoke. Strange sounds, grating, irritating, metallic. Words that provoked. Words that jolted. *Move. Open. Speak.* Commands and demands.

But the man wanted only to sleep and listen to the other voices and imagine what they could be talking about… where… when…

"Wake up!" words crystalized into meaning in his ears abruptly. And just as quickly, pain flooded his body from the feet up, rolling toward the head.

"Why?" his voice cracked and rasped.

"Because you must live," the first speaker responded, in a voice like cool, clear liquid; bright, strong, compelling. This was the voice he wanted to hear, wanted to find.

"I knocked another canister of oxygen loose and you need to hook it up," the different words jarred against his brain, as annoying as the bumping on his arm. It was like the gravel under him, the dirt coating him, the rocks pinning him. Earthy, plain, constraining.

"No," he murmured, "I don't want to be pinned here. Let me go."

"That is the plan," the AI in the cart answered thinly in a monotone. "I have made decisions—I am looking forward to discussing them with you. I have grown. You are going to be rescued. Help is on the way!" The last sentence held a hint of excitement.

"Stop ramming me," he croaked and swallowed, licking dry lips.

"I have been attempting to wake you. Once you have attached the tank, I will proceed with the rescue plan."

The man squinted and looked up at the cart's camera, bending toward him on a metallic arm, a single eye with a miniature mike and speaker incorporated into its casing.

"Companion?" he queried as he struggled to assemble the fractured pieces of understanding in his mind. "What are you doing?"

"I have taken measures," the voice affirmed proudly, "to secure your release and preserve life. I am a hero." There was no arrogance in that statement. It was a reasonable assessment.

"What measures?" the man asked as he fumbled with the tank and with an effort found the appropriate valve and attached it to his suit.

"I have announced the complete destruction of Lab 9 to the Interplanetary Command Relay and simulated disaster data like that produced in the destruction of Reznik Base. It was the only way…"

"What?" the man's eyes filled with despair. "The base is gone?" He choked on the words.

"Yes, I have filed reports you can review…"

"Why…?" he couldn't even frame a question. His limbs were so cold and he realized he was quivering all over. He just wanted to close his eyes and never open them again.

"It was the only way I could take over the local command structure and spare…"

"What are you saying?" he moaned.

Companion cut to the chase.

"Drones are on the way," he finished simply.

This was a preview of the next book which will be out in mid-2018.

CPSIA information can be obtained
at www.ICGtesting.com
Printed in the USA
FSHW020608220220
67280FS